"Out of curiosity, how big is this network of yours?"

"If you mean in terms of people, I'd have to consult my records. I do know that we have assets in 127 countries so far."

She caught me just as I was sipping my *chai*, and escaped the blast only because I was looking toward the batik hanging on the wall at the time. Fortunately, the spray didn't get that far.

"*One hundred twenty-seven* countries?"

"Yes. It's amazing how quickly a grass-roots movement grows when it fulfils a deeply felt need."

I'd thought her offer was bigger than it seemed but this was ridiculous. At first words failed me, and then I thought of the right term.

"You're an anti-Moriarty."

She laughed, but my timing was off. She managed to get the cup away from her lips before she sprayed me with *chai*.

"That's rather good. I'd never thought of it that way before, but yes, I'm the mastermind at the centre of a web of agents who thwart criminals. The Napoleon of crime fighters." She arched her eyebrows, and lowered her voice. "My spies are everywhere. Or, at least, by number of countries, about 66 percent of everywhere." She drained her cup. "The appellation is particularly interesting considering the name of our group."

"Which is?"

"BSI." I raised one eyebrow. "I'm confident that you'll figure it out."

I wondered if all private investigators had such crazy lives, or whether the universe just had it in for me. What was next, being offered a position by MI-6?

Of course, from what I'd read, MI-6 had around 3200 personnel, so the BSI might be bigger than them.

Madre de dios.

THE STABLE VICES AFFAIR

Book One of the Chandler Affairs

by

G.W. Renshaw

Javari

Javari Press
Calgary, Alberta
2014

The Stable Vices Affair

Javari Press,
Calgary, Alberta, Canada.
http://www.javaripress.ca/

ISBN: 978-1-895487-05-3 (pbk)

First paperback edition, November 2014.

Set in Gentium Book Basic
Printed in the United States of America

DEDICATION

For my primordial Fan Girls, Sandy and Jenna, without whose support, encouragement, and love my life would be infinitely more bleak.

ACKNOWLEDGEMENTS

Thank you. Yes, you, for reading this book. I greatly appreciate your support, and hope that you enjoy it as much as I enjoyed writing it.

A novel like this wouldn't be possible without the generosity of those experts who gave up their valuable time to answer just one more question from a sincere, but sometimes clueless, author.

Those people whose names are in italics are fellow members of the Imaginative Fiction Writers Association.

In alphabetical order:

The lovely and talented Peggy Adams, retired criminal prosecutor, bon vivant, and a rich source of knowledge about both the Calgary police and RCMP.

Harold Cardona, whose native knowledge of Colombian culture and language was invaluable.

My lovely wife, *Sandra Fitzpatrick*, my financial, tax, and biology consultant, without whose love, ruthless editing, and encouragement I might have been another wannabe.

Susan Forest, who answered my many startling questions about school procedure.

Ron Friedman, my source of knowledge about all things Israeli. !שָׁלוֹם

Det. Darren Hafner, truly one of Calgary's Finest, who provided several rather obscure details about the Calgary Police Service.

Jenna Miles, who has tried to educate me in the finer points of being a teenage girl, as well as beating me up in aikido, Krav Maga, and baton class. The cake is a lie, the popcorn is truth.

Michael Shepherd, actor and professional Santa, who provided insight in to the complicated world of working with small children.

Jennifer Sykes, LLB., culinary artist, and karate sensei, who supplied odd answers to my odd legal questions.

Michael Thompson, *Chef de Cuisine*, and master psychologist, whose explanations of certain disturbing psychopathologies were never accompanied by "and how does that make you feel?"

Thanks also to my beta readers, all of whom freely gave their time to winnow the chaff, and thresh the author: Jenna, Janet, Peggy, Sandra, Danita, and Ann. What can I say? A lot of my friends are talented, intelligent women. It's my cross to bear.

Any variances between the information given to me, and what appears in my writing, are mine. All mine. I refuse to share the credit with anybody else.

If they want credit, let 'em make their own mistakes.

ALSO BY G.W. RENSHAW

Hic Sunt Dracones: Being a True Account of the Rescue of Professor George Herbert Endeavour from Misadventure

Odd Thoughts: An Anthology of Speculative Fiction

The Chandler Affairs

The Stable Vices Affair
The Prince and the Puppet Affair
(coming 2015)

PROLOGUE

The name's Chandler: Veronica Irene Chandler. You can call me Veronica or Ms. Chandler.

If you have the normal love for keeping your limbs attached to your body, do not call me Your Imperial Majesty or Mrs. Anything. My patience, never one of my strong points, has worn thin.

From an early age I had a detailed plan for my life, and to say that it hasn't worked out the way I thought it would is beyond a gross understatement. Quite a few years ago – never mind how many – all I ever wanted was to be a private investigator. To recover the lost and expose the faithless.

That's pretty good isn't it? Maybe I should put it on my business cards. Assuming, of course, that I ever have use for them again. Between then and now my life has become a bit complex.

Right from the start of my career I attracted unusual cases. Cases that would have gotten people burned at the stake in the 17th century. Or, for that matter, in most modern university physics department meetings.

When it became obvious how things were going, I had brief fantasies that it would be handy to be a superhero or a wizard. Unfortunately, I have no powers, and all the best names are taken. What would I call myself? Super-, naw. Hyper... Chick? Wow, lame.

I'd make a terrible wizard. The only magic I ever learned involves making a knot in a piece of string.

Superpowers aren't my style anyway. Despite everything that's happened, I like to cling to the belief that I am a mostly normal, Canadian, teenage girl. I even have a lot of human friends. At least, for some value of human.

Personally, I blame most of my problems on that damned dwarf.
And the aliens, of course.

CHAPTER 1

Fifteen Minutes of Fame

The second hand on the wall clock insisted that time was moving at a normal rate. My keen, investigator's instinct informed me that the clock was lying.

The previous week I'd had this great idea of getting the local campus radio station to interview me as free advertising. Advertising equals work equals money equals food. So far my business accounting had been all out and no in.

It had seemed like such a good idea at the time. Now, I wasn't so sure.

The waiting room (or "green room" as the perky production assistant had called it) was painted industrial beige. The chairs were ones that the college had decided were practical, durable, and cheap. Comfortable they were not. They were probably excellent for keeping students awake during classes. My butt was slowly going numb.

There wasn't much in the room other than a few of the torture chairs, a low table with magazines almost as old as me, and the clock. I tried not to stare at the only other person present. That would have been rude.

He'd come in a few minutes after me, and was average: average height, average weight, average looks somewhere in his forties. I guessed that he was here for the program segment after mine.

He had no problem being rude, and kept leering at me when he thought I wasn't watching. It was creepy. I have no illusions about being supermodel beautiful or being well-endowed. At first I wondered if he'd ever seen a woman before.

In this case, though, he didn't look like he was checking me out. He looked annoyed. As far as I knew we'd never met, and my new theory was that maybe he just didn't like women.

I glanced at the clock, which had advanced by a whole 40 seconds since last time I'd checked. It would be nice to get this over with.

Mr. Average was still glaring at me, so I gave him a five second eyeball-to-eyeball stare, then smiled insincerely, and ignored him completely until I was called.

Eleven tectonically-paced minutes went by before the perky PA returned.

"Ms. Chandler? Mr. Stickler? We're ready for you."

What the...? I was sure I'd been told that I'd be the only guest. My stomach did even more of a dance than it had been as I smoothed my navy blue skirt. Not that it would make any difference on the radio.

The girl led us down the corridor to a door with a red light over it and stopped. After a moment the light went out, and the door opened.

Ziggy Mendolia was shorter and darker than I'd imagined. From his voice over the radio, I had pictured someone more like a young, hard-bodied Prince. From the look of Ziggy's shirt, the six pack was still a distinct possibility. I became glad that I'd tried to make myself presentable. Maybe this wouldn't be so bad after all.

"Hello," he said with a big smile. "Please come in." He had a light Jamaican accent that added charm to his voice, and listeners to his audience. No, not bad at all.

The sound booth had blue, corrugated panels on the walls, sort of like egg cartons, or the underside of mattress foam. A round table with four microphones on short stands sat in the middle. One wall had a large window showing us the engineer's booth where a guy wearing headphones was sitting at a mixing console.

We sat in equally spaced chairs around the table.

"One minute," said a voice in midair. I jumped slightly. Ziggy gave me a reassuring smile. Out of the corner of my eye I caught the engineer leaning back from an overhead microphone.

"Relax," Ziggy said. "This isn't a job interview, it's just a conversation. Take a deep breath."

"Okay," I said, wondering why I was so nervous. Stickler was trying to look bored, and not quite succeeding. I guess I wasn't the only one with nerves. That made me feel a little better.

"When you speak," Ziggy said to both of us, "speak directly toward your microphones, regardless of who you are addressing. You don't have to lean in or speak loudly."

"Got it," I said. Stickler said nothing. Whatever.

"Five seconds," the engineer's voice said. In his booth, he held up five fingers, then four, three, two, one...

"Welcome back, my friends," Ziggy said to his microphone. "This morning I'm pleased to have two special guests. Ms. Veronica Chandler is the youngest private investigator in Alberta, while Mr. Orval Stickler is an independent candidate for Calgary North East who will be running in the upcoming by-election. Ms. Chandler, what led you to become a private detective?"

That was easy.

"My mother."

Ziggy made a stretching motion with his hands. Oh.

"She's a homicide detective with the Calgary Police Service."

"Why didn't you become a policewoman like her?"

"She wanted me to, but the police only deal with criminal matters. I wanted to help the people the police can't. I guess the obvious example is people with cheating spouses. That's a civil matter, not a criminal one."

"If I may say so, you look too young to be peeking into motel bedroom windows."

"Firstly, I don't peek in bedroom windows. That would be illegal. There are other investigative techniques available. Secondly, I'm hardly an innocent child."

Stickler jumped in before I could continue.

"You see, this is a perfect example of what is wrong with our present government. How can an eighteen-year old girl be a licensed investigator?"

I gave both of them a dirty look, then spoke to my microphone.

"An eighteen year old *woman* can easily be a licensed investigator if she is dedicated, and works hard enough. It's not that difficult."

"Clearly, the industry needs better regulation. I certainly wouldn't send a child out to do a man's job, especially one as dangerous as this."

Holy crap, the guy was a dinosaur. I understood why Ziggy had put him on the show with me – it made for good radio. That didn't prevent me from wanting to tear our host a new one later for not warning me.

"Mr. Stickler, I assure you that the industry is quite well regulated. As far as being a child..."

"In British Columbia the requirements are much more..."

"We aren't in B.C. We're in Alberta. Any resident, male or female, can take the investigator's course at any age, and write the provincial licensing examination at 18. True, most PIs are older and are ex-cops, but that's not a requirement. If I was unqualified the word would get around quickly, and nobody would hire me. Incompetence would be self-correcting without any need for government regulation."

I smiled to convey how friendly and relaxed I was pretending to be. My temper was under control for the moment, although the urge to punch him remained. Doing that on the air was probably not the kind of free advertising I wanted.

Stickler opened his mouth again, but Ziggy beat him to it.

"He does have a point, Ms. Chandler. Most provinces require a PI to have industry experience, or serve an apprenticeship. Does Alberta have anything similar?"

"Not formally, but I spent two years prior to licensing as an intern with the CPS. That, along with the investigator's course, gave me a thorough grounding in investigative work."

"I can't believe that you were hired by the police at the age of 16," Stickler said, mocking. I didn't like his tone.

"They didn't. It was an unpaid internship."

Stickler threw his hands in the air, although the gesture was lost on our audience.

"Well, there you are. What did you do during your 'internship?'" I could hear him put quotes around the word. "Make coffee?"

I took a deep breath, and let it out. The urge to hit him was definitely getting stronger again.

"Mr. Stickler, I have no idea what I did to pi – upset you, but if you can't have a civil conversation I'm leaving."

He snorted.

"I certainly wouldn't hire an investigator who runs away from a confrontation. This is just another example of the current government's incompetence..."

I cut him off. "I've never run away from a fight, Mr. Stickler. Nor do I need to. I have practised Krav Maga since I was nine, I'm licensed to carry a baton, and I've had firearm training. Believe me, I can take care of myself."

Stickler gave me an over-the-top shocked look, and I realized that his over-acting was designed to piss me off so I'd become flustered.

"Are you telling me that our government allows *teenage girls* masquerading as private investigators to wander around with guns?"

I shouldn't have mentioned guns. Dammit, I was going to have to keep my temper under control.

I took another deep breath, and let it out. He looked smug. I would be damned if I was going to say something stupid that he could use against me. My heart was pounding. I ignored it as well as I could, and tried to speak in a calm, quiet voice.

"Have you ever been a police officer, Mr. Stickler?"

"No, but that's hardly..."

"Have you ever been in the armed forces?"

"I haven't had that honour." He said it like a rehearsed line.

"I'm not a girl. I'm an adult woman. I'm not wandering around with a gun playing cops and robbers. That would be both illegal and unnecessary. If you'd bothered to do your research, you'd know that private investigators in Canada aren't allowed to carry firearms. Despite that, I have shot and killed a man in the line of duty, which I think gives me a better perspective on the dangers of guns than your completely civilian one."

"I find it difficult to believe that even the Calgary Police Service would issue a firearm to an unpaid, underage intern. You can't seriously think that people will buy that story."

He'd insulted my friends in the force. I went dead calm, the same as I would in a physical fight.

"They didn't. The circumstances were unique. I used a constable's pistol to shoot a subject who was an immediate danger to others."

He gave me an unpleasant smile. Like a predator who thought he was closing in.

"And what was this constable doing while you were allegedly doing his job for him?"

I ignored his gender assumptions.

"Lying on the ground unconscious with a fractured skull and broken arm, both courtesy of the subject."

"A civilian should never take the law into their own hands. When I'm elected..."

"What would you have done?"

"*Clearly*, the responsible thing would have been to call 9-1-1 instead of trying to act like a hero."

"Then you would have died, as would the constable, and several bystanders. I was there. You weren't. The subject was insane and carrying a baseball bat with which he'd already murdered a man."

"Hopefully this alleged incident took place somewhere where other people weren't in danger."

"I wish. It was in downtown Calgary."

"Good heavens, you could have killed someone!"

"I did," I said very, very evenly. "The man I was aiming at."

"And we're taking a break," Ziggy said. "We'll be back after the news." He leaned back in this chair, and the ON AIR sign went off. I leaned forward, my eyes fixed on the candidate across from me.

"Since you are obviously a *real* man who knows just how things should be done, and I'm just a silly little teenage girl, how about if we meet outside later and you can show me how you would have handled the situation?" His eyes were fixed on mine, like a mouse watching a hawk. He swallowed.

"You can't threaten me," he said.

"I didn't," I said. "It was a polite invitation."
For once he didn't have anything to say.

CHAPTER 2

Crash Course

It's strange how quickly life can change. One moment I was a sixteen year old girl who was happily looking forward to a career as a private investigator. The next I was a cold-blooded killer.

The conversion started with a flash.

Constable Danielle Shuemaker and I had spent a tedious morning at the court house, and now we were in hot pursuit of lunch before returning to the police station.

Danielle drove north on Fourth Street in an attempt to escape from downtown Calgary's warren of one-way streets.

At Sixth Avenue, we were half way through the intersection when I saw a flash of something to my right moving faster than I'd have believed possible in downtown traffic. I almost had time to turn my head toward it before the world exploded. There wasn't enough time to draw in a breath, let alone warn Danielle, or do anything to protect myself.

You have to have been through such a thing to understand the violence of what we experienced. The noise alone would have been enough to make me scream if I'd had time. The impact tossed us around in our seat belts like a chew rope in a Rottweiler's mouth. I had no control over anything. No time to even think of bracing myself.

My head hit the side window before the air bag could go off. When it did, I was violently thrown toward Danielle. Her head smashed into my shoulder when we met. My ears were ringing, my head hurt and my shoulder felt broken. She rebounded back into her own seat.

Amid the impacts, the screaming metal, and exploding air bags, I barely registered that the street outside the car was spinning madly in a circle. Most of what I did remember came to me later. I didn't have time to process much while I was in the moment.

It was a miracle that our car didn't collide with anybody else as we came to rest, now facing south instead of north. Snow slurry had sprayed up on the windows, and all I could see outside was a blur. Everything inside my head was a blur too.

I think that Danielle asked me if I was all right. I could hear sound but I didn't understand the words.

"I'm okay. You?" I didn't really hear the words as I spoke them.

She released her seat belt, then hit the switch to turn on the light bar on the roof.

"Stay in the car." Her mouth moved, and her hand gesture made her meaning clear. Since I was just an intern that was fine by me. I could just sit there and hurt while the professional took care of things.

She hit her door with her shoulder several times before it opened. By then the ice was running down the warm windshield, and I saw that the other driver had crawled out of his broken driver's side window, and tumbled to the pavement. He staggered toward us, blood oozing down the side of his head. He had something in his hand.

Danielle was watching the traffic in case some moron ran into her. She wasn't expecting an attack. The northbound cars that had been behind us had either already cleared the intersection, or stopped when they saw the collision. One idiot on the cross-street decided that he could make it through. She held up her hand to stop him, and his pickup truck slid to a halt blocking Danielle's view of the guy coming toward her.

"Danielle, look out!" I yelled. She finally spotted the driver, who lurched around the stopped truck waving a baseball bat. For no obvious reason he hit the truck grill a few times as he passed. My hearing was coming back, and he was screaming so hard that his voice was distorted. I couldn't understand anything he was trying to say. It was all just noise, like a wild animal trying to mimic human speech.

Danielle, left palm outstretched and right hand on her holstered gun, ordered him to drop the bat as she side-stepped to get clear of the truck. Its driver grabbed the opportunity to take off in a panic, spraying her with slush as he went.

The screaming man ignored both the truck and her command, and she took a step back to give herself more room, as well as to manoeuvre so that nobody else was in her line of fire. He kept coming as she ordered him to drop the weapon again, and drew her gun.

On her next step her feet flew out from under her. She fell heavily, the gun still in her hand. I was helpless to do anything to stop him as I watched the aluminium bat whistling toward her head. Her hand came up, maybe to fire, maybe to stop the blow, and I heard a horrible crunch as the bat met her forearm before pushing through to connect with the side of her head. She collapsed unmoving in the street. The blow sent her Glock bouncing off the open car door to land somewhere out of sight. I stared out the door, stunned by the violence, and the sudden realization that I was alone, unarmed and trapped in the car with a psycho outside.

I shoved on my door, but it had been horribly mangled by the collision, and wouldn't open no matter what I did. The window controls didn't work. There was nothing to break the window so I could crawl out. The only way out was through the driver's side door.

I wasn't a cop, and I wasn't trained for any of this. After seeing Danielle go down, I'm ashamed to say that I panicked.

The madman howled as he saw me, and hit the window of the open door with his bat. I closed my eyes as small cubes of glass sprayed my face. He swung his bat a few more times, hitting the car, then realized on some level that he couldn't get to me that way.

I fumbled with my seat belt, trying to get it undone so I'd have some chance of defending myself.

The seat belt buckle popped open. I pulled my feet up on the seat, trying to stay as far away from him as possible. He dropped the bat, and, instead of doing the obvious thing and coming through the door, he lunged at me through the broken window.

There was nowhere for me to go. The prisoner barrier behind the front seats prevented me from getting into the back. He grabbed my leg, dragging me toward him. I kicked at him, but the steering wheel got in the way. My next try caught the dispatch computer on the centre console. His yanks on my leg threw my aim off, and made it hard to get a clear shot at him. Everything I tried to do hit equipment instead. My left boot caught his head once and cut him, but it was like he didn't even feel it. As he hauled me across the driver's seat my open coat was rucked up to my armpits. The dispatch computer gouged my ribs. Small cubes of glass grated my skin.

Taking off my seat belt was a mistake. If I'd left it on he wouldn't have been able to pull me from the car.

I slammed my free foot against the door, and he lost his grip just as he was about to pull me through the window. He staggered back while I fell out onto the cold street. Like Danielle, my feet slid and I fell flat on my stomach in the slush beside her. From under the door, I could see him trying to pick up his baseball bat again.

He screamed something else unintelligible, and raised the bat over his head.

I didn't think of how useless it was to cover my head with my arms. I just ducked and whimpered. There was a loud bang as the bat came down, and smashed the window frame instead of me. He was still howling like an animal. I was so frightened that I wasn't far from that myself.

He was completely insane, and hit anything he could get to: the door, the fender, our windshield. Every time he missed me, his rage seemed to transfer to whatever he'd hit. If he'd kept any ability to reason, he'd have just come around the broken door that was acting as my shield and killed me. I thought of playing dead, but I was terrified that he'd just keep beating us anyway.

He raised the bat over his head again, and screamed like a feral creature in pain. There was no time for me to dodge, pray, or anything else. At the age of sixteen, I knew that was going to die.

The bat smashed into the top of the window frame again, denting it downward. He howled in frustration, then hit it a few more times, venting his rage on the twisting metal.

My brain didn't bother me with the details of what it planned. The next thing I knew, I was trying to crawl under the car. There was a sharp pain in my foot as he struck my boot. It was a glancing blow, but it still felt like my foot had been crushed.

I was pulled out from under the car just as my hand closed on something cold and solid.

Looking back on it, I think my brain had finally gone to its happy place, and was pretending that it was playing a video game where the worst thing that could happen was that I'd get a lower score.

Danielle's Glock was cold and heavy in my hands. As he raised his bat again, we were so close that I could smell that he hadn't bathed for several weeks. My brain was so overloaded that I think the two shots caught me as much by surprise as they did him. Two holes appeared in the centre of his chest. The training sergeant would have approved of the perfect double tap. Just like I'd done while fooling around in the simulator. Just like every first-person shooter video game I'd ever played. Just like on television. Completely unlike any of them.

God help me.

Pain. Cold. Wetness. Silence. Blood.

A real person, not an image on a screen, looked surprised as two .40 calibre bullets tore through his body. A real person, not a game avatar, crumpled to the ground.

In that instant, I don't think I knew what had happened. I was just happy that he had stopped trying to hit me.

The Glock was still pointing upward as I lay in the street gasping for breath. After a while it occurred to me that I could lower it, and my arms felt better. I tried to suck air into my lungs, but for some reason they weren't working properly. I felt light-headed.

He'd splashed me when he fell, adding to the mess the wet snow had made of my clothes. I spat out wet, salty, dirty slush. Every part of me that was, or had been, in contact with the ground was wet and agonizingly, bitterly cold.

My ears had completely shut down from the gun shots. All I could hear was a high-pitched whistling sound.

After some time, I looked up, shivering, and saw people on the sidewalks moving in near silence. Some were running away. Others had their mouths open, probably screaming. Some were doing both. Nothing else was moving.

The shock paralysed me. This couldn't be happening. The small part of my brain where the lights were still on was trying to cope by telling me that I had to get moving and do things. Anything to postpone reality.

That didn't work either. There were so many things to do that sheer indecision froze me. I remember putting my bare hands down into the wet cold, and forced myself to my knees. It was hard to keep my balance, or maybe the whole world was moving. I couldn't tell which.

The world proceeded in a series of film clips with blanks in between as I faded in and out. An older woman appeared out of nowhere, and said something to me. I couldn't hear her.

The snow by Danielle's head was turning red. Her radio on her duty belt. Eventually my brain recognized those as important things.

I dropped the gun beside Danielle, then crawled around her and fumbled with frozen fingers.

On top of the radio was the tiny, orange Code 200 "officer in trouble" button. I managed to press it, then tried to stand. I had to use the door for support. My wet fingers tried to stick to the metal. I reached into the car, and pulled the trunk release lever. My hands were nearly useless. It took me a few tries.

The woman was still trying to speak to me, her hand on my arm. I ignored her while I felt my way along the side of the car to the back, trying not to touch metal with my bare skin. The trunk lid had opened: a minor miracle. I started pulling out the emergency blankets. The good Samaritan figured out what I was trying to do, and helped me to wrap them around Danielle. She seemed to understand that we should move her as little as possible. I could feel more cold, salty tears in my eyes when I saw movement under the blanket. Danielle was still breathing.

The radio was squawking, so I had to be able to hear again. The microphone was clipped to her lapel, just visible beneath her. I managed to get it unhooked without moving her much, and tried to push the talk button.

It was so difficult. I was surprised to see blood on my right hand. I didn't remember injuring it. It was too cold to hurt.

I never knew that my head could be spinning around in circles while simultaneously made of unmovable lead.

It's a good thing that push-to-talk switches are big. My hands were ridiculously clumsy. I pressed the button in.

"This is, uh…" I couldn't remember our unit number. "There's been an accident."

"Calling officer, say again," came from the speaker. I must have remembered to let go of the button so I could listen.

"We had an accident. We're at…" I looked around, trying to process what I was seeing.

"Knox United Church," the nice woman said.

"We're at Knox United Church. Officer down. I – I had to shoot him."

Sirens were approaching, summoned by the Code 200 "officer in trouble" button I'd pushed earlier.

"Are you saying that you shot a police officer?"

"Are you all right, miss?" The nice lady was still standing there, concern on her face. Trying to have two conversations confused me to the point where I couldn't speak.

God, there was so much to do. I completely forgot about how I'd gotten to this point, and what had actually happened. One thing at a time. The radio was most important. There was somebody on the radio who could help. I coughed to clear my throat, then took a breath, and focused as well as I could.

"Dispatch, this is, um, Veronica Chandler. We need an ambulance at Knox United Church. Constable Schuemaker was hit with a baseball bat. She's unconscious and bleeding."

"What was that about shots fired?"

"I had to shoot him." I said it once, calmly, then the reality slammed into me, roaring over me like an avalanche, and my head spun. It was like the car crash all over again. "I had to shoot him. I…"

It's strange, I remember the microphone dropping from my fingers as I finally looked at the unmoving man lying next to Danielle. There wasn't as much blood around him as I thought there'd be. His face was toward me, and he looked like he finally was at peace.

Movement caught the corner of my eye and I cringed, remembering how his car had come out of nowhere, but it was the red and blue lights flashing as at the responders pulled up. One car was threading itself through traffic going the wrong way along Sixth. Another was inching its way along the sidewalk to get around the stopped vehicles. There were blood spatters everywhere. Where had those come from?

Pain. Cold. Wetness. Noise. Blood.

Somebody started screaming. I wondered who I needed help now.

That was weird. Whoever was screaming sounded like me. The world flew apart into scattered shards.

Everything after that was black and still.

CHAPTER 3

The Great Santa Scam

My strangeness started before kindergarten. Other little girls played with dolls, were deeply fascinated by Pokémon, and had sleep overs where they and their friends talked and giggled a lot. They had normal lives.

I was never normal. Not in the "Veronica is our special child but we love her anyway" sense of the term. I just didn't think about the world like other children.

One of my earliest memories involves being in a stroller. We must have been in a toy store, but only one thing remains clear: the *thing* that almost looked like a person. Daddy held it up to me, and it *started talking*. I tried to escape, but the straps in the stroller held me too tightly. Years later, Mum told me that I cried and screamed so much that the manager asked us to leave the store. Mercifully, nobody ever tried to buy me a doll after that. Creepy things.

The kids in school were crazy about Pokémon. I found the whole idea unsettling, although it was a few years before I could explain why. I couldn't understand the appeal of a game with the goal of enslaving creatures, and forcing them to participate in gladiatorial combat. It seemed too much like bullying. Everybody, except for a few adults, looked at me like I was crazy if I said anything about it. After all, it was only a game. Maybe I'm the reincarnation of Sojourner Truth. Stranger things have happened to me recently.

Sleepovers were okay. I liked playing with others, and having friends, except for one minor detail: we had little in common. They liked little girl things. I liked adult things.

My dad was a professional chef, and by the age of five I was helping him in the kitchen at home. Looking back, I probably wasn't all that helpful, but I tried and Daddy was always patient with me. The paring knife he let me use seemed huge at the time. I'd chop easy things like celery, and he taught me to hold the knife by the bolster for better control. He was always there to make sure I didn't cut myself. I never have. I also stirred sauces, and measured ingredients for him.

One day, all by myself, I made a lemon mousse for dessert. I wasn't strong enough to whip the cream by hand, so Daddy supervised my use of his stand mixer. Mummy and Daddy pronounced the mousse delicious. It was one of the proudest moments of my life to that point.

The other girls in our neighbourhood were lucky if they knew how to pour cereal into a bowl. It seemed weird to me that not everybody knew how to cook. Come to think of it, it still does. We spend several hours a day eating. Why not learn to make the adventure as pleasurable as possible?

The other adventures in my life were the ones that Dad would read to me before I went to sleep at night. He'd lie in bed beside me so I could see the words as he read them.

We went through all the adventures he'd read as a boy: *Treasure Island, Robinson Crusoe*, and, of course, *The Annotated Alice*.

By the time I started kindergarten I could read *Alice* quite well, although I still preferred to have Daddy read it to me. He never wore any kind of aftershave or cologne in case somebody at his restaurant had an allergy, so he just smelled like Daddy. It was a smell that I found comforting.

Mum and Dad were both avid readers. Our house was full of books when I was growing up and by full, I mean that the only walls without bookcases were the ones in the kitchen and the bathroom. Even the windows were surrounded by shelves. They correctly assumed that I'd be a reader too.

I loved the time Dad and I spent together, but in some ways my mum was even more interesting.

She was a police detective.

As far as I know, Mum's Glock was always either locked in her gun safe, or was on her hip, so despite what some people think there was never a problem having a gun and a small child in the same house.

Much later, I learned that a lot of people are overly paranoid about gun safety. They lock up the guns, which is reasonable, and then threaten their kids with all kinds of punishment if they go anywhere near the gun safe. Sometimes that backfires, if you'll pardon the expression, and makes the kids even more curious. That's when problems happen.

Mum had a completely different approach. Just after I started kinder-garten, when she thought I was old enough to understand, she took me to the shooting range.

She showed me her service pistol, explained how it worked, and explained why she had it. Then she emptied a clip into the paper target while I watched. Even with the ear protectors, it was loud and scary. The gun jumped in her hand like something alive that was trying to get away. I remember being in awe that my mother could control that much power. It was one of my first lessons that being female had nothing to do with being weak.

At the end of our adventure I got to fire the gun. Several years later, she admitted that she'd loaded one bullet, a Simunition round, so even if I did something wildly wrong I wouldn't do any permanent damage. She showed me how to hold the gun, and how to stand just like she did. The Glock 22 was huge in my little hands. It was almost too big for my finger to reach the trigger, and it was really heavy. She knelt behind me, her hands nearly touching mine, and helped me to squeeze the trigger. When the gun went off, it kicked enough that it almost hit me in the head. I remember dropping it.

After that, I had no interest in even thinking of playing with firearms, just like I didn't play with the stove after I'd burned myself once on a hot skillet before Daddy taught me how to cook.

The girls at school talked about dresses, parties, and things they'd seen on television. I talked about Daddy letting me use a knife, how we made a souffle together, and how Mummy let me fire her pistol. The other girls thought that I was strange. Some of their parents complained to the school that I was a bad influence on their precious indigo children.

I didn't care all that much because there was something better than playmates. By the age of seven I was reading things that some people considered completely "unsuitable" for my age. While my classmates pretended to be scared after reading Goosebumps, I read the works of Dashiell Hammett, Anthony Bidulka, and Sir Arthur Conan Doyle. To those I added a good measure of Edgar Rice Burroughs, Robert J. Sawyer, Robert Heinlein, H.P. Lovecraft, and many other masters of science fic-tion, fantasy, and mystery.

My parents never censored the books I read. If I wanted to read it, I could.

They weren't easy books to read. They were meant for adults, and assumed that I knew things that I didn't. The first time I read The Maltese Falcon I had a lot of questions, so I went to find my father. I found him sitting in the living room, reading a copy of a food magazine.

"Daddy, I have a question."

He put down the magazine he was reading, and patted his knees. I climbed up into his lap and settled in.

"What would you like to know?"

"What's the difference between a .38 and a .45?"

He looked confused.

"Between what?"

"In this book I'm reading, the private eye uses a .45 and the bad guy uses a .38. What's the difference?"

He paused, and looked at me oddly. Then he cleared his throat.

"I think that's a Mummy question."

That was fair enough. My parents never hesitated when I asked something, but some things were Daddy questions, and others were Mummy questions. I asked Mummy about the guns.

Over the next several years, I asked her a lot of questions about guns, adultery, cocaine use, and men with boyfriends. I assumed that a detective with the Calgary Police Service must know everything, (except about cooking, restaurants, and business, which were Daddy things), and I must say that she rarely let me down.

I became a voracious reader, in the same sense that starving piranhas are voracious eaters. I went through children's books so fast that it wasn't worth checking them out of the library. Young adult novels might last me a few hours. The typical four-hundred page bestseller would last me a few days, unless it was a weekend when I could read all day. I had more familiarity with Victorian London, the ethnic cuisines of Saskatoon, the jungles of South America, the layout of the Royal Ontario Museum, the grimy dives of San Francisco, and the geography of Barsoom than with the rules for hopscotch.

The girls at school liked to pretend they knew a lot about the world. The more weird stuff they thought you knew, the higher your status. I didn't have to pretend. My big problem was that it drove me nuts when people got something wrong. It took me a while to figure out that constantly correcting people did not lead to happiness.

All of this got me bullied a lot. Apparently, the dear, sweet, little girls only liked you if you were exactly the same as them.

Part of my problem with them was that they did the same thing that a lot of adults do. Instead of saying something like "I don't like that TV show," they'd say "that show is stupid." Most people don't seem to understand that they are being insulting when they say something like that, and it doesn't allow a lot of room for discussion.

I came home crying far more often than any child ever should. Never let anybody tell you that girls are only about psychological bullying. A lot of times I was crying because I'd been in a fight. I was small for my age, so despite being motivated I never won.

I was also too stubborn, or stupid, to run away. Come to think of it, I still am.

Mummy and Daddy tried to make things better. Daddy would hold me and tell me that I'd done nothing wrong, and that the other girls were just mean. That didn't make me feel much better because I already knew that. The hugs, however, were wonderful. As long as Daddy loved me I could imagine things getting better. Never underestimate the healing power of your daddy's arms as a remedy for sadness.

Mummy, as usual, took a more direct approach. She gave me similar talks and hugs, but she also asked for the names of the bullies. Then she visited their parents in an official capacity. For some reason, it makes parents nervous when somebody wearing a badge and a gun comes to talk to them about the behaviour of their evil brats.

Many of the parents were reasonable, and agreed to punish their kids for being bullies. A lot of the overt intimidation at school stopped. What Mummy and I didn't realize at the time was that we'd violated an unwritten law of childhood. The girls hated me more for being a snitch than they did for being weird. The bullying became more sneaky, like someone anonymously tripping me from behind when I was walking down the hall.

A few months into the new year, when I was nine years old, the bully-ing stopped. At Christmas I'd come out of the closet.

At first my father took it hard. The crisis came after supper on a bit-terly cold evening in mid-December.

"Sweetie, I have something for you," he said.

I looked up from the book I was reading. It was unusual to get a present just before Christmas, and I was hoping for a book. Instead, it was a flat cardboard box. Maybe there were books inside.

I opened the box. Inside was a new dress. It was pink, knee-length, with spaghetti straps, and an empire waist.

I have to explain something. I loathe pink. I always have. It reminds me of Pepto Bismol, idiot princesses who need somebody else to save them, and really old, smelly bathrooms. Mum agrees with me. We aren't pink girls. Never have been. Never will be.

You'd think that would be clear enough, wouldn't you? Especially for an intelligent man who had lived with us for many years.

The problem was that my father was somewhat delusional. One of his enduring, irrational beliefs was that all girls love pink.

I looked up at Dad, who was smiling like he'd done something clever. I didn't want to hurt his feelings, but I didn't know what I could say that wasn't a lie.

"What do we say?" Mum prompted.

"Thank you," I said. I hoped that I didn't sound too much like I was being tortured by Nazi dentists. I told you that I read inappropriate things.

"Try it on, then we'll go see Santa."

He had to be crazy. The weather report on TV said that it was -27 Celsius. Nobody in their right mind would go outside at that temperature. Mum had been saying during supper that she'd had a rough day and was tired. She was also looking at him like he was 10-21. That's a police code for somebody who is a few galleons short of an armada.

Mum and I took the dress to my room. At least Dad had gotten the size right. We looked in the mirror. It wasn't too horrible except for the colour. Maybe Mummy could dye it or something when he wasn't looking.

When I started to take it off Mum stopped me.

"He'll want to see it. And try not to roll your eyes like that when you are downstairs."

When we returned, Daddy was beaming.

"You look beautiful," he said. "Turn around."

I pirouetted clumsily. He'd already grabbed our coats from the closet, and was putting his on.

"Shall we?"

Mum and I looked at each other. We hadn't been consulted, but apparently it had been decided that we were all going to see Santa.

Yippee.

Chinook Shopping Centre in Calgary has always suffered from a common retail dilemma. Being surrounded on all sides by major roads, it inhabits a strictly limited area. To be competitive it needs lots of stores, but to accommodate that many customers it needs a vast parking space. It's constantly at war with itself, and seems like it's always under construction, an activity that further limits both the shops and parking. We circled the mall for what felt like hours until Daddy found a spot to leave the car. We walked a long way from there to the warmth of the stores. My legs almost froze off.

People jammed themselves into the mall, all of them desperately intent on giving in to their compulsion to over-spend themselves into debt in the name of peace and goodwill among men. Over the roar of the multitude the PA system played the same Christmas playlist, over, and over again. The people working there must have been ready to go mad.

We fought our way to the line for Santa. Mummy and Daddy were on either side of me, holding my hands so I wouldn't be swept away by the torrent. I nearly got bowled over a few times by obsessive shoppers who weren't looking where they were going. I shivered, despite the body heat and bright lights. In this weather, any sane person would be wearing ski trousers instead of a skirt. For goodness sake, my mother was wearing slacks and a parka.

We moved forward one step. An eternity later we took another step. After an infinite number of eternities, one of Santa's helpers ushered me to Santa's throne.

Santa's helpers were a couple of older women dressed as elves; they probably were high school students trying to make money for Christmas. Santa himself was one of the better ones I'd seen. At least his beard and hair looked real. My legs were still cold and his velvet suit was warm against them. I decided that made it worthwhile to sit on his lap.

Apart from the cold, the dress and the music, there was another reason why I wasn't excited to be there. I'd come to a shocking conclusion during the past year – Santa Claus was a fake. Close inspection showed that, instead of one Santa, there was a different one at each mall. Somehow, despite the lack of a fireplace in our house, presents appeared under our tree. The black threads I'd strung around the living room on Christmas eve to catch him remained undisturbed in the morning. After reading Mummy's copy of a book by Naomi Wolf, I realized that Rudolph the Red-Nosed Reindeer was a song about bullying, and gaining favour with the alpha male in a patriarchal dictatorship at the expense of one's natural companions. As far as I was concerned, the clincher was that it would take some serious magic to make his delivery schedule work. If magic that powerful existed, my grandma wouldn't have died of cancer when I was eight.

The revelation about Santa scared me. I'd already been bullied at school for being different. Everybody else I knew seemed to believe in the reality of Santa Claus. I decided that, if anybody would be on my side, it would be Mummy.

One day, when we were alone, I asked her to come to my room. I closed the door, and had her sit on my bed. The people in stories tended to faint a lot when they got shocking news, and I didn't want her to hurt herself.

I presented her with my evidence, carefully building my case. She listened attentively to my report, then hugged me.

"Veronica, let's just keep this a secret between us. Try to pretend that you still believe in Santa when you talk to your father. Okay?"

I was as I feared. "Daddy believes in Santa?"

"No, dear, but it's complicated. He needs *you* to believe in Santa, just for a while longer. Can you pretend to do that for him?" She brushed my hair back behind one ear with her fingers.

It made no sense to me, but I agreed to the deception. Much later I understood that fathers have certain innate beliefs about their daughters. My father's addiction to pink was one example. Another, probably more universal belief, is that daughters will be little girls forever. When puberty destroys that illusion, they switch to firmly believing that their daughters will always be virgins. He did eventually figure out that one, just as I'd figured out the truth about Santa Claus.

"Hello, little girl. What's your name?" Faux-Santa asked in his hearty voice.

"Veronica Irene Chandler," I said. "Would you like me to spell it for you?"

Honestly, I wasn't trying to be sarcastic. A lot of people seem to have trouble spelling even the easiest names. I was glad that I didn't have a name like Qarrynn Smyth at school. His eyes flicked toward where my parents stood, then he ho-ho-hoed.

"That's all right, Veronica. What would you like for Christmas?"

I'd been bored, standing in line, so I thought about why Daddy had dragged me here. If Mummy was right, and Daddy didn't believe in Santa Claus either, then the only purpose he could have for bringing me here was so that the man in the red suit could ask me that question. A question that, for some reason, Daddy didn't want to ask me himself. Fathers can be so 10-21 at times.

"I want a baton."

"Ho, ho, ho," fake-Santa boomed again, "you want to be a majorette, do you?" I had no idea what a majorette was.

"No," I said, "I want a twenty-one inch ASP baton, like my mummy's." I spoke loudly and clearly so I could be heard over the background music. Both of Santa's elves stared at me like I'd said something strange. I defiantly stared back at them. I had no intention of taking any crap from a pair of old ladies.

Santa's eyes flicked toward my parents again, and I followed his eyes.

Mummy had stepped behind Daddy where he couldn't see her. She hid her mouth behind her hand, and for some reason her shoulders shook. Daddy looked sad. I thought that maybe I'd done something wrong. Was Mummy crying?

"Her mother's a detective," Daddy explained to Santa in an odd voice. Mummy's eyes sparkled, like she had tears in them.

The light went on in pseudo-St. Nick's head.

"Oh, you want one of *those* batons."

I nodded, my eyes still on Daddy's unhappy face, and Mummy's moist eyes. What had I done wrong?

"I'll see what the elves can do, but they're better at making toys. Is there anything else you want, just in case they can't get a baton ready in time?"

He must have thought I was a child. Batons come from ASP, not elves at the North Pole.

"No."

"Maybe something smaller?"

"I'll grow into it," I said, being stubborn. "My mummy says that a larger baton is more versatile, and feels better when it's extended." Mummy turned completely away, her shoulders shaking even more. Daddy looked uncomfortable. The elves' eyes grew round, and one of them smirked. What was their problem? Like either of them knew anything about how batons felt. Santa cleared his throat.

"Well," Santa said as he locked eyes with my father, "we'll see what we can do."

We got the required family picture with Santa. Mummy and Daddy didn't say much in the car on the way home. I really thought that I was in trouble, but had no idea why.

When we got there, Dad disappeared into the kitchen. It was his version of a man cave. Mummy took me to my room, and we sat on my bed for another talk. Now she looked like she was trying hard not to laugh.

"Did I do something wrong?" I was close to tears. I hate not understanding what's going on. It's one of the reasons I wanted to become a PI.

"No, Veronica," she said gently as she hugged me. "I think that your daddy finally understands that you will be whoever you are, not the little pink princess he expected. Don't worry, he'll get over it. Why do you want a baton?"

"You said it took you *months* for you to learn how to use yours, so if I start now, then I'll be ready when I become a private detective," I said, using the term I'd learned from books.

"Is that really what you want to be?"

I nodded.

"You like cooking with your father. Maybe you'd like to be a chef."

"I can be both," I said with the confidence of a nine year old that whatever I could imagine was possible. Except Santa Claus, of course.

Mummy gave me another hug. "All right, dear. I'll explain it to your father. Everything will be all right."

On Christmas morning I came bouncing down stairs to the living room. Since we were staying home, I wore the pink dress to please Daddy. I was proud that I'd thought of that all on my own.

We had a plastic Christmas tree, but it looked wonderful with little twinkling lights, and shining balls hung from it. Daddy had sprayed something on it so it almost smelled like a real tree. By family custom, I got to open one present before breakfast. I dug into the pile beneath the tree, branches poking me in the head and back. I didn't care.

Ignoring the other boxes that promised wonderful things, I came out with a small, heavy present that had been near the trunk. The tag said "To Veronica, with love, Daddy." I tore the paper off, and inside was a box with an Armament Systems and Procedures logo on it. I thought I'd die from the suspense. Inside the box, I found my first tactical baton. I ran my fingers along it, feeling the cool, black steel and foam rubber grip. It smelled faintly of machine oil. Daddy even hugged and kissed me when I squealed, and thanked him for it.

All was right with the world. I was out of the closet as a private eye, and my daddy still loved me. Mummy was smiling as I hugged her too.

It was time for Daddy and I to make pancakes together.

CHAPTER 4

Clients

It's difficult to pay attention to a client when your thong is leaping across the living room. The private investigator's manual really needs a module on dealing with animate lingerie.

It was a Monday afternoon in the middle of December. The provincial private investigator's licensing examination was two months behind me. I'd written it on my eighteenth birthday, the minimum age for licensing in Alberta.

My not-particularly luxurious apartment doubled as my office, an arrangement that saved me a lot of money. That was good, because I still had no clients, and rapidly shrinking savings. A frugal diet had become old. To cheer myself, I'd decided to make porchetta for supper.

Whole suckling pigs don't fit well into a normal oven, especially the ones they put in one-bedroom apartments. Besides, they are expensive. I made do with a piece of pork tenderloin.

Adding olive oil to the rub makes it to stick to the meat more evenly, and helps to hold in moisture. The drawback is that the preparation is messier. I scooped a blob of spice mixture from the prep bowl with my fingers. The mingled smells of anise seed, thyme, rosemary, pepper, lemon, and garlic rose to caress my nose with the promise of wonders to come.

That's when my cell phone rang in the living room. Dammit, I'd left it on the coffee table.

The bowl nearly leaped off the counter as I scraped the spices off my fingers. There was no time to wash my hands, so I grabbed a side towel and dashed for the phone, wiping as I went.

"Chandler Investigations," I said in a slightly breathless version of my professional voice. It was probably a telemarketer, but you never know. Despite my best efforts, the phone slowly slid through my still oily hand.

"Is this the private investigator?" The woman's voice sounded snooty and condescending, which is to say, rich. I can live with snooty and condescending as long as I get paid on time. My heart beat faster.

"Yes, this is Chandler Investigations," I said, thoroughly professional now. I'd already said that, but I can live with deaf too.

"An *acquaintance* suggested your services to me." From her tone, clearly none of her *friends* would have lowered themselves to making such a suggestion. I wondered what acquaintance we could have in common. Maybe it was somebody one of my cop buddies knew.

I heard the quiet tapping sound of tiny claws on Formica coming from the kitchen. Yoko Geri (pronounced with a hard G, not Jerry – it's Japanese, not a Spice Girls reference) had jumped onto the counter, circumnavigated the sink, and was tentatively extending his feline nose toward the defenceless pork roast. I balled up the side towel and threw it at him. He jumped backward as it hit him, sending the prep bowl spinning toward the edge of the counter.

While my attention was distracted the phone made a break for freedom, finally sliding from my oily grip. I had to grab at it with both hands. There was a skittering of claws trying to find purchase, and a thud as my cat hit the linoleum floor. The bowl wobbled to a stop almost half way over the edge, looking like it would fall if a fly landed on the rim. I got the Evil Eye from Yoko, and he gave voice to a series of irritated chirps as he trotted out of the kitchen, around the corner, and into my bedroom.

"Sorry, what was that?" I said into the phone as I went to rescue the bowl.

"I said, I need to see you immediately."

I looked around the apartment. Damn. I needed to stall.

"I'm booked until this evening..."

"What time?"

"One moment." I stared at my 1941 Maltese Falcon movie poster for a count of five in lieu of consulting an empty appointment book.

"How about six thirty?"

"Good." She hung up before I could ask her name, or if she had my address. Damn again.

Then I jumped up, pumped my fist in the air, and did my happy dance. At least that's what I call it. I've never actually learned how to dance, and I suspect that I look like a crippled, epileptic elephant.

My first case as a private investigator! I squeezed the phone too hard, and it flew out of my hand again, bouncing across the counter, and into the living room. I put it back on the counter.

My elation was immediately followed by a moment of panic. *Who am I kidding? I'm not ready for this. I'm eighteen years old!* Getting a high mark on the provincial exam was one thing. Adequately performing services for a live client was another.

Yoko Geri stomped out of my bedroom dragging a cream-coloured silk blouse in his teeth. I distinctly remembered putting it in the laundry hamper. He stared at me with his golden kitten eyes, and I got the message. *Nice blouse. It would be a pity if something happened to it, say, if I don't get some of that porchetta.*

I know when I'm beaten.

"Well, predator, I guess we're having supper early."

I had barely started to spread a second handful of oily glop onto the roll-fileted roast when the phone rang again.

This was ridiculous. For a second I was going to ignore it, but it could have been my new client calling back for directions.

Scrape the fingers, wipe the hands, juggle the oily phone. It would be a pain cleaning it later.

"Chandler Investigations," I said a trifle less professionally.

"You sound pissed," a familiar voice said, and my mood immediately improved.

"*Hola, chica.* How's my favourite sister?"

"Your *only* sister," Kali reminded me. "I wondered if you'd like to come over for dinner."

"Sorry," I said casually, "I have a client meeting at 6:30."

"Oh, my gods! A real, paying client at last? I was beginning to worry."

I fought back the nerves at hearing my own doubts echoed. "Thanks for the vote of confidence, *hermanita.*"

"I didn't mean that," she said. "You'll be awesome. I did have an ulterior motive for asking you over, though."

There was a second of silence that caused small alarm bells to go off in my head. Kali was many things. Hesitant was not one of them.

"I have a situation that seems to need a private investigator."

That wasn't good. "What's wrong? Maybe I can reschedule with my client."

"Don't you dare. It can wait."

"Are you sure?"

"It's for a friend of mine. It's nothing life-threatening or anything."

"All right, how about after my meeting? I can probably make it by eight or nine."

"That'll be great. Have fun with your client."

After she hung up I wondered which of her friends was involved. It was going to bug me until I knew. Insatiable curiosity was part of the price of being a PI.

An hour later, Yoko Geri graciously accepted a small slice of porchetta and gravy while I savoured a considerably larger portion. I did *not* share the mint peas, the new potatoes aux herbes de Provence, or the smooth, home-made red beer. I love my cat, but I have my limits.

After supper I tidied the apartment, and sprayed to clear the air of the delicious smells. It was a shame, but I thought that clients would respond better if they thought that this was solely my office. I also changed out of my flannel pyjamas. They never actually mentioned it in the investig-ator's course, but I'm pretty sure that most investigators wear real clothes during a client interview.

Unless, I suppose, the interview was at a nudist resort. I wondered if I'd ever get a case like that. I had a brief image of frisking hot male sus-pects for unconcealed weapons. I have a bit of ADD. When I get nervous my mind wanders in weird ways.

At 6:15 the intercom buzzer sounded. The client must be impatient. I buzzed her up, then stuck the tasteful, magnetic "Chandler Investiga-tions" sign on the outside of my door. I stared at it for a few seconds until I'd convinced myself that it was straight. In theory, ours is a resid-ential-only building, but after I batted my lashes at the superintendent he relented, and told me that I could put up my sign when I was expect-ing a client. He drew the line at putting "Chandler Investigations" on my buzzer button outside, though. I settled for just "Chandler."

Unless the elevator is already at the ground floor, it takes at least half a minute to get to my apartment on the fourth floor. I used the time for a last look around. Laptop and tissue box on the coffee table: check. The last time I'd looked, Yoko was sprawled on my bed asleep. Bedroom door closed: check. Bathroom door closed: check. I sniffed my hands. Oil and spices removed: check. Since I'd cleverly waited to dress until after sup-per, I didn't have to worry about spots on my blouse from the gravy.

As I expected, she walked in without knocking. I gave a friendly smile as I saw my very first client. She didn't quite wrinkle her nose.

"Mrs. Sofia Reinkemeyer to see Veronica Chandler," she said, glancing around my apartment/office, then dismissing it from her mind. She star-ted to remove her leather gloves.

"I'm Veronica Chandler." I extended my hand.

She paused, the second glove half off, then finished removing it.

"Really? You look much younger than I expected." She did not shake my hand.

She should talk. If she was more than twenty-two, I wanted to know where she kept the portrait that aged instead of her. I caught the scent of Shalini perfume, a bottle of which would keep me in food for at least four months.

"Thank you, I get that a lot. It has benefits in certain investigations. Won't you have a seat?"

I'd salvaged a cool coat rack from a 1930s-era office that was being demolished. It looked like it belonged in Sam Spade's office. I hung her coat on it along with my fedora and trench coat that Dad had bought me as licensing presents.

She accepted my offer of a seat on my IKEA couch, where she perched as if fearing contamination. Her mid-back length blonde hair fell over one shoulder of the short Armani dress that probably cost more than my month's rent. She canted her legs to the side to keep her knees together. That just happened to nicely display her mid-heel Gucci boots that definitely cost more than my month's rent.

It's not what I would have chosen to wear on a cold winter evening, but to each her own. Maybe being cold was her natural state.

I sat across the IKEA coffee table from her in my IKEA comfy chair and picked up my refurbished, non-IKEA computer.

The laptop felt warm on my thighs. With any luck, my Sears pant suit and Payless shoes would pass muster.

"What can I do for you, Mrs. Reinkemeyer?"

There was another pause, and her lips pursed slightly.

"It's about my husband, Frank."

She hesitated again, and I caught the first hint that her calm wasn't as deep as she wanted me to believe.

"We were married three years ago. At first, he was wonderful: buying me presents, and taking me on vacations all over the world. Then he changed."

She sniffled artistically, dabbing at the corners of her shockingly blue eyes with a tissue from her purse so she wouldn't damage her make-up. It's very important, I'm sure, not to damage your make-up when you suspect that your life is dropping into the toilet.

"How old is your husband?" I asked, making notes on the computer.

"Forty-three. He's the owner of a high-end computer consulting firm. He was quite athletic when we married, but now he's let himself go. And – I think he's having an affair."

Her last sentence really brought out the tears, and her chin quivered in a way that's difficult to fake. I could relate; my first boyfriend had cheated on me. I waited for her to cry herself out.

"When did you first become suspicious?"

"A month ago, when he started working late. Why would he have to work late? He owns the business. He has people to do that for him. I don't know what I'll do if he leaves me." The words came tumbling out in a stream of consciousness jumble. Her distress seemed genuine.

One thing was certain: if he was seeing someone more than a few years younger than his wife then a divorce would be the least of his problems. He'd be up on a paedophilia charge as well.

"Do you have a recent picture of him?"

She dug through her Versace shoulder bag that perfectly matched her eyes. I didn't want to think about what that had cost. My own eyes are sort of hazel, my hair sort of brown (currently dyed darker so I can mention my hair colour without prefacing it with "sort of"). On the other hand, I'll never have to worry about my breasts drooping.

The formal head shot of Frank Reinkemeyer looked like it had been taken for a company brochure. It showed his public persona: a confident, strong, friendly, trustworthy businessman who could get things done for you. It also tried, but failed, to disguise that he had at least a double chin, and a neck in peril of overflowing his shirt collar. Even with the most talented photographer head angle, make-up, and good lighting can't hide everything.

That's when I noticed the thong.

Yoko Geri was at the all-legs stage of kittenhood, and he must have sneaked out of the bedroom before I'd closed the door. I must have missed one of his toy stashes in the living room itself, probably hidden under the couch. He threw a lacy black thong into the air, and then danced on his back legs to catch it as it floated down. Damn it, he'd been raiding the laundry basket again.

So much for professionalism. If he moved slightly toward me he'd be in her line of sight. Trying to tackle him would be a bit obvious, as well as futile. He was fast when he thought he was being chased. He might take the thong with him, parading it around the room, or he might not.

Either way, my chances of stopping his play weren't good.

The wisp of nylon floated to the carpet and he crouched, his feet spread wide. With a small chirp, he pounced on the offending underwear, and threw it up into the air again, his paws waving menacingly to catch it as it descended. He'd managed to get the toss just right, and the thong looked like a tiny three-cornered parachute. I needed a good distraction.

"Would you like some water?"

Sofia sniffed and nodded, too self-absorbed to notice Yoko's almost silent acrobatics on the floor beside her. I tried to grab my thong in midair on the way past, but he beat me to it, running a few steps away with it in his mouth. He dropped it, and this time I managed to pin it to the carpet with my toe before scooping it up. That earned me an indignant chirp from my sidekick. He scampered after me into the kitchen, thoughts of more porchetta dancing in his head. Hope springs eternal in the kitten stomach.

After tossing the thong into the mostly empty freezer to keep it well away from Yoko, I grabbed a bottle of water from the fridge. While I was there I also put a slice of porchetta in his dish to keep him busy.

I handed her the bottle, and the art film of her internal monologue rolled across her face. *What the hell is this? Water comes in plastic? What's a "Kirkland Signature?" Where's the San Pellegrino label?* She gave me an insincere smile and sipped. *Ugh. I didn't know they made unflavoured water.* She tried to be gracious.

"Thank you, Ms. Chandler."

"Please, call me Veronica. I assume that you'd like me to find out if your husband is having an affair, and to bring you proof either way," I said gently. She nodded. Despite her care, her make-up now the worse for wear. I felt considerably more sympathy for her as a grief-stricken woman instead of a trophy wife out for blood.

We went through questions about where his office was, his hobbies, habits, and schedule. By the end I had enough to start surveillance.

It only took me a minute to type the details into my contract template and print it. She took a long time to read it, and I tried not to fidget. In high school, I'd never earned more than fifteen dollars an hour, and I only got that because I worked at my father's restaurant. I like to think that I'm pretty self-confident, but asking a stranger to pay me fifty dollars an hour plus expenses, with a thousand dollar retainer, made me uncomfortable despite her obvious wealth. The shrink I'd seen a few years ago had gotten me into the habit of questioning my reactions, so I thought about why the money was an issue for me.

It struck me then that this had nothing to do with money. This was the real graduation, the loss of another virginity. Before this meeting, I was a teenage girl who had a part-time job, a dream of becoming a private investigator, and whose parents would bail her out if I got into trouble. As soon as we signed the contract, I would be an adult professional with a private investigation agency for whose performance I was solely responsible.

I took a deep breath, knowing that my nerves were stupid. This moment was what I'd been working toward since I was a small girl. Still, I studied the computer screen, and pretended to make more notes so she wouldn't see my jitters.

Yoko, just to prove that sometimes he's actually a loving companion instead of a fiend from hell, jumped into my lap. He sat purring on the keyboard. It forced me to stop typing, and start stroking his back with one hand. That helped, and my mind drifted.

I felt a little like Ernst Blofeld. Too bad Yoko is the exact opposite of a white Persian. Maybe I should get a grey Mao jacket. Or perhaps Auric Goldfinger would be more appropriate: *Do you expect me to sign? No, Mrs. Reinkemeyer, I expect you to pay.* In a masterful use of mental mixed film metaphors, I pictured myself putting the end of my pinky to the corner of my mouth. I firmly stifled a nervous giggle. I hate it when I giggle.

My client finally flipped to the last page, signed, and took an envelope out of her handbag.

"I believe you require a thousand dollars for your retainer?"

I glanced inside the envelope briefly, and saw a thin stack of new hundred dollar bills. My first income as a PI. I tried not to salivate.

"Perfect," I said. She started to rise, so I tried to place Yoko on the floor, the laptop on the table, and get out of my chair, all without looking too clumsy. Sofia rose smoothly from the edge of the couch, and accepted my business card. Women who are tall, willowy and graceful should be shot.

"Call me the next time he says he'll be working late. I'll be in touch as soon as I have anything to report." I offered her my hand again, and this time she accepted it. I was afraid to squeeze too hard. It was like shaking hands with a water-filled condom.

I don't like people with soggy handshakes. So much for us ever becoming friends.

CHAPTER 5

Girl Power

I had a few friends when I was nine years old, but almost all of our interaction was at school. Most of the girls never came over to our house, and those who did often didn't come back a second time. To them, "coming over to watch TV" seemed to be a code phrase that meant endlessly talking about other things while the television played in the background. Silly me, I thought we'd actually watch it, and talk about the show afterwards. The girls talked during Doctor Who were never invited back. Some things are sacred.

On Boxing Day, Mum gave me my first lesson with my new baton. It was both exciting and disappointing. Faux-Santa had been right: A twenty-one inch baton was a lot for a little girl to handle. Mum spent a lot of time trying to teach me the flick needed to extend the baton in my hand without it flying off into the distance. The problem wasn't the motion. I could do it just fine with something smaller in my hand. The problem was that the handle was just so damned big, and I wasn't very strong. Mum could do it so effortlessly that I got more and more frustrated.

"Maybe we should put this away until you're a little older," she said. Even as an adult, I would have given her at least a glare for making such a suggestion, no matter how reasonable it was. Nine year old me got really pissed at the thought of not being able to use a baton like Mum. I insisted that we keep trying. After an unfortunate incident involving the living room lamp, we moved practice sessions into the basement.

I needed more strength and more size. Intellectually, I knew that time would make me bigger, but I've never been very patient. "Next year" might as well have been forever. At least strength was something I could work on now, and I told her so.

"All right," Mum said, "if that's what you want, I'll see what I can arrange." I assumed that she'd bring home weights, or maybe we'd go to a gym to use some of those machines you see on TV that seem to make people bulge with muscles overnight.

Instead, the next day she called me to my room, and presented me with a new outfit that matched hers: sweat pants, a t-shirt, and a gym bag.

For the past few years, Mum had been going out twice a week during the evening. She'd always referred to it as "going to class," so at first I thought she went to school like I did. Now that I was older I realized that it was something she did for fun.

Going to school for the fun of it. Who'd have thought?

"I spoke with my teacher, and he said that you can try coming to class with me. He doesn't have a children's course, so you'll be practising with the adults."

I was excited before I even knew what I'd be getting into. I squealed and hugged her.

I tried on the new outfit. It was a little big on me, but that just meant that I could grow into it.

Our first class was just after the New Year. She drove us over to the community centre, and I felt really grown up as we walked across the parking lot and into the building with matching outfits and bags. I walked beside her, matched her stride so we were in step.

The class was held in a room in the basement where the entire floor was covered with rubber mats.

Several people were already there doing stretching things. There was no fancy equipment; just some locked cupboards. I recognized one of the students as Nick Holley. He was a constable who lived near us, and picked Mum up for work every morning.

The teacher was shorter than Nick, but he still looked huge to me. He could probably lift Nick with one hand. All of a sudden I felt shy.

"Janet," he said to my mother, "so this is your daughter." He had an accent, a bit like Russians I'd heard on television but nicer, I thought.

"Yes," Mum said. "Veronica, this is *Madrich* Ish-shalom."

"Veronica," he repeated, shaking my hand. He pronounced my name as "VayrohneeKAH." I thought that it sounded cool that way. "I would like to get an idea of how much you can do before we start so that you don't hurt yourself. Do you know how to do push ups? How many can you do for me?"

I got down, and did my best. By the time I'd done seven push ups my arms were tired. Nine were almost impossible. Although I really tried, I got half way through the tenth push up and collapsed.

"Good! How about sit ups?"

I rolled over and did as many as I could while he gently held my feet down for me. Being both skinny and light, I didn't give up until I'd done forty.

"Excellent!" He knelt down beside me. "When we do our warm up in class, I want you to do no more than one quarter of what I ask the adults to do. Do you understand?"

I nodded. Inside I was annoyed that I was being treated like a child. "Yes, sir."

"Call me *Madrich.* Can you say that?"

I tried, pronouncing it madreesh. He corrected me and I tried again. This time I got the Scottish "ch" sound more or less right.

"Excellent!" He said again. "That means teacher in Hebrew. It is very important that you do not try to do too much right away, or you will hurt yourself. After a while, we will increase the amount you do as you get stronger. Before long you will be keeping up with the other students, but for now, no more than one quarter." He wiggled his forefinger at me but was smiling. I got the feeling that he knew what I was thinking.

"Yes, *Madrich.*" I pronounced it correctly, and more respectfully.

He looked up at Mum. "You keep an eye on her. She has a lot of spirit, and it isn't good to push a young body too hard."

The first hour of the class was the "warm up." Even though I was only doing a quarter of what the adults were, I felt like even The Hulk couldn't have kept up. At the end, everybody was covered with sweat and panting. The one exception was *Madrich* Ish-shalom. He did everything he asked the adults to do, and looked like he'd been quietly sitting reading a book the whole time.

During the second hour we practised drills with a partner. My first partner was a non-police women named Lacey who was only a bit taller than me. She showed me what to do, and she was really gentle with me compared with what I saw Mum doing with Nick. Every few minutes we changed partners. By the end of the first night I was exhausted but I felt good, like I was on my way to accomplishing something.

After class we went out to the car. I climbed in and fastened my seat belt. My next memory was waking up in bed with the morning sun shining through the window.

I slowly got out of bed, hurting in places I wouldn't have believed *could* hurt.

Later, Mum told me about *Madrich* Raanan Ish-shalom. He'd moved to Calgary from Israel, where he'd been in the *Sayeret Matkal,* the special forces branch of Israeli intelligence. He'd been injured during an operation the same year I was born, and had to retire. Nick was the one who had convinced him to teach a civilian Krav Maga class. It was a small group, only about a dozen students, most of whom were police officers.

It was fun having a mother-daughter activity, even though a lot of the protective equipment that was stored in those cupboards smelled like old sweat. It was sort of like going shopping together, but with body armour, knives, and fake guns instead of Calvin Klein.

Some mothers are much cooler than others.

By the age of twelve, there were three kinds of girls in my school. Some didn't care about their marks, and would probably grow up to do little or nothing with their lives. Most were in the middle, the normal girls who did as little as possible to get by in school with reasonable marks. A few were the freaks, who were cray-cray smart. The others lumped me in with them because I was reading all the time, but my lack of plans to go after a PhD. made me an outsider among the brains too.

Many girls ran around in "clubs" (to keep the school from freaking out about gang activity). Going by what I'd read and seen on television, the clubs weren't at all gang-like, but you know how adults are. The girls still pretended to know far more about life than they really did.

School was easy for me. I was used to reading three or four books a week since I was in kindergarten. The "clubs" held no interest for me, partly because I really did know a lot about life, at least theoretically. They also didn't do anything that I found particularly fun.

The girls played games like hopscotch, which I found boring. I played with the boys instead. They had better games than the girls did, and if one of them annoyed me, I actually gained respect from the group by punching his lights out. Unlike the girls, the boys tended to talk about things they knew about, or at least thought they knew about. The big hole in their education was girls, who seemed to be the ultimate mystery to them. On this subject they considered me to be their resident expert. Unfortunately, I didn't really get what most girls were about either.

By then, I was big enough to use my baton, and I was getting good with it. My big disappointment was that I wasn't allowed to take it with me, either to school, or when I went out to play – even if we were playing cops and robbers. It wasn't fair.

Dad started being weird about things again. In particular, he didn't seem to like who my friends were.

"Where are you going?" He asked one fine summer day as I was going out the door.

I had to stop to swallow the cookie I was eating before I could answer. "Robert's house."

"Can I talk to you for a minute?"

That's never a good sign. If it had been something normal such as "can you help me make supper tonight?" he'd have just said "can you help me make supper tonight?"

I came back inside, closed the door, and sat on the end of the sofa.

"I'm a little worried about you," he said, sounding almost like he had when he and Mum had sat me down for The Talk About Babies two years earlier. "You seem to be spending a lot of time with these boys."

What was he talking about? "Don't you want me to have friends?"

He cleared his throat. "Of course I do, but don't you think that it would be more appropriate for you to spend time with your other friends?" I was outraged by his use of the word. I'd gone through a big argument with a librarian the year before when I tried to check out some books that she thought were "inappropriate."

"Appropriate? Did you actually say 'appropriate'?"

Dad's not stupid. He can tell when he's stuck his foot in his mouth, even if he isn't always sure why.

"I mean, wouldn't you rather hang out with your girl friends?"

"No. Most girls are boring. Why would I hang out with them?"

"I don't want you getting hurt, that's all."

What the hell was he talking about?

"Dad, I've been taking Krav Maga for over two years. Nobody is going to hurt me."

"That wasn't what I meant." I think he realized that he was getting in over his head. "You are getting to the age when the boys are going to start thinking of you as a girl."

That was just stupid. "I am a girl." Then it clicked.

"Eww. Dad, that's gross. Robert would never do anything like that."

"Veronica, I just want you to..."

"Have 'appropriate' friends? Read only 'appropriate' books? Or are you like some of my inappropriate friends' parents who want me to act 'appropriately' for a twelve year old girl? Whatever that means."

He gave a deep sigh.

"All right, I can see that I've hit one of your buttons. Just be careful, okay?"

"Dad," I said with the full gravitas of a twelve-year old's dignity, "when have I not been careful?"

Don't ever get the idea that my dad is stupid or a male chauvinist pig. Like Lazarus Long in Heinlein's novels, he believes that it is a man's job to protect women, although he does admit that they should be able to take care of themselves too. And, no matter how annoying his Neanderthal attitudes were at times, I knew that he loved me.

It sounds like Dad was completely isolated from the reality of my life, but that's far from true. Dad owned his own restaurant, Maison Chandler (pronounced "Shondlair" by the pretentious and Chandler by us). If the Michelin guide inspectors ever visited Calgary, I'm sure it would have gotten three stars. Dad and I spent a lot of happy hours in the kitchen together, and it meant a lot to us that we shared a passion for fine food and its preparation. It also gave me another, less lethal, knife-related parental activity.

My great teenage rebellion against my father was that I preferred beer to wine. Mind you, it had to be *good* beer. Starting in my late teens, I was brewing my own for home consumption, my bubbling fermentors sitting next to Dad's wine cellar in the basement. Dad grudgingly agreed that what I brewed was pretty good – for beer.

Between us, Dad and I did all the cooking at home, which was fortunate for all of us. As far as Mum was concerned, if a recipe said to bake for an hour at 300 degrees, she should be able to cook it in half an hour at 600 degrees. In her world, the microwave oven had one setting – high. Mum could just about manage a grilled cheese sandwich, but anything more complicated had a high probability of setting off the smoke alarm. After a while, we just forbade her to set foot in our kitchen.

Everybody was happier that way (including the smoke alarm), but sometimes I wondered if she was just manipulating us into cooking for her. Detectives can be sneaky that way, and Mum was a very good detective.

CHAPTER 6

When Shall We Three Meet Again?

My interview with Sofia Reinkemeyer took less time than I'd expected. The case should be a straight forward surveillance of an allegedly cheating husband who, we hoped, had no idea that she suspected him. That made things much easier for me.

It was only 7:30 when she left. I removed the sign from my door, and headed out to my next appointment. Binky, my white Chevy Cavalier, started right away despite the temperature that was in the low minus twenties.

A few blocks north, a few blocks west, and I was heading down Crowchild Trail to Kali's house. I like to think that being spiritual sisters, rather than biological ones, has made us even closer. We didn't have to compete for anything while growing up.

Fifteen minutes later I turned onto Thirty Third Avenue. Marda Loop used to be a Calgary hot spot, between the end of an old streetcar line, and the armed forces base. Dad had told me that it had drooped when the Currie Barracks closed. Now it was booming again, with boutiques, coffee shops and, of course, Kali's occult shop. I headed south toward the ice cream shop, and pulled into Kali's driveway a few minutes later. The concrete pad had a built in heater so it was bare and dry despite the piles of snow on the street. Ditto for the walkway. It was shortly before eight o'clock, and I wondered again why Kali might need a PI.

Since she was expecting me, I used my key and walked right in. There was no immediate sign of her, so I dropped my laptop bag on her couch.

"Yo, witch," I called.

"In here, boiling children," she said from the kitchen.

"How many times do I have to tell you: children should be sauteed, not boiled."

"Like you'd know anything about cooking children."

The house itself was less than a year old, and looked as close to a castle as she could get away with in that neighbourhood. She'd wanted a modest place to live so she'd had one built: Three bedrooms, four bathrooms, and a kitchen the size of my living room. I thought it was a bit much. Honestly, these days, how many eighteen-year olds want or need a formal dining room? Mind you, compared with the places she'd lived with her parents, this *was* modest.

Kali, as always, was the most notable thing in the room. As I came around the corner, I saw her standing at the stove, stirring a sauce pan full of something that smelled wonderfully herbal, but not at all delicious. It was somewhat medicinal, and seemed to go right up into my sinuses. Her outfit was typical for her when hanging around the house: a black baby doll, black fishnets, and combat boots. Over it all she wore an apron.

I'd always admired her rich, Mestizo Colombian skin tone. Tonight her black hair was brushed out loose, and the dyed blood-red tips fanned out across her back. The middle third of her hair was held by a pink, plastic, Hello Kitty clip. Sometimes that girl worries me.

"Have a seat," she said, "this is almost done. Have you met Keith?"

It took me a moment to switch mental tracks, then I turned. There was a cute guy sitting at her kitchen table. He looked uncomfortable. I wondered if he and Kali were sleeping together, and what her boyfriend George thought about that. Her outfit might point in that direction. If they weren't, maybe I could borrow him. He was really cute.

"Keith, this is Veronica Chandler. Veronica, Keith Bonsell."

He smiled shyly, and I recognized him from her shop.

"You're one of Kali's customers, aren't you?"

"And a friend," Kali said. "Would you like some tea?" She was straining her concoction through cheesecloth.

"Um, that doesn't smell very good."

"Not this, *miquita.* This is a purification potion for a house-cleansing ritual. I'm making it for a client."

She carefully poured the steaming liquid into a spray bottle, and stored it in her refrigerator.

True to the hard-boiled detective image I'd like to think I have, I usually drink black coffee. Kali, despite being Colombian, had more refined sensibilities. She preferred teas of various exotic types. I had to admit that a lot of them were interesting.

There were three mugs ready on the counter. I sat at the table while she poured from what was obviously an industrial-sized coffee maker.

"What happened to your tea maker?"

"It was too small. Manufacturers must think that tea drinkers use shot glasses."

She brought the mugs over, put one in front of each of us, and sat across from me. I smiled at Keith, and he looked down at his cup.

I looked from one to the other, and back again. Neither of them were talking. "All right, spill it."

Now it was her turn to toy with her cup before answering me.

"Keith's having problems with his boyfriend."

Darn, so much for my investigative instincts. No wonder Kali didn't mind prancing around in front of him in that outfit. And so much for borrowing him. I looked at Keith. He was still studying his cup.

"And?"

"I've known them for about three years. He and Parker are a completely committed couple. A few months ago Parker proposed, and they've set a date in June."

"Congratulations," I said to Keith. He was still looking down. "But those don't sound like problems to me."

"In the last month, Parker has started acting – weird," Keith finally spoke. "We've always been honest with each other, but now he acts like there's something he doesn't want me to know. Evasive. Ashamed. Maybe guilty. It's not like him."

"Have you tried talking to him?"

"Yes. I didn't get anywhere. Parker insists that nothing is wrong, but Kali and I can both see it. I think he's in some kind of trouble, and doesn't want us to worry."

I took a sip of my tea. It was time for me to be insensitive.

"Could he be seeing someone else?" Keith looked like I'd slapped him.

"You have to know Parker," Kali said. "He's the most monogamous person I've ever met. He makes our parents look like swingers."

A mental image with our parents, loud music, lacy underwear, leather corsets, and a big pile of naked people flashed through my mind. I repressed it immediately. There are some things we were never meant to see, even in our imagination.

"We love each other," Keith said. I could hear the pain in his voice. His eyes glistened.

"All right, what would you like me to do?"

"Find out what's going on," Kali said. "Please."

"You want to hire me professionally?"

Keith nodded.

"I know that investigators are expensive," he said, "and I won't have much money until I get a new job." He blushed more than anyone else I'd ever seen. "The place where I worked went under a few weeks ago. Would you accept instalments?"

"I'll pay the bill," Kali said.

"No! This is my problem!"

"Get real, Keith. You and Parker are my friends. You are so right for each other, and I want to help."

"I can't let you..."

"It's not like I can't afford it..."

"That's not the point..."

"Enough!" I ordered. They both shut up.

"Keith, you obviously don't know how stubborn Kali can be. Why don't you let her handle the initial bill, and then you can pay her back when you get work? It's really no different from paying me in instalments."

They both glared at me but Keith cracked first.

"Fine," he said.

"Fine," Kali repeated.

"Fine," I said to make it unanimous. "Give me a second to get my computer. I'll need the details." I retrieved my bag from the living room.

I opened a new case file, trying not to show my excitement. After months of sitting around staring at the phone, I had two paying clients in one day.

I just wished that the cases were more, I don't know, exciting. Memorable. A girl's first cases should be exciting and memorable. I'd probably just get a few billable hours out of each one for taking a few pictures.

Where's a good Maltese Falcon when you need one?

CHAPTER 7

Alien Mutation

For some parents, it would be the ultimate horror: Their daughter was about to become a teenager. Within two months of my thirteenth birthday, three things happened to me: One was good, one was bad, and one was weird.

The weird one was that I turned into a freaking mutant. It started with two puffy lumps on my chest. Over a period of several weeks they grew into cones. I was sure that there was something wrong, although Mum assured me that I was normal.

Suddenly, I couldn't quite lie flat on my stomach on the floor. My hips got wider, and I felt clumsy, especially when doing Krav Maga. After a while, the cones became mounds, which at least looked less weird.

Hair mysteriously started growing everywhere. Well, it seemed like everywhere. To top it all off, the ickier aspects of that theoretical discussion about reproduction a few years earlier suddenly applied to me, very personally.

So this was the cherished "growing up" I'd been looking forward to for years.

Yippee.

Then there was this unbelievably bizarre moment when I was walking to school, and aliens took over my brain. As usual, there were a few kids ahead of me on the street. Some were boys, some were girls. Whatever.

Suddenly, the boy in front of me became different. It's hard to explain, but instead of being just a moving blob, he became a *male*. In a moment, he somehow became important to me. Someone who had something I wanted, or needed, or something. I didn't even know him. The day before I might have described him as looking okay, if anybody asked. Now I thought he was kind of cute. Somehow, that was an entirely different thing.

It was incredibly confusing. I spent the whole day distracted by all the *males* in my classes. I knew all about the theory, but nothing I'd ever read prepared me for it happening in my own head. It freaked me out.

After a while I learned to mostly ignore the problem, except when it ambushed me. It ambushed me a lot. I wondered if this was normal, or if I was going mad.

The bad thing that happened was that my playmates started mutating too. I had noticed the boys staring at me strangely ever since my breasts started growing. My playmates were acting oddly, and I wondered if they were going through something like the same mental weirdness that I was.

I also wondered what it meant if they were.

The Bow River valley had been carved by the melting torrent at the end of the last Ice Age. What was now a quiet river about 100 metres wide had been a mighty flood almost four kilometres across where it went through what would be Calgary. The hillside north of downtown used to be one of the river banks.

Now it's just a grass-covered slope leading down to Riley Park: eight square blocks of lawns, flower beds, a wading pool, and the cricket pitch. On summer weekends you can find a lot of families there, picnicking, splashing in the pool, or playing catch. Not to mention the cricket club in their white uniforms.

On the day when things came crashing down around me, my friends and I were having a game of Ultimate in the park.

The day was sunny and hot. I was sweating like girls, for some reason, aren't supposed to. We had just pulled to the other team, and I was running down the field when the disc came sailing toward my target, Ken Tolly. He jumped to catch it and missed. I caught it as it passed him. It should have been an elegant catch and re-throw. Both of us were watching the disc more than each other, and we smashed into each other with arms and legs everywhere. Lying on the ground, his hand was on my chest, cupping what there was of my right breast. I hadn't started wearing a bra yet.

I pushed him away, and when we got up he had a stupid grin on his face as he stared at my chest.

"What?" I looked down to see if there was blood on me or something.

"I just wanted to make sure you're all right," he said, then the idiot reached out and *tweaked* my nipple. Damn, that hurt and pissed me off. My breasts had been feeling sensitive for a day or so, a sign that my new

Monthly Friend would soon be on her way. I very carefully explained to him that his actions were socially unacceptable by planting my foot in his crotch. He was quiet for a few seconds, then his howls as he rolled on the ground brought everybody else over.

"What's wrong?" Asked Paul Milani.

"He groped me, so I kicked him," I said reasonably. My arms were crossed over my chest, protecting the nipple that was still throbbing. He'd pinched it hard.

"Are you all right?" Paul said to his friend. What the hell? Before the Great Mutation, the boys would have made fun of Ken for being beaten up by a girl. Now they were on his side?

Ken shook his head and moaned. He was still on the ground, and still curled up.

"You didn't have to hurt him," someone said from behind me. I turned around but couldn't figure out who in the group had spoken.

"Hey, this is Veronica we're talking about," Robert Sherling said. He was the one boy who hadn't been turning into a creep lately. "Show some respect."

"We'll have to stop the game until Ken can play," Paul complained.

"I don't believe this," I yelled. "He hurt me, and all you care about is the stupid game!"

Everybody, except Robert, was looking at me like I was at fault.

"Hey, Veronica, it's no big deal," Devin said. He was the biggest boy on my team, a good head taller than me. He'd transferred to our school a week before, so he didn't know me as well as the others did.

He put his arm around my shoulders, then let his hand slip down toward my waist.

"Don't," I said quietly. I could feel my anger building.

He laughed and squeezed.

I ignored his arm. Instead, I held hands with myself and used the power of both arms to ram my elbow into his side. The "I'm so cool" grin vanished from his face as his breath exploded outward, and he doubled over. I'd purposely missed his ribs, so nothing should be broken. I considered that being polite.

I stepped away from him, ready to rain down a world of hurt if necessary. It suddenly dawned on me that I was probably PMSing, and maybe I should calm down before there were more bodies on the grass.

Part of me said I shouldn't.

"Don't - touch - me," I said, shaking with general rage at them, for being idiots, and myself, for losing control. Most of the boys backed up a few steps. They might outnumber me thirteen to one (eleven to one if Ken and Devin stayed down), but apart from today's demonstration, they'd seen me fight before, and nobody wanted to be the next casualty. Robert didn't back up. He stood beside me.

"Not cool, guys," he said. "Veronica, can I walk you home?"

I looked at my former friends, and all I saw were the eyes of *boys* fixed on my chest. Robert was the only one looking at my face. Not trusting myself to speak, I just walked away. Robert followed.

Behind me I heard somebody say "now what are we going to do? We're four players down."

I quickly walked across the grass toward Tenth Street, not wanting to spend any more time than necessary getting out of the park. Feelings were bouncing around inside me that I didn't like at all. I could feel my eyes getting moist, but there was no way I was going to cry within sight of those morons, and give them any kind of satisfaction.

We reached the sidewalk and I turned south. Robert walked quietly at my side. I kept it together until we got to the next intersection, but as soon as the light turned green the tears started. There were all kinds of reasons, but a big part of it was that I didn't know who I was any more. It seemed like only last week that I was one of the guys. Now? Had I changed that much? Into what?

"Are you sure you're okay?" Robert asked as we crossed the street. He had the good sense not to try to hug me or anything.

I angrily swiped the tears from my eyes with the heels of my hands. "I'm fine." I took a deep breath, and thought about it. "Maybe I overreacted."

Robert took a moment before answering.

"No. I know I'd be upset if somebody grabbed my – um – "

"Crotch?" I thought it was cute that he was embarrassed. I'd known him since grade three, and this was the first time I'd thought of him as cute. I'd noticed that the alien was a bit less crazy around my period, but I still wished Robert would put his arm around me. Just for a friendly hug, you know. My tears had mysteriously vanished. The aliens had turned off the bozo rays that were scrambling my brain. Or maybe they'd turned them to a different setting.

"Yeah. I don't think you overreacted. Well, not much." His smile was tentative, and I returned it.

"You do realize that we can't walk home from here. I need to call my dad to pick us up."

"I know. I just thought that 'can I walk you home' sounded better than 'can I get you out of here before you kill them all?'" At least I laughed at that instead of crying. I was acting like a mental case. What was wrong with me?

We walked down Tenth Street to Kensington Road in silence, enjoying the summer sun. Kensington is the home of a ton of little shops: book stores, fancy coffee places, wine shops, and of course, the Plaza Theatre where art films go to see and be seen. The whole Kensington thing spills over onto Tenth Street: The United Brotherhood of Carpenters and Joiners (I wonder if they let women in?), a talent agency, a motorcycle shop. Not to mention Calgary's oldest surviving occult shop, and a hardware store with a window display that never seems to change, but somehow has been there forever.

The alien was back in my head, whispering that Robert was sweet and cared about me, and I should do something about it. I just wasn't sure what it was suggesting. Apparently, some boys thought that grabbing my chest was a sign of affection, but there was no way I was going to start grabbing any part of him. That would just be a weird thing to do to a friend.

I arched my back as I clasped my hands behind my back. Only because the stretch felt good after all that exercise, of course. I noticed that I was swinging my hips more than usual, convincing myself I was just being playful. The reason why I would want to be playful at that moment escaped me.

"How come you aren't staring at my chest?" I blurted. I want to be very clear that I was just curious. I wasn't trying to send an invitation or anything. Robert seemed really uncomfortable with my question.

"Can you keep a secret?" He finally said, his voice quiet.

"Always. You're my friend. Probably my only one, now."

"I'm not really interested in girls' chests."

It took me a moment to get it. "You're gay?" I blurted. A couple of women in their thirties were passing by. One gave me a dirty look, then kissed the woman beside her. She'd misunderstood my tone of voice, and I thought about how what I said might sound to Robert. "That's so cool," I added. He shrugged, and I realized how dumb that was. I guess if you're gay then inside you aren't cool or not cool. You just are, like everybody else.

The alien was annoyed that he was gay. Wow, I really was possessed.

"Still friends?" He looked as if he thought I might hit him so I did, punching his arm gently.

"Of course, dummy. I'll call Dad."

It took half an hour for him to arrive. In the meantime, we found a small café that served ice cream.

Parking on Kensington is one of those urban myths where everybody knows somebody whose friend says they've done it, but they've never actually found a spot themselves. Dad stopped on the street, and we piled into the back seat before too many people started blowing their horns.

"You're done early," Dad said as he navigated through the stop-and-stop traffic. I didn't answer.

"There was an argument," Rob said. My elbow poked his side as a hint to shut up.

"With whom?"

"Just some of the guys," I said.

"About what?"

"Nothing important."

By then we'd gotten out of Kensington, and were in a more residential area with actual side streets. In one fluid motion, Dad abruptly signalled, turned, and parked on one of them.

"Veronica, what's going on?"

Crap. Dad wasn't going to let this go.

"Two of the boys groped me."

He was looking at us in the read view mirror, so all I could see was his eyes. His hands tightened on the steering wheel.

"Robert, would you mind waiting outside for a minute?"

"It's okay. It wasn't a big deal." I grabbed Robert's arm to keep him from bailing out of the car.

"All right. What exactly did they do?"

"Ken groped my chest, and Devin put his arm around my waist."

"Ken *what*?"

"It's okay, Mr. Chandler," Robert said. "Veronica handled it."

Dad started the engine. He did not look happy.

"What are you doing?" I asked, panicking.

"I'm going to have a talk with them."

"Dad, no! I handled it."

"How?"

"I just did."

"Robert?"

"Um..." He decided he was more afraid of my father than me. "She kicked Ken in the balls, and nailed Devin with her elbow. They were still on the ground when we left." He sounded proud of me.

"And your part in all this?"

"I offered to walk her home before she killed them all," Robert said.

"I see."

Dad drummed on the steering wheel with the fingers of one hand. We waited to see what would happen.

"Very well. I hope you hit them hard," Dad said after a while. Wow, where was the man who thought violence never solved anything?

"Oh yeah, Mr. Chandler," Robert said, "she explained their mistakes to them *very* carefully."

Dad turned around to look at Robert.

"May I assume that the lesson was not lost on you, either?"

"Yes, sir," Robert said with a straight face. "I have no interest in groping your daughter."

I turned to look back at him, and he winked. I giggled at his double meaning. I hate it when I giggle.

"Good. Thank you for looking after my daughter, Robert," he said.

"I don't need anybody to look after me!" I snapped.

"No problem, sir."

When we got to my house, I invited Robert in for juice and left-over pizza. We watched some DVD, I forget which. I just know that it was nice having a friend who didn't see me as a pair of tits with a girl attached.

We're still friends, even though his family moved to Vancouver at the end of that school year. E-mail is a wonderful invention. Phone calls and texting long distance cost too much.

The good thing happened after school began. It started with a black eye, a visit to the principal's office, and a ride home in a police car.

CHAPTER 8

Steampunk Vampire

As long as you were in the sun, the September air still held a remembrance of summer. It was the kind of weather where you want a light jacket, and to ignore the threat of a coming winter. For me, grade seven had started two days before. My fourteenth birthday was just over a month away.

My school took students from the "gracious country living" subdivisions southwest of Calgary, so there was a long line of yellow school buses outside. Fighting the buses for the limited parking space on the street were the usual swarm of helicopter parents in SUVs. It wouldn't do to let their children walk four or five whole blocks to get home, would it?

The final bell of the day sounded. Within a few minutes, several hundred kids streamed from the doors, the waiting vehicles absorbing only a fraction of the flood.

By the time I got outside, a crowd of fifteen or twenty kids were clustered around a moving spot by the athletic field. They were cheering at whatever was in the middle like they were watching a sports match.

Obviously, it was a fight. I walked past, ignoring the whole thing until I heard some boy yell "get her, Ashley!"

I'm sure that most schools have a girl like Ashley Borenstein - pretty, stupid, entitled, and mean. The jocks loved her (in more ways than one, I'd heard - she'd developed early) so she never had to worry about boys beating up on her regardless of how cruel she was to them. She was 18 centimetres taller than me - 173, even at that age. She was physically big enough to fight most of the other girls, and she did so every time one of them offended her in any way. When a girl was too much for her to handle by herself some of her minions took care of it for her.

In short, she was a petty, vindictive bitch. I hadn't had a run in with her since grade one when we'd been in the same class. She was one of the few girls whose mother hadn't punished her for bullying me. I pushed my way through the crowd.

Her victim was a Latina girl I'd never seen before. She was dressed like she was going to a Victorian funeral. Ashley was repeatedly hitting her while the girl was just trying to protect herself and get away. The blows probably hurt more emotionally than physically. It was obvious from her wild swings that Ashley had never had any training. I hadn't noticed that in grade one, but at the time I didn't have any training either.

If you haven't guessed, I don't like bullies.

The girl was about to get hit again when I stepped in, deflected Ashley's arm, and simultaneously hit her in the face with the heel of my other hand. Between the shock, and not knowing how to fall properly, she went down on her big butt. I hadn't hit her as hard as I could have, so she was more surprised than hurt. She wasn't even bleeding. That should have been the end of the fight.

"Bitch!" someone yelled, and I was tackled from behind. I tried to roll as I fell forward.

Judy White was one of Ashley's minions. She'd caught me off-guard, and was trying to deliver a beating to protect the virtue of her leader. I fell on Ashley, who at least was soft, and the whole pile of us collapsed to one side in a tangle. Ashley was wiggling around, trying to hit anything that moved.

From the sound of their cheers, the crowd loved our show.

Judy ended up on top, sitting on my stomach while she pinned my hands to the ground, a typical bully move but not at all bright. Most people will instinctively try to push up, which is useless if the person sitting on you is anywhere near your size. Instead of struggling against her weight, I quickly moved my arms clockwise against the grass, like I was turning a big wheel, and flipped my hip. Judy went sailing off to the side, straight into Ashley who was just getting to her feet. If I'd been bowling it would have been a strike.

The crowd thought this was hilarious, and started heckling all of us equally.

Before I could roll away, somebody's stray knee caught me in the face. For a moment I saw stars. Judy and Ashley were getting themselves sorted out, and it was time for me to get serious unless I wanted to get hit again.

They were both going to pile onto me, so I rolled aside and stood up. Obviously, they weren't plugged into the boys' gossip network, or they'd have known what Mum and I had been doing for the past five years. Maybe they were too stupid to understand.

They rushed me at the same time.

Ashley was bigger so I went after her first. As she lunged for me I stepped to the side, pulled forward on her arm, and brought my knee up fast like a male dog at a hydrant. She made an explosive puking sound, landed on her knees, and fell over trying to gasp for breath. While she was busy I pivoted to face Judy. Ashley was on the ground between us. Judy ground to a halt, breathing heavily, and trying to look tough while staying out of my reach. She had no idea what else I could do, but seeing her *führer* on the ground made her think twice.

I ignored the jeers of the crowd, and circled her slowly while keeping Ashley between us. I didn't have to look for an opening; there were plenty. I just didn't want to make it easy for one of their other friends to jump me from behind.

This was not what I'd had in mind. I guess I had assumed that I'd hit Ashley once, spoil her fun, and that would be the end of it. I had *so* not thought this through. The fight should have been over, but now Judy and Ashley couldn't walk away without losing cred. If I tried to leave they'd think I was chicken. They'd either try to jump me now, or catch me later.

I began to be sorry that I'd interfered, and wasn't sure how I was going to get out of this without hurting them badly enough that they'd *have* to quit. In class with Mum, I'd taken on four police officers and gotten out in one piece. The thought that these *girls* would actually be able to hurt me, except by accident, never entered my mind.

At least the Latina girl had slipped away while she could, for which I didn't blame her one bit.

"What's going on here?" The boys' gym teacher, Mr. McElwaine, waded into the crowd, most of whom suddenly remembered that they had homework to do.

I was saved from my own heroic intentions. Now all I had to do was get the administration to believe that I was the good guy.

We were marched to the office to see the principal, Mrs. Forest. Of course, Ashley told her that I'd started it, and Judy supported her story. We got dumped on the bench outside the office while the principal called our parents.

Judy looked scared. I didn't blame her. For as long as I can remember, regardless of what Judy did or didn't do, her mother blamed her for it.

Judy's skin was a beautiful shade of medium brown, and she could have been really popular if she didn't have a chip the size of a redwood forest on her shoulder. Mrs. White believed that all the problems in her life were caused by people blaming her for having a half-black daughter.

Like anybody cared.

Her father had left soon after his daughter was born, which I didn't think was at all cool of him. On the other hand, I couldn't imagine living with Mrs. White without wanting to run away too. Judy was the first one to make me realize that not all parents were as sane, or as loving, as mine.

Ashley looked smug, probably figuring that she could sweet-talk her way out of anything, and her mother would back her. All I knew about her father was that he had walked out on them several years previously. See previous comments about parents.

I sat on the bench and hummed *Still Alive* to myself. Neither of them had met my mother. Back when I'd been bullied, Mrs. Borenstein had refused to meet with Mum about Ashley's behaviour, so they'd just talked on the phone. She probably didn't even remember the conversation. Yet.

The school secretary looked up when I started humming. I smiled at her, and she quickly went back to her paperwork. I guess that's the first rule of being a bull in the Big House: Don't fraternize with the prisoners.

After a while, Mrs. Borenstein arrived and stormed into the office without being invited. She didn't bother closing the door so we could hear her yelling at the principal before Mrs. Forest quietly closed the door. The gist was that her perfect daughter couldn't possibly be at fault for anything. Judy relaxed a bit, assuming that if Ashley got off, so would she.

Mrs. White came in next, and as soon as she spotted her daughter the first words out of her mouth were, "what have you done this time?" Despite the bruise on my eye, I almost felt sorry for Judy.

At the time, my mother worked downtown at the combination District One and Police Headquarters office. Usually, she'd catch a ride to work with Nick Holley who lives a few blocks from us. Fortunately, on this day, he was also free to give her a lift to the school.

I liked Nick. His lovely northern English accent reminded me of Christopher Eccleston in Doctor Who. I kept expecting him to say something like, "Hello Veronica, nice to meet you. Run for your life." He was a head taller than Mum, and outweighed her by almost fifty kilos. It was no surprise to me that he'd been a night club bouncer in Bradford before joining the West Yorkshire Police.

Sometimes I watched when he and Mum sparred together at the gym. It wasn't for show. They wore thick body armour, and went at each other like the Spartans and the Persians. Despite the armour, more often than not, they both came away with some really impressive bruises. One time, after he'd kicked her so hard that she hit the wall before hitting the mat, I asked her why they tried so hard to kill one another. She took a long pull at her water bottle before answering.

"In a fight, the most important thing is the will to win. If you don't have it, you'll lose every time. The outcome has very little to do with who knows more techniques. That's one reason why Krav Maga is so simple – fancy stuff is mostly a waste of energy. The average man is bigger and stronger than the average woman, so given similar skill levels the only way for the woman to win is to overwhelm his will. Sparring with Nick isn't just about improving my skills. It's about training myself to have the will to go at him like a honey badger on crack, regardless of what he does, so that he loses his belief that he has the ability to put me down. Once he starts having doubts, he leaves openings that I can exploit to put *him* down."

"Okay, so how come he still wins sometimes?"

She smiled as she towelled the sweat off her head and neck, then winced as she moved her shoulder in a way that didn't make it happy. She watched two other people across the room playing judo for a moment before answering.

"Nick was brought up to be a gentleman. When he was a bouncer he took pride in never hitting a woman, no matter how obnoxious she was. He'd just pick up the girls, and carry them out of the club, taking a few hits rather than hitting back. When we spar, he's training himself to be able to come at anyone, regardless of size or gender. That's how he's training his will. Someday, he might run into a crazy woman with a knife, and what he's learning from me will save his life. I don't let him win. I *make* him win."

I'd seen some girly girls at school who let people walk all over them because standing up for themselves wasn't "feminine." I decided that I'd rather be a honey badger on crack.

Mum entered the school office wearing a navy blue pantsuit with her jacket unbuttoned. Ashley's mother glared at her.

If Nick had been in a pinstripe suit and fedora instead of a police uniform he'd have looked exactly like a bodyguard in a mob film. All he needed was a Tommy gun. He took up position outside the door of the principal's office, not saying a word. He did a great imitation of a granite slab.

We three prisoners were invited into the principal's office. Before anyone else could speak, my mother took charge. I was surprised that Mrs. Forest was allowing her to take the lead in a school matter.

"Let me get this straight," Detective Chandler said to the principal. "My daughter was beating up these two other girls?"

"That's what they allege." Mrs. Forest was serious, but there was something odd about her voice. Maybe it was the tiniest hint of emphasis on the word "allege."

Mum turned on Judy.

"Why did Veronica attack you?"

"Who do you think you are?" Mrs. Borenstein said.

Mum fixed her with The Look, and put her hands on her hips. By mere coincidence, that brought her jacket back to reveal her duty belt, complete with badge, extra ammo clips and handcuffs. It was, I'm sure, pure chance that it also revealed her Glock in its holster.

"Ma'am, I need you to be quiet while I'm conducting this investigation." The tone of her voice held the finality of the Grim Reaper announcing that the game was over, and there would be no overtime.

Ashley's mother opened her mouth again like a fish, then closed it. So that's what the will to win looked like. I wondered if Mum was holding out on me and could do the Jedi Mind Trick as well. That would certainly explain some of my childhood experiences. She turned back to Judy.

"Well?"

Judy tried to meet Mum's eyes and failed. I concentrated on keeping the smile off my face. I'd grown up with this, and it was kind of fun to see someone else on the sharp end of an interrogation.

"Um, well, I guess she was attacking Ashley. I was trying to help."

"You were trying to help Veronica attack Ashley?"

"No! I mean, she jumped Ashley, and I tried to stop her." Judy was flustered.

"I see," Mum said. "How did that work out for you?" She suddenly turned on Ashley. "Why did Veronica attack you?"

Ashley was about as sharp as a sack full of wet mice. I guess that, with her looks, and her mother's protection, she'd never needed to develop any skills in constructing plausible alibis.

"I don't know. The bitch is crazy." She sounded surly.

"So no reason you can think of?"

Ashley shrugged. I glanced at Mrs. Forest. She was sitting with her hands clasped on her desk. To me, she looked suspiciously like she was trying not to enjoy the performance.

"Where were you when she attacked you?"

"Out by the football field."

"What were you doing there?"

"Just hanging out, you know, before going home."

"Hanging out with whom?"

"I dunno. Just some of my peeps."

"All of whom ran away when a teacher showed up. Were you selling the drugs, or just taking them?"

Ashley looked far more scared than surprised by the accusation. That was interesting.

"Ashley?" Her mother said, horrified, but not surprised.

"No! I don't do that any more."

"So you admit that you *used* to do drugs," Mum said.

Ashley and Mrs. Borenstein just glared at her.

"We'll get back to that in a moment. Who was the girl?"

"What girl?"

Mum smiled at Ashley, reminding me of a Great White shark.

"The girl who was seen being beaten by you just before Veronica stepped in to stop you."

Ashley licked her lips before answering.

"I don't know anything about that."

"I notice you didn't say it didn't happen, just that you've somehow forgotten. Let me refresh your memory. There was a girl in a black dress on the ground with a bleeding nose about two metres from your fight with my daughter. We have a witness."

I'll give Ashley this: she didn't give up easily.

"Your witness must be somebody who has it in for me. That never happened."

"Mrs. Forest?"

The principal turned her laptop around so we could see the screen. On it was playing a video of the whole fight. Mrs. Forest could have settled this at any time by herself. My guess was that she'd tried to reason with Ashley and her mother before. Now she wanted someone more official than her to put the fear of God into them without quite making it a police matter. *Well played*, I thought.

"Next time you want to be a bully, try not to do it in front of a CCTV camera," Mum said. "And next time you want to be stupid, don't lie to a police officer. Veronica, please wait outside."

I managed to make it outside with a straight face.

"How'd it go?" Nick asked as I closed the door behind me.

To my horror, I giggled like a school girl. Okay, I was a school girl, but there's such a thing as dignity.

"I think Mum is reaming them a new one."

"Ah, yes," Nick said in his lovely accent, "your mother is an expert in forensic proctology. It can be a very effective treatment."

Through the door, we could hear a muffled argument going on inside the office. We couldn't quite make out the words, but most of it was Mrs.

Borenstein's hysterical voice with the occasional, decisive phrase from Mum or Mrs. Forest. Then there was silence.

A few minutes later, the door was wrenched open, and Mrs. Borenstein marched out, her lips compressed to a fine line. A miserable-looking Ashley followed her. In her hand was a slip of paper that looked suspiciously like a citation. An angry Mrs. White, and an almost relieved-looking Judy followed. Once they'd left, Mum waved us in. Mrs. Forest was standing in front of her desk, looking very principal-like. I liked Mrs. Forest. Not only was she a good principal, she was the same height as me. Usually, when I was in a group of people, I felt like I was standing in a freaking forest. Talk about ironic symbolism.

"Miss Chandler," the principal said, "while I generally try to enforce a zero-tolerance policy with regard to fighting on campus, in this case I'd like to commend you for your actions. You showed admirable restraint in your use of force to help a fellow student."

"Just don't make a habit of it," Mum added sternly.

"Yes, officer," I said meekly.

"Detective," she corrected.

We filed out of the principal's office with appropriate solemnity, until we were at the front door of the school. Then Nick spoiled the moment by bursting into laughter.

"Veronica, we'll make a copper of you yet."

That's how I ended up being taken home in a police car.

"What are you thinking?" Mum asked through the plastic shield that covered the space between the front and back seats.

I was sitting in the back seat. Mum and Nick had just gotten in the front. Nick started the engine as I tried to put my thoughts in order.

"Judy's mother always assumes that she's at fault for everything, but you never once even hinted that you thought I'd started the fight."

"Was Judy to blame?"

"Well, yes, this time."

"And who does she hang out with?"

I thought about it.

"Yeah, I see your point."

"Even if your principal hadn't told me about the video, I know my daughter. I trust her never to have started a fight without a good reason."

I thought about that for a moment, too.

"You know," I said, "it's really creepy when you talk to Veronica in the third person."

Nick snorted. Mum gave him The Look, then turned back to me.

"Since you want to be an investigator, I hope you were taking notes about interrogation technique," she said. "Start with the weak member of the team, and don't ask a question to which you don't already have a good idea of the answer."

"How did you know to ask about the drugs?"

"I looked up Ashley's record after your principal called me. I knew that, even if drugs weren't involved this time, at least it would throw her off her game." She paused. "I assume you know that her record is confidential information. Spreading it around school would be a bad idea."

"Yes, Mum." I also knew when to lose the smart-assed replies. Don't piss off the senior honey badger.

"After you left the office I gave them a choice. I could arrest Ashley, and have her tried for assault, or I could give her a ticket for disorderly conduct. In the second case they could consider it a warning that there would be no further chances."

"Do you think it worked?"

"Ashley isn't as tough as she seems. Mostly, her attitude is a result of her mother treating her like a princess. Mrs. Borenstein seems to believe that she herself is royalty or something, and therefore her daughter should be able to get away with anything. Except, of course, tarnishing her mother's good name by getting arrested. I think that Ashley will be kept in line from now on. Judy's just a follower whose self-respect has been massacred by her mother. What little remains is measured by the status of the people who let her run with them. With Ashley's fangs pulled I doubt that she'll be any problem. I chose to ignore what she did as defence of her friend. I'd suggest that you do the same."

"I can do that."

Nick let us off in front of our house. I waved as he drove away, and he blipped the siren in response.

Mum gave me one more piece of maternal advice before we went inside.

"By the way, that black eye was completely unnecessary. Keep your arms in front of you when you are on the ground so you can block."

It was my turn to make supper so I started slicing the meat, onions, and mushrooms for beef stroganoff. The only further excitement we had that evening was when Dad came home from the restaurant, and saw my black eye. By that time, I had a really cool-looking bruise. He freaked out, which was kind of sweet. Mostly, he was worried that his little girl had been hurt. Fighting was not what Little Princesses did, although when we got him to understand that I'd been defending someone else, he was proud of me too. Fathers can be so schizo.

The next morning at school, my eye looked awesome. The whole area surrounding my left eye was red, and starting to turn purple. It didn't hurt too much, which gave me the best of both worlds. I could look like a bad-ass, but didn't have to put up with a lot of pain. I saw Ashley in the hall, and for a moment she looked at me like she wanted to kill me. Then she lowered her eyes and scuttled away.

"Hello," an accented voice said behind me while I was getting books from my locker.

The Latina girl was of medium height, which meant about eight centimetres shorter than Ashley and 8 centimetres taller than me. She had long, straight black hair dyed blood red at the ends. Her dress looked like she'd stolen it from a Steampunk vampire; black with red lace trim that matched her hair. All she needed was a top hat with brass goggles. From her colouration and accent I guessed that she was from somewhere in South America. Her nose looked puffy, probably from the fight. Her eyes widened as I turned around.

"Oh no, that isn't because of me, is it?"

There's no point in looking like a bad-ass if you whine about it.

"It was my fault. I didn't block somebody's knee."

"My name is Kali. I wanted to thank you for your help yesterday."

"Veronica," I said, "and don't mention it. Is Kali your first name?"

She laughed. "Kali is my only name. It's the name the goddess herself gave me when I became one of the Wicca."

I could see why Ashley might think that she was weird, but my gut feeling was that Kali was a really cool person. Apart from the Romantigoth outfit, that is. Or maybe, partially, because of it.

"I don't remember seeing you around before."

"We moved here a few weeks ago. Yesterday was my first day in this school."

"I'm sorry you had to run into Ashley. She's needed an attitude adjustment for a long time now. Hey, you want to get together at lunch?"

"I would like that," she said with a big white smile under her brown eyes.

There was something peaceful about Kali, like a Zen garden. I immediately liked her. The class bell cut our conversation short.

Over the next few weeks we became best friends. I heard rumours that we were lesbians, that were probably started by Ashley. It wasn't true, and we didn't care. Neither did anybody else. Ashley's stock had taken a dive.

You know how there are some people you just click with? Meeting Kali was like meeting a sister I never knew I had. Even our birthdays were close together: Hers was October twenty sixth, mine was the nineteenth.

I wished she really was my sister, until she told me her story. Then I was glad that we hadn't grown up together.

CHAPTER 9

Dulce Vida

It's likely that most Canadian children, at some point or another, have heard an adult say something like "eat your Brussels sprouts, there are starving children in Africa." Another good adult line, usually associated with something that seems terribly commonplace, is "I hope you realize how lucky you are."

I've never met anybody under the age of twenty five who has truthfully admitted to thinking anything other than "if they want them so badly, send those sprouts to Africa." No child who has lived in Canada all her life suddenly thinks "wow, I'm so lucky to be here."

It isn't that young people are selfish and horrible. It's just that these are the only lives we know, and we have nothing to compare them with. Television doesn't count – it's always showing strange and terrible things. Unless you've been there, there's no real emotional difference between seeing news reports of riots in the streets somewhere, and the destruction of Alderaan in Star Wars. As soon as we're old enough to recognize that most of the images are unreal, everything on TV becomes fantasy. A child is more likely to cry over something happening to an animal in a nature show than over an entire village being massacred on the news. At least animals are something we can identify with. When was the last time rebel soldiers ran through a Calgary neighbourhood slaughtering everybody?

What we don't realize is that not everybody has lives like ours.

About two months after we'd met, Kali and I were in my room after school. We were teenagers, and we ate like ones. The kitchen didn't stand a chance when we rolled through looking for supplies. We had a

Costco-sized jar of peanut butter, and an entire box of crackers between us on the carpet. We'd eaten crackers on the bed once, and I wasn't stupid enough to repeat *that* mistake.

So far, Kali hadn't said much about her life in Colombia, or why they'd come to Canada. She'd talk about anything else for hours. It was driving me nuts, so I went the direct route.

"What's Colombia like?"

She paused, a cracker in her fingers, on their way to the peanut butter jar.

"Mostly it was all right. I grew up in Bogotá, which is the capital. My mother is a doctor. She's studying to take the examinations so she can practice in Canada."

"That seems weird. I mean, if she's already a doctor why can't she just start treating people?"

"She said that there are differences. Some drugs she's used to prescribing aren't available here, or they have different names. There are differences in government regulations, and culture, that she has to learn. Also, some countries don't train doctors as well as they do here, or in Colombia. Everybody has to take the examination."

She stopped talking. That was also unusual. We both ate crackers piled high with peanut butter. Crackers and peanut butter are sort of like Oreos where you put up with the cookie so you can get to the filling.

"What about your dad?"

"Papa is a geologist, and I suppose that rocks are the same all over the world. Years ago his family was involved in finding the emerald deposits near Muzo. That is how they made their money. He's working for a mining company now that we are here."

She used a cracker to scoop a big blob of peanut butter out of the jar. If you use knives and plates you have to wash them later. Our way was so much more efficient.

"And?" I drew the word out, hoping to suck more information from her.

"What else can I tell you? I went to a private school in Bogotá. It was a Catholic school for girls only. Our family went on vacations in Santa Marta, which is almost at the northern tip of the country."

"How come you aren't going to a private school here?"

"Papa and Mama thought that it was important for us to be involved in Canadian culture instead of keeping to ourselves."

She licked the peanut butter from the edges of her cracker.

"One big difference is that here we have no bodyguards."

"You're kidding. You had actual bodyguards?"

"Of course. They were needed to prevent members of our family from being kidnapped. My family has money, and none of it comes from illegal drugs. That is somewhat unusual, and meant that we did not have the protection of a cartel. All of us were targets."

"I can't imagine having bodyguards around all the time. Did they ever have to stop any kidnappers?"

"No, they were very good, and we all were very careful." She stared at the peanut butter jar. "That wasn't enough, though." She looked so sad.

"I had an older sister, Ana Lucia. She was beautiful, and funny, and wonderful. I remember once, when I'd broken a plate, I was hiding from our parents under my bed. She lay on top, talking to me. When our parents asked where I was, she pretended that I wasn't there. She would have been 21 now."

In her eyes, the reflections from the window changed. As I watched, one tear overflowed her right eye and crawled down her cheek. She instinctively brushed it away.

"What happened?" I said very quietly.

"Do you know about *FARC*?"

She spat it out like a swear word. I shook my head.

"*Fuerzas Armadas Revolucionarios de Colombia*. They used to be the army of the Communist party but now they live in the jungle and deal in drugs, extortion, kidnapping, and terror."

"We have a mall in Bogotá, *Centro Andino*, where many rich people shop. *FARC* drove a van full of explosives into the underground car park, hoping to destroy the whole building. Ana Lucia and her boyfriend were at the cinema."

She stopped her story. More tears rolled down her face. She sniffed, and I gave her a box of tissues from my night stand. It made me feel a bit less helpless.

"The driver was stupid, and put the van too close to the entrance. When the bomb went off, most of the explosion went out into the street. There was almost no damage to the building itself. It was fortunate, except that Ana Lucia, her bodyguard and Alberto had left the cinema, and were crossing the street to a restaurant when it happened."

Her voice caught. I hugged her.

"You don't have to..."

"Yes, I do. I couldn't speak of this to Mama and Papa, they were hurting too much. I want you to know."

She blew her nose. It was a startlingly loud sound.

"They were all killed instantly. *FARC* had sent a message to the government just before it happened, hoping that the army would be sent to evacuate the mall, and be caught in the blast. The soldiers arrived a few minutes before the bomb went off, but since the building was untouched none of them were injured, even as they evacuated the stores. The worst injury was a man who sprained his ankle trying to run down the escalator."

I didn't know what to say. I couldn't imagine what she was describing. I had nothing to compare it with in my own life.

"You have to understand, most people in Colombia are just like anyone else. They want to live in peace, love their families, and go about their business. It is the drug cartels and terrorists who make our country unbearable."

"We learned what had happened when soldiers came to our house. They said that my sister was a terrorist, and that one of the soldiers had shot her as she fled. They said that he had found a gun on her body. It was impossible."

"It took almost a month, and much money, for Papa's own investigators to prove what had happened. The soldier had planted the gun on her, then he shot her body to support his story. During all that time the army was investigating our family for connections to *FARC*. There were hours of interrogations. At one point I did not see either of my parents for three days."

She paused to blow her nose again.

"That's crazy!" I said. "Why would somebody do something like that?" I couldn't believe that this had actually happened in real life. It sounded like something from a bad action movie. I realized something terrible that had never occurred to me before: these things happen in action movies *because* they happen in real life. She smiled bitterly.

"Papa told me that, twenty years ago, it was a practice in the army to try to gain favour by pretending that one had killed a terrorist. A soldier would shoot someone, claim that they were a terrorist, and get a promotion. He said that there was a big scandal when the practice was uncovered, and it was stopped. They called it a 'false positive.' That soldier wanted to advance his career, and didn't care what it did to our family. So he – he shot my sister's body as she lay bleeding on the ground."

I held her in my arms as she sobbed, giving voice to a pain she'd kept inside for over a year.

I cried too. I cried for Kali, who had had lost someone she loved. I cried for her Ana Lucia, who never had a chance to live. I cried for my own loss of innocence. For thirteen years I'd taken my ability to walk safely to school for granted. I could go shopping without fearing for my life, without taking along an armed bodyguard to protect me. Maybe the helicopter parents were right after all. I could no longer look at life the same way, and that scared me.

A long time later I felt her grip relax, and we separated.

"My father decided that it was too much. He sold almost everything we owned, and chose Calgary because it is far away from Colombia. We moved here, and it is strange not having a bodyguard accompany me everywhere I go."

She sniffed and blew her nose again.

"I lost more than Ana Lucia that day. Our family have always been good Catholics, but I could not reconcile a God of love with what had happened. I looked for different answers. I found Wicca, the way of the old gods. My sister might not approve, but, I think, perhaps she understands. That's also when I became a RomantiGoth."

She smiled. It was a weak and ironic thing, but at least it was a smile.

"The music brings me peace. Also, I wanted nothing more to do with the way I had to dress at Catholic school: the white blouse, the knee socks. You must admit, I make these clothes look very good."

It wasn't that funny, but we laughed anyway. It was the kind of laugh where you can't stop, because if you do you'll start crying again. We were still laughing when dad knocked on the door, and told us that it was time for supper.

We were quiet during supper. I couldn't stop thinking about Kali's life. Every problem I could imagine facing suddenly seemed trivial. I promised myself that I would try not to whine about anything ever again.

"What's wrong?" Dad asked me.

"Nothing."

"You and Kali didn't have a fight, did you?"

I looked at Kali just as she looked at me.

"No."

"Well, your mother wants to see The Bourne Ultimatum tonight. Would you girls like to go to the movies with us?"

Kali looked horrified. She dropped her fork, and ran out of the kitchen crying. My parents looked surprised. I put my fork down very carefully.

"How could you?" I said to my father. Then I hurried after Kali who had retreated to my bedroom.

Fathers can be so insensitive.

An hour later, her parents sent a driver to pick her up. My dad offered to drive her home, but her parents had already made the arrangements. They said that they did not want to put Dad to any trouble.

I wondered if the driver was armed.

Kali's parents were rich, and had bought a house about as far west as you can get without dropping off the edge of Calgary. She would have had to bus in to school every morning if they hadn't had their "man" drive her to school. I'd never met anyone with servants before.

We hung out at my place a lot after school because it was closer: five blocks instead of eight kilometres. When she was ready to go home, her driver would pick her up in their Mercedes.

A few days later I received a hand written invitation card from her parents:

"*Señor* Diego Acisclo Hernandez Gomez and *Doctora* Laura Jaquinda Rojas Muñoz wish to have the pleasure of your company for a family dinner on Friday, the Second of November, at seven o'clock. Dress is casual. RSVP."

The hand writing was all swirls and gold ink. I'd never received a formal dinner invitation before. Kali said that dinner with the family is a really big deal in Colombia, and with her help I wrote a reply: *Gracias. Estoy encantada de asistir.* I wanted to make a good impression, but being a child of the computer age, my handwriting was embarrassingly bad and I knew it. To make up for it, I spent a lot of time on the internet and muttering to myself.

The card had a map printed on the back. At 6:30 on the day, Mum drove me to Kali's house. A stone wall surrounded the property, and a camera peered at us when we stopped at the wrought-iron gate. There didn't seem to be any kind of intercom like you see in movies, but the gate opened by itself anyway. That was kind of spooky, and I hoped we were in the right place.

The driveway wound through a stand of aspen, then down into a coulee that hid the house until the last moment. Suddenly we came out into an open circle with a fountain in the middle, and there was the house.

Wow.

It was a freaking castle. Three stories tall, made of grey limestone blocks with dark wood trim around the doors and windows. A round tower on the left reinforced the image. It certainly looked too big for a family of three. I wondered just how many servants they had.

The front door was under a portico, and was wide enough that we could have driven the car in. We sat there for a minute, gaping at it.

"Nice house," Mum finally said.

We got out, still hoping that we were in the right place, and went to the door. I paused with my finger on the door bell.

"Well?" she prompted. I pressed the button. I kept going over things in my head, and wondering if my idea was as good as it had seemed when I was in my room at home.

The only sound the door made when opening was the slight whoosh of air due to the excellent weather stripping. I wasn't sure if I was relieved or disappointed that it didn't creak like something from a horror film.

The woman standing in the doorway certainly wasn't Igor. She looked exactly like Kali, plus about thirty years, and minus the red tips on her hair.

"Hi," Mum said, "I'm Janet Chandler, Veronica's mother." She stuck out her hand, and Kali's mother shook it.

"Laura Rojas," she said, pronouncing her first name with an *ow* instead of an *oh*, and a rolled r on her last name. Her accent was just rich enough to make her sound like she should be in a James Bond film.

"I'll be back to collect Veronica at ten thirty, if that's all right."

"Perfect. I look forward to seeing you again."

"Have fun," she said, holding her arm out to give me a hug. For some reason I felt a bit shy about hugging her in front of Kali's mother, like it was a little girl thing to be doing in public.

I watched her restart the car, and waved as she drove away. Then I turned back to my hostess.

She and her daughter shared the same glossy black hair, the same full lips, and the same height, dammit. *Doctora* Rojas was wearing a knee-length navy blue skirt and cream blouse with an emerald brooch at her throat. She smiled.

"Welcome, Veronica."

I tried to swallow so my own voice wouldn't come out as a squeak. I was mostly successful.

"*Gracias, Doctora Rojas. Encantada.*" I held out my hand and, instead of shaking hands I grasped her forearm. She returned my gesture, one eyebrow rising as she smiled even more. She turned to yell back into the house.

"*¡Diego, Liliana Marina, vengan acá! Tenemos una invitada que tiene mejores modales que ustedes! ¡Ahora!*"

I'd only caught about three words, something about "guest", "manners" and "now!" but she was still smiling, so I figured I hadn't said anything too weird.

"*Por favor,*" she said, stepping aside to let me in. I entered the foyer, and she closed the door behind me. For a moment I busied myself removing my shoes and placing them on a wooden rack.

The inside of the house was even more amazing than the outside. Marble floors, a sweeping curved staircase, oak panelling on the walls. Holy crap, this place looked like it belonged in a movie. I wondered if they had a butler in a tuxedo. I'd worn slacks and my good blouse but I began to wish I'd worn a dress instead.

Just not a pink one.

"*Mi hija no nos dijo que usted habla español.*" She held out her hands, offering to take my coat.

I was about to give her my prepared bail-out line when it occurred to me that I still had something in my hand.

"*Esto es para ti,*" I said, handing it to her just as Kali and her father appeared.

She looked at the small, unwrapped box of chocolates that had cost me over fifty dollars. According to my research, if I'd wrapped it she'd have had to open it later.

"*Muchas gracias,*" she said warmly.

"*De nada.*"

"Hey, when did you learn to speak Spanish?" Kali said, giving me a hug.

"*Señorita Chandler,*" her father interrupted, "*bienvenida a nuestra casa.*"

I caught *bienvenida*, welcome, and *casa*, home. It was time to bail.

"*Gracias, Señor Hernández. Perdóname, no habla Español.*"

He looked at me with exaggerated shock, then looked at Kali. She shrugged.

"I only learned a few phrases this week," I said. "I wanted to honour my friend's parents."

He laughed and put his arm around his daughter.

"You have excellent taste in friends, *mijita.*" He extended his arm and waved me forward. "We shall get along splendidly. Come."

We sat in the living room, Kali and I sharing a small couch. The carpet was so thick that it oozed over the toes of my socks.

"So, you are the other student at our daughter's school," *Doctora* Rojas said.

I must have looked confused.

"Other student?"

"She's only talked about two, one of whom tried to beat her, so you must be the other one," her father added.

"Papa!"

"Liliana Marina has told us about you rescuing her," her mother said. "Thank you."

Liliana Marina?

"In fact, I understand that you have formidable fighting skills," her father said.

"I'm still learning," I said. "I want to be a private investigator. My mother and I take lessons together."

"She must also be a formidable woman."

"She's a detective with the Calgary Police," Kali said.

"So? Perhaps we could interest you in a job as our daughter's body-guard?"

I laughed, expecting everyone else to join in. Nobody did. Kali looked horrified.

"You're kidding, right?" I had the feeling that I'd missed something.

"Not at all. It was not feasible for us to hire armed bodyguards before we came to Canada. Nor did we think it necessary. The fight at the school proved otherwise."

Kali groaned and rolled her eyes.

"Papa, I don't need a bodyguard here."

I had a mental picture of me in a black suit, wearing dark glasses and following Kali around school, suggestively tapping my palm with a baton whenever someone looked at her the wrong way, and talking into my cuff radio. Cool.

Not cool. Among my research into Colombian customs I'd read an article about business negotiations, and wondered how I was going to say no without saying no.

"I am honoured," I said, "but I think that it would be in Kali's best interest if you found someone with more experience for such an important position. We don't have any classes together, so I wouldn't be able to be with her most of the day." Damn I'm good.

"Hmm, perhaps we should have a word with the school about that."

"Papa!" Kali was turning red under her permanent tan.

Doctora Rojas started laughing, followed by her husband. Kali rolled her eyes again.

"You were joking?" I asked.

"Perhaps," he said.

An older woman appeared in a doorway wearing, I kid you not, a maid's uniform like the ones you see in movies.

"*Señor, la cena esta servida.*"

"*Gracias, María,*" he said, then added for my benefit, "supper is ready. Shall we?"

We followed Kali's parents into a dining room that was the size of our house. The table could probably have sat thirty people. There were four place settings at one end.

Kali sat down immediately. I took a step to sit beside her, and then waited, looking at her father. He nodded with satisfaction.

"Manners indeed." He showed me to my seat, pulled it out for me, and held the chair while I sat. He then seated his wife and himself.

Maria appeared with a soup tureen and bowls on a trolley. I felt like I'd wandered into a Jane Austen novel.

"*Ajiaco,*" she announced. She began ladling the soup into bowls and placing them before us.

"*Buen provecho,*" *Señor* Hernández said formally, the Colombian equivalent of *bon apétit*.

"*Gracias*," I replied. This was fun, as long as they stuck to the phrases I'd memorized.

Ajiaco was a chicken soup with pieces of corn and asparagus, and garnished with coriander leaves, although in Spanish they would call it *cilantro*. It was amazing, and I wanted the recipe. I had a hard time remembering to leave some in the bottom of my bowl, as politeness dictated.

The next course was announced as *Sancocho de Cerdo*, allegedly a stew but more like pieces of pork and cassava root slow cooked in a sauce.

"Okay, show them your trick," Kali said when the bowls had been set before us.

"Trick?" *Doctora* Rojas said.

I took a forkful of the pork, let the aromas whisper to my nose, and then put it in my mouth. After it had spoken to me I swallowed.

"Pork, garlic, cumin, onion, tomatoes, cor – *cilantro*," I said, then paused while the minor notes developed. "Bell pepper, beer, carrots of course, pepper, salt. Is that *achiote* seeds too?"

"Remarkable!" She said. "That's my mother's recipe, and the only thing you missed was the scallions. Given that their flavour would be masked by the onions I think perhaps I'll forgive you for that. Are you familiar with Colombian food?"

"No, *Doctora*. My father is a professional chef. He taught me a lot about fine food. He would have been able to tell you the proportions as well."

"Perhaps you can teach Liliana Marina how to cook," her father said. "I seem to remember her burning water once or twice."

"Papa!"

Okay, this was driving me crazy.

"Liliana Marina?"

"I'm shocked. You haven't properly introduced yourself to your friend? Shame on you!" Kali's mother said to her. "*Señorita* Chandler, may I present my daughter, Liliana Marina Hernández Rojas."

"Kali," Kali said.

"Liliana Marina," her father said. Kali sighed again.

"She is as stubborn as her mother, and just as beautiful."

Kali glared at him. He smiled back at her.

Dessert was *Bananos con Salsa de Naranja*. I wouldn't have thought of cooking bananas in orange sauce. I certainly would in the future.

"Would it be too much trouble to ask Maria for the recipes?" I asked, looking wistfully at the last piece of banana. This custom of leaving a little on one's plate was a killer. Kali kicked me under the table.

"Mama's the cook, not Maria," she whispered.

Oops.

"I'd be delighted to show you how to prepare them," her mother said graciously. "Perhaps your father would be interested as well?"

"I'm certain that he would." I noticed that the slightly formal way they had of speaking English was rubbing off on me. It made me feel more like an adult.

"We'll have to have your family come over for a Colombian cooking class. Is your mother a chef as well?"

I couldn't help it. I laughed, then felt my face grow warm.

"From what you've said, she cooks almost as well as Kali."

She kicked me again, harder this time.

"*Traidor.*"

I didn't need the internet to translate that one.

After supper we went to Kali's room. It had been decorated by parents who thought of their daughter as Liliana Marina, then re-decorated by a girl who thought of herself as Kali. As a result there was a pink duvet on the bed with stuffed animals and lace-trimmed pillows, along with band posters for *Lycia* and *Love Spirals Downwards* on the walls, along with a huge picture of Stonehenge. In a walk-in closet with room for a hundred pair of shoes, she had two pairs of combat boots and a pair of black fuzzy slippers.

Her family welcomed me like an extra daughter. For the next four years I spent about half of my life in their house, as she spent the other half at mine. Sleepovers were common. I'm afraid we shamelessly let Mum, Dad and Maria's husband, Ramón, shuttle us around like royalty. Such are the ways of teenagers.

Kali also introduced me to a new hobby. Believe it or not, this native Calgarian girl had never been on a horse before. Kali couldn't believe it, and she fixed that omission at the first opportunity.

I know that all girls at that age are supposed to be crazy about horses, but I was used to cars. Cars don't try to buck you off, or suddenly decide to run away. Of course, they also don't respond to bribes.

There's also the size. A half tonne of horse seems much bigger than a tonne of vehicle, especially when the look it gives you tells you that it knows you are a newb who can be manipulated.

Brushing and saddling the horse was kind of fun, once I was shown how. My problem started after the cinch was tight. It's amazing the way horses grow. From the ground, Snip wasn't much taller than me. Once I was in the saddle, she seemed at least twice that height. I had a death grip on the saddle horn but, fortunately, Snip was perfect for a beginner. I wasn't really in danger of falling, especially as she refused to move faster than a walk. After a while I suspected that I could actually get to enjoy riding.

The next day, the muscles on the inside of my legs wanted me to know how wrong I was about that. I thought I would never walk again. Kali persisted in taking me riding, and my legs eventually got over it.

Our parents also got along, especially when *Doctora* Rojas and my father discovered that each knew Spanish recipes that the other didn't. *Sr.* Hernández and my mother shared an interest in the law-enforcement differences between their two countries. When the two families got together the only reasonable word to describe the result was fiesta. Dad, Kali's mother, and I did the cooking while Kali, her father, and my mum were our enthusiastic fans.

Occasionally, *Señor* Moreno and his wife (a.k.a. Ramón and Maria) joined our parties. They had worked for the family for over thirty years, and, instead of dismissing them when the family moved, Kali's parents had brought them to Canada. Although they did some work around the house, they were now semi-retired and were more like friends of the family than employees.

Those were simple times, some of the best of our lives.

CHAPTER 10

At Least He Doesn't Sparkle

By the time we were almost sixteen years old, Kali and I had spent hours together planning exactly how the rest of our lives would go.

I was going to open my own private investigation business. She was going to open an occult shop. We were both extremely focused on our goals.

Her Wiccan faith was important to her. I tried it for a while, but just couldn't get into the whole "the Earth is our mother and magic is alive" thing. I respected her beliefs, but the existence of magic didn't make any more sense to me than it had back when I'd blown the whistle on Santa Claus.

August 27, a week before our grade-ten year would start, was a day for being lazy. The sun had raised the temperature to somewhere around 30 Celsius with very few clouds. The first hint of a storm was the front door slamming, and the delicate stomping of a teenage girl in combat boots.

By the time I got to the living room, Kali had flumped down on the couch. Her hair was wet and stringy with streaks of dried salt. It was difficult to tell in her black clothing, but she looked like she was soaking wet. It was not difficult to tell that she looked pissed.

"What's wrong?" I could almost see the thundercloud over her head.

"My parents," she said, "are –" She waved her hands, trying to find the words.

I looked out the living room window. There was no car outside.

"How did you get here?"

"I walked."

"You *walked*? That's like eight kilometres!"

She glared at me, so I sat down, and waited for her to speak. When she's angry Kali's like a bear with a sore paw. She'll take your head off if you push her.

"Mama was hinting that I need to think about university. I told them that I already have plans for my life after high school."

She went silent again. This time I thought I could get away with a short question.

"So?"

"¡*Malparida vida!* They don't think that opening an occult shop is 'suitable.' They're sure that I'll 'grow out of Wicca', and remember that I'm really a nice Catholic girl, destined to be a doctor or something. When I told them that this isn't a phase, they went crazy. ¡*Mis papas son unos cerrados de mierda!*"

Ouch. I wondered if she'd used that kind of language at home.

"They yelled at me, I yelled back at them, and then I came over here where nobody had better do any yelling," she yelled, then glared at me again, challenging me to yell. When I didn't, she wiped the sweat off her forehead with her hand. "I could really use a drink."

We went into the kitchen and rummaged through the refrigerator. We found two cans of Canada Dry, which we took into our back yard. There's a big poplar tree near the back fence that casts a lot of shade. A slight breeze helped to cool things down slightly.

We sat down on the grass, and inhaled the slightly spicy poplar smell. Kali took a big swig of her ginger ale, like she was in a bar trying to drown her sorrows. She tried to look grim, but her attempt to be a badass ended a few moments later with the loudest burp I'd ever heard from anyone.

She was as startled as I was, and we completely lost it. I laughed so hard I fell over. When I hit the ground I burped too, which set us off again.

Mum appeared at the back door looking stern and parental.

"Kali, your mother is on the phone, and would like to speak with you."

Kali stopped laughing, and was going to say something with attitude, but as soon as her mouth opened she burped again. We didn't stop laughing until several minutes after Mum had disappeared inside. I wondered how she would translate the conversation to *Doctora* Rojas.

Kali's parents eventually got over it, mostly. I could relate. My own plan to become a private investigator made my parents nervous as well. They were very nice about it, but Mum wanted me to join the police service, so I'd have a steady income instead of going private right away and starving to death. Dad was worried about me getting hurt either way, and hinted that he needed another sous-chef at his restaurant where it was nice and safe.

It took a while, but once our parents were more or less on board, or at least had given up trying to change our minds, we had life all figured out.

It was really kind of sweet, the way Kali was insulated from the evils of boys. Despite her exotic appearance and dress code, she was completely clueless about the hints that I could see them dropping around her. Some guy would ask her if she was going to a dance, and she'd say "no" as a matter of fact, not getting that he was hinting that he wanted her to go with him.

I, on the other hand, had simply decided that I was above all this tawdry teen sexuality, despite the fact that thoughts of sex dominated a lot of my day. I saw the actions of my former male friends as betrayal, and it still stung. I could appreciate hotness like David Tennant, or Stephen Merchant, but I couldn't really see any use for boys my own age in my life.

That didn't mean that either of us was innocent. I'm told that, back in the old days, boys were the only ones who had any real access to porn because girls didn't want to be seen buying the books and magazines in stores. The internet changed all that. It's a lot easier to hide a browser history from your parents than a bunch of magazines under your mattress. Kali and I were able to supplement our parents' theoretical lectures with considerable research into the practical aspects of sex, without having to deal with any store owners, bodily fluids, or embarrassing hardware. It was fun to find stuff online that grossed us out, and swear we'd never do anything like that.

Then the aliens abducted me again.

The first day of grade ten was also our first day in Central Memorial High School. It was a lot further away from my place, so Kali convinced Ramón to pick me up "on his way" to the new school. Otherwise, I would have had a half hour bus ride, or a thirty five minute walk, twice a day. Getting a ride from our chauffeur was, of course, nothing at all like the helicopter parents I'd been ridiculing earlier.

After a lot of wandering around, paperwork, and confusion, I was sitting in my home room, reading a book that Mum had bought me, and waiting for class to start. I'd just gotten to a really interesting chapter when –

"What are you reading?" When I looked up, a boy was sitting down at the desk next to me.

He was gorgeous, with warm brown eyes that seemed to penetrate my soul, and dark, thick hair. He oozed confidence. Taller than me by about a head, his arms were muscular without being gross. I could easily ima-gine that he had a six pack under his shirt. I caught myself wondering how hard his muscles were.

I'm pretty sure that my next word was something like "blugh?"

He smiled, showing beautiful, white teeth, then reached over with one finger, and raised my book so he could read the title. A faint smell wafted toward me, far more musky and sensual than the cheap body spray that everybody thinks is a babe magnet.

"*The Canadian Private Investigator's Manual*," he read aloud. "Interest-ing. I'm Adam." I stared at him, not knowing what to say. "What's your name?" He prompted.

"Veronica," I said far too quickly, like I'd sneezed. What was wrong with me? He was just some boy. A charming, handsome, beautiful boy who wanted to talk to me and –

The class bell rang. Everybody shuffled to their seats so our teacher could take attendance. When the teacher got to "Veronica Chandler" on the roll, I put up my hand, and Adam smiled at me. I felt my face grow warm, then I shivered. Maybe I was coming down with something.

A moment later the teacher called "Adam Cullen," and I stared. His last name was "Cullen?" What kind of sick joke was that? Thank God his first name wasn't Edward! I could just imagine: Mrs. Veronica Cullen. How horrible!

Wait, what?

I was distracted all day, and didn't learn much. Every time I caught sight of Adam my mind would wander, and I'd get lost in warm and fuzzy feelings. It didn't help that he smiled at me every time he caught me staring. I had to be coming down with something.

At the end of the day he showed up at my locker.

"Hey, Veronica."

Again, I stared without saying anything.

"I was wondering, which way do you go home?"

For the life of me I couldn't remember any street names. I really must have been coming down with something. I pointed in the general direc-tion of my house.

"Cool! Me too. Can I walk you home?"

I think I managed to nod.

We were several blocks from the school when I remembered that Ramón was supposed to pick us up. I'd forgotten because Kali hadn't come to find me at my locker. That was odd. Where was she?

"Sorry, what did you say?"

"I said, I'm trying out for the football team this year." His dark eyes were so warm. I felt flushed.

"I have to call somebody," I said abruptly.

Kali picked up on the first ring.

"*Hola, chica.*"

"Kali, I'm so sorry. When you didn't show up at my locker I forgot about getting a ride and..."

"It's okay, I know."

I could feel my face getting hot.

"Know what?"

"About the cute guy. What's his name?"

"Um, Adam." For some reason I found myself turning away and whispering. I glanced at Adam who was pretending not to be listening.

"Is he still there?"

"Um, yeah."

"I'll call you later so you can tell me *everything*." She hung up.

Adam lived in North Glenmore Park, which, despite its name, is just a community north of the north side of Glenmore Park. If that makes sense you must be a city planner. We walked most of the way together. When we got to the corner where he'd have to leave me we stood, and talked about stuff. Mostly, he wanted to know about me. He acted like it was all fascinating to him.

When I got home Dad was in the kitchen.

"It was your turn to make supper tonight," he said as he cut some broccoli.

"Um, sorry. Kali and I missed each other after school, and I had to walk home. How can I help?" It was strictly true even if not completely accurate.

After supper, I called Kali from my room. That was really embarrassing. She kept asking me for all the details about Adam, and what we'd done. She seemed disappointed that there wasn't more to tell. I had no idea that she was such a voyeur.

Adam and I became, as my mother put it, "an item." Dad kept looking like he wanted to tell me something, but he never did. I guessed that it was another lecture about the dangers of boys, and how they only wanted one thing from a girl. Dad can be such a Neanderthal at times. It's a good thing he didn't know what was going through my head, or he'd have locked me up to protect the boys.

Adam was sweet and kind, and really seemed interested in my plans to become a private investigator. We went to movies, and studied together, and even took walks in the park. He let me include Kali in some of our plans, and paid more attention to me than to her when we were together, which made me feel warm inside. Kali admitted that she thought he was nice, but I sensed that she was keeping an eye on him. Maybe it was just because she was shy around boys.

A few days after we met, he kissed me for the first time. Sure, I'd kissed people before. At least, I'd kissed people on the cheek. I'd never put mouth to mouth before, and I was nervous about it. I mean, it's not exactly obvious that literally swapping spit with another person is going to be anything other than gross.

Wow. Just, wow. Not gross. Really amazing. Not at all gross.

Did I mention, wow?

Adam really respected my feelings, never pushing me, but somehow leading me to want more. I really wanted more. Kisses became caresses. Depending on where we were at the time, some of them were on bare skin. Exquisitely sensitive bare skin. I think I had bare skin where I didn't even know I had bare skin. I had no idea that another person's hands could feel so – different.

December wasn't that cold, and it was only minus five or so that evening.

Adam had borrowed his father's SUV, and we'd gone out for dinner at a great little Indian restaurant on Northmount Drive. We chatted about school and laughed a lot. Then, at the end of dessert, Adam held my hand and smiled at me.

"Veronica, would you like to go somewhere and talk?"

I looked at him as he waited for an answer. The alien was beaming its bozo rays into my brain, and my stomach fluttered. I don't believe that I really thought about what I was doing. This was my boyfriend, and whatever he wanted had to be good.

"Sure. Where did you have in mind?"

His smile got bigger.

There hadn't been a lot of snow yet, so driving up the little service road to the "lookout point" on Nose Hill wasn't a problem, especially for the SUV. We parked some distance away from the other "sight seers," and Adam turned off the engine. At first we actually looked out the window at the city lights below us. A few minutes later the windows started to fog over, but by that time we weren't interested in the view anyway.

The shifter on the centre console was in our way. It was only logical that we should move to the rear seat. It wasn't Adam who suggested it. By that time, the windows were completely white with fog, and we were in our own little world that was warm, dark, and private.

Each step was completely sensible and reversible. Our winter coats were too warm, so we took them off. I was wearing a sweater but after making out for a while it was also too hot, so I took that off as well. I wanted to run my fingers over Adam's chest, so he removed his shirt. It took only seconds to get it off, so it was only reasonable that it would take no more than a moment to put it back on if necessary. By the time I realized that these little steps were leading somewhere specific, all I was wearing was my panties, and I was hornier than I'd ever been in my life. It was getting chilly with the engine off, so the sensible thing was to press our bodies together for warmth. It was all right, though. He was so sweet and gentle that I was sure that we were in love.

I wish I could say that the first time we did it there were choirs of angels, I instantly converted to the Church of Nymphomania, or even that I got somewhere near an orgasm. The truth is that I was too tense to get much enjoyment from it.

From what other girls had told me, it seemed that, for teenage guys, sex is simple. There are endless months or years of wanting it, and then they do it. All that's left is, maybe, bragging to their friends later. I knew Adam wouldn't do that.

For girls, sex is the definition of "it's complicated."

First, the obvious one – babies. Most guys get that those are a bad idea when you are sixteen. What they don't get is that, these days, pregnancy is almost the least of our worries. At least there are easy ways to prevent that. If we aren't made completely stupid by the fog of hormones clouding our brains, at least contraception is something girls have control over. I'm really glad that Adam had thought to bring along a strip of condoms because, as much as it embarrasses me to admit it, I think I'd have just gone ahead without one. The aliens are powerful and incredibly stupid.

Another, bigger problem is that the first couple of times can hurt, and you have no idea how much until you actually do it. For some girls it's maybe a bit uncomfortable, for others it's like being stabbed, and there's blood everywhere. Riding horses, doing gymnastics, or any of the other stuff that's supposed to make it easier doesn't always work, so we have a fear of possibly being badly hurt in a really tender place, plus the fear of the unknown.

Then there's something that boys don't seem to get at all. There's nothing metaphorical about us "letting you in." This isn't just sharing our thoughts or feelings, we're letting you actually put something inside our bodies, in a sensitive place that we've been taught for years is private. We're teetering on the edge between thinking the whole thing is horrifying and disgusting on one hand, and wanting it more than we've ever wanted anything in our lives on the other.

You try relaxing under those conditions.

Speaking of relaxing, imagine somebody tries to stuff a cucumber into your mouth while you are keeping your lips tightly closed. Ouch, right? If girls are scared, our muscles tighten, and I don't just mean some butterflies in the stomach. Now imagine that the cucumber gets in, but your mouth is completely dry. Double ouch.

On top of all that, there's the way a lot of girls get their self-esteem shredded. They think that they aren't tall enough, or pretty enough, or have big enough breasts, or whatever stupid messages keep getting pounded into them all their lives. Go ahead, think about taking off your clothes for the first time in front of somebody else who, by definition, is judging how attractive you are. Girls have a lot of parts and we worry about all of them. Too big? Too small? The right shape? Too hairy? Not hairy enough? It never ends.

What did Adam expect me to do? Whatever it was, would I know how to do it when the moment came? Would I know how to do it well enough? What could I expect him to do? If I wanted him to do something, should I ask for it? How should I ask for it? What if he thought it was gross?

Oh, yes, then there's worrying about whether somebody would see us, and call the police. "Oh, hi Nick. Fancy meeting you here. That's all right, don't bother calling Mum." Of course, he would have to. I was above the age of consent, but I was still a minor.

It's no wonder that the whole subject is a complete freak show for us. At least I didn't have to worry about sexually transmitted diseases. We were both virgins.

The grand event probably took about five minutes. It's funny, but the thing that bothered me the most was seeing him dispose of the condom afterwards. It was like some dead, creepy specimen in biology class held between his thumb and forefinger. Not at all romantic. He threw it out the window and the blast of sub-zero air on my naked, sweaty body wasn't a bundle of laughs either.

What with one thing and another, the experience rated a "meh," somewhere between uncomfortable and whatever.

The thing that I did like was the cuddling and kissing afterwards. It made me feel really close to Adam. It just didn't last long enough, because somebody with a large truck and a booming stereo drove up a few minutes later, spraying all the cars with its monster headlights. Our windows became big white, glowing panels all around us. I knew that nobody could see in, but suddenly we could see each other with perfect clarity. Even after what we'd just done, now I felt completely naked, not just nude. Talk about a mood killer.

Getting dressed in the back of an SUV isn't as easy as you think it's going to be, especially when you are hurrying, and your clothes are mixed up with another person's. Everything is inside out and backwards. It takes a lot longer than you thought it would.

We got home around 10:30. We made out in the car for a while before I went inside.

Dad was just coming out of the kitchen when I walked in.

"How was dinner?"

I felt myself blush so I turned away from him, toward the coat closet.

"It was okay." I pulled my coat off, and opened the closet door.

"Where did you go?"

"An Indian restaurant on Northmount." I hung my coat up, and felt a slight tug at the back of my neck. Dad was right behind me.

"You must have been in a hurry to leave for your date. You put your sweater on inside out. Good thing your hair hid the tag."

I bent down to take my boots off, my face now burning.

"God, that's so embarrassing. Thanks for letting me know."

I knew that my sweater on the right way when I left. Now I worried about what else I'd gotten wrong. There had been a wonderful, rich smell in the SUV while we were doing it, and I had a sudden, horrifying thought that maybe Dad could smell that I was no longer a virgin.

"I'm going to take a shower now."

I ran upstairs, leaving Dad standing there. Did he suspect? I was lucky that Mum wasn't there. I was certain that she'd have figured it out as soon as she saw me.

I couldn't smell anything on my clothes when I took them off, but I sprayed them before putting them in the laundry basket anyway. Now I was feeling completely paranoid.

Dad never mentioned anything and, slowly, I realized that we'd gotten away with it. More than a week went by before Adam and I did it again. By that time, the minor physical damage had healed, and there was no soreness at all. Mentally, I was flipping back and forth between less and more paranoia about my sexuality. I was still too embarrassed to talk about it so all I could do was wonder. Did I do the right things? Was I was good enough for him? Were my various parts attractive enough that he'd want to do it again? Was it okay that I was so short? Did he really not mind my A-cups with big nipples? By the time the subject came up again, I didn't know what to think, except that I might like to try it again, especially the post-cuddling. Maybe Veronica Cullen wouldn't be such a bad name after all.

We were at his house the second time we did it. His parents were out for the evening, and they trusted us not to get into any trouble while "studying." I guess it depends on your definition of trouble.

It was a lot better for me than the first time. The simple fact that he wanted to do it with me again relieved some of my fears. For another thing it was warmer. This time nothing hurt. I had a bit of confidence that I wasn't going to make a complete fool of myself, at least as long as we stuck to the things we'd done before. On the other hand, there was more light, and I really was shy about my small breasts. One thing that was a lot less stressful was being in a real bed behind a closed door, instead of in a glass box outside.

Fifteen minutes or so later, I concluded that sex was probably almost as good as people said it was. The only problem was that we had to get dressed as soon as he was done in case his parents came home early. Damn it, I wanted that cuddling! An orgasm would be nice, too.

The third time we did it was also at his house, and something inside me clicked. I relaxed enough that the angel chorus was singing in five part harmony. That elusive orgasm showed up, and brought a bunch of her friends to the party. I thought I was going to melt. Sex was *way* better than people said it was. I could see doing this a lot for the rest of my life. Like, several times a day whenever possible. Could boys do that?

Welcome to the Church of Nymphomania. Please leave your brain in the offering plate.

For the next few weeks everything was wonderful. A few days after our study date I had a confidential talk with Mum about my new hobby. She took it calmly, and told me that she would make an appointment for me to see my doctor about birth control options. I told her we were using condoms, and she expressed her belief in the wisdom of belt and suspenders. Her only concession to being a normal mother was that she repeated that part of The Talk about STIs. I assured her that Adam and I were each others first, and we were exclusive so it wasn't a problem. It occurred to me afterwards that Mum was using her "friendly cop" interrogation method, and had gotten a lot of really personal details out of me before I caught on. For some reason she seemed dubious about some of what I was saying. That was annoying.

Remember that episode of Doctor Who where the Doctor tells the Prime Minister that he can bring down her government with just six words? My mother's better – she only used three.

"Adam is so sweet and wonderful," I was saying. "He makes me so happy, and he's really taught me a lot."

"Who taught him?"

Her question didn't make any sense to me. "What?"

"Who taught him?"

"Nobody taught him. I guess he's just naturally good at it."

"Right." It's amazing how much negation a mother can put into one word of agreement.

"Or maybe he read Sex for Dummies or something."

"Right."

Mum's attitude pissed me off. I didn't want to think about it, but her question began to bother me. I only had Adam's word for it that he had been a virgin.

I trusted him, didn't I?

Why did I trust him? We were in love, right? That was enough, wasn't it? Was it?

None of this hit me right away. It crept up on me over a few days. Paranoia came and sat on my shoulder, whispering bad things to me during the night.

It was a complete mood killer. I didn't feel like doing it again until I got my head on straight.

Almost at once, I started noticing little things. Suggestive things. Things that might indicate that Adam wasn't quite as excited to be around me as he had been before we'd done it. Was that smile as sincere as it should have been? Were we going for fewer walks in the park? He seemed confident in what he did to me. Was that just his confidence, or was it experience?

My mother would never say "I told you so." In fact, she said nothing at all. She was just very eloquent about it.

I was too proud to ask her for advice, and I didn't want Dad to freak out. Instead, I talked to Kali.

She accepted that dating Adam meant I'd be spending less time with her, and she was mostly happy for me. When I told her what was going on she took it very seriously, and gave me good advice. Dammit, I didn't want good advice. What I wanted was my best friend to tell me that I was being foolish, and Adam was just as wonderful as I wanted him to be. Kali's words were a slap in the face.

"No matter how painful, it is always better to know the truth. Maybe it is nothing. Maybe it is something. You want to be a private investigator – investigate."

When I got over being annoyed with her, I remembered how I'd questioned everything as a child. I felt a cold shock as I realized that, somehow, I'd allowed Adam to lull me into a state of contentment where the only thing that mattered to me was that I was his girlfriend. What had happened to Veronica Irene Chandler, the crack-fed honey badger who exposed the Great Santa Claus Scam? When had she been replaced by Veronica the "yes, dear, anything you want is fine as long as you tell me that you love me and screw me stupid" girl?

I got out my copy of the private investigator's manual, reviewed the chapters on surveillance, prepared a kit, and waited. I would *prove* that he was good for me. A disturbing thought occurred to me that this was probably how one turned into a crazy stalker girl friend, but I convinced myself that this was different. I wasn't stalking; I was investigating. Completely different.

I didn't have long to wait.

The most suspicious thing that had been happening lately were the "errands" he sometimes had to run during lunch periods instead of spending the time with me. He'd only started this in the past month or so. The errands always sounded plausible, but I began to wonder where he was really going.

That Tuesday, Adam said that he had to go get something for his mother from the store. As soon as the bell rang, he gave me a peck on the cheek, and then took off.

Almost as soon as he turned away I dug into my backpack, put on the hoodie I had inside, flipped the hood up, and followed him.

Immediately, I saw that he was acting oddly. He kept looking behind him as he went outside without his coat, then doubled back, and went in the side door nearest the auditorium. I kept to the crowd, and looked down to hide my face. With the hood up nobody could see my head at all.

As the crowd thinned out, I had to resort to moving from one recessed classroom door to the next. I wore sneakers, and walked mostly on the balls of my feet so they made almost no sound except for a slight squeak from the melting snow on them.

When he went around the corner, I used a small mirror to keep an eye on him. Now I was really acting like a stalker, and I felt so guilty that I almost gave up on the project. Adam stopped by the auditorium doors. He took one last look around and slipped inside. That was just weird. What was in the auditorium?

If I followed him he'd probably either hear the door open, or see me. I tried looking through the crack between the doors, but all I could see was the weather strip. There were doors to the auditorium near the stage, but without knowing where he was I could walk right into him.

It's amazing how the answers to problems depend on asking the right question. I didn't need to follow Adam; I just needed to see where he was.

Between the two sets of auditorium doors was the door to the projectionist's booth. It was unlocked, and I ran up the stairs without turning on the lights. The booth smelled like old machinery and dust.

There was enough illumination through the small projection windows that I could see where I was going. I looked out, and could see almost the whole auditorium below me.

Adam was down by the left side of the stage. Taking a last look around, he went into the prop storage room. My throat tightened. Whatever he was doing, he wasn't going to the store. He had lied to me.

As soon as the door closed behind him I ran down the stairs, and into the auditorium. I could feel my heart pounding. As much as I wanted to believe that this was a waste of time, there was no good reason why he would be in there.

The storage room door muffled the voices inside. I could barely make them out as I put my ear against the cool surface.

"We don't have long," I thought I heard a male voice say. It had to be Adam, but the door muffled the voice enough that I couldn't be sure.

"Hurry up, I really need you," a higher pitched voice said, also unrecognizable. Who was in there with him?

There were some non-specific sounds, some laughter, then a definite female moan. I knew that sound. I'd made noises like that myself, so it was all too easy for me to imagine what was causing it.

My heart was pounding so loudly that I couldn't hear anything else. I felt light-headed, and thought I might faint. I leaned my hot forehead against the cool door, and I could feel my eyes getting wet.

Silent tears rolled down my cheeks as I slid to the floor, turning to sit with my back to the door. After a while there was a sharp, wailing female cry from inside the room that I could hear even without my ear to the door. I flinched, then hugged my knees. It rose quickly, and then trailed off in a happy sounding moan.

For what felt like a very long time, I floundered in a sea of self-loathing while giant piranhas tried to take big chunks out of me. What did the other girl have that I didn't? Why wasn't I as good as her? There had to be something if Adam was with her instead of me. Maybe she was prettier, or had bigger breasts. I caught hold of a tiny piece of floating hope. Maybe there was another explanation for what I heard. Hope slipped away again. The sounds could only be one thing. Maybe I had a crappy personality. How could he do this if he loved me?

After a while, other thoughts started appearing between the bouts of drowning in misery, and I started swimming rather than floundering. My parents and Kali's were two excellent examples of couples who really were in love: mine for over twenty years and hers for over thirty. People who were truly in love didn't do this kind of thing to each other. I was in love with Adam, but he didn't love me.

I tried to cry quietly so the lovers behind the door wouldn't hear me. Then I wondered why I cared what they heard. That was easy: I didn't want him to know how much he'd hurt me.

If he loved me he wouldn't be cheating on me. If he didn't love me, then he was using me, and I had no use for him. If Adam was honest, he'd tell me we were through and then move on, not move on without telling me. I started to wonder if sleeping with me might have been just a game to him. I pictured him bragging to his friends about another conquest. Worse, I pictured him bragging to whoever the girl was in there with him. The more I chased those thoughts the more my sorrow was turning to being pissed off.

At some point, Veronica the girl gave up driving the misery bus, and Veronica the PI took over. I would be damned if I was going to let somebody treat me like a disposable pet, especially if that pet was a sex kitten.

There's an old movie called Pitch Black that I'd seen on TV, and I remembered a casual comment from the bad-ass character just after he kills one of the monsters: "Did not know who he was fuckin' with." I'd told Adam everything about me. He should have known exactly who he was fucking with. I stood up, angrily wiped my eyes with the back of my hand, and prepared to reclaim my self-respect. Behind the wheel of the misery bus, Veronica the PI narrowed her eyes, downshifted, and stepped on the accelerator, aiming for Adam in the middle of the road.

The door opened easily; they hadn't even bothered to lock it. I braced myself for the sight of my ex-boyfriend doing another girl. I had my phone out, recording video as soon as the door was open wide enough for my hand to fit through. I wanted proof of what happened here in case somebody disagreed with my version of the facts later.

There was thing that I wasn't prepared for. The girl he was with was Ashley Borenstein.

CHAPTER 11

Tutti-Frutti

The surveillance of Frank Reinkemeyer promised to be easy. According to his wife, up until this last month his routine had been set in concrete. Each weekday morning he drove to work at seven o'clock, and drove home at five. Except for his supposed extra-curricular activities, that was the extent of his exercise. No wonder he was pushing three hundred pounds. All I had to do was show up around quitting time, and follow him from the office to where ever he was going.

The next afternoon I got the call that he would be "working late." Around quarter to five I pulled into his company parking lot, and found an empty spot where I could watch the main doors. I draped a city map across the steering wheel as if I was studying it. If anyone asked why I was there I'd play the poor lost soul, and then move to my alternate surveillance location in the hotel parking lot next door.

It wasn't difficult to spot Frank when he came out, right on schedule. So much for him working late. He looked even fatter in real life, and waddled as he walked.

He levered himself into the silver BMW parked in the CEO's stall. I was about to follow him when another Beemer stopped right in front of me so the driver could chat with a female co-worker who had just come out of the building.

I beeped my horn, and he glanced at Binky, clearly assigning me to the loser category, before turning his charm back to the co-worker. His more reasonable girlfriend looked at me, and said something to him. Mister Personality inched forward, not amused but wanting to impress her with his compassion for the poor. While he did so Frank turned left from the parking lot, instead of right toward his home. As I pulled out of the stall I rolled down the window to say something rude, but the co-worker beat me to it with some fine passive aggression.

"If you're a contractor you should be parking in the west lot," she said with the most insincere helpful smile I'd seen in a long time.

Did I mention that I hate bullies?

"I'm not a contractor. I'm a client." I let my smile drop a few degrees, and shifted my version of The Look to him. "Or at least I was. Next time you act like an ass, remember who pays your bills."

The expression on Mr. Personality's face was worth it. He must be in sales. It gave me a warm feeling to think of the hours he'd waste on the phone, trying to figure out which client I was so he could try to mend the bridges he thought he'd just burned. I peeled out of the lot before either of them could start apologizing. If I was very lucky I hadn't lost my target.

The street we were on was mainly a service road. It had plenty of intersections, but most of them led deeper into industrial territory. It wasn't likely that Frank was going that way. I caught up with him three blocks later when he stopped at a traffic light. I had no choice but to stop right behind him. As long as he didn't look back and notice my face, everything would be fine.

Of course, he looked back.

I could see him staring at me in his rear view mirror. Sometimes, being young and vaguely attractive is inconvenient, and this was certainly such a time. I watched him mentally undressing me, and I carefully avoided his gaze. Shit. So much for a low profile surveillance. It was time for plan B.

The light changed, and we moved forward. The road was only two lanes, so dropping back and losing myself in other traffic wasn't an option. The key to successfully tailing a subject is to make sure that the target never knows that someone is following him. Once you've been made, staying with him becomes a matter of who is willing to drive most dangerously. I had to change the rules before he got suspicious.

I don't know who sets the traffic signal timing in Calgary, but the next one was red too. In this case it worked in my favour.

I drove through the gas station on the corner, and exited onto the cross street. There was a row of industrial bays on the left. I turned into the service lane between them. As expected, the lane went all the way to the next street. In the meantime, Frank was stuck at the light for the next few seconds.

Time was of the essence. I braked to a sliding halt, grabbed a dark grey hoodie and a brown baseball cap from the back seat. It's faster to change standing up, so I jumped out of the car. The hoodie went on over everything else, which left me looking bulgy in a non-female way, and I stuffed my hair under the cap that I put on sideways, yo. Back in the car, I raced to the next street, and turned left just in time to see Frank sail past. Big sunglasses that would have caused Kourtney Kardashian a case of terminal envy joined the rest of my disguise as I entered the traffic flow two cars behind him. In that outfit, I looked like a fourteen year old boy trying to channel his favourite pop star.

Several blocks later, and now only one car behind, we crossed Six-teenth Avenue, and entered a residential area. The buffer car between us turned off, and we ended up together at another red light. I'd tuned my radio to a teen pop station, cranked up the volume, and was jumping around like a real head banger while singing along with lots of energy and no talent. When Frank looked back at the thumping, bouncing car behind him it was only for a split second. If someone had asked him to describe the driver behind him I'm sure he'd have said "I don't know, just one of those punk kids." Theoretically, he might have recognized my car, but people see a thousand cars on a typical city drive, and generally notice them only as "thing in the lane" unless they do something remarkable or are exotic. This is one of the reasons why investigators drive neutral-coloured beaters: A red Lotus is not a good surveillance vehicle. My car had cost me $900, so I doubt that he even registered its existence, let alone that he'd seen it before with a different looking driver.

After the light, I turned the radio down before my ears started bleed-ing, and let him get a hundred metres or so ahead. A block later he turned left. I slowed down, then followed when I saw that he hadn't stopped. He turned right at the next block.

I played a cautious game of follow the leader through several more turns until he pulled up in front of a bungalow with no driveway. I'd have to check the map, but it seemed to me like he'd taken the long way around to get there. Maybe he suspected a tail. There was nothing I could do about that now.

The house was one of the few remaining ones on the street built at a time when Oxford Brown wood trim and white stucco were king. Most of the houses were bigger, more modern, two-storey yuppy palaces with brick facades and double garages.

By now it was fully dark. In another half hour the residents would be home, and thinking about supper. I parked on the street, but left the engine running so I could stay warm.

Right away a detail became apparent that I hadn't thought of. I turned out the headlights – which stayed lit. It hadn't occurred to me before that Binky was equipped with daytime running lights that would stay on until the engine was turned off. This sucked. A car sitting in front of somebody's house with the lights on for any length of time was bound to attract attention. I made a mental note to talk to Doug, my genius mechanic, about installing a running light cut-off switch for stakeouts.

I had to move. The good news was that he was looking down at something when I drove past his car. He didn't look up.

The bad news was that the street was a cul de sac. I got to the turn around, and shut off the engine, watching Frank's car in my rear view mirror. With any luck he'd go into the house, and I could leave before somebody wondered why I was sitting in my car and blocking their driveway. Maybe yuppies aren't expected to have social events because the builders never allow for street parking. Unless you park in a driveway you are guaranteed to block somebody.

Five minutes later he was still sitting in his car. I couldn't see what he was doing, if anything. Maybe he was having second thoughts or, at this temperature, cold feet. My windows were already fogging over. I made another mental note to ask Doug about window coatings that might prevent that.

Crap, a vehicle turned into the street, coming toward me. I quickly started my engine, and turned around to head back toward Frank. It would look suspicious if I stopped, so I had to keep going. At this rate, sheer repetition would cause him to notice me.

As I approached his car, Frank finally got out, and went up the walkway. I continued on to the next block, quickly turned around and parked.

I gave him ten minutes to get comfortable before seeing if I could catch him in the act. I kept the hoodie, swapped the ball cap for a black toque, and walked up to the house like I was expected in case a neighbour was watching. As I had anticipated, there were no pedestrians visible. Sensible Calgarians ignore the outside world in December.

The bungalow was one of the few houses on the street without any Christmas decorations, not even a single string of lights. That helped me stay hidden while sneaking around. Drapes were drawn over the living room windows. I could see that the lights were on, and there were vague shadows moving around inside, but no details.

It looked like the mail carrier had cut across the lawn several times, so I followed the existing footprints in the snow, and went around to the side facing the neighbouring house. The ground there was bare, the narrow gap between buildings shielding it from snow fall. The gas meter was conveniently located under a window with no curtains, so all I had to do was to use the meter as a step ladder, and take some pictures of Frank smooching, or whatever, with his girlfriend. Although unlikely, maybe I'd learn a new position.

My head was out of sight under the sill, and I held my phone just above me so that the camera lens peeked through the window. In that position, I could see what the camera saw. It let me make a video of what was going on inside without revealing myself, or the camera, to anyone who casually glanced toward the window.

The screen was small, and my angle was awkward. I could see movement, but it took me a while for me to process what was happening. Call me old-fashioned, but I prefer soft kisses, cuddling, and actual sex.

If that made me vanilla, Frank was definitely tutti-frutti.

CHAPTER 12

Pony Club

In some ways I caught a lucky break. Frank Reinkemeyer's hot date was taking place in the living room.

I had to move my camera a little to avoid being blocked by the faucet, but otherwise I had a good view.

The room was typical of suburbia: couch, chairs, paintings on the walls, and a sound system. There was no coffee table; the middle of the living room was cleared for action. There was also no television. An old rotary-dial telephone sat on the side table next to the couch. That was also good. It was usually easy to find the name of the owner of a land line.

At first I thought Frank's girlfriend was a child, but that's only because she made me look like a giant. She was an honest-to-goodness dwarf. At most, she was maybe 120 centimetres tall, with wide eyes, and knee-length chestnut hair held back in a pony tail. Her face looked as young as mine. Her figure, however, was more like that of an old-school Playboy model. Looking at her, there was something that gave me the creeps. Maybe it had to do with her outfit.

She wasn't naked as I'd expected. Instead, she was wearing a full English equestrian outfit, complete with velvet-covered helmet, shiny black boots, and the old-style trousers with big thighs. Taking all that as a given, the only odd thing about her clothes were her spurs. Those made later than about 1700 have rowels with blunt ends so they don't cut the horse. These were big, and looked needle-sharp.

She was currying the thick hair on his back with a horse brush. The man was a freaking bear.

What really gave me the ickies was that Frank was standing, quietly bent over at the waist. On his hands and forearms he wore lace-up leather sheaths that ended in realistic-looking hooves, and were long enough for them to touch the floor. On his feet were things that looked like stiletto-heeled fetish boots, but without the heels. They also had hooves instead of soles. The boots forced him to stand on his toes. I bet that most women who wear high heels couldn't have been comfortable in something that extreme. I wondered how Frank managed. To complete his outfit, he had a horse's tail. From my angle I couldn't see how it was attached, and given that he didn't appear to be wearing anything other than the gloves and boots, I had no interest in finding out.

She put the brush down, and picked up a bridle equipped with a spade bit. I couldn't figure out how she was going to get it on him, then I saw that the harness had been modified to fit a human head. He passively opened his mouth to accept the bit. Without the gap that a horse has in its mouth, the steel bit was jammed between his teeth. It must have hurt.

After putting the bridle on, she arranged what looked like a tiny saddle pad on his lower back, followed by the smallest English saddle I'd ever seen. That was nuts. Humans don't have the anatomy to take a real horse saddle. It would crush their ribs. Not only that, but only a person with an amazingly strong back would be able to take a rider. Her only concession to biology was to put the saddle further down his back, near his hips, so that it was around his abdomen instead of his ribs. The girth was wider than normal, too. With his big gut, I was amazed that she could tighten the billets enough to keep the saddle on without him passing out. She even used the trick of kneeing him in the stomach when she tightened them. From the way he lurched when her knee hit, it wasn't a token blow either.

She was tiny enough that she'd actually have to mount him instead of just putting her leg over his back. She didn't put her foot in the stirrup and mount normally from the side. Instead, she put her hands on his hips and vaulted onto his back from the rear, expertly clearing the high cantle, and landing in the seat. He staggered, and if she'd been any heavier I think she'd have broken his back. She took up the reins to quiet him, then tucked her crop under her left arm. She removed a remote control from the pocket of her jacket and waved it at the stereo, then brought her riding crop to hand again.

Even from outside, I could hear the stereo begin to play Strauss' Radetzky March, well known to anyone who has ever seen an equestrian competition.

No. Freaking. Way.

Yes, way. She dug her spurs into his flanks, leaving red dots that slowly oozed blood, and Frank started to do a dressage routine. It looked like his gloves had some kind of spring-loaded controls in them so he could raise his horse knees when required. Otherwise, they were locked straight.

When he made the slightest mistake in his gait, or in a movement, she'd reach back to whip his flank with the crop several times, restart the music, and have him do the whole thing again from the beginning. I could see angry red welts forming on his buttocks where she struck him.

I'd heard of pony play where people dressed up like ponies, and were trained to do things like trot on a longe line, or draw a sulky. One difference between that and this was that this wasn't pony play. There was nothing playful about it. This was pony deadly serious.

As he moved around, I could see everything. As I'd guessed, his tail was attached to a plug stuck in his butt. To add to the list of oddities, he didn't appear to be at all excited about what they were doing. Why would he do it if it wasn't exciting? It wasn't like somebody her size would be able to physically force him to do it.

Once, he stumbled, and as she pitched forward she dug the spurs into his sides hard, leaving wounds that bled freely. I could hear his scream, even though it was muffled by the bit and the window. The blood dripped off his legs onto the carpet. She didn't seem concerned. Maybe she'd make him clean it up later.

It was a good thing I was recording this. Otherwise, there was no way I'd believe that I wasn't imagining it. I hoped that my client would be equally incredulous. I'd really be grossed out if she said something like "oh, yes, we usually do that every Tuesday, but with ferrets."

I've met a few people who were into BDSM, and the theory is straight forward, even if personally uninteresting. What was happening here didn't fit the pattern. There was no sign that Frank was getting anything out of it. He wasn't a bottom, he just looked to be in pain and oddly passive. Why would he consent to this?

The woman also looked like she was just doing a job. There was no sign that I could see of excitement on her part either. She was like a jeweller creating something beautiful from inert raw materials for which she felt no kinship. She was not somebody playing with a lover. She showed no concern that Frank wasn't enjoying anything she was doing. It wasn't even a mistress/slave relationship. It was as if she was interested in Frank solely as livestock. She was methodically training an animal to do her bidding for some purpose. It was creepy as hell.

The music finally ended, and Frank collapsed under the woman's weight. Given his fitness level, I was surprised that he'd lasted that long. As he fell, she gracefully jumped from the saddle.

He was out of breath, and having a lot of trouble getting air with the girth done up. He couldn't curl up, so he had to lie on his side like a horse. Standing beside him, she ran her crop along his side, from head to, well, tail, then paused as if she was listening to something. She slowly turned her head to look directly at my camera lens, even though it was impossible that she could have seen anything in the darkness beyond the window. She smiled with lots of teeth, then returned her attention to the horse she was training. I was being paranoid. She had to have been looking at a clock on the kitchen counter or something.

After allowing him a short rest, she struck him repeatedly with the crop until he managed to stagger to his feet again. That seemed to be very difficult while wearing the fake forelegs. He had to rise much like a real horse, with his forelegs splayed out in front of him. There were welts all over his shoulders, and the spur pricks on his sides were still bleeding. Again, she mounted him from behind, and brought out the remote control.

I'd had more than enough. I jogged back to my car, and disappeared into the night. I felt like I was expecting someone to chase me, and I kept my eye on the rear view mirror. There was no sign of pursuit through the back streets, nor along Sixteenth Avenue.

I confess that I drove somewhat above the speed limit. It took me until Edmonton Trail until I was calm enough to drive normally.

I was passing North Hill Mall, and was almost home. Without really thinking about it, I pulled in and parked in the first available stall.

That's when I started shaking. There was something terrifying about that woman, a psychopathic purity of purpose that considered other humans only as objects to be moulded to her needs. Legally, there was nothing I could do as long as he didn't complain, and she didn't kill him. Despite my distaste for him, and my loyalty to my client, I hoped he complained before he wound up disabled or dead. I had a feeling that "flogging a dead horse" was a phrase invented for her, if she thought there was the slightest chance of resurrection.

Why was she doing this? I've never believed in those Emperor Ming-like villains who do bad things just for the hell of it. Everything that real people did was done for a reason. That reason might be crazy to everyone else, but it always made sense to them, and in their eyes it was usually right.

Half of me was annoyed at my reaction, which was not that of a hard-boiled PI. The other half wanted to stay as far as possible from her, or preferably forget about her completely.

I wondered how they'd gotten together. Yes, she was beautiful, but so was his wife. From what little I knew, pony play was rarely about physical sex as such, at least between pony and trainer. People involved in it would consider that bestiality.

My gut feeling was that Sofia would do almost anything if it meant keeping her lifestyle, so how did that woman convince Frank to let her turn him into a horse? Or did he approach her? Was this his secret fantasy? The evidence so far suggested that it wasn't. Was she blackmailing him?

The answers could directly affect my client, which meant I had to find them. My omniscient gut, however, was telling me that I really didn't want to know.

This was not the kind of "more interesting case" I'd been hoping for.

CHAPTER 13

Semper Fidelis

Ashley Borenstein was lying on the floor, a slab of open-cell foam under her back as a makeshift mattress. Her arms and legs were wrapped around Adam.

She must have seen the door open, because as soon as I entered the room her eyes grew big. She squeaked as she recognized me. I saw her limbs instinctively squeeze him, as if holding on tighter was going to save her. Bitch.

Adam managed to turn his head enough to see me. "Shit..." was as far as he got as he struggled to free himself from The Bitch and grab me. If there had been any lingering doubts in my mind about what I should do, his attempt to subdue me ended them.

I wanted Adam to be quite clear on the new status of our relationship, but my foot caught him high up on the inside of his thigh instead of dead centre. Kicks, even properly done, ruin your balance so Krav Maga isn't big on them. That, and outrage, are my excuses for missing. Oddly, it was The Bitch who screamed as I connected. He just quietly crumpled to the floor out cold. I guess I was close enough.

I looked down at the scum-sucking pig whom I thought had loved me, and couldn't think of anything bad enough to call him. I settled on *perro granhijueputa*. Swearing in Spanish seemed more satisfying, somehow. Less commonplace.

The Bitch scuttled backward like a crab, while simultaneously trying to cover herself, and hide in the corner. You can imagine how graceful that was. It would have been funny under other circumstances. I glanced around, making sure that I knew where all the hazards were located just in case either of the lovebirds wanted to prolong the fight. I'd be happy to oblige. What I found while looking around disgusted me even more.

Their clothes and her purse were on the table. Beside the pile was a small mirror, a credit card, a drinking straw and a couple of lines of white powder beside the faint residue of two more. He did drugs? When did that start? I began to wonder if I knew anything about him at all. I propped my phone on the table, so I'd have both hands free if I needed them.

By then, *El Perro Granhijueputa* had woken up, and was rolling on the floor moaning and holding himself. I kicked him in the ribs just hard enough to get his attention. Okay, maybe a bit harder than that.

"Stay," I said, pointing at him. He stayed.

The Bitch cowered in the corner whimpering. I got in her face so closely that her hair moved when I spoke.

"You stupid, pathetic little bitch. I see you are back to using again. Can't you get your own boyfriend? Or did you have to bribe him with drugs to get him to do you?"

There had been some people I didn't like, but this was the first time in my life that I clearly understood that there was a real difference between dislike and hatred. It was a terrible difference.

Two years before, our families had gone to Vancouver Island together on vacation. It was a windy day as I stood on a promontory above the ocean with Kali. The waves smashed into the rocks with awful power. A huge wall of water shot up in front of us, far enough away that we almost stayed dry, close enough that the sound and elemental fury filled the world. I was terrified that one of those walls would grab me, and suck me into the depths to disappear forever.

The feeling rising inside me as I looked at The Bitch was such a wall, obscuring everything else.

I wanted to hit her. More than that, I wanted to obliterate The Bitch for all the pain she'd caused over the years to dozens of girls, including Kali and myself. In that moment, I understood how a crime of passion was possible and, for a moment, I wished I had my baton or a brick so I could smash her head to a pulp with it, regardless of the consequences to me, her, or anybody else.

I think that I was about to give in when the raw feeling was sucked away by a sudden realization that I'd gone insane. The mindless rage fell into the abyss of my id, leaving an empty place inside me filled with nothing but horror, sickness, and adrenaline that made me shake from the physical reaction. My head and chest pounded, and my stomach wanted to throw up the lunch I hadn't eaten. How could there be anything that violent inside me?

I took a deep breath, then let it out. Again. And again. The Veronica I knew and loved slowly returned.

When I'd recovered enough, I made sure that I got lots of video of The Bitch, and her drug paraphernalia. I dumped my sandwich out of its plastic bag, wrapped my hand in a tissue and collected the evidence. The sandwich I threw away. I wasn't going to feel like eating any time soon.

The Bitch whimpered again as she watched me. She misunderstood what I was doing.

"Please, don't hurt me. You want more? There's more in my purse."

I'd been wrong all these years; there was a Santa Claus. I now had a record of her giving me permission to search her purse.

It didn't take me long to find the plastic bag of white powder. I remembered what Mum had taught me about identifying drugs, so I made sure of what I had by getting a tiny amount on my finger tip, and touching it to my tongue. It tasted bitter, and that spot on my tongue went numb. It was either cocaine, or a similar narcotic. I spat, then used my sleeve to scrub the end of my tongue until it was almost raw. I wanted nothing inside me that was in any way associated with The Bitch.

El Perro Granhijueputa had sort of recovered, but seemed to be too scared of me to do anything but lie on the floor trying to cover himself. He knew how I'd met Kali and now, too late, he remembered exactly what I was capable of doing to him.

Once I had the evidence bagged, I picked up most of their clothing, and my camera before I left. From behind me, I heard "hey, wait!" from The Bitch as the door closed.

I stashed the clothing under an auditorium seat, so it wasn't immediately visible. Then I went to the school office.

It felt like I was having an out-of-body experience. I watched myself make plans, and carry them out while another part of me was still crying and screaming.

"Is the SRO available?" The secretary looked up from her lunch, then at the School Resource Officer's door. From her desk she could see into his office.

"He's having lunch right now. Can it wait?"

I pulled the bag of evidence out of my pack and jiggled it.

"I think he may want to see me now."

Constable Malvern didn't mind having his lunch interrupted at all.

"What can I do for you?" He said as he closed the door behind me. I placed the bag on his desk.

"That belongs to Ashley Borenstein. She and Adam Cullen were doing lines in the auditorium prop room. They should still be there. I handled everything with a tissue. Fingerprints should be intact." That earned me an odd look. "My mother is a detective."

He put on a pair of blue examination gloves, then pulled a package out of his desk drawer, and tore it open. He sprinkled a tiny amount of the powder into a test tube, then broke an ampoule into it. The mixture turned blue. After breaking a second ampoule into it, the mixture turned pink. A third ampoule formed a pink layer over a blue layer.

"Do you know what this is?"

"I'm guessing that it's cocaine," I said.

"The test agrees with you. Where did you say the students are?"

"They should still be in the prop room. I hid their clothes under a third-row seat in the auditorium."

"How did you get their clothes?"

I pulled out my phone, and cued the video. He watched for a few seconds, then picked up his phone.

"Mrs. Forest, could you come to the SRO office please?"

He hung up, then handed my phone back to me.

"I'll need your phone's memory card," Malvern said, holding out his hand. I dutifully removed the card from my phone, and handed it to him. It went into its own evidence bag, sealed, signed, and dated.

"Can I get that back later? There are some family pictures on there."

"I can't make any promises. You should have thought of that before recording evidence on it." Just wonderful. The part of me was still in logical mode made a mental note to always put a fresh card in my camera when I was doing surveillance.

He took a form from his desk drawer and passed it over.

"I need you to fill out this witness statement. Just explain the whole thing in your own words." He handed me the form, and I started writing as he keyed the lapel microphone on his radio.

"Dispatch," he said.

"Go ahead," a female voice replied.

"This is 14378 at Central Memorial High School. Please make me up a 10-38 call, and send two units for transport. One of them needs to be a PW. I have two 10-18s under arrest, one female. Both are 10-17."

"Copy that. Units dispatched."

Mrs. Forest came in at the beginning of his radio call, and waited until he was done, looking at me curiously.

"Mrs. Forest, can you keep an eye on this young lady while I deal with some other students?"

"Certainly. Anything I should know?"

"She's a witness. You can ask her for the story." He sealed the rest of the evidence in bags, signed and dated them, then locked them away in his file cabinet along with my completed witness report.

After he'd left, Mrs. Forest sat down beside me.

"What's going on?"

I told the story for the third time.

"Are you all right?"

"Fine," I said.

"Why did you hit Adam?"

"He was attacking me."

"Why did you take their clothes?" I tried to answer like a responsible, law-abiding citizen.

"A crime had been committed, but I had no way of arresting both suspects at once. I did the next best thing, and made it unlikely that they would leave the scene before the proper authorities had been notified."

She raised one eyebrow, and I tried not to blush. I'd tried to fool myself, but as usual I wasn't fooling Mrs. Forest at all.

"I'm a little disappointed in you, Veronica. The evidence says that you acted in self defence – again – but you can't solve every problem with violence. Assuming that either of them ever return to this school, there had better not be any more incidents."

Her eyes held just as good a Look as my mother's.

"No, Mrs. Forest, there won't be any more incidents."

Cst. Malvern returned. Mrs. Forest asked him if she could leave to make some phone calls to the school board.

A few minutes later another male constable, whose name tag read "Winter," appeared at the door. Malvern unlocked his file cabinet, and retrieved the evidence. Winter signed his name on the bags below Malvern's, noting the time at which the evidence had been transferred to his custody.

"They're getting dressed," Winter said.

"All right, Ms. Chandler," Malvern said, "you can go."

I went outside to get some fresh air, still uninterested in lunch. I was just in time to see The Bitch and *El Perro Granhijueputa* being led out of the school in handcuffs. A third male constable was leading *El Perro*, a female constable leading The Bitch.

By now it was near the end of lunch hour, so there was a crowd of at least a hundred students watching the circus. Mrs. Borenstein had arrived. She was screaming and waving her arms at the officers as they escorted the sobbing Bitch, and limping *Perro Granhijueputa*, to separate cars. A sergeant had arrived as well to supervise.

Kali appeared beside me, and held my hand, not saying anything. I guess that the presence of the police told her most of what she needed to know. If it hadn't been for the big hole in my heart where *El Perro* used to be, the show would have been massively entertaining. Especially when the sergeant took The Bitch's mother aside, and quietly explained reality to her. I saw him touch his handcuff case at one point. After that, she stopped yelling, and was very polite to the officers.

I should have just gone home that afternoon. I could have called Ramón, and had him pick me up but it never occurred to me. For all the sense that the teachers made, I might as well have been living in a *Peanuts* cartoon. The empty seat beside me kept drawing my eyes and attention. Veronica the PI considered her job done and left. Veronica the Girl was back in the driver's seat, and she felt like complete crap.

Kali called Ramón, and told him not to bother picking us up after school, that we'd walk to my place. When the final period ended, we headed for my house as quickly as possible to avoid people staring at me. A block later her plan to give me some processing time failed as a car pulled up beside us, and Mum unlocked the doors.

I'd kept it together really well all afternoon. As soon as the car door closed the balloon burst, and I completely lost it. It was that loud, wailing crying you make when your heart is breaking, and you don't care what you sound like. Kali held me, saying nothing, while Mum drove. They both waited until I wound down.

"Your principal called me at work," Mum said. "I'm sorry I couldn't be here sooner, but there was a new case, and nobody else was available. Can you tell me what happened?"

I told her the whole story, punctuated by more bouts of crying. I wanted to be strong, and give her a report worthy of Investigator Veronica but Girl Veronica refused to get out of the damned driver's seat. I'd get a few sentences out, and then my throat would tighten up to the point where I physically couldn't make a sound, and the tears would start again. I was feeling hot, sick, violated, and humiliated.

By the time we got home I was too exhausted to cry again. Mum helped me inside, followed by Kali with our homework books.

"Kali, would you mind waiting here, please?" Kali looked at me before answering. I must have looked like complete shit as my eyes pleaded with her.

"I think Veronica would prefer me to be with her, if you don't mind."

At that moment I knew that Kali loved me more than *El Perro Granhijueputa* ever had. I guess that wasn't saying much.

We sat on the sofa with me in the middle. Both Mum and Kali held my hands. At one point I wondered what I was looking at, and realizing that my eyes were just tracking the second hand on the mantle clock as it made its way endlessly around the dial.

"I'm so sorry, Veronica," Mum said. "How do you feel?"

I sighed. "Hurt. Betrayed. Like my heart's a bleeding mess on the floor."

My eyes stung again, and Mum handed me the box of tissues. I was too tired to feel grateful, but I murmured "thanks" anyway.

"When you think of Ashley and Adam, do you use their names?"

I blew my nose, and looked at her with as much self-respect as I could. With a runny nose and red eyes that probably wasn't much.

"I wouldn't dignify them with names."

"What do you call them?"

I hesitated. My parents had never been freaky about swearing, but somehow it wasn't something that was done at home unless the situation really warranted it.

"The Bitch and..."

"What?"

"*El Perro Granhijueputa.*"

Kali blushed, even through her permanent tan.

"What does that mean?" Mum asked.

Kali and I both blushed.

"Um, literally, 'big cheating son of a whore.' But it's much worse in Spanish."

Mum smiled. There was no humour in it.

"I see. The problem is that by doing so, you give them more power over you. If you have to call him anything, call him Adam. He doesn't deserve the effort it takes to stay angry with him."

I was too exhausted to argue.

"Okay, I'll try."

"How else do you feel?" Mum said.

I waved one hand vaguely. At that moment, all I felt was numb and tired.

"Satisfied?" Kali asked.

I looked at her like she'd grown an extra head, then thought about it. I wasn't sure if I was allowed to feel something like that.

"Yeah, a bit."

"Revenge is not a simple thing," Kali said quietly. "For some people in Colombia, it is a way of life. It almost always makes things worse. But what you did was not revenge, not really. It was justice, and taking back control of your life. Having control is important, as long as you don't let it control you."

Even after all these years, Kali continued to surprise me. I spoke without thinking. "How did you get to be so wise?"

It was a stupid question. She looked at me so sadly with her big, brown eyes that I was sorry that I'd reminded her of her family past. When she spoke, it was very quietly.

"Believe me, justice is important."

"I'm afraid that there's one more thing," Mum said, stroking my hair. "We need to get you an appointment with the doctor." That confused me.

"Why? I'm not injured."

"Was Adam using a condom with Ashley?"

It took about two heartbeats for me to start the uncontrollable bawling again. It didn't register when I was in the prop room, but when I thought about it, I hadn't seen any condoms. The thought that I might have gotten some disease from Ashley made me want to throw up.

A few minutes later, Mum called my doctor, and explained the situation. I sat on the couch feeling completely humiliated. The lab requisition would be left at the front desk, so I could pick it up without an actual appointment. Kali couldn't go home without a ride anyway, so she came with us. I was grateful for the company.

The requisition was in an envelope with just my name on it, which allowed me to pretend to myself that the receptionist who handed it to me didn't know exactly what was in it.

We just had time to make it to the lab before closing time. I thought I would die of embarrassment, again, when the receptionist looked at my requisition, but she was professional and didn't bat an eye. Neither did the woman who took the blood samples.

I left the lab, sure that everybody in the waiting room was looking at me, and walked out to the car between the two most important women in my life.

"Please, don't tell Dad." Mum squeezed my hand.

"I'm sorry, but he needs to know."

My life just kept getting better and better.

It would be at least a day before we got the results. I hate waiting.

Two days later the phone rang. Dad answered it.

"Veronica, it's for you." He had a "look how not curious I am" look on his face as he passed me the phone.

"Hello?"

"Veronica Chandler?"

"Yes." The bottom dropped out of my stomach.

This is Doctor Vogt's office. We have the results of your blood work. All the tests were negative."

The relief was so great that my stomach heaved again.

"All of them?"

"Yes."

"I don't need to see the doctor?"

"Not unless there's something else you want to discuss with her."

"No, that's fine. Thank you."

I managed to hang up before bursting into tears again, this time from relief. It was getting to be a habit, and I really hated it. It took Mum and Dad several minutes before they got the good news out of me. Then I called Kali.

I got over Adam faster than I thought I would.

Within a few days I was sleeping through the night, and no longer wanted to burst into tears or screams every time I thought of him. Though I still wouldn't have minded beating the crap out of him.

There was one thing that I didn't tell anybody because it was really weird and embarrassing. I really missed the sex. I mean, I *really* missed the sex. I thought I knew what a drug addict must feel like when her supply is cut off. Taking things into my own hands helped, but not as much as I thought it would.

A week later I was at my locker when Blaine, one of Adam's friends, tried to ask me out. It was obvious from his hints that Adam had told him that I put out, which pissed me off. I was proud of the way I handled him. For once, I didn't burst into tears, or beat him senseless. Instead, I just told him very loudly I'd rather clean out the zoo cages by hand than go out with anybody who associated with Adam and his slut. I also said that a lot of the girls agreed with me.

I had no idea whether anybody else agreed with me or not. I hadn't talked about it, not wanting Mrs. Forest to be mad at me, but word of what had happened had spread through the school. After all, at least a hundred people had to have seen Adam and Ashley being taken away by the police.

There were about a dozen girls within hearing distance in the corridor who had suffered at Ashley's hands over the years. One of them started clapping, and the rest joined in, accompanied by assorted cheers, and one girl who yelled "fuck yeah!" For a fleeting moment, Veronica was popular, and the jocks were nothing.

Blaine muttered something under his breath, and slunk away like he wanted to be invisible. From the look on his face, the poor boy was seriously rethinking his "bros before hos" philosophy.

Okay, that was revenge. Just this once, it tasted nothing at all like cocaine.

That did help. Just a little.

CHAPTER 14

Internship

Four months later I had a big assignment for grade ten social studies, and it was a pain. I was trying to find a reliable website for research, and not having much luck.

There was a knock on my open bedroom door. "May we come in?" Mum asked.

Both parental units entered, looking serious, and sat on my bed. Oh, oh.

"What's wrong?"

"Nothing's wrong," Mum said, although Dad gave her a quick look that told me that he didn't necessarily agree. "We just wanted to discuss your summer plans with you."

"I don't really have any, other than working at the restaurant." I looked at Dad. "*Am* I still working at the restaurant?" It would be bad if I wasn't. I needed to save a lot of money so I could start my business after I graduated.

"For as long as you want," he assured me.

"Are you still determined to become a private investigator?" Mum asked.

"Yes." I tried to sound as firm as possible to prevent any re-opening of the discussion about my career goals.

"I was speaking with Staff Sergeant Mott about your plans," Mum said, "and he had a suggestion. How would you like to do an internship with the police service?"

That was an amazing offer. Most private investigators were retired police officers, and they started their second careers with years of investigative experience. I had been listening to Mum's stories since I was old enough to understand them. I'd read the Investigator's Manual dozens of times, but even after I took the investigator's course I'd be starting with a lot of theory and no real field experience.

An internship would let me do some police work without being a sworn officer. That was important to me for reasons I was too embarrassed to ever tell Mum.

"So I'd be working with you?"

"Sometimes. You won't be paid for this, but you'll get to move around among the units, learning how each one does things, going on ridealongs, maybe assisting with paperwork. Possibly the most valuable part will be talking to working officers, hearing their stories, and making contacts. If you really want to be an investigator, having a lot of friends on the force will be important to you."

I think I squealed as I tackled them both. It wasn't dignified, but I didn't care.

"We'll take that as a yes," Dad said in a somewhat strangled voice. He pried my arm away from his neck so he could breathe. "There is one condition, however. The deal is off if you can't do your internship and maintain your grades once school starts in the fall."

"That shouldn't be a problem."

"This isn't going to be easy," Dad said. "During the summer you'll be working with the police until five o'clock, then at the restaurant until ten. When school starts you'll do your homework, then work for the police part-time when possible, and at the restaurant on weekends. That won't leave you with much free time. You might decide that being a private investigator isn't what you want to do."

"Or you may decide that police work is what you love after all," Mum said. They never stopped trying.

"When do I start?"

Kali thought it was cool, too. We were sitting on her bedroom floor eating leftovers from plastic containers when I told her about my internship.

"That's amazing," she said. "So, you'll be like a real police officer?"

"Yes and no. I'll get to do some things that they do, but I won't be arresting anyone, or stuff like that."

"Do you get to carry a gun?"

Something must have gone across my face when she said that.

"What?"

"The thought of carrying a gun freaks me out."

"Don't private investigators carry guns?"

"Not in Canada. That's why I have a baton."

"Didn't you say that your mother took you to a shooting range when you were little?"

The discussion was making me really uncomfortable. I chased the last bits of *Sudado de Cerdo* around the bottom of the container rather than answering.

"Veronica?" Kali can be very stubborn.

"I'm going to tell you something, but you have to promise *never* to tell Mum, okay?"

She put down her fork, her expression matching my seriousness.

"I promise."

I found a bit more stew and finished it.

"It isn't really guns that freak me out. I was scared of them for a while after I fired Mum's but I got over it." I ran out of words.

"If it isn't the gun, what's the problem?"

The sentence built up inside me until the pressure forced it out.

"I'm afraid I'll have to shoot somebody."

Kali was ready to be sympathetic, but I could see she didn't get it. Now that I'd come this far, I was desperate for her to understand.

"I don't mind beating the crap out of somebody."

"Just ask Ashley and Adam," she said.

"Yeah. So did some boys when I was a lot younger. I can even see myself using my baton on a bad guy, somebody who actually deserves it. But pointing a gun at somebody..."

I took a long breath and let it out.

"Just thinking about it scares me. I mean, it's difficult to kill somebody just by punching them a few times. It's easier with a baton, but still hard to do. With a gun it's different. It's like, 'I'm not fooling around any more. Game over.' When a cop uses her gun, the situation has gone so far that she's justified in shooting to kill. The fact that most cops never shoot anyone in their careers doesn't make a difference. It could happen. For me, guns themselves aren't a problem. The problem is me firing a gun at another person intending to kill them. I feel sick just thinking about it. I'm a born fighter, but I'm not a born killer."

"That's why you don't want to become a police officer like your mother."

I nodded, not trusting myself to speak for a moment.

"You can't tell Mum about this, ever. She'll think that she traumatized me as a child or something. That it's all her fault that I don't want to join the force."

There was a moment, a brief instant when I was sure that she still didn't get it. Then she leaned over, hugged me fiercely, and whispered in my ear.

"Our secret."

My first day as a police intern started bright and early at seven A.M. I wasn't really awake yet. Mum brought me up to the Major Crimes Unit, and introduced me to her Staff Sergeant, Lawrence Mott. We spent the next while talking about what I'd be doing, signing non-disclosure forms, liability waivers, and a stack of other paperwork. Then SSgt. Mott kicked me out of his office to start work.

As I'd been told, I didn't work exclusively in homicide with Mum. Instead, I was the dogsbody for the entire building. That included the District One office as well as Calgary Police Headquarters.

Just like real police officers, a lot of what I dealt with was paperwork. Detectives on TV are always saying "her phone records show..." a few moments after requesting them. In real life they spent hours sitting at a desk with a stack of printouts, or endless streams of numbers on the computer, looking at each line for meaningful patterns. That part wasn't fun, but it was important. As soon as I found something of interest, the person in charge of that investigation would check my results, and put the new evidence in place. In the meantime, that person was able to do other work that moved the investigation forward. There was a lot of that, especially in Commercial Crimes.

In between assignments I got a chance to talk with a lot of the detectives and constables. Lunch time was the best. I got to sit and listen to all the old war stories. Since I was "Janet's kid", the officers seemed to feel like they were teaching me how to be a good cop rather than a civilian investigator. I was willing to swallow my pride, and be the District One mascot if it meant that I could call on several dozen people for help later in my career.

On one particular day I was having lunch with Nick Holley, and a bunch of his buddies who had also been recruited from Yorkshire.

"I have a question," I said during a lull in the conversation about the Yorkshire Ripper investigation in the 1970s. I loved hanging around with the English constables; it was like being on the set of Doctor Who, but with less running. "Some officers think that 'cop' is a rude word but you guys use it all the time. Why?"

Nick put down his sandwich, dabbed his mouth with a serviette, and cleared his throat.

"Now you've done it," Stan Watkins said, then buried his face in his hamburger.

"The term cop, in reference to a police officer," Nick began, "is a recent contraction of the proper noun copper, meaning 'one who cops.' It is therefore a completely proper term for a constable. Of course, 'to cop' is a Northern English verb meaning to catch or grab, from the Middle French *caper*, 'to seize or take,' and ultimately from the Latin *capere*, 'to take.' We still use it in that sense when we speak of 'copping a plea' or 'copping a feel.' The use of copper as a generic term for police officers dates back to 1846. Our fellow constables who feel that it is derogatory simply don't speak the Queen's English properly."

"That's what you get when you ask a question of someone with a master's degree in English," Stan said. I was astounded.

"Nick, you have a master's?"

"You didn't think I was a knuckle-dragging gorilla who used to be a bouncer because he lacked the intellectual capacity for more sophisticated employment, did you? I was a knuckle-dragging gorilla who used to be a bouncer so I could pay my way through university. Ask Stan about his degree."

"Oh thanks, mate. I'm not confiding in you ever again."

I looked at Stan until he sighed.

"Medieval English history."

At that point I changed the subject back to something safer: Northern English terrorism during the heyday of the IRA.

My job also involved a lot of fieldwork, although I wasn't allowed to handle evidence, or enter crime scenes, until the Identification Unit had finished with them. That was fine by me. I knew that a defence attorney would have a field day if a half-trained civilian teenager was given any chance to contaminate evidence.

That didn't mean I couldn't ask questions or answer them. Certain officers delighted in giving me pop quizzes about whatever aspects of police work they thought were important at that moment. On several memorable occasions, I got to interpret blood spatter patterns while an Ident technician corrected me.

Then there was the Fire Arm Training Simulator, hidden under the Public Library downtown.

It's a pity that most people never get to play with the FATS. It's the coolest video game in the world, although occasionally painful. It makes commercial interactive games look pathetic.

In simple terms, the simulator is a holodeck. The room has a projection screen across the front where the scenario plays out, and you get a laser gun built to look and feel exactly like a real Glock 22. The gun is air-powered, and kicks like the real thing when you fire it. A sadistic training sergeant puts a computerized scenario on the screen, and you react to it, saving bystanders, clearing rooms, or shooting the bad guys as needed. A computer system watches the screen, and sees where your laser hits when you fire so it knows if you took the bad guy down or not. It's the best video game ever.

As with any good video game, there are catches that make it harder to win.

Firstly, the bad guys shoot back. There's an air cannon above the screen loaded with 3/4 inch hard plastic balls. A camera linked to the cannon tracks where you are in the room, and if bad guy shoots back at you, he really does. The trainer can set the cannon anywhere from "ouch, that stings" to "holy crap, that's going to leave a permanent mark," depending on the point he's making. Try to imagine what happens if you make a mistake, and the bad guy has a machine gun. Trust me, you want as little bare skin as possible showing when you are in the FATS. Shooting goggles are mandatory. A scarf isn't a bad idea either.

Another kink is that the training sergeant can change the scenario in real time, depending on how much he hates you that day. Maybe the bad guy has a knife. The next time the bad guy in the same scenario might have a pistol. Or a machine gun. Or he's an innocent office worker carrying a stapler, and the bad guy is behind you. Sometimes that innocent bystander you thought you were saving is the bad guy. Sometimes there's no bad guy. Sometimes there are several. If you are doing well, and have the situation under control, I guarantee that it will change. Training sergeants are evil, but by the time they get through with you, almost nothing surprises you. That's the whole point.

The last thing to put a smile on the training sergeant's face is that, unlike real bullets that become flattened blobs, all those plastic balls from the shoot-back cannon just sit on the floor like round little banana peels. I'm not the only one who's landed on her butt, and heard laughter from the observation booth.

I didn't spend a huge amount of time in the FATS because, duh, it was mostly used for training real officers. I was there enough to know that using a gun well in real life combat is a lot harder than it appears on TV. In particular, holding the gun like a gangsta gets you hit in the face by your own weapon and/or killed. Using two hands in a modified Weaver stance is your best friend.

Shooting was a skill I'd never use in real life, but at least I got an appreciation for the basics of that part of the job. As I told Kali, I was more than happy to leave the idea of shooting bad guys to someone else.

Dad was right about the work load. Once school started I had no spare time at all. About the only time I saw Kali was at the restaurant, where she also got a part-time job, and after school when we did homework together.

Boyfriends were a distant improbability at best. The alien kept suggesting that I really, *really* needed one, but Adam's treachery had made me wary. A few guys tried to hit on me, but it's amazing how well an excuse of "sorry, I have to go to the gun range tonight with my mother" works to make sixteen year old boys run away. Assuming I ever found someone who wasn't a complete pig, there was plenty of time for that later.

Everything was going fine, and I was really happy with my life.

That is, until some moron got a traffic ticket.

CHAPTER 15

Once More Into the Breach

The rest of my work on the Reinkemeyer case should have been routine: Identify the mistress or whatever she was, present my report to my client, and get paid. I was close to using up my retainer on this case, so I should make over a thousand dollars. At least I wouldn't be living on the street next month.

Curled up on my couch the next morning with Yoko Geri, I hit the internet to find the owner of that telephone. 411.ca showed no phone at that address, not even an unlisted one. I sighed. Why was nothing about this case easy?

I sat in my car outside Horse Girl's house, drinking coffee from a Thermos, and trying not to burn my mouth. The postman dropped something in the mail box, but a quick look showed nothing but junk mail addressed to Occupant. At least I now knew approximately when the post was delivered. Maybe there would be something with her name on it the next day.

By supper time I was starving, really had to pee again, and still had nothing on the woman. If she was in there she wasn't showing herself, not even to adjust the drapes.

A fictional PI would call her police contact, who would invariably whine about doing favours for somebody who wasn't a real cop, the PI would beg, and the cop would "see what she could do." Eventually the information would be forthcoming.

The difference between real life and fiction is that books ignore little details like FOIPP, the Freedom of Information and Protection of Privacy Act, and PIPA, the Personal Information Protection Act.

I had a lot of friendly contacts in the police service, but without a warrant, or an active investigation number, those laws would come down on them even harder than it would on a civilian.

I wasn't desperate enough yet to take a chance that any of them would be fired because of me. I would have to come up with a means of getting the information some other way.

That's why I'm paid the big bucks.

While my cunning subconscious mind worked on the Horse Girl problem, I decided to pursue Kali's case. According to Keith, Parker was increasingly prone to "working late," and curiously evasive about why. As with Frank, these late nights were an obvious point of attack on the problem.

Around three o'clock, Keith sent me a text message that Parker said he would be out late that night. Fortunately, Sofia and Frank were going somewhere together, so I didn't have to be in two places at once. Maybe the date night would do their marriage some good.

Parker worked at Kimu Visuals, a high end camera store on Tenth Avenue. The parking lot was L-shaped, so I could wait for him to leave with a good view of his car, but it was highly unlikely that he'd notice me.

He was supposed to work until six and, sure enough, a few minutes after quitting time he came out, got in his Toyota, and headed west. I'd learned from my experience with Frank, and took my time following him. I was one car behind him at the turn north onto 14th Street.

It's a good thing that the city has finally put a traffic light at that intersection. It used to be almost impossible to make the turn during peak traffic, and getting more than one car around the corner at a time was nearly unknown.

Fourteenth north is pretty much a parking lot during rush hour, so I had no trouble keeping up. From the corner of Tenth, Fourteenth crosses the Bow River to meet Kensington Road. The total distance between the intersections is a bit over eight hundred metres.

Five minutes later, we were almost at Kensington. A jogger who had crossed at the Tenth Avenue traffic light just before we turned was standing at the corner checking the pulse in her neck. She'd beaten us by fifteen seconds.

North of Kensington, things became a bit faster. We made it up the hill to Sixteenth Avenue in only five more minutes. Parker turned east.

Sixteenth is a lot better at rush hour now that a third lane has been added, but it is still slow. We crawled toward Deerfoot Trail, then up the other side of the Nose Creek Valley toward a familiar intersection. I thought how funny it would be if Parker had a mistress (or would the term be a mister if you are a gay man?) in the same neighbourhood as Frank. One stop shopping for all your clandestine affair needs. Maybe I should move there. In a city of over a million people the probability was close to zero.

Parker turned at the same intersection. Huh.

After a while, he turned left at the same place Frank had and, yes, immediately right. The rest of his route was identical, turn for turn. He pulled up to the same house. I watched in disbelief from the end of the street.

What the hell was going on?

Everybody said that he was as thoroughly into men as I was, so why would he be going to see Frank's mistress? Could he be doing Frank while Frank was involved with Horse Girl? That didn't feel right either, especially since Frank wasn't here. If it was me, I'd definitely choose Keith over Frank, and anyway Parker was supposed to be head over heels in love with Keith. Maybe he and Horse Girl were conspiring to blackmail Frank. That was almost a reasonable theory, but then why was he making so many trips over here?

It was already dark, so I didn't wait. A few minutes after Parker entered with his own key, I was balanced on the gas meter again, getting video through the kitchen window.

Parker was getting undressed while a tiny figure in an English equestrian outfit walked around him, occasionally encouraging him to hurry with the riding crop. The figure turned toward the kitchen, so I got a clear shot of her face.

His face. It wasn't Horse Girl, although there was a close resemblance. This one was male, although with an androgynous beauty about him. The only real differences between him and Horse Girl was that Horse Boy's hair was only shoulder length, and he didn't have the curves. In fact, he was wearing the more modern, form-fitting riding trousers. They left no doubt at all that he was male.

I watched through the camera screen for half an hour, after which I stumbled back to my car. While the engine idled I tried to absorb some heat and reality.

This was ridiculous. The Horse Kids looked enough like each other that they could be fraternal twins. Fraternal dwarf twins in a suburban house running an exclusive BDSM club that catered to men in committed relationships who wanted to be forced into being dressage horses. If they were related, I wondered what their childhood had been like. The thought was incredibly nasty.

I toyed with the idea that Horse Boy was Horse Girl pretending to be male. Maybe wearing a breast band, and with a banana stuffed in her trousers. That seemed even less likely. Her breasts were far too big to hide completely in an equestrian outfit, and hiding hair that long under a wig would be difficult and pointless.

I went over part of the video again. The Horse Twins were just too similar: They had to be brother and sister. There was something else that I noticed. Parker was crying, and definitely not excited. Like Frank, he appeared to be there against his will, but somehow unable to just walk out. What did they have on him?

Wonderful. Now I had two mysterious people to identify. The good news was that they were somehow related, probably by blood. To find one was to find the other. Surely that couldn't be difficult. How many fraternal dwarf twins were there in Calgary? How could I find out?

I didn't think Keith would react well to specific questioning about what I had so far. To have any chance of understanding what was happening, I was going to have to hope that Kali could give me more information that I could use.

When I called Kali before heading home all I got was her voice mail. I left a message for her to meet me at my place. The message was short and cryptic in case Keith was nearby when she listened to it. As they say in the movies, I wanted her to come alone.

By the time I got home, cooking wasn't high on my list of exciting things to do. I thawed some breaded chicken breasts with lime-butter sauce that I kept in case of emergencies, made some Colombian *arroz amarillo*, and left the two to finish heating while I took a quick shower. Kali phoned just as I was washing my hair. It's a law of the universe.

She arrived half an hour later. She used her key, and walked in just as I was sitting down in my comfy chair to eat. I was wearing my sinfully thick, floor-length terry cloth robe. Yoko Geri had wedged himself in beside me to keep an eye on the food. Tea and cookies waited for her on the coffee table.

Kali flumped down on the couch. For once she wasn't wearing a dress. I'd seen her in jeans before, but it still looked odd. Yoko Geri immediately abandoned my chair to sit on her lap and purr. The ungrateful animal.

"Have you found out anything about Parker?" She asked after clearing her mouth of crumbs with a sip of chai spice tea.

"Yes, but it's not good."

Kali digested that thought.

"How bad can it be?"

I directed her to play the video on my laptop.

"*¡Pichar!*" She said bitterly. "How could he do such a thing?"

"It's either better, or worse than we think. This is directly tied to another case I have. Horse Boy has a twin sister who is doing exactly the same thing with my other client's husband. I have an almost identical video of Horse Girl and the husband."

She shook her head slowly. "Who are these people?"

"I wish I knew. Somehow the dwarf twins have managed to convince two people in committed relationships to become dressage horses." I paused. That's not a sentence I ever thought would pass my lips. "If you watch carefully, Parker is crying. He knows what's going on, but he seems really docile, like he's drugged or hypnotized. The husband is the same way. It's like they don't have any will of their own, and they aren't happy about it. I have no idea what's going on, but I don't believe for a moment that this is consensual."

Kali closed her eyes, then shut the lid of the computer, cutting off the video.

"How do we stop them? Keith is going to want to know what's going on, but I think that seeing this would kill him."

"I have a few ideas about that. The good news is that I can't tell him anything about this, regardless of what Keith may believe."

She paused with another cookie in her hand.

"Why not?"

"The original idea was that he would hire me to surveil Parker. That didn't actually happen. Instead, you're the one who signed the contract, and is paying for the investigation. You're my client, and I can't breach confidentiality to report to Keith. Whether you tell him is up to you."

"Until he pays me back."

"No, you're still the client of record. It's none of my business if some-body gives you money for a perceived debt. Of course, if you want to, you can give me written permission to discuss it with him after the case is settled."

"You," she said, "are a crafty devil."

"Thank you." Yoko Geri decided that Kali wasn't a source of acceptable food, and came sniffing around my plate. I gave him a small bit of chicken to win back his affection.

"Can you think of anywhere that Parker might have met this guy?"

"Not really. Ever since they met, Parker and Keith have been pretty much joined at the hip. The only time they've been apart for any length of time is when they're at work. Keith got a new job working downtown for an oil company."

"All right, so they must have met at Parker's work. It's a good thing that Horse Boy is so distinctive. It makes him easier to check out."

"What are you going to do, ask Parker's co-workers if they've seen a dwarf with a riding crop hanging around the store?"

"I wish I could, but I don't want Parker to know that I'm looking for his – whatever he is. Even if Parker's not there, his co-workers could tell him that someone is asking questions. If the Horse Twins get wind of the investigation, they could disappear before we find out who they are, and what they're doing. The lack of closure wouldn't be good for anyone. I'll save the co-workers as a last resort."

"How are you going to find these people?"

"I'm not sure. As far as I can tell, the only time either of them show up is when one of their victims is at the house. I don't know – yet – where they are the rest of the time but nobody exists in a vacuum, especially people as physically distinctive as these two. They can't be sitting around in a secret bunker waiting for one of their victims to show up."

"Unless they belong to a league of super-villains." I ignored her.

"Somebody, somewhere, knows these people. I just have to find them."

Kali took another cookie while I put my plate on the floor. Yoko Geri jumped down, and began licking at the remains of the lime sauce.

"My cat, the mighty carnivore," I said. He ignored me.

"What can I do?"

"Be Keith's friend. Don't ask, but if the subject comes up normally, try to get any other details about Parker from him."

"Okay. What's your next move?"

I took a cookie.

"When I figure that out, I'll let you know."

CHAPTER 16

Traffic Court

There was no high school on Friday. While the teachers had a professional development day, so did I.

"Veronica," Mum called from her desk. I had been going through some very old reports for SSgt Mott for the past hour, looking for a reference that he needed, and I was ready to do anything that didn't involve paper. When I got to Mum's desk there was a uniformed constable there.

"This is Constable Shuemaker. She has to appear in traffic court this morning. I thought it would be instructive for you to go with her."

The constable was about 45, taller than me (big surprise), and had a really nice smile. She kept herself in shape and her short, brown hair had very little grey in it. She held out her hand to me.

"Call me Danielle. I hear you want to be a private investigator."

"That's why I'm here: to get some experience."

"An interesting choice. At least you won't be getting fat, lounging behind a desk all day like some detectives I know."

"At least some of us work for a living," Mum said, then turned deliberately to her computer screen. We had been dismissed.

"Seriously, why a PI and not police?" Danielle asked as we went down stairs to the car park.

"I think I can help people who either won't or can't go to the police," I said. "Domestic problems, for example. A cheating spouse hasn't broken any criminal laws, so you can't do anything. Who's going to help their families?"

There must have been something in my voice. Danielle looked at me oddly.

"Who was the cheating SOB who pissed you off?"

I snorted, then started laughing.

"I didn't know I was that funny," she said.

"My first boyfriend cheated on me with the school bad girl. I called him something very similar to that until Mum convinced me he wasn't worth the effort. That doesn't mean I don't have a point."

"True. I've had the odd relationship like that myself."

"Sucks, doesn't it?"

"Ain't that the truth."

We could have walked to the court house if we didn't mind the weather, or made our way through the maze of +15 walkways, which would take forever. Danielle had looked outside before coming to collect me, and signed out a car.

Mid-January in Calgary is the traditional time for a week or so of cold weather. The temperature might have been hovering around freezing over Christmas and New Year when suddenly, for no obvious reason, it plummets. And by plummet, I mean minus thirty.

By Friday afternoon, the outside temperature had "warmed up" to minus fifteen Celsius. The roads were nasty. It made me glad that I didn't drive yet, although that was a skill I would have to acquire soon. Many of the roads were ploughed and gravelled, but the extreme cold had hardened every lump and ridge of snow into an obstacle course. Flurries the day before had hidden the patches of ice under a layer of powder, which made walking an exciting adventure. Now that it was "warmer" the salt on the streets was beginning to turn them slushy as well. Occasionally, a car would throw a wave of muck at passing pedestrians.

Maybe the Calgarians who move down to Arizona for the winter have the right idea.

Once we were at the court house, Danielle handed some paperwork to a clerk and we waited. An hour and a half later, sitting in the cafeteria nursing cups of coffee, we were still waiting.

After about two hours the clerk found us.

"You can go. He didn't show."

Danielle smiled at the clerk, thanked him and we left.

"Ass hole," she said once we were in the safety of the car. "Most people either pay their fine, or ignore it until they're caught. Some want a court date because they know that it's a pain in the ass for us to drop what we're doing to show up to testify. If he'd shown, and I hadn't, the charges would have been dismissed for lack of evidence."

"So why did this guy ask for a court date, and then not show?"

"Maybe he thinks it's a joke. We'll see how funny he finds the bench warrant for his arrest."

She put the car in drive, then looked at her watch.

"We should have gotten lunch while we were there. What would you say to a side trip to Peter's? I'm buying."

My stomach gurgled audibly at the thought of Peter's Drive-In and Danielle snorted.

"I'll take that as a yes."

We turned north on Fourth Street, and were approaching Knox United Church on the corner of Sixth Avenue. I had a question about bench warrants.

"So, what happens..."

Pain. Cold. Wetness. Sound. Blood. Fear.

Between one instant and the next, the universe was overwhelmed by screaming madness throwing me around, dominated by the indescribably loud and piercing shrieks of rending metal. Every tiny shred of control was torn away from me. There was no time to even think of trying to brace myself. My head hit the side window hard enough that I was surprised that neither the glass nor my head broke. Then I was thrown to the left by the air bag exploding. There was a sharp pain in my left shoulder as Danielle's head bounced off it before she rebounded back into her own seat.

I'm almost certain that's what happened. In that instant there was no time to think.

The outside world disappeared in a spray of dirty slush coating the windows. Most of the force of the impact went into making our car whirl like a roulette wheel. Amid the spinning, the noise, and exploding air bags, all that registered was chaos.

Once the car stopped, there was a gaping void in the world as everything stopped. For what felt like a long time I had almost no idea who or where I was.

The snow slurry on the windows slowly began to slide off as the warm glass melted it. I saw the other driver crawl out his broken side window. He was driving some kind of sports car.

My brain came into focus, and I realized that he was hidden from Danielle by a truck stopped in the middle of the crossroad. She didn't know he was carrying a baseball bat.

"Look out!" I yelled. My ears were mostly working again. She spotted the driver, who came around the stopped truck, hitting it several times in a rage as he passed by.

The most terrifying thing about him was his voice. His screaming was so out of control that his voice wasn't human any more. It was like seeing a hungry, rabid bear running toward us.

The guy in the truck did something right and drove away. Danielle backed up, and ordered the crazy man to stop. I felt a moment of relief as she drew her gun. To my shame, I only thought about her protecting me.

She backed away again and slipped. Utter horror washed through me as her inhuman attacker swung the bat at her.

Serious injury hadn't been part of my childhood. I had no idea that the sound of breaking bone was that loud.

My door was hopelessly mangled by the crash and refused to open. I couldn't get out. I cowered on my seat, trying not to be noticed by the madman.

He howled as he saw movement, and tried to smash his way in, despite the already open driver's door.

He dropped the bat and, ignoring the open door, dove through the window at me while I tried to disappear.

He reached for my foot, and I kicked at him. It wasn't much of a kick, and didn't do anything other than make my foot a better target for him to grab. His strength was incredible. It felt like he might have broken my ankle just by squeezing it.

He wiggled back out of the window, dragging me along despite my best efforts. I tried fighting back, but there was too much panic and not enough room.

The centre console gouged my ribs, and glass cubes on the seat scoured my back as my coat rucked up.

I was desperately trying to free myself. I only managed to connect with him once, and he didn't even notice. How strong did he have to be to shrug off a boot to the face? He was like one of those movie monsters. An invincible killing machine that keeps coming through a storm of bullets.

He was about to pull me through the window when I finally got my other foot planted. He lost his grip, and I fell through the doorway to land awkwardly on my stomach in the icy muck.

I felt burning wetness on my legs, and wondered if I'd peed myself. It wasn't until later that I realized that pee should be warm instead of searingly cold.

There were tears in my eyes, and my body insisted on making whimpering noises. My fear controlled me, overwhelming my ability to think and act to try to protect Danielle or myself. It was a horrible thing to discover about myself.

I was a coward.

This wasn't a training scenario in a gym, or a fight in the school yard. This wasn't even a mugger who might leave me alone if I didn't have what he wanted. This was an insane stranger with a weapon who wanted to kill me just because I happened to be in a car that got in his way.

Against untrained school bullies I was a hero. Against friendly opponents in class I did well. But given a real killer in the real world, I was fall-ing to pieces. I was disgusted with myself, but I couldn't do anything about it. I was sick with fear. He swung the bat and, uselessly, I covered my head with my arms.

The car door shielded me.

That was my salvation. I couldn't live with myself as a coward. My grandmother hadn't been a coward when she fought her cancer to the end. My mother wasn't a coward when she'd faced murderers every day at work. Danielle wasn't a coward when she went out to confront this guy. Kali had survived more than I could imagine, and wasn't a coward. The only way I would survive, physically and spiritually, was by con-trolling the fear instead of letting it control me.

From the way he was acting, he might not have the brains to find me if I could hide from him. I wiggled madly to get under the car, letting the panic drive me.

There was sharp pain in my foot as the bat struck it, but my boot absorbed most of it. I wiggled harder. My coat got caught on something, and I strained to get away. Just as he grabbed both of my legs, and hauled me out into the street again, my hand grabbed something hard and cold.

There was no thought of consequences as I came out into the sunlight. Danielle's gun was heavy in my frozen hands as I raised it to the looming shadow overhead.

At that range it would have been almost impossible to miss. As he screamed again I squeezed the trigger. A hole appeared in his chest. He looked surprised.

I managed to squeeze off another round as he began to crumple straight down. It reminded me of video of a building being demolished with explosives.

Two rounds. Centre of mass. Just like in the simulator. I would have shot him more times if I could have gotten my fingers to work faster. I wasn't consciously trying for a double tap.

The sound of the shots was deafening. Afterwards, all I could hear was a high-pitched whine in my head. My ears were not impressed by all they'd been through in the past few minutes.

I couldn't breathe. Maybe it was the cold.

Pain. Cold. Wetness. Silence. Blood.

For a blessedly long time I lay there staring at Danielle. Waiting for the monster to rise again from behind her.

Slowly, I started noticing other things. People on the sidewalks were running away, or standing with their mouths open. They were probably screaming, but I couldn't hear anything but that whine.

I was exhausted. Part of me knew that it wasn't over. I had to move.

I rolled, and put my bare hands down into the wet cold. I forced myself to my knees, but it was hard to keep my balance. Or maybe the whole world was moving. I couldn't tell which.

I think I kept blacking out or something. The world lurched forward in a series of short video clips with blanks in between. An older woman appeared out of nowhere. She looked concerned, and her mouth moved. I couldn't hear what she said.

There was blood staining the snow by Danielle's head. That triggered something in my stomach, and I turned to vomit in the street.

The woman who had been speaking was still there. She put her arm around me.

"I threw up," I think I said. For some reason it was important that I explain myself to her. I could still hear the high-pitched whine. Through it my voice sounded to me like I was speaking underwater.

I pushed the Code 200 button on Danielle's radio, then got blankets out of the back of the car to wrap her in. The nice woman helped me.

The whole time I refused to look at the other body lying in the snow.

We were wrapping Danielle when my hearing started to come back. I heard the dispatcher on the radio, and managed to tell her what was going on.

I could hear sirens, then police cars started arriving. I looked past Danielle and forgot to ignore the other body.

Pain. Cold. Wetness. Noise. Blood.

Like a video that suddenly comes into focus the world caught up with me. I started shivering, and hurting everywhere. I was overwhelmed by the wail of the approaching ambulance, the squawking radio, the officers directing traffic, people trying to talk to me.

There were blood spatters everywhere.

The man who had tried to beat us to death was lying still, his eyes still open, and it finally hit me that I'd killed him.

Somebody started screaming, and I wondered what was going on now.

Whoever it was sounded like me. Somebody in a paramedic's uniform stood beside me. When had I gotten to my feet? He held me as I crumpled to my knees again.

I'd had enough of this.

I went away.

CHAPTER 17

Recovery

At some point after that I woke up. It was one of the worst ideas I've ever had.

I felt like I was floating in a bath of warm pudding, both mentally and physically. It was kind of nice for a while.

My shoulder started hurting. It was soon joined by my head and my chest. My fingers joined the chorus. My throat was raw and dry. I tried to swallow and started coughing. That made me move things that didn't want to be moved. Although I was warm, I was afraid to open my eyes in case I was still on the street.

Once I stopped coughing, the pain leeched away into the pudding again. I still hurt, but it didn't really matter to me.

"Take it easy, honey." I heard my daddy's voice from a long way off. "Would you like some water?"

Something touched my lips – a straw. I sucked. The cool water felt wonderful going down my throat.

If Daddy was there then I must be safe. I dozed off again.

Some time later, I opened my eyes again and blinked. Everything still hurt. It took a while for me to focus on the blur in front of me. Eventually, it turned into a familiar figure, and a hospital room.

"Daddy?" I said. Inside my head it was a firm question. What I heard coming out was a weak, croaking voice that sounded like I was a hundred years old.

"I'm here, Veronica." He was on my right side, and I felt pressure on my hand. It hurt. When I looked, he was resting his hand gently on mine, which was wrapped in a neat, white bandage.

Now that I was more aware, I saw three other people in the room. If a tailored white coat and stethoscope around her neck were any indications, one was a doctor. The others were men in suits. I didn't recognize either of them. It took me a moment to figure out what was missing.

"Where's Mummy?" I finally asked.

"She'll be here later."

"Veronica," the woman said, "I'm Doctor MacMillan." Ha, I was right. It gives you some idea of my mental state that I was proud of my deductive skills. She looked like she was from India, but had the most wonderful Irish accent. "I'm your attending physician. How are you feeling?"

"I hurt," I said and then more of my memory came back. I was still feeling fuzzy, but now I was only partially wrapped in pudding. I struggled to sit up. "Danielle, he hit her and..."

"It's all right, Veronica," she said, her hands warm and gentle against my right shoulder, the one that didn't hurt. I let her push me back onto the pillow. "Constable Shuemaker is just down the hall. She's going to be grand." She looked toward one of the men. "This is Mr. Larsen from SIU. Do you know what that is?" I felt a lump in my chest.

"Special Investigations Unit, the people who investigate the police."

"Very good. Do you feel up to answering some questions?"

I tried to nod but my neck hurt. I must have grimaced.

"You have a mild concussion, and a touch of whiplash," she said. "Try not to move your head too much for a while."

I focused my eyes on Larsen. My memory was slowly coming back, and I felt tears on my cheeks. They itched as they ran down my face, but I couldn't move my left arm. It seemed to be in a sling. The right one had a tube taped to it that I was afraid to disturb.

Larsen pulled up a chair beside my bed, and sat down. He took a voice recorder from his pocket, and turned it on. Like a bad reflection, the other man did the same on the other side. Larsen read from a notebook.

"Samuel Larsen, Calgary SIU, January nineteenth, 2008 at 1335, Foothills Hospital. Deposition of Veronica Irene Chandler, age sixteen, in the shooting of Ronald Brandau, case number 1177538637. Present are Quin Chandler, Ms. Chandler's father, Doctor Trinity MacMillan, attending physician, and Mr. Howard DeSanto, attorney for Ms. Chandler. Veronica, can you tell me what happened?" He spoke gently. That confused me. Everything I'd heard about SIU made them sound like ogres.

I tried to take a deep breath, but my ribs hurt. I let the air out slowly, trying to keep my distance from the feelings linked to the memories. As long as the feelings were far away they couldn't hurt me. In all that pudding, it seemed almost too easy.

"After we left the court house –" For some reason, it was really easy for me to tell the whole story. None of it seemed to bother me much, and that bothered me a bit. I could remember being scared at the time it happened, but the fear wasn't touching me now. Larsen was listening to every word, and nodding occasionally to encourage me. Doctor MacMillan stood behind him, her eyes on me. The man who hadn't introduced himself, Mr. DeSanto, I guessed, was also focused on me. I thought that I should be more worried, then I wondered what was wrong with me. Whatever it was, it didn't worry me much.

Daddy stood by me the whole time, holding my hand. Once I felt something wet on my fingers. A tear had dropped from his cheek. I wondered why, and then the question floated away. I went back to telling my story.

When I got to the part where the driver was shot, Daddy's hand squeezed mine. A pain shot through my palm. For some reason it didn't seem important, so I continued until the end when I didn't remember anything else.

"Thank you, Ms. Chandler," Larsen said as he put the recorder back in his pocket. "Your statement matches the other depositions we have from witnesses. I don't think we'll need anything more from you." He stood up and looked at Daddy. "You have a remarkable daughter." He nodded at Mr. DeSanto. "Howard." DeSanto nodded back.

"Thank you," I remember saying, just before he left. It seemed like something I should say. Mr. DeSanto shook Dad's hand, told me to get better, and then left.

"Where's Mummy?" I thought about it. "Did I ask that already?"

"She couldn't be here while Mr. Larsen was taking your statement," Daddy said. "She's in the waiting room."

That reminded me of what I'd been told about SIU. An officer who was involved in a shooting was kept isolated until she'd given her statement, and any evidence was collected. Since I was a minor in hospital, they'd allowed my father and doctor to be with me. Mr. Santos must be a lawyer who worked for the police union to represent the officer under investigation.

That was me, even though I wasn't a sworn officer.

"I can get her if you wish," the doctor said.

"Please," Dad said. She left us alone.

"Daddy, is something wrong with me? I feel like I'm not really here."

"It's okay, sweetheart. You bumped your head in the accident, and have a lot of bruises. You also had hypothermia, and mild frostbite on your hands. They just want you here overnight to make sure you are all right."

"Oh." Another thought crawled through my mind. "Why do I feel like I'm floating?"

"You had a big shock yesterday, and they gave you a sedative. You'll feel more like yourself tomorrow."

"Oh." I couldn't quite understand why I was concerned over my lack of concern, then I gave up being concerned about it.

"Oh God, Veronica, I'm so sorry." Mummy rushed into the room, followed more slowly by the doctor. Mummy put her arms around me and started crying.

That bothered me too, in a distant sort of way. Mummy never cried. Why was my mummy crying?

"What's wrong?" I asked her.

"I'm so sorry. If I hadn't made you go to court..."

"Constable Shuemaker would be dead," Doctor MacMillan interrupted. Mummy looked up at her.

"I was here during Veronica's deposition. Without question, Veronica saved the constable's life, and probably the lives of several other people, including her own. I spoke with the sergeant who came in with them. The driver who hit them had overdosed on cocaine, killed a man, and then stolen his car. Given the effects of a massive dose of cocaine, he was probably trying to get away from a psychotic delusion when the collision occurred. If Veronica hadn't stopped him he'd have kept going, ploughing through anyone who might have gotten in his path. We'll never know what his delusions were, but from the way he was acting after the accident it seems likely that he'd have killed everyone he encountered until the drugs wore off, assuming that he survived the overdose."

Mummy had stopped crying but she still looked really sad. The doctor pulled the chair out, and sat beside me.

"Veronica, it's going to take a while for you to process what's happened today." She put a card on the night stand beside my bed. "When you are feeling better, I want you to come to see me, so I can help you to make sense of it all. Okay?"

On some level her words meant something to me, but mostly they floated over me like butterflies. Another thought came to me, and I grabbed at it before it flew away.

"Where's Kali?"

Mummy and Daddy looked at each other.

"I didn't call her, did you?"

"We're in such trouble."

The next morning the sedatives had mostly worn off. It was nice to be able to hold onto a thought for more than a few seconds. Being on drugs once was an interesting experience, but in general it sucked. I was dozing when I heard a burst of high velocity Spanish. Kali came sailing into my room, Romantigoth gown flowing behind her, followed by a determined looking nurse.

"Only family members are allowed to visit. Leave now before I call security."

Kali sneered at the nurse. Wow, I'd never seen anyone actually do that before.

"It's okay," I said. "She's my sister."

That stopped the nurse. She looked from me to Kali, and back again. She seemed dubious.

"She's adopted," Kali said with a straight face.

The nurse glared at us and left.

Kali flumped onto the chair beside my bed. "Your parents didn't call to tell us what happened until this morning. I may never speak to them again."

"Don't be too hard on them. I think this whole thing really scared them. Besides, I was spaced-out on painkillers yesterday that had me floating around the room. Most of the time I didn't know if I was here, let alone anyone else."

She blew a blast of air out her nose to let me know what she thought of that, but seemed to consider it.

"Where are *tus padres*?"

"At home. The hospital won't let anybody but family see you to keep reporters out."

"Reporters?"

"You are famous but mysterious. The whole thing was on the news. By the time the reporters got there you'd been taken away, and nobody would tell them who you were."

"If your parents are at home, how did you get here?"

"I persuaded Rámon to bring me when he went shopping." I could imagine. Poor Rámon. Kali could be very persuasive.

She suddenly looked very small. "Please, don't do such a thing again. I've already lost one sister to madmen."

It was a good thing that I'd been given some non-floaty painkillers when I woke up that morning, otherwise the hugs we gave each other as we cried on each others shoulders would probably have hurt like hell. As it was, I barely felt anything.

At least, not physically. It had finally hit me, despite what SIU thought, that I'd murdered a man.

Doctor MacMillan came in around eleven. Her good news was that I'd be going home just after lunch. She removed the IV cannula herself, and gave me several pages of psychological and medical advice. She frowned slightly when I told her that I was fine. Kali promised to watch over me. Knowing her, she meant it.

Kali found a wheelchair, and pushed me up and down the hall. Not that I'm admitting anything, but there may have been some sound effects from my driver as we accelerated or turned corners. The nurses weren't amused, so we took a road trip out to the elevators where there was more room. Just before noon, one of the nurses caught up with us, and said that Danielle wanted to see me.

She looked like hell. Part of her hair had been shaved where she'd received a long row of stitches. Her right arm was in a cast. The bruising on her face made her look like those posters you see of battered wives.

"I hear you're going home today," she said, her speech slightly slurred as she tried to talk without moving her jaw too much. "I just wanted to thank you for saving my ass."

"No problem," I said. "You'd have done the same for me."

"Yeah, but I get paid to be stupid. You should ask for a raise."

"I don't think my boss will go for that. He probably thinks I'm getting too much as it is."

"At least you get two weeks paid vacation."

"What?"

"It's standard policy after a shooting. Two weeks administrative leave with full pay and benefits while SIU completes their investigation."

I was glad I was in a wheelchair. My head started swimming like I was going to pass out.

"Hey, what's wrong?"

"Nothing," I lied. "I'm fine." I managed to pull myself together a bit. I think I managed some sarcasm in my voice. "So I get a vacation from not being on duty, with the usual zero pay and zero benefits. That's excellent. I should do this more often."

We chatted a bit about other things until she felt too tired. With all the understated emotion and sarcasm in the face of imminent death, I felt like a real member of the police service: We Band of Brothers, the Thin Blue Line, Us against the Bad Guys. Except for one tiny, nagging thing.

I'd killed someone. Somewhere inside, a little girl was still sitting in the snow screaming.

Mum and Dad arrived a while later. Kali insisted on being my wheelchair chauffeur on the way to the car. She wasn't allowed to run, but she did do a wheelie when we got outside. I squeaked when I tipped back, which earned her a sharp word from Dad about my whiplash.

Everything was great until I got out of the wheelchair. I held onto the open car door and...

...was on Sixth Avenue, lying in the slush, the Glock in my hand. A madman raised his baseball bat, and there was the smell of burnt gun cotton.

"Veronica, what's wrong?" Dad said, suddenly beside me. How had he moved so quickly from the rear other side of the car?

"What?" I had no idea what just happened.

"It looked like you zoned out for a few seconds," Kali said, worried. "You were just standing there like a zombie, even when your dad spoke to you."

"I'm not sure. I'm fine now." I said, easing into the warm interior. Mum was sitting behind the wheel, watching the whole thing intently.

"I think we'll make an appointment with Doctor MacMillan sooner rather than later," she said.

"I don't want any more drugs," I said. Once was more than enough.

"Didn't you read her card? She's a psychologist as well as an MD."

On Wednesday, Dad drove me to my appointment at Doctor Mac-Millan's office. Rather than being in a bustling professional building somewhere, it was buried on a quiet side street off Bow Trail, in an unmarked and unremarkable house.

I'd never gone to a psychologist before. I didn't know what to expect, and I was nervous. It didn't help that the clinic looked just like every other house on the street, with no signs to indicate that we were in the right place.

The front door opened into a living room that had been converted into a waiting room. There were several couches, a coffee table, and the inevitable stacks of old magazines. A corridor led to the rest of the house. We sat down, not knowing what else to do. There was no receptionist, bell, or anything. Several of the magazines were lingerie catalogues, which I thought was strange for a doctor's office.

A few minutes later, Doctor MacMillan popped around the corner.

"Hello, Mr. Chandler. Veronica, won't you come in?"

Dad and I rose at the same time but the doctor gestured for him to sit.

"Unless Veronica has an objection, I'd like to speak with her alone. The three of us can talk later."

Dad sat down. He looked a bit worried, and I realized that this was new to him, too. It made me feel a little better to know that it wasn't just me who was nervous.

Her office was a small room with a desk, file cabinets, book shelves, and several comfortable chairs. The colours were warm and cozy.

"Please, have a seat."

I picked a chair and sat, then ran my damp palms along my thighs in case she wanted to shake hands.

"Nervous?" She said. I nodded.

"Perfectly understandable. However, I'm not going to get you to lie on a couch, ask you to tell me about your dreams, or your childhood, or do any of that other psychological stuff that you are probably expecting. I want you to know that this is a safe space for you. Whatever you tell me will go no further than these walls, unless it involves the safety of yourself or others. Not even your parents will know the specifics unless you give me written permission to discuss our sessions with them. Is that acceptable?"

"Yes, Doctor MacMillan," I said.

"To start, I'd like you to call me Trinity. Doctor MacMillan makes me feel much too old and stuffy."

"Your name is Trinity? That's different."

"I was born in Dublin, and I'm named after the college. Now, what we're going to do today is called a defusing. It may seem a bit odd, but it's like first aid for your emotions."

"That does seem weird. I'm feeling fine now."

She had that fleeting frown again at the word "fine."

"An emotional trauma is just like a physical trauma. The sooner we can clean the wound, and put a bandage on it, the sooner it will heal. Your parents told me about the flashback you had outside the hospital. Does that seem 'fine' to you?"

I didn't know what to say, so I shrugged. Ouch. I'd forgotten that moving my shoulder was a bad idea.

"Have you had any more flashbacks since then?"

"One, I guess."

"What were you doing at the time?"

"Watching TV. NCIS."

"Let's start with the facts. Tell me what happened on Friday."

"Do I have to? It feels like I've gone over it at least a dozen times."

"Humour me, and pretend that you think I know what I'm doing."

"You sound like my mother. All right, Danielle and I left the court house..." I think it took less time to tell. Maybe practice makes perfect.

"All right. Now, how did you feel about what happened?"

I like to think that I'm a good patient. When a doctor gives me a prescription I take it on time, and finish the whole thing. I tried to do what Trinity asked, but it was like touching something with boxing gloves on. I couldn't quite grab on to what I'd been feeling at the time.

"Let's try it this way. Start at the court house. How did you feel when you arrived?"

"Excited, I guess. It would have been the first time I was in a real court room."

"And when you had to wait?"

"Bored, after a while. There wasn't anything to do except sit around in the cafeteria, and watch people going in and out."

She led me through the whole experience, one step at a time. Things seemed to be going well.

"How did you feel when you saw the car coming toward you?"

"Scared, I think. I don't know. I only saw a flash before it hit us. I didn't think anything could move that fast."

"What about when the cars collided?"

"Loud. It was really loud. I didn't understand what had happened until we stopped spinning. It was too fast. My shoulder hurt where Danielle bounced off it. It still does."

We kept going, and I remembered more and more about what had happened, both little details, and how I felt about them.

What I really felt at that moment, sitting in her office, was increasingly scared. Like I'd done something wrong, and people were about to find out about it. Trinity kept a close eye on me. Every time I tensed up she had me do some breathing exercises until I relaxed again. It made for slow going.

"What did you feel when he reached into the car?"

"Terrified. It was like those dreams you have as a child, where you're hiding somewhere, and the monster comes to get you. There was no way out, and nothing I did seemed to hurt him."

"That's no reflection on you. Cocaine is an anaesthetic. You could have torn his arm off, and he probably wouldn't have felt it."

"I didn't know that at the time. It was like being in a Terminator movie. I felt so helpless. And..."

"And?"

I was too ashamed to continue.

"You were terrified," she said. "An unstoppable, inhuman monster was coming to get you. What did you do next?"

My vision blurred, and I could feel little wet feet walking down my cheeks. I could barely hear myself say, "nothing."

"And how do you feel about that?"

"Ashamed. I'm a coward."

"You think that makes you a coward?"

I sniffed, then nodded a little. I didn't think I could speak.

"You're wrong."

She waited until I looked at her, then continued.

"May I assume that you are familiar with James Bond?"

"Yes," I managed, puzzled by where this was going.

"And has he ever been taken off guard?"

I nodded again.

"And is he a coward?"

I shook my head. What was her point?

"Even a well-trained professional who is in a situation known to be dangerous can be surprised. At this point in your life you are neither well-trained nor a professional. Nor were you expecting the situation to become dangerous."

"Surprise didn't stop Danielle from going out to face him."

"True, but she's both well-trained and a professional. Have you heard of fight or flight?"

Again, I nodded.

"That's two thirds of the equation. The other third is to freeze. Earlier you described your assailant as an inhuman killing machine. One you couldn't fight. Could you run?"

"No. I was trapped in the car."

"So what was the only instinctive reaction left to you?"

It still didn't seem right to me.

"Freezing, I suppose. But..."

"But what happened as he was dragging you from the car?"

"I tried to kick him."

"So you fought back. If you were a coward you would have gone limp, and prayed that he didn't do anything more to you."

"But..." I tried again.

"You had no options, so you froze. As soon as you had options, you fought. What happened when you were being dragged out?"

I touched my side. Under my shirt I could feel the bandages. "I suppose that's when I hurt my ribs. I didn't think of it at the time, but he dragged me over the centre console. Danielle's gun was outside. He could have grabbed it and shot me." I shivered.

"But he didn't."

"Yeah, but he could have."

"Yeah," she said, mimicking me, "but he didn't. Don't start 'what iffing.' You're alive, and relatively unharmed. With that much cocaine in his system, he probably couldn't have figured out how to use the gun even if he'd noticed it. Chalk it up to good luck or good management and move on. How about after you were dragged out the door?"

"The slush was cold. I remember thinking how stupid kids are to leave their coats open in winter, like freezing to death makes you cooler." She smiled. "You know what I mean."

"Of course. Where was the other driver?"

"Just on the other side of Danielle and the door. He had the baseball bat, and he was going to hit me. Or her. I'm not sure now." My mind leaped ahead to the gun going off but Trinity leaned forward, put her hand on my knee and spoke forcefully.

"Stop right there. I want you to concentrate on his image. What do you see on his face?"

"I don't understand." His face swam before me, and I didn't want to look at it.

"Is he happy? Sad? Angry? What do you see?"

"He's angry, I think. Really angry."

"Anything else?"

"Just really angry, like crazy angry." Suddenly I recognized what I was seeing, and I flashed back to that moment in the prop room when I wanted to obliterate Ashley Borenstein. "He was completely out of control, like he'd snapped, and wasn't human any more. I don't think he saw people at all. Just things that he had to smash."

"Anything else?" I studied the frozen scene again, noticing details that hadn't really registered at the time.

"There are red stains on his coat and bat. Oh God, it's blood, so much blood. All that couldn't have come from Danielle..."

"It didn't. It was from the owner of the car he stole. I'm told that he kept beating him until he was completely unrecognizable. Make no mistake, you saved Constable Shuemaker's life as well as your own."

There was no air in the room, and my head felt woozy. Trinity led me through the breathing exercises again until I didn't feel like I was going to pass out. It was a horrible sensation while it lasted.

"Let me ask you this: What would have happened if you hadn't had the gun?"

"I don't know."

"Really?"

She just sat there, waiting for me to give her a reasonable answer.

"He would have killed us. He would have killed Danielle, and me, and anyone who tried to help. Maybe everyone on the sidewalk too until he was stopped."

"Are you sure?"

"Yes." It took a lot to say that one word. The knowledge sat in my mind like a big rock, pushing down into my chest, and squeezing the breath out of me again. Despite the relaxation exercises, my hands tingled.

"How do you know?"

"I just do. He wasn't human, he wasn't even an animal. Danielle, the car, me, it didn't matter. All he saw was things that he had to destroy."

"Veronica, what is a hero?"

The change in subject caught me off balance.

"What?"

"What is a hero?"

"I don't know. Somebody who does something really good, I guess."

"Like slaying dragons? Saving the princess? Defeating evil?"

"Yeah, I suppose."

"And what did you do on Friday?"

"I..." I saw where she was going, but the conclusion felt ridiculous.

"Who slew the dragon that was killing innocent people? Who saved the lives of Constable Shuemaker and yourself? Who stopped the madman from murdering again?"

"The police were coming..."

"Only because you radioed for help *after* stopping a murderer. There was only one person who was in a position to do all those things. Who was it?"

"I don't..."

"Who was it?" She was as relentless as my mother.

"Me," I whispered. Something modest inside me rebelled against the label. Heroes are always somebody else.

"Don't confuse your normal reluctance to take a life with being in the wrong. I'll let you in on a secret. Heroes aren't the people who have no problem slaying dragons. They are the people who are terrified and horrified by slaying dragons, but who do it anyway because it needs to be done. I've counselled several police officers over the years who were forced to take a life in the line of duty. Not one of them found it easy. They moved past the experience by learning to focus on the positive instead of the negative. On Friday you stopped a murderer, and saved at least two lives. More, if he'd been allowed to continue. Focus on that."

Some part of me really wanted to believe her. "You make it sound easy."

"It's simple but it isn't easy. Just remember that you have people who love you, and who will support you. You have people with whom you can talk about what you are going through. Over the next several weeks, I expect that you'll think about what happened a lot. It wouldn't surprise me if you dream about it."

"They aren't dreams, they're nightmares."

"That's perfectly normal. You need to process what happened and that takes time. What will surprise me is if those episodes don't decrease in intensity fairly soon. Give yourself a break, and remember that there is nothing wrong with you. You are having the normal reactions of a normal person to an abnormal situation."

"I'll try. Thank you."

"We'll get together again in a few days to see how things are going.

Don't stand on ceremony, though. Give me a call any time if you need to talk between appointments. I'll let your father know the same thing. Unless there's anything else, I think we're done for today."

"There is one thing that kind of bothers me about the whole thing. We must have been out there for twenty minutes before help arrived."

She flipped through her notes to a computer printout.

"I received a transcript from the accident investigation and dispatch call. According to the on-board diagnostics, your car's air bags went off at 11:37:40."

"Okay," I said.

"The Code 200 button was pressed at 11:40:23, not quite three minutes later. The first cars arrived almost two minutes after that."

"That's not possible."

"You were in shock. A lot happened in a short time. It fooled you into thinking that it took longer than it really did. Don't worry, that's normal too."

I wondered how normal she's think I was if I told her about my other reaction to the incident.

"Is there something else?" Crap, now she was a mind-reader. I looked past her, out the office window. There was no way I was going to talk about that. It was far too embarrassing.

"It's nothing."

"Then why are you blushing? "

If she wanted crazy, I'd give her crazy.

"It made me horny." I waited for some sign of outrage. Horror. Anything. What kind of sicko gets turned on by killing someone?

"What did, specifically?"

"I don't *know*. Just the whole thing." I started crying again. I felt like such a freak.

"Did you act on your feelings?"

"What, you mean by screwing the football team or something?"

She just waited.

"No. But I feel like I want to."

"What you are experiencing is quite common for people in life-threatening situations. Think about our ancestors who lived in small groups. The loss of even one member of the community could threaten the survival of everybody. How did they cope?"

Despite my shoulder injury, I shrugged instead of speaking.

"They replaced the victims as quickly as possible. Does the thought of the accident turn you on?"

"No, it's scary."

"How about the shooting?"

"God, no."

"Then don't worry about it. It's just an instinct, but acting on it could get you in trouble. It'll go away after a while."

"Then I'm not psycho or something?"

"Not at all. Give yourself some space to get your head together before you start calling yourself names."

That evening, Dad and I were watching a movie on television. He was sitting in his recliner while I sprawled on the couch. At 8:29, according to the DVD player's clock, there was a commercial break. Being half past, there would probably be at least a few minutes to get a drink. The commercial caught my attention – and Danielle and I were lying in the street again.

"Veronica? Did it happen again?" Dad was sitting beside me on the couch. I glanced at the television. The commercials were over and the movie was on again. The remembered cold made me shiver.

"I think so."

"I'm calling Dr. MacMillan."

"No, don't! I'm fine!" I felt stupid bothering a doctor because I'd been daydreaming for a few seconds. I looked at the mantle clock. It must be wrong, but the clock on the DVD player agreed. It was now 8:52. I grabbed Dad's wrist and looked at his watch. It agreed with the other two clocks.

Where the hell had I been for over 20 minutes?

Dad looked less anxious as he went to the phone, keeping his eyes on me the whole time except when he was dialling the number on Dr. Mac-Millan's card. I guess he took comfort that help was just a few rings away. Meanwhile, I caught myself biting my nails. I hadn't done that since I was eight.

"This is Quin Chandler. I'm sorry to bother you, but Veronica had another flashback." There was a pause while the doctor said something. "Here she is."

He carried the phone over to me, then turned down the volume on the TV.

"Hello?" Even I heard the quaver in my voice.

"I understand you had another flashback."

"I guess."

"Do you know what caused it?"

"I think it was a commercial. The one that's supposed to be a Canadian high-speed chase with both cars spinning their tires in the snow."

"I've seen it. Did it remind you of your experience?"

"Not really. I guess so. I don't remember what happened, but I think I was out of it for about 20 minutes. Are you sure I'm not brain-damaged or something?"

"Quite sure. All of your neurological tests are normal. Your mind is still trying to make sense of what you went through. How do you feel now?"

"Scared."

"Remember the breathing exercises we did? Let's do that now."

After a few slow, deep breaths, I was feeling a lot better.

"This is the important part. I want you to go back to watching television. If the same commercial comes on again, just watch it. Remind yourself that it's just a commercial, and has nothing to do with what you experienced. If you have another flashback, do the breathing exercises, and remind yourself of where you are. All right? Can you put your father back on?"

From Dad's side of the conversation, Trinity must have been telling him to keep an eye on me, and to remind me of where I was after a flashback.

I felt like a helpless little kid.

Over the next two months, the blackouts went from several times a week, to once a week, to never. I got very good at the breathing exercises. Sometimes I dreamed about the shooting, but after a while the dreams started to focus on rescuing Danielle instead of the monster hitting things, and dragging me from the car. I could even talk about it without having a panic attack. Mum and Dad were wonderful at home, giving me space to work things out, and being there when I wanted them.

I wanted them a lot.

Kali and her family were unbelievable. After she heard about the flashback during the movie, she stayed with me for three days straight in case I woke up with nightmares. The thing that woke me up the most was her snoring. Her parents brought big pots of food over so none of us would have to cook. I think that it gave them a sense of being able to do something, a feeling they hadn't had when Ana Lucia died. It was a bit awkward, though. One of the items on Trinity's list was that I should resume my normal activities as soon as possible. I missed being in the kitchen.

An awesome moment happened on Monday, ten days after the incident. On Mondays I got out of school early; my study period being the last period of the day. I had some work at the station that needed to get done so I took the bus downtown to District One. Usually, I ran up the stairs to the tenth floor, but various parts of me still hurt so I treated myself to a ride in the elevator. On the tenth floor the elevator dinged, and the doors opened. I took a few steps before realizing that something was different.

Tom at the front desk must have called up to let them know I was coming. Everybody from homicide was standing by the elevator doors, and when they opened I was met with applause. I stood in front of the elevator like a stunned banana as the doors closed behind me. Even Danielle was there, sitting in a wheel chair, with Mum standing behind her. Danielle couldn't applaud with a broken arm, but she was smiling.

"Welcome back, Ms Chandler," Staff Sergeant Mott said. "On behalf of the Calgary Police Service I'd like to express our appreciation for your actions. Not only did you save the life of one of our officers, but you showed yourself to be the kind of courageous and resourceful individual we'd be proud to call one of our own."

"Unfortunately, I can't put a commendation in your service record, since you don't have one. Nor will you be getting the Calgary Award for your actions. The mayor feels that your actions, while entirely deserving, are not the kind of thing we want to encourage others to emulate. The Ninth Floor agrees."

I didn't know what to say. The ninth floor was where the police chief's offices were. And the mayor knew about me?

There was a moment of silence during which he turned to pick up a neatly folded bundle from the desk beside him. I looked at the faces of my co-workers, and saw things that shocked me.

Acceptance and pride.

"This is the only thing we can give you to commemorate your heroism. However, be assured that none of us shall ever forget what you did."

He handed me the bundle, and everybody broke into applause again. I just stood there, overwhelmed. I had no idea what to say or do.

"Put it on," Danielle called out.

When I unfolded the bundle it was a police windbreaker. I took off my coat, and put it on. It even fit. Everybody seemed to be waiting for something.

"Um, thank you," I said. I couldn't think of anything else to say.

"Don't let it go to your head," Mum said. "You still have filing to do."

"Back to work, people," SSgt. Mott said. "The bad guys won't catch themselves." The mob began to disperse. Everybody came over to shake my hand, mindful of the bandage, before going back to their desks.

I thought I was kidding myself when I was talking to Danielle in the hospital, but it was true. At their best, the police were a Band of Brothers, the Thin Blue Line. It was Us against the Bad Guys.

Despite my age, despite my officially civilian status, and despite my often repeated desire not to join the force, they accepted me as one of their own.

I felt tears quietly pouring down my cheeks. This time, I wasn't afraid or sad at all.

CHAPTER 18

Survey Says...

I was sick of surveilling the Horse Twins house without learning anything new. It was time to find some real information about them.

From a PI's point of view, one of the wonderful things about modern technology is that tricks that would have required a skilled forger only a few years ago now required only a graphics program and a colour printer. It's one of the things that keeps private investigators like me in business.

I spent an entertaining half hour creating a masterpiece for myself, and slipping it into a plastic ID holder with a nice string. Legally, what I was about to do was a bit on the grey side, but as long as I had no intent to defraud I was still on the side of the angels. Probably the worst that could happen was me getting a stern letter from a lawyer about copyright violation.

I started late on Wednesday morning on the theory that people who weren't home during the day wouldn't be able to tell me much anyway.

My first stop was at the end of the block to establish my credentials in case people compared notes later. I was carrying an official-looking clipboard with questionnaires, and wearing the ID around my neck for a fictitious department at the university. I was also wearing a blonde wig and hipster glasses.

Most people, even the bad guys with something to hide, have truly terrible security habits. "Password" and "secret" are still the most commonly used computer passwords, and a disturbing number of people will answer personal questions from a stranger at the door, especially personal questions about other people.

People wonder why identity theft is on the rise.

Nobody answered the door at the first three houses, which was about what I'd expected. I got a response at number four. My target was number six.

"Yes?" The word was clipped, and my best guess from her appearance and accent was that the woman was Filipina. She had that nervous look when answering the door that was common with new immigrants who didn't speak much English. I gave her my best friendly smile, and spoke a bit more slowly.

"Hello, we're doing a research survey about the effects of social media on community values. Do you have a few minutes to answer some questions?"

She looked at me like she was translating in her head, her eyes glued to my authentic-looking fake university ID. She nodded.

"Do you use social sites such as Facebook, Tumblr or Twitter?"

She thought about it, then shook her head.

"Do you know your neighbours?"

Again, she thought, then nodded.

"Let's start with the neighbour on the left...," I said, pointing at house three. It was a good rehearsal of my patter, but the woman didn't know anything of interest. I thanked her for her time and moved on.

An elderly gentleman answered the door at house five. He had to be at least ninety, although he was pretty spry for his age.

"Hello, we're doing a research survey about the effects of social media on community values. Do you have a few minutes to answer some questions?"

"Oh, yes," he said cheerfully, "please come in."

The living room was stuffed with an amazing collection of antiques. It wasn't messy. Just cluttered in that way you see in Victorian houses.

Almost before I'd managed to sit down, I'd learned that Mr. Galvan's wife had died twenty years before. She had been the true love of his life, and he'd never dated afterwards. He seemed lonely and I felt sorry for him, but he was exactly the sort of person a PI wants living next door to a target. He wouldn't stop talking as he made tea, and all I had to do was gently steer the topic.

"What can you tell me about your neighbour on that side?" I pointed toward the Horse Twin's house.

"Oh," he said quietly, "that was so sad. They bought the house two, no, three years ago, but then you know how the economy is these days. Their children were so polite."

I tried to wade through his grammar.

"I'm not sure I understand. A couple with children is living there?"

"Eric and Crystal Lamb, a lovely young couple. Their children are twins, you know. Jason and Kim. Four years old, I think, although they'd be older now, of course. Fraternal twins, not identical, although it's hard to tell at that age. I let 'em help me with my garden. They couldn't really do much, but they did their best. Like most children they enjoyed digging in the dirt. I don't know if they ever joined Beavers. Did you know that they let girls in now? Did I mention that Kim is the girl? Would you like cream?"

Mr. Galvan would be a treasury of information if only I could keep him focused. I expected the tea to be in mugs, but he insisted on serving it from a formal silver service. He offered me real cream, and sugar cubes served with silver tongs. Sadly, the tea itself didn't live up to the Royal Doulton china cup into which it was poured. It must have been some generic house brand.

"Do they still live there?"

"Oh, heavens no. Eric lost his job. Downsizing, they call it these days, as if that makes it any easier on the families. You know, I was a boy during the Great Depression. I remember my father and I driving from our farm in our Bennett buggy to get supplies in town. The whole Depression just sucked the life out of him. He was never the same after. Fortunately, our farm didn't have a mortgage, and we could at least grow most of our own food. A lot of our neighbours weren't so lucky." He fell silent as the old memories marched through his head.

"How did the Lambs make out?"

He looked confused. "We didn't keep lambs. There wasn't much of a market for 'em at the time, unless you could sell the wool. Some people did take up spinning so they could make their own clothes, but it wasn't that common. It was all good Alberta beef cattle on our farm. And a cow for milk, of course. My father was very traditional so we called her Bessy."

It was my turn to look confused. "Sorry, I meant the family living next door. What happened after Eric lost his job?"

"Oh, they both tried to find work, but with two children and a mortgage they had to sell the house. Back then children could work, but they aren't allowed to do that now."

The time shift made me blink.

"When was this?"

"1930, 32."

"I meant, when did Eric and Crystal sell the house next door?"

"It must have been last year. It was bought by some Chinese fellow who was going to tear it down, and build something else. Probably one of those big houses people like now. It makes no sense to me. My Julianne and I raised four children in this house. If it was big enough for us, it should be big enough for two people, don't you think?"

"Who is living there now?"

"Where?"

"Next door, the house owned by the Chinese fellow."

"What with the economy the way it is he couldn't afford to tear it down right away. Nobody lives there now. You know, in this economy I wouldn't be surprised to see Bennett buggies making a comeback."

Old people have always fascinated me. They've lived through so much, eye witnesses to history that I barely know anything about from school. I didn't have the time for stories at the moment, but I couldn't resist asking one question.

"Bennett buggies?"

"Most people used 'em. Nobody could afford gasoline, you see, so we'd take the engine out of the truck, and attach a single tree so it could be drawn by a horse. A lot of people who'd bought cars in the twenties did that during the Depression. We called 'em Bennett buggies after the Prime Minister."

I had a brief, post-apocalyptic vision of Deerfoot Trail at rush hour, with six lanes of cars and trucks pulled by horses. At least it would cut down on high speed collisions. Something that he said bothered me so I double checked.

"Who lives there now?"

"Like I said, nobody. There hasn't been anybody there since last spring. I remember waving to the twins as they drove away. It was so sad."

That was weird.

"Have you seen anybody else around the house lately?"

"There's a large fellow who comes by in the evenings sometimes. I've said hello once or twice, but he never says a word. Maybe he works for the new owner, an architect or something."

"Anyone else? Another man or maybe a woman?" Mr. Galvan thought about it.

"You know, I believe I've seen a young fellow dropping by recently. I didn't like the look of him; he looked nervous, like he's guilty of something. I'd think twice about hiring him if I was an architect."

"Nobody else?"

"No, just those two. And the Chinese fellow, of course. He comes by after every snowfall and shovels the walk. I'll give him that, he doesn't let it build up until people nearly break their necks. Not like some on this street I could mention."

I finished my tea, leaving the thin mud of tea leaf dust in the bottom. I stood up before he could start another train of thought.

"Thank you for your time, Mr. Galvan. You've been very helpful."

He seemed perplexed for a moment. I think he'd forgotten that I was supposed to be taking a survey.

"And thank you very much for the tea."

"My pleasure," he said as he escorted me to the door. "Do come again. I've enjoyed talking to you."

Mr. Galvan really was a treasure. Now it was time for a horse of a different colour.

I pushed the doorbell button at the target house. There was no sound from inside which might mean anything. Nobody came to the door. I tried knocking several times, but the only result was a set of sore knuckles. I went around to the kitchen window, climbed up and looked inside.

The house was completely empty. Nothing on the walls, no furniture. Nothing except the carpet in the living room.

How the heck did she move an entire house worth of belongings in and out under the inquisitive nose of Mr. Galvan? There was no way that he would have failed to notice a moving van, unless it was a stealth move in the middle of the night. Usually people drove up on the lawn to load furniture, but there were no tire tracks in the snow.

Somehow, between yesterday and this morning, the Horse Twins had bugged out. Did Frank and Parker know, or would they come by and wonder where their riders had gone?

There was nobody in the houses on the other side, either. It was now late afternoon, and time to call it a day.

I was almost home when my phone rang. I pulled over to answer it.

"This is Sofia Reinkemeyer. Frank just let me know that he'll be 'working late' tonight." She did a good job of enunciating the quotes.

I looked at my watch. Damn, it was after 4:30. I thanked her for the information and hung up.

Ploughing through the rush hour traffic, I barely made it to his office in time. Given my last adventure there, I parked in the alternate location next door. It was a lot more difficult to see people coming out of the building, but at least I'd catch him as he turned onto the road.

This surveillance should be interesting. I'd either tail him to Horse Girl's new house, or I'd see an amusing reaction when he found that the house was empty.

Once again, Frank turned left after he left the lot. I was able to follow at a more reasonable distance this time.

He hadn't gotten the memo that his trainer had moved, and went back to the same house. Again, he followed the oddly wandering route to get there. I wished that I knew what that meant.

I expected him to either stand outside until he gave up on getting a response from the doorbell, or maybe go in with his own key, and then come right back out.

He had his own key, and he didn't come out. Just as he reached the door, I could see the lights come on behind the living room drapes. They must be on a timer.

What the heck, I might as well see what was happening. Maybe he was sobbing on the empty living room floor or something. I didn't feel like watching whatever he was doing live so I just held my camera up to the kitchen window, and shot a few minutes of video before going back home. I guess my sense of humour wasn't as sadistic as I thought.

I waited until I was sitting warmly on the couch before playing the video. What I expected was a forlorn man wandering around the empty house, or maybe just standing there in disbelief. What else could he be doing?

What he was doing was getting into his horse boots, or whatever they were called, and the woman was whipping him across the backs of his thighs to make him go faster. From my point of view, that wasn't the strange part.

All the furniture was back in place. I compared stills from the two videos, and as far as I could tell everything was exactly where I'd last seen it: carpet, chairs, stereo, paintings, all of it. Even the mysterious unlisted telephone was back.

What the hell was going on? Either I was going totally nuts, or somehow an entire empty house had been furnished within two hours. There was no way that Mr. Galvan could have missed it unless he was out, had been drugged, or was in on it.

More to convince myself than anything else, I looked at the stills I'd taken of the empty house, proof that the furniture had been gone that afternoon.

If I was going crazy, I was doing a really professional job of it. I wondered if Trinity ever charged her patients hazard pay.

CHAPTER 19

Hot Stuff

Now was the summer of our content, made glorious by this being the last year before graduation from high school. See what I did there? And you thought that learning Shakespeare in school was a waste of time.

I'd been an intern with the CPS for just over a year, and apart from one obvious exception, it had been a lot of fun.

Summer started early that year. The custom in Calgary is to wait until the Victoria Day weekend to put plants out in the garden. I've seen it snow after that, but it's rare. Of course, everybody starts their long-season plants indoors long before that.

Despite tradition, Dad planted his herbs outdoors at the end of April. It was that sort of spring. Even though a lot of my days were spent indoors, this promised to be everything a summer should be.

The biggest news was that Kali had finally found a boyfriend. His name was George Hallford, and he met the stringent standards of both her parents and myself.

Sr. Hernandez didn't even have to threaten him to be good to her. I took care of that myself, warning George what I would do to him if he hurt my sister. On my seventeenth birthday I had joined Mum and Nick's Abuse Club sessions at the gym. Kali and I were going out for pizza afterwards, so I told her to invite George as well.

She was annoyed with me for a week or so afterwards. Apparently, he'd become even more respectful of her after seeing what I did for fun. For several days she had trouble getting him to even hold hands with her. She said she was in no hurry to repeat my mistakes (ouch!) so, although I got all the juicy details of them making out, they hadn't gone any further. Kali was no longer Catholic, but she was still a good girl.

In comparison, I felt like a slut. So far I'd dated four guys in total and slept with three of them. Only one had worked out – sort of.

Simon had come along a few months after Adam. By then I was climbing the walls. I found out later that he knew one of Adam's friends, and had been told that I put out. Fortunately for me, he had even less patience than I do. At the end of our first date he tried to stick his hand between my legs without prior permission, so I dropped him.

Literally.

He played basketball, and was benched for three weeks while his elbow healed. I assumed that someone who played sports would have known how to fall properly, and it almost made me feel slightly guilty. I promised myself I'd try to be less impulsive, as well as swearing off jocks. No matter how hot they might be on the outside they weren't worth it.

The next boy was Chris MacBryde. Sleeping with him was an awful mistake, and I ended up hurting him terribly. It was his idea to be friends before anything else, but I was feeling lonely (girl-speak for horny). *Very* lonely. I kept hinting in increasingly obvious ways that I wanted him. I couldn't figure out why he was slow to jump at the chance to have sex without any strings attached. Wasn't that what boys did?

He taught me the hard way that not all boys are the same. If I'd let him set the pace, I'd have discovered before it was too late that his upbringing had given him an absolutely black and white view of relationships. In his mind, the only girl he was destined to sleep with was The One that God Intended Him To Marry.

I didn't know that, and was frustrated. I finally managed to seduce him – once. He acted terribly shy so I took the lead. All right, I practically tore his clothes off. Stupidly, it never occurred to me that he was a virgin. Too late, I put the brakes on when he refused to have sex again until we were married. He was a really nice, sweet guy, but there was no real spark between us. Marriage had never entered my mind. It was all hormones.

After our one night stand, he started calling me several times a day. Since we really didn't have that much in common, he didn't know what to say. After several awkward minutes of silence I would try to hint that I had things to do, but he didn't get it. I'd end up hanging up on him.

After a while, he started calling Kali to ask about me, then ran out of things to say to her too. Since she was just the uninvolved friend, she had no problem getting her father to take the phone, and suggest in strong terms that he not call again. He didn't stalk me in the usual sense. He just followed me around like a duckling, or a lost puppy, hoping that I'd take him back.

Kali let me know that my morals were not up to standard. By then that was obvious even to me.

It took a lot of effort to keep my parents from finding out about the situation so I could handle the problem myself. For once, violence wasn't an option. It wasn't his fault that I was a hormone-crazed moron.

He finally got the hint, and left me alone. I went out of my way to avoid him at school because every time we saw each other he got this hurt puppy dog look on his face. I felt like a rapist. It took a long time before I admitted to myself that a rapist was exactly what I'd been. This did very little to improve my self-esteem. I promised myself to try not to make the same mistake again.

Jordan Bier was definitely not a jock. He was a science nerd with whom I shared a love of Doctor Who, and certain video games involving psychotic female artificial intelligences.

Jordan was cute, with a little boy smile and an unconventional view of relationships. Unlike Adam and Simon who had thought they knew how to treat a girl just because they were Real Men, Jordan had done extensive research on how to make girls happy. He'd then tested, and refined that knowledge with several research subjects, all of whom were still friends with him. By the time we hooked up he could make my toes curl just by the way he kissed my neck.

Jordan could have been an egotistical jerk who thought he was God's gift to women. Instead, he preferred having friends with whom he could have sex rather than just having sex with random girls, and you had to be interesting for him to consider you a friend. We hit it off immediately, but didn't start sleeping together until two weeks after we'd met. It was a mind-blowing experience. He made Adam look like a complete amateur.

Also mind-blowing was meeting the other two girls he was currently sleeping with. He wasn't cheating on any of us. He was completely honest about it. He wouldn't sleep with me until all three of us had agreed to being Jordan's friends with benefits.

On the flip side, none of us considered him our boyfriend. Jordan treated us all like friends first, and no, there was never any sex between us girls. Looking back on it, the most remarkable feature of our relationship was that it worked for us.

Jordan insisted that we all use condoms in addition to whatever else we used for birth control, which was smart. None of us were virgins coming into this arrangement, and one of the girls, Heike, also had a real boyfriend. I never did meet him and talk to him about the arrangement, but Jordan had. He knew and had agreed.

Now that I knew what real death looked like, I wasn't going to (if you'll

pardon the expression) screw around with my future. If we'd been older
we could have gotten regular STI tests so we could lose the rubbers, but
at our age that would have involved parents. I think that mine could
have been okay with it, but the others, including Jordan, had parents
who weren't so practical.

Jordan was a lot of fun, and was very good at dealing with my raging
teenage lust, but there was something lacking in our relationship. We
didn't have that *je ne sais quoi* (I'm Canadian, of course I speak French:
fromage fort, gagnez, canneberge, mélange du jus) that our parents enjoyed.
There was no danger that I'd think I was in love with him, and think
about marriage. We were just good friends with amazingly great benefits.

We got together occasionally to see movies, talk about books or have
sex. We even hung out or double dated with Kali and George a few times.

One of the best things about Jordan was that he didn't try to do anything to make me "his girlfriend." I was free to be Veronica, the kick-ass
chick who would some day be a private investigator. I felt no need to
write Jordan's name in my notes accompanied by little hearts. It was
refreshing and educational to be having a relationship with a boy
without losing my identity in the process.

Our biggest problem was probably common to all active teens – finding places for us to have sex. See how far I'd come since Adam? Now I
could call it "having sex" instead of blushing and call it "doing it."

We sometimes solved the location problem by taking what I later realized were ridiculous chances. Certain parks were usually deserted after
dark. Half-built houses could be fun if you watched out for nails and
splinters. His place was great when his parents were guaranteed to be
out, but that made us nervous. They were devout something-or-others,
so getting caught by them having sex before marriage would have been
the end of his world. We used my place when Dad was out so that he
could pretend that I was still a virgin, regardless of the incident with
Adam.

Later I found out that Dad knew exactly what was going on, he just
decided to leave the administration to Mum. We were in a situation
where he was pretending not to know what I was doing while I was pretending not to be doing it. Fathers and daughters can be so weird at
times.

Yes, my mother allowed me to bring Jordan home to jump him. We
had a long talk (translation: she talked) about it. She acknowledged that I
was old enough to make up my own mind about my sexuality. While she
hoped that I wasn't doing anything that would get me hurt, she also felt
better knowing that I was doing it (her words!) where help was available

if necessary. I tried to be adult about it, even if it did seem weird, and thanked her for her concern.

At first, I thought she was being overly paranoid. By this time I was really good at Krav Maga, and something good had come of that incident outside Knox United. With Trinity's help, over the past several months, I'd turned that feeling of "oh God, I'm a murderer" into a feeling of "Black Widow has nothing on me." She'd convinced me that freaking out under those circumstances didn't make me a coward; it made me sane. At least I'd gotten myself together in time not to die. I still had mental twinges occasionally, but when I sparred with Mum or Nick, I won about a third of the time because I was willing to do whatever it took, and I never gave up. I'd figured out how to access my will to win. Beware the crack-fed honey badger.

On the other hand, Danielle had taught me by example that even a trained professional with a gun can be taken down if the stars are against her.

I trusted Jordan more than I'd ever trusted Adam. But maybe a little paranoia wasn't a bad thing.

CHAPTER 20

Creepy

Friday was clear and bitterly cold, the temperature pushing minus twenty-eight with a miserable, gusting wind that blasted my face into numbness within seconds of me leaving the apartment building. I vowed that the next place I live would have heated indoor parking.

Back at the Horse House, I put on my surveyor wig and glasses, and tried the survey ruse. Nobody was home, either there or on the other side. Or at least nobody was answering the door. For completeness, I also tried canvassing the other side of the street, figuring that the people there would have a better view of anything interesting. I caught five people at home, one of whom shut the door in my face, and four of whom had nothing new to add. Two of them had noticed Frank and/or Parker entering and leaving the house, but they weren't as detail-oriented as Mr. Galvan. After that I settled down in my car for a full day of surveillance.

The result was nothing but boredom, and a pile of food wrappers on the seat beside me. My buddies at District One had entrusted me with the secret of how cops pee when they're on a stakeout, something that somehow never comes up in TV shows. Or in the investigator's course, for that matter. Suffice it to say that a wide-mouthed plastic bottle with a tight screw lid is your friend. There's a reason why relatively few women volunteer for stakeouts. Trying to manoeuvre into position in a Cavalier, while wearing winter clothes, and making sure nobody reported me for indecent exposure, was definitely an acrobatic workout. Regardless of what Freud thought, it was the first time in my life that I envied men for having parts that could be easily aimed.

When I became completely bored, I drove through the back lane to check for tire marks. The house didn't have a garage, but the fence line was indented to make a parking space in the back yard. The snow in that area was undisturbed, as was the snow in the back yard. It didn't appear that anyone had used the back door since winter began. So much for my alternate theory of how the furniture was moved.

Even though it was futile, I checked the back several times. Each time I returned to the front, I tried the door bell, and knocked in case someone had come in while I was gone. There was no response and, for once, the kitchen blinds were drawn. I had no idea if the furniture was there or not, but at least that proved that someone had been in the house lately. I'd have gone home if this wasn't my only lead.

Around 8:30 that evening, I could see faint light behind the living room drapes. I'd given up being astonished. There was no way for anyone to have entered the house without me seeing them, yet apparently someone had. Either that, or somebody had been hiding in the house all this time. I wasn't quite at the point where I'd believe that somebody had dug a secret tunnel connecting with the storm drains.

According to Kali, Parker would be at home tonight, and it was much later than Frank's usual arrival time. At worst, I'd have to deal with two dwarfs if I tried the door. I wondered what they did when their ponies weren't there, then wished I hadn't.

I grabbed my clipboard and ID once more, turned off the engine, and braved the cold.

I made a last moment adjustment to my wig, then rang the door bell. This time I could hear the chime.

The door was thrown open so quickly that I heard the air being sucked back. For the first time, I was seeing Horse Girl in something other than her riding outfit.

I'd been slightly off in my estimate of her height. Standing in the doorway in her bare feet, the top of her head was just above the level of the door knob, making her about 112 centimetres tall. Even standing a step above me in the open doorway, she had to look up to meet my eyes. For once in my life I felt huge. There were no visible signs of dwarfism, just a perfectly miniaturized woman with a killer body. There was no question about that at all because, despite the weather that had me bundled up like a Yeti, she was wearing a sheer baby doll with nothing under it.

"Who the fuck are you and what the fuck do you want?" She screamed. I almost took a step back, not because she intimidated me, but because her psychotic rage reminded me of Ronald Brandau, the man I'd shot.

I plastered my most sincere fake smile on my face and forged ahead.

"Hello, we're doing a research survey..."

"What kind of bullshit is this? What gives you right to disturb me like this? Do you have any idea who I am? Do you?" She yelled at my face. She was on the top step, had to stand on tip-toe to do it, and was still a bit short. If the Arctic temperature bothered her, she didn't show it. The only visible effect was on her nipples.

"No, ma'am," I said, putting pencil to paper, "who are you?" When she didn't answer I let my eyes pointedly flick down her nearly naked front. "If you're busy, I can come back another time."

She laughed, a musical sound that would have been charming under other circumstances. She nodded like I'd passed a test.

"I like you. You don't scare easily. Come in, you look cold."

I returned her smile, *pro forma*, and went into the house. That wasn't as rash as it sounds, even though nothing was changing my impression that she was a creepy, raving nut case. She might have a riding crop stashed somewhere, but I had my baton in my coat pocket. If I kept my hand on it, I could draw and extend it in less than a second. For once, I had the advantage in height and weight in a fight. It was a strange but pleasant feeling. As long as I wasn't stupid enough to turn my back on her, or let her brother jump me from behind, I could take her down even if she had a knife hidden somewhere.

It certainly wasn't concealed on her.

The snow on my boots was beginning to melt, leaving puddles on the linoleum.

"Come," she breathed in an unnecessarily sexy voice. She went into the living room. "Don't worry about your boots," she added as I started to remove one with the toe of the other.

I sat on the edge of the couch, keeping my feet in close so I could get up quickly. I looked at the telephone, and noted that a number was written in the centre of the dial.

She sat in a chair facing me, one foot draped over the arm. She was posed like a hardcore porn star, and showed about the same amount.

"What can I do for you this evening, Miss...?"

"Leia Woolsey. And you are?"

"Fascinating," she said, swinging one small, bare foot back and forth in the air, "Woolsey, as in pulling the wool over my eyes?"

I hoped that I didn't look as startled as I felt. I wondered what might have given me away, assuming she wasn't just playing head games.

"Your name is 'Fascinating'?"

She smiled like she was pleased with my question.

"It probably should be," she said, "but I'm sure you have places to be. What is it that you want to know?"

I began my spiel.

"Our project is to research the effect of social media on personal social interactions. Do you use social sites such as Facebook, Tumblr or Twitter?"

"Oh, no," she continued in her sexy voice, "I believe only in *intimate*, personal interactions." She trailed one hand down her front, like a spaceship navigating between two planets. The hand hovered over Endor for a moment, then dropped to her side.

I tried to figure out her game. It didn't take a genius to see that she was hitting on me. Maybe she just wanted to see what my reaction would be. She had an amazing body, and I might have fallen for it if I'd had a gay bone in my body. Some other straight woman might have freaked out. Either could work to her advantage, and tell her something she wanted to know. It was a smart move on her part. The possibility that made me most uncomfortable was that she wanted to recruit me for her stable. No way was I falling for that. It didn't help that, bundled up as I was, I was starting to sweat. There was no way that I was taking anything off while in her presence.

I tried to ignore her display, and marked her answer on my form.

"Okay, that eliminates most of the rest of the survey. Can I get your name, please?" I paused with my pencil hovering over the appropriate part of the form, and looked at her expectantly.

"Do we really need names?" She licked her beautiful, full lips and ran one forefinger around her right nipple. Talk about laying it on thick.

"I'm afraid that I do. It's a requirement in case we need to follow up with any of our respondents."

She smiled and my skin crawled. It was a dazzlingly beautiful smile, but didn't involve anything but her mouth. I pressed my forearm against my coat to make sure that the baton was still there. The hard bulge was comforting.

"Beleth." It took me a moment to realize that she'd answered my question. I wrote it down.

"Is that your given name or family name?"

"Both, I suppose. Like Prince or Plato. Perhaps you've heard of me. I co-authored a mathematical treatise with Cham ben Noah. He never did understand zeta functions." Her voice became even more husky. "Or sexy primes." She moistened her lips with her tongue again. Her tongue was pink and very wet. It was getting a lot hotter in here.

Once again, apart from the obvious, there was something weird going on. I could feel myself becoming interested, drawn in like a swimmer trying to escape from a whirlpool. Her lips were so full and red, her hair a dark cascade across her shoulders. I wondered what it would feel like to bury my face in it. Or between her full breasts.

I felt like I'd dozed off, and then suddenly awakened from an erotic dream. This was definitely not me. I'd never been sexually attracted to another woman in my life.

In a way, it reminded me of my drug experience in the hospital. I knew that something was wrong but couldn't bring myself to care as much as I should. Instead, I tried to ignore my emotions and act rationally. I took a deep breath and let it out.

"Sorry, I'm not really into mathematics." Her lips quirked in a tiny smile, like she knew what was going on inside me.

"That's a pity. It's probably why you are having trouble getting things to add up." She swung her bare leg around in a wide arc, like a burlesque of a woman wanting to flash an onlooker. She got out of the chair so quickly that I almost went for my baton. She had the front door open before I could get off the couch.

"Oh well, it's been pleasant, and I'm sure you have more questions, but it turns out that I'm expecting company very soon. We'll have to continue this another time."

I managed to get myself together through the fog of horniness, and went to the door. She was standing in the middle of the entryway, again heedless of the cold, and I had to squeeze past her. She did it on purpose. I made it to the front step without quite touching her.

"Very well, if you'll give me your phone number we can set up another time..."

"Leave now."

The shift in mood was bizarre, like a small child who had abruptly become bored with one toy and picked up another.

I kept my cover enough to say "thank you for your time" and left, still uncomfortable about my reaction to her attempted seduction. I loved Kali as much as any woman could love another but I'd never felt any desire toward her. Some women are attracted to bad boys, so I suppose attraction to a bad girl was possible, but Beleth was just plain creepy. Why did she turn me on? It freaked the hell out of me.

It didn't make me happy that she was behind me, either. The spot between my shoulder blades felt like ants were crawling on it as I went down the walkway.

My attention was completely focused on any sounds behind me until I heard the door close on another of her laughs. I turned quickly to confirm that she had gone back inside, and wasn't sneaking up behind me.

I took several deep breaths of the cold night air, trying to clear my head. I had a vague theory that maybe I'd been drugged somehow. Perhaps some kind of gas or spray. The frigid air burned my throat, and I had a brief coughing fit. When it subsided I felt normal.

At least I now had a name that might or might not be hers, and one phone number. It wasn't impossible for her to have only one name. Apart from the obvious media stars, and Canadian senator Nancy Ruth who'd renounced her last name, a lot of cultures don't use family names.

As I walked away, Frank Reinkemeyer's car pulled up in front of the house. He must have actually been working late.

He completely ignored me as he quickly waddled up the walkway and let himself in. His arrival at that moment was troubling.

Either his arrival was an amazing coincidence, or Beleth had somehow known exactly when to throw me out so I wouldn't quite bump into him.

At last, I had some promising leads on the mystery woman.

I sat on my couch with my feet up, trying to work around Yoko. He was determined to be on my lap, bunting my hands with his head. I managed to type Beleth's phone number into 411.ca after only four tries.

Crap. The number existed, but it belonged to a business in the south end of Calgary that had been around since 1924. It couldn't possibly be hers.

It took me only two tries to type "Beleth" into the search engine. Yoko was getting bored with giving me subtle hints about petting him.

Beleth was a popular name. For now I ignored the articles defining Beleth, most of them nearly identical, and concentrated on the rest.

There was a Polish black metal band called Beleth, but none of the member photos matched. I checked Facebook, Tumblr, Twitter, and all the rest, but none of the Beleths were the one I wanted. Most of them were just people who wanted to seem scary.

After several hours of searching, I had nothing.

I went back to the definition articles. Most of them seemed to have been copied from each other. I picked one from an academic site, and immediately got the crucial point: Beleth was the name of a demon king or sometimes queen.

Wonderful, my only clue to the mistress's identity was that she thought she was a gender-confused demon. Yoko was still sitting in my lap, so I read the salient points aloud to him. It never hurts to get a second opinion.

"Fierce and powerful fallen angel... preceded by trumpets and loud music of all kinds... rides a pale horse... kills those who fear him... true form is a small, doe-eyed girl. What do you think, sidekick? Psychopathic and delusional?"

He scratched the side of his head with one foot, then responded to my question by attacking my hand in an attempt to disembowel it. With some difficulty I saved it from total annihilation.

"Ow, you need to have your claws clipped. It looks like our Beleth had a demon fetish, and is a few blocks short of a Jenga tower. We'll have to dig deeper." Yoko started washing himself. "Why am I telling you this? You don't have any investigative training."

He stopped washing, chirped at me, then jumped down and went to investigate his food bowl.

"I stand corrected."

Assuming for the moment that Beleth wasn't a real demon queen, there wasn't much more that I could do unless I could find out her real name.

Damn. It was time to call in the big guns.

"Detective Chandler," said the voice on the phone.

"Hi Mum, it's your favourite daughter."

"Sorry, which one is that again? Kali?"

"For that you shall feel my wrath, female parental unit."

"Many have threatened me, and I'm still here. What can I do for you, whoever-you-are?"

"I hate to ask, but I need some help with this case. Two cases, actually."

She lowered her voice. "It's about time people started flocking to you. What do you need?"

"I'm following a cheating husband, but I've run into a stone wall finding out who the girlfriend is."

"Name? Address? Phone number? License plate?"

"The only name I have is Beleth, though that may be an alias. The only place I've seen her is at 147 Millward Place North East. It's probably a rental, but according to a neighbour it should be empty. I saw a land line but the number on the phone is bogus. No car that I've seen."

"Has she done anything illegal?"

"Technically, no, other than squatting if the house really is supposed to be empty."

"You don't make it easy, do you? I'll see what I can find, but it might be awhile. I might not be able to give you much."

"I know, Mum, thanks anyway. I hate to ask, but this is a weird one."

"That's probably good. If the first one's weird they can only get better, right?"

"You mean like Adam?"

She barked a laugh, then stifled it. I imagined the other detectives in the bull pen looking at her. It served her right for the favourite daughter crack.

"I'll call you when I have something I can share."

I hate waiting.

CHAPTER 21

The Duty

The summer was over. Our extended family had spent a lot of time perfecting the art of picnicking in the mountains. These weren't your typical "cold fried chicken and potato salad from Safeway" picnics, either. Dad, *Doctora* Rojas, and I tried to outdo each other in preparing a variety of ethnic feasts to delight the eye, nose, and palate. They were a bit like eighteenth-century, European upper-class picnics, but without the horde of servants to carry everything for us.

After lunch, Kali and George took quiet hikes while holding hands. Sometimes Jordan would come along, and he and I would wander off as well.

As soon as we were out of sight of the parents, Kali would drag George into the nearest bushes for a make-out session. Jordan and I were a bit more discriminating in our locations.

Kali's father developed a habit of calling George "hore-hay," as if he'd suddenly lost the ability to pronounce English. He told me privately that it was his way of showing approval of his daughter's "friend." George put up with it to get along with his girlfriend's father. Kali glared at her father every time he did it. I thought it was funny but wisely tried not to show it when Kali could see me.

On Labour Day weekend, known primarily among students as the last weekend of freedom before school starts, *Señores* Hernández went to the Chateau Lake Louise for their own make-out session. Kali could have stayed home, but it was more fun for her to spend the weekend with us. We wanted to have a girls' weekend so George and Jordan had to make do with their parents for a few days.

On Sunday afternoon we were in the kitchen. I have a great recipe for peanut butter, coconut, and chocolate chip cookies, and I was teaching her how to make them. Mum was in the shower after doing some gardening. Dad was in the living room watching the Food Network when the doorbell rang.

I heard Dad get up and open the front door.

There was a silence.

"Yes?" he said.

"Mister Chandler, I'm Staff Sergeant Lawrence Mott. I believe you know Constable Holley." A familiar male voice said. What was our boss doing here with Nick? And why was he being so formal?

"Hi, Nick. What's going on?" Dad said.

"We're looking for Liliana Marina Hernández Rojas." SSgt. Mott said.

There was another pause, and I could picture Dad trying to remember Kali's real name. Kali looked at me, startled.

"She's in the kitchen with Veronica."

I looked around the corner, and saw the two police officers in their full uniforms. SSgt. Mott *never* wore his uniform unless he was making a statement for the press. They looked deeply serious and – oh God. A knot formed in my middle.

"May we come in?"

"What's this about?" Dad asked.

Kali was looking at me like I'd seen a ghost. I hoped that she was wrong as I dropped the spatula in panic, and ran into the living room.

"Dad, go get Mum."

He turned at the sound of my voice, unsure who to look at.

"NOW!" I yelled. He looked at my face and then, without a word, he ran upstairs to the master bath. I could feel the tears starting as I saw the look of sympathy on their faces. Oh shit, oh shit, oh shit...

Kali was standing in the kitchen door, holding a tea towel. There was a fleck of cookie dough caught in her hair. She was picking up my panic, and I tried really hard to calm down for her sake.

"What's wrong?" She asked.

"Kali," Nick said very gently, "please sit down."

She looked like a deer in headlights, unable to move or speak. She knew something must be dreadfully wrong but had no idea what. I could tell she was looking at me, but I couldn't see any details through the blur of my tears.

I remember her taking my hand as I sat beside her on the couch.

Mum came downstairs at that moment, her hair still wet from her shower, and wearing her dressing gown over her pyjamas. I guess they were the closest things at hand when Dad dragged her out of the shower.

Dad followed her, still confused, and almost ran into her when she saw who the visitors were, how they were dressed, and their expressions.

"Oh, God, no," she said, like it was a prayer. There was only one reason why they would both be here, in full uniforms, and looking at us that way.

Nick had met Kali several times when he'd come to pick up Mum, and he obviously had claimed the duty as he knelt in front of her.

"Kali," he said more gently than I'd ever heard the big man speak before, "there was a traffic accident. I'm sorry, but both of your parents were killed."

There's something missing from our rational, civilized Canadian society – a depth of passion that still exists in pure form in other cultures. If Nick had been kneeling in front of me instead of Kali I'm almost certain that I'd have asked if he was sure, cried for a while, and then asked what happened.

Kali's eyes widened, and she began hyperventilating. A soft moan started in her throat, and rose in pitch.

Until then "keening" had been a word I'd seen once or twice in old stories. I'd never looked it up, but got the idea that maybe it was like a synonym for crying.

What came out of her wasn't a moan, or a shriek or anything else with a name. It was a raw wall of sound that filled the entire room in a way that mere crying couldn't possibly have done. It went on and on until she was out of breath, then she sucked air in like she was drowning, and it began again.

Every muscle in her body was rigid, and I tried to hold her as best I could while the feeble drops of my tears were added to her tsunami of grief. The sound wasn't constant, and after a while I could distinguish something like words, repeating over and over again.

"*¡Yo quiero a mi mamá! ¡Yo quiero a mi mamá!*"

The world consisted of the two of us. Kali was in my arms, her face buried in my chest. I wiped my eyes with one hand as Nick stood up. He towered over us, his uniform a symbol of the law, order, and control that was supposed to govern our lives. His eyes were wet, and he looked as lost as we were as he sat on the other side of Kali.

Dad and Mum had their arms around one another. I couldn't tell through the blur if one or both of them were also crying.

I felt completely helpless. I wanted to change reality, to take away her pain, to take away all our pain, to somehow make things better. I had no idea how that could ever be possible. This wasn't like the shooting had been for me. Then, my mind was on autopilot, and did what it needed to do to survive at that moment. Now it kept jumping all over the place, filling with almost random, terrible thoughts.

Diego and Laura were gone. What would happen now? I assumed that they had family back in Colombia. Would Kali want to move back? Would some long-lost relative force her to move back? Would she be placed in a foster home? Would I ever see her again?

I began to understand, a bit, how she had felt when Ana Lucia was killed: Lost, alone, and powerless before forces that could sweep her family away.

Maybe Mum and Dad could adopt her, or something. From reading mom's copy of the Canadian Criminal Code, I knew a fair amount about criminal law, but next to nothing about family law. Wait, they had named Mum and Dad as Kali's guardians if anything happened. Wouldn't that mean she had to live with us? I clung to that hope as Kali clung to me.

I didn't know how long she could keep keening, and I tried to bury her face further in my chest. A quick glance at the mantle clock showed that it had been almost half an hour since this hell had begun. I felt like a traitor that I had any thoughts for myself, but my arms were burning with fatigue from supporting her in one position. At least she was becoming quieter, and I hoped that was a good sign. She was still repeating "*yo quiero a mi mamá*," but now it was more of a mumble than a wail, and her voice was hoarse. After a while she was silent, her breathing ragged, and her eyes closed. I raised her head and looked at her. She didn't move. She was asleep.

"Poor dear, she's exhausted," Nick said quietly. "Do you think we should put her to bed?"

"No," I whispered. "I don't want her to be alone if she wakes up." He nodded in agreement. "Can you hold her up while I move?"

Nick gently supported her while I slid out from behind, my arms aching and almost useless. He managed to lay her down on the couch without waking her.

I felt completely drained; almost afraid to try standing. If I was too tired to cry any more I couldn't imagine how she must have felt. We all moved into the kitchen so we were close to Kali but could talk quietly.

"What happened?" Mum asked SSgt. Mott. Her eyes were red, but her voice was steady. Professional.

"A propane transport going west on the highway by Lac des Arcs lost control and jumped the median. Her parents were coming back to Calgary, and it smashed their car against the rock cut. We think that they died instantly. They may not have even seen it coming."

"I can't believe that Diego and Laura are gone," Dad said. His eyes were red as well.

"It turns out that being killed on impact was a good thing," SSgt. Mott said. "The truck caught fire. The explosion a few minutes later incinerated everything within a hundred metres, and sent pieces of the truck at least 800 metres. The forest on the mountain side is still burning, but is under control. It's a minor miracle that the death toll was a low as it was."

"Oh my God," Mum said, "how many?"

"Seven, including the truck driver. The RCMP has shut down the Trans-Canada from Canmore to Seebe, and is routing all the traffic along Highway 1A until the fire is out. It will be at least sometime tomorrow before traffic can move normally. You should probably try to keep Kali away from news reports for the next week. If she ever wants to see the video she can request it from the news station. For now, I wouldn't recommend it."

"From what we're told, the truck rolled onto its side so it partially shielded the car from much of the fire and explosion. That allowed them to recover the bodies, and make positive identifications. The RCMP contacted us to find their daughter, and we insisted that we be allowed to do the notification. We didn't want strangers doing it."

"Thank you," Mum said, wiping tears from her cheeks.

"What will happen to Kali?" I said.

"That's a good question. Does she have any other family in Canada?"

"No. I don't know if there's anyone in Colombia either," Dad said.

"Do you think she'd want to go back?"

"I doubt it. She and Veronica are like sisters. Hell, we've all become close."

"That won't matter if relatives insist that they assume guardianship."

"Diego and Laura named us in their will as guardians in case anything happened," Dad said.

SSgt. Mott shook his head.

"That's good, but it may or may not mean anything. The courts tend to prefer relatives over friends where minors are concerned. You might get a sympathetic judge who would consider the will and Kali's wishes, or you might not. Of course, we'll do anything we can."

"Please," I said, "they can't take her away from us. We're her family." Dammit, I wanted to be strong for Kali. I hated it when something overwhelmed me, and I became just a girl again.

"There is another alternative," Nick said. "Alberta doesn't have laws about emancipated minors. However, a minor over fifteen years old can become independent simply by moving out of her parents' house, and paying her own way. If she maintains a separate household, and has some means of supporting herself, she's effectively an adult, and nobody can force her to do anything."

My head snapped up. "Mum?"

"It's up to her, but we have a guest room. She spends half her life here anyway. Quin?"

"Absolutely. As Janet said, it's up to her."

"Of course she'll stay," I said, clinging to hope again.

"She still needs to demonstrate to Children's Services that she can support herself," Mum said.

"What about her parents' money?" I hated myself for even thinking it. It felt too much like being a vulture who couldn't wait for dinner.

"It would be better if she could establish that she was independent before her parents' death," SSgt. Mott said. "Children's Services will have to be convinced that she's not existing on charity."

"She's worked part-time at our restaurant for several months now," Dad said.

"That could work," Nick said.

"All right," SSgt. Mott said, "After careful investigation, Ms. Hernández is self-sufficient, and has been living in her own household since...?"

"Last month," Dad said.

"Last month, then. I see no reason to bother Children's Services, or the courts at this time, do you Constable Holley?"

"Not at all, sir."

"Thank you," I said. I hugged Nick, who kind of expected it, then SSgt. Mott, who didn't. He put up with it well, though.

"Don't do that at the station," he said.

"No, sir."

"Take all the leave you need," he said to Mum and me.

Nick spoke very quietly to me. "One question, do you know what Kali was saying?"

Dammit, I started crying again. I choked out the words as softly as I could in case Kali woke up.

"I want my mummy."

CHAPTER 22

Emancipation

Nick, being the biggest, carried Kali up to my room, and we slept together until late the next morning. I woke to see her facing me, her eyes red and puffy.

"It wasn't a dream, was it?" She said very quietly.

"No. I'm so sorry, Kali."

We cried ourselves back to sleep, our arms wrapped around each other.

It was two days later when she felt able to face the world. We had a family meeting to explain the plan to her. She was quietly grateful for our kindness, as if she'd suddenly been possessed by her father's formal dignity in such circumstances.

"We've been thinking about this." Mum said to her. "If it was up to us, you'd have a home without any question. However, Children's Services will want to see that you are making enough money to support yourself as if you were living with strangers."

Kali nodded but said nothing.

"Quin says that meals should cost about $200 a month. If we charge you another $200 for your room, that should satisfy them."

"Fortunately, if I give you a few more hours at the restaurant, you'll be making about $600 per month. That pays your bills, and gives you money for yourself."

"We know that working as well as going to school will be difficult for you, but it's only for the next year. After that, you'll legally be an adult, and your parents' estate should be settled."

Kali nodded again. After a moment she cleared her throat.

"What about their wills? Didn't they name you as my guardians?"

Mum sighed.

"We spoke with your family lawyer about that. The courts would probably take that part of the wills into account, but it isn't guaranteed. Apparently some cousin in Colombia is already trying to be declared your guardian. Do you know Ricardo Martinez?"

"I've never heard of him."

"Well, he's heard of you. Mr. Flynn is certain that he just wants to get his hands on your family's money. The problem is that, if we petition the courts to be named your guardian, then you lose your independent minor status. The courts prefer to place minors with family rather than friends so it's possible that you could end up being sent back to Colombia to live with this cousin. However, if your are living independently then you are pretty much guaranteed to stay here with us, as long as we can convince Children's Services."

"Then we have no choice," she said.

We agreed on a date when she'd moved out of her parents' house in case anybody came snooping. Dad and I went to get her things, with María's help. She and Ramón were as devastated as we were, and would be staying at the house as caretakers, at least until Kali formally inherited it. When María answered the door she was wearing black, as was Ramón. They agreed to say that Kali had been living with us for a month.

Dad put Kali to work as soon as she felt able to function. I had to admire her strength. It would be a week or two before the life insurance paid out, and nearly a year before probate was completed on the estate. Most of the insurance money would go toward taxes owed by the estate and other expenses. Kali would see little if any of it.

In the meantime, working at the restaurant kept her from drowning in her grief. I was sure that I couldn't have functioned that well if something like that had happened to me.

Our grade-twelve year was much better because nobody died. I know exactly how horrible that sounds.

SSgt. Mott encouraged me to write some articles for the police association newsletter about my experiences. This increased my reputation among the officers as someone who understood, and cared about, police officers. If I'd planned it, I might have felt guilty for manipulating people, but he was right. It would help me later in my career.

It was also the year when I took the private investigator's course.

In Alberta, you can take the licensing exam at eighteen, even though most private investigators are ex-cops with years of experience. The nice part was that I could take the course online, which meant I didn't have to be the only seventeen-year old girl in a classroom full of fifty year old men I didn't know.

The course was a piece of cake, given that I'd been reading the manual for almost two years. Not to mention a dozen detectives who kept quizzing me on the details of being an investigator.

The other thing I had to do was to be certified to carry my baton. I'd have to re-certify every three years.

Kali's life consisted of going to school, spending two or three hours at the restaurant, then doing homework. Every two weeks she made a little ceremony of coming home with the cheque that Dad had given her at work, and presenting it to Mum at home. Apparently that made it an arm's length transaction, which was important for legal reasons. Although the amount was always more than her theoretical room and board, she insisted that Mum take the whole thing. The only money she kept for herself was what she earned from the tip pool.

It was exhausting for her, and I wished there was something I could do to help. Unfortunately, Children's Services had heard about her family situation, and they were lurking nearby, keeping an eye on her to make sure she was actually self-sufficient. Ricardo Martinez kept prodding the Alberta government to Do Something. Unfortunately for him, all the evidence pointed to her being self-sufficient: renting her own place, and paying for her own food. He kept trying, though. I guess he thought of it like buying lottery tickets. If he won, he'd win big.

The up side of working at the restaurant was that Dad's sous-chef occasionally had a moment to teach her something. He never said anything, but I wondered if Cliff was acting on a Dad's orders. Between lessons at work, and me teaching her at home, she was slowly learning the restaurant business, and becoming a good cook. If her plans for an occult shop fell through, she might end up in the sous-chef's position that Dad had hoped I'd want.

Our lives for the next year revolved around one immutable principle: that the four of us were a family. Kali and I considered ourselves to be sisters. Mum and Dad considered Kali to be their daughter. The government – well, who cared what the government thought as long as Children's Services didn't make too much of a nuisance of themselves. Someone with no sense of humour would come by every month to check up on her.

About a month before final exams were due to start, Kali and I were talking in her room. She was freaking out a bit. We couldn't figure out how she'd have time to study for finals while working.

Our doorbell rang.

At the sound of the bell we gave each other a nervous look. That's the worst part of going through the things we'd experienced. Once the world has threatened your safety, it's all too easy to become paranoid about every little thing. I wondered who was at the door, and what had gone wrong this time.

We could hear people mumbling downstairs but couldn't make out any words.

"Girls, could you come down here please?" Dad called out.

We went down to a crowded living room. Mum and Dad were talking to Ramón and María as well as a man in a suit I didn't recognize. I felt Kali tense beside me. Dad got right to the point.

"Have a seat. Kali, I think you know your parents' lawyer?"

"Mr. Flynn," Kali said quietly.

"Hello, Liliana. I'm so sorry for your loss."

She nodded with her father's dignity, not trusting herself to speak. He opened his brief case, and consulted some papers.

"There are some things you need to be aware of regarding your parents' estate," he said. "After moving to Canada, your father purchased a house and other items, then set up a trust as a tax shelter. The bulk of his net worth went into that trust, with a separate bank account for contingencies." He paused.

Kali and I looked at each other. We didn't really get what he was saying.

"Myself, your mother and the Morenos were named as trustees. You and your mother were also named as beneficiaries." He paused again. We still weren't getting it.

"And?" Kali asked.

"We didn't want to burden you with details after the accident, but now we agree that it would be best if you understood the financial arrangements."

I lost patience. "Could you please speak English? What's going on?"

He glanced at the papers again.

"As I said, the bulk of your father's money was put into the trust. The trustees have a specific set of instructions regarding disbursement of the funds. On your eighteenth birthday, you become a trustee, and your vote overrides the others with the exception that the Morenos can always draw their pension from the trust. Until then, you can draw any amount that the trustees agree to. Given that you have no immediate need for large expenditures, I would recommend keeping your income below $35,000 this year to avoid a tax burden."

It took us both a while to figure out what was going on.

"So, Kali doesn't need to work at the restaurant?"

"No," he said. "If she follows our recommendations, this year she can make $35,000. For the rest of her life, she'll be independently wealthy."

"I thought we had to wait for the estate to go through probate," Kali said. She sounded shocked.

"That only applies to the non-trust portion of the estate: the house, vehicles, and bank accounts. That's relatively minor and only adds up to –" He turned a page. "– about 9.8 million."

"My God," I blurted, "that's *minor*? How much is the trust?"

He consulted the paperwork again.

"At the moment, approximately 167.4 million. The investments are getting somewhat over five percent so that will double in about thirteen years, assuming no large disbursements."

"You never told me your family had that much money," I said.

"I knew that papa was rich, but I had no idea of the numbers."

There was silence for a minute as our brains tried to wrap themselves around this new reality.

"Are you telling me that I can get $35,000 just by asking for it?" Kali said slowly.

"Yes."

"And when I turn eighteen I can have it all?"

"Yes."

"Over 177 million dollars?"

"Give or take a few hundred thousand, yes."

"And that by the time I'm thirty, I'll have over three hundred fifty million dollars?"

"In round numbers, yes, assuming you don't use a significant portion of it. Your parents were quite frugal in their spending. Not more than a few hundred thousand a year."

"*Madre de dios*," she whispered. "How quickly could I get a few thousand dollars?"

"Right now, if you wish. May I ask what you want it for?"

"I want to pay my room and board for the next few months."

"You don't have to do that," Mum said.

"Yes, I do. Mama and papa always paid their debts, and I shall pay mine."

Mr. Flynn took out a cheque book.

"How much do you need?"

Kali counted on her fingers.

"Six thousand dollars. Please make it payable to Mrs. Janet Chandler."

He glanced at Ramón and María, who nodded. He began writing.

"That's too much," Mum said. "Your room and board is only about four hundred a month, and you've been paying almost six hundred."

Kali's mouth took a determined set, and her eyes narrowed.

"Shut up, Mum," I said.

"But..."

"Shut up, dear," Dad said. "Let her have her pride."

Mr. Flynn handed her the cheque.

"Thank you."

"What about Ramón and María?" Kali asked.

"They remain the caretakers of the country house until you decide what you want to do with it. After probate you can keep it or sell it as you choose."

"*Ustedes nunca tendrán nada de que preocuparse, yo me encargo de eso,*" Kali said to Ramón. "You will never have anything to worry about."

"*Muchos gracias, chiqui,*" María said.

Having quit her job, Kali had extra time, both to study and get more sleep. A few days later we were in her room. She was working on her computer while I was reading on the bed. There was a buzzing sound, and her phone danced beside her on the desk.

"Hello?" There was a long pause. "You must be joking."

She pushed a button to activate the speaker phone. The person on the other end was an annoyed-sounding woman.

"Not at all. You're a minor, and an immigrant. If you don't have the means to support yourself we'll have to place you in foster care, or send you back to Colombia to live with your cousin."

I was about to explode when Kali held her hand up to stop me.

"I'm in the middle of final exams. The reason I quit my job was so that I'd have time to study."

"That's very commendable, but the fact remains that you don't have any income."

"Are you sure about that?"

"Are you saying that you have another job? I have no record of that."

"No, I'm saying that you have no idea what I have. Get Mum." It took me a second to figure out that the last was directed at me. I got Mum in the time-honoured method used by girls everywhere.

"MUM!" I bellowed without getting off the bed.

"What was that?"

"My landlady is on the way. I'll let you talk to her about how I'm meeting my obligations."

Mum appeared at the doorway, and Kali held out the phone.

"Mrs. Chandler, this woman wants to put me in a foster home because I quit my job."

Mum got The Look and took the phone, turning off the speaker.

"This is Detective Janet Chandler, Ms. Herndández's landlady. What's this about her not paying her way?"

There was a long pause. All we could hear was an indistinct "blah blah blah."

"Are you aware that she just paid me $6000 for the next few month's room and board while she writes her exams?"

Indignant squawks from the phone.

"Were you further aware that she has a considerable inheritance that she can draw upon at any time?"

More subdued muttering.

"May I suggest that you avoid the rush, and close the file now? In six months she will be eighteen. In the meantime, she has more than paid her way. She has, and will continue to have, a roof over her head. She also buys, and makes, a third of the meals on my family's table. Good bye."

That's a problem with modern technology: All you can do is swipe a touch screen when you hang up on somebody. I bet that the old phones that you could slam down onto the switch-hooks were much more satisfying.

"I don't think she'll be bothering you again," Mum said.

We both wanted to do well in our exams, not because we had to, but because we wanted four parents to be proud of us. A lot of other kids were really stressed about exams, but Kali and I had a secret weapon. The majority of them were leaving school to find jobs, or to try to get into university. Kali and I were going into business for ourselves – we didn't need to impress an employer or a university registrar. Even if both our businesses failed, Dad would hire us without question. We both wanted to get good marks but we didn't need to get good marks.

It made the whole process much more relaxing.

CHAPTER 23

Graduation

This was the day that parents looked forward to as the end of them having to say "have you done your homework yet?" Graduation Day.

The ceremony itself took place in the Corral at the Stampede Grounds, and involved a lot of pomp and circumstance – literally, in the case of the processional music played by our concert band. We were all dressed in academic robes, and paraded in the applause of our parents before going up on stage a class at a time to receive our diplomas.

There was no throwing of mortarboards into the air and cheering at the end because we had no mortarboards. Somebody at the school board had decided that students had to be kept completely safe under all possible circumstances, and somebody might get hit in the eye if they looked up while a cap was coming down. Of course, they could have told people not to look up, but then maybe somebody would get a concussion from a piece of cloth and cardboard. It didn't make sense to us, but that's the way it was. Several people had brought bags of confetti, and threw that instead. I imagined that the caretakers would be unhappy at having to clean it all up. Mrs. Forest was not amused either.

Of course, at this point, what were they going to do? Give us detention?

Kali, unlike every other girl there, had brought a big backpack instead of a purse. She was also very quiet through the whole thing.

"What's wrong?" I whispered when we got back to our seats, diplomas in hand. She just shook her head.

"Later."

Later was the graduation party. I'd opted for a black, ankle-length

formal dress, thinking that I could use it later for professional engage-
ments. It's not like I wear dresses every day, and black goes with
everything.

The band was pretty good. I just wished it wasn't so loud that I had to
yell to talk to anybody.

"You look great."

I turned and Jordan was there, arm-in-arm with Miranda, another
member of his team of girl friends-with-benefits.

"Thanks. Where's Heike?" I yelled.

"She's here with her boyfriend. I think they're dancing." He dropped
Miranda's arm, holding out his hand to me. "Would you like to dance?"

"I don't dance."

"Come on, it'll be fun." He tried to take my hand. I gave him The Look.
He withdrew his hand slowly, like he was afraid I'd bite.

"Where's Kali?" Miranda asked.

"I'm not sure. She's here with George somewhere." My eyes wandered
around the crowd, trying to spot her.

"I'm going to get some food," Miranda said. "You coming?"

"I'm good," Jordan said.

"Me too."

"Okay, see you later." She disappeared into the crowd.

"You don't look like you're having much fun," Jordan said in my ear.
Otherwise I wouldn't have heard him.

"Big parties always make me feel like a gnome in a forest. And I hate
having to yell."

At that moment, random movement caused an opening in the crowd,
and I saw Kali and George by a punch bowl. I started toward them, Jordan
following.

Kali's dress was long and dark green. She looked gorgeous in it.

She also looked unhappy. She was still clutching her backpack with
both hands like it was her life-support system.

"Okay girl, what's wrong?" I yelled, almost in her ear.

"I wish my family were here."

Oh crap, of course. George looked as sad as she was. He had one arm
around her waist.

"I have an idea," Jordan yelled. "Let's blow this off and see a movie."
Jordan had borrowed his parents' car for the night so we had transporta-
tion.

"Which one?" George yelled.

I herded everybody outside. I could feel my eardrums moving back
into position once the door was closed on the noise.

"How about *Thor*?" Jordan said. "It's at a cheap theatre."

"I want to see *X-Men: First Class*," Kali said.

"Why?"

"James McAvoy is in it."

"Who?"

"He played Mr. Tumnus in *The Lion, The Witch and the Wardrobe*."

"Let's do it," I said, my throat a bit sore from the previous yelling. Jordan looked at me like I was crazy. I gave him what I hoped was a Meaningful Look. He shrugged, then agreed. George would go anywhere Kali did.

What the boys didn't know was that the Narnia movie was the one Ana Lucia had gone to see just before she was killed. If Kali wanted to see a movie with the same actor, we would see it, even if the two of us had to ditch the boys and go alone. Chicks before dicks.

We had just enough time to make it to the early show. The movie was pretty good, with lots of explosions and heroics. Kali and I sat next to each other, flanked by the boys. They held our hands. We held each others. I wondered what was going through her mind, watching the same actor that had been the last thing her sister had seen.

I guess I was in a mood for symbolism. Super powers might have let Kali save her sister. They might have allowed me to stop Ronald Brandau without killing him. Being Mystique would certainly be useful when I was an investigator.

Unfortunately, we weren't mutants. We were normal, ordinary girls. In extreme circumstances, that pretty much sucked.

But that was another message in the movie. What is normal and ordinary? How do you keep going when your best isn't good enough? I had no idea. I suspected that nobody really did.

"Where now?" George said when we got outside after the movie.

"Ice cream," Jordan said. That's why I like him: he understands.

MacKay's ice cream in Cochrane is a landmark. It's possible that Jordan may have been driving slightly over the speed limit to get us there before they closed. We made it with about a minute to spare, and as we went in they locked the doors behind us. As custom dictated, we ate our cones on the benches outside the shop.

"What would you like to do now?" Jordan said as we piled back into the car.

"Let's go for a walk," Kali said. "I want to go up on Nose Hill."

Jordan shrugged and started the engine.

We drove back to Calgary, more slowly this time, and parked in the same area where I'd parked with Adam. This time it was a lot warmer, and the company was a lot nicer. We started hiking up the hill.

Kali seemed to know where she was going. Nose Hill is a wilderness area, and hiking in our graduation dresses made for some tough going. I could imagine Mum's reaction when we came home with seeds and burrs all over us.

Kali wasn't just walking, she had some goal in mind. I asked but her only response was "you'll see."

Her destination was one of the coulees, in a dense clump of aspens with a small clearing in the centre. It was difficult to get to, and not at all scenic. As nearly as I could tell in the growing darkness, it was hidden from view from all directions. It would have been an ideal make-out spot if we'd had sleeping bags. The ground was entirely too lumpy and prickly otherwise.

Now that we were out of the glare from the city lights, we'd have been completely blind if it wasn't for the full moon. Kali opened her pack in the middle of the clearing, and started bringing things out.

First was a flashlight with a red filter on it. She used that to check a small compass, then she distributed four small glow sticks around the edge of the clearing, breaking and shaking each as she dropped it. Going clockwise from north, they were green, yellow, red and blue.

Suddenly, I knew what we were doing here. The boys might not know what was going on, but this was something that she and I had done before. I knelt beside her to help.

I lit the end of a sage bundle with a disposable lighter. When it was smouldering well, I walked around the circle clockwise, fanning the smoke outward. I paid special attention to smudging the boys and Kali, then myself. It might not be something I believed in, but if I was going to do it for Kali, I was going to do it well.

She had brought out a plastic bowl, added salt from a few of those packets you get with fast food, and water from a bottle. She sprinkled the salty water around the perimeter, and on each of us as well.

George seemed to be okay with all this, so maybe she'd briefed him.

"What's she doing?" Jordan whispered to me.

"Kali is Wiccan. She's casting a circle to create sacred space. I think she's going to honour her parents and sister. Just go with it."

"We aren't going to summon the dead or anything, are we?"

"Don't be an idiot."

Kali brought out her ceremonial knife, and walked around the circle, speaking quietly in Spanish, invoking the Guardians, and her favourite God and Goddess. Although Spanish wasn't an "exotic" language to her (or to me either, for that matter), I had to admit that it sounded more magical than the English equivalents.

She sat on the grass, followed by me, George, and Jordan. Kali spoke softly but firmly in English.

"We are gathered to honour our dead." She paused for a moment, then pulled a photograph from her purse, holding it before her.

"Ana Lucia, my sister, there is not a day when I do not miss you. I have a new sister now, but she is a new sister, not a replacement. You will always live in my heart. I wish you well on your journey, and may you find the peace and love you deserve. Hail and farewell."

I repeated the "hail and farewell," followed a moment later by George. I had to nudge Jordan to join in.

She drew out another photo.

"Mama and papa, you gave me life, and love, and joy. I cannot express my gratitude, even though I am now on a different path from yours." I heard a catch in her voice. "I wish you well on your journey. I love you."

Tears ran down my face and my throat was tight. I managed not to make any sound. Kali looked at me and I hoped that I could speak. I had to clear my throat several times to get it to work.

"*Señor Hernández, Doctora Rojas, adiós. Yo también los amo.*"

Kali looked at George, and he also cleared his throat.

"I only knew Kali's parents for a few months, but they were cool. They treated me like a man instead of a boy. I miss them."

Jordan looked at the ground for a while before speaking.

"I didn't know them very well, but George is right, they were cool. Kali's mother made the best cookies."

I think we all smiled at that. Kali cleared her throat, and drew out another photograph.

"Tonight, we also honour Ronald Brandau."

It took me a moment to recognize the name, and then I became angry. Why would Kali mention a homicidal drug addict none of us had ever met in the same ritual as her family?

"Ronald, none of us knew you except Veronica, and she saw you at your worst. You made some terrible choices in your life, but I have to believe that you can learn from your mistakes. I wish you peace."

She looked at me, offering the picture to me. I glared back at her.

How could she do this? Danielle had come within millimetres of dying at his hands, and it hadn't even been personal. She just happened to be in front of him when he went insane from a drug overdose. Danielle had a husband and two children, and she was alive only because I was there to distract him from her. If I hadn't...

Why was I so angry? Trinity had worked with me to get past the shooting. I no longer had flashbacks or nightmares.

Why was I so angry? I took the picture that she was holding, and looked at it.

I don't know where Kali had gotten the photo, but it was a Ronald

Brandau I'd never known. He was younger, and dressed nicely. He looked happy.

Sometime between when that picture was taken, and the day I'd killed him, something terrible must have happened in his life. I wondered if it was one big trauma that had ruined him, or whether it was a series of small events that led him down into destruction. The man in the picture looked like he wouldn't hurt anybody. What had changed?

I thought I was past it all, but I was only ninety percent of the way there. There was still a part of me that resented what he'd done to Danielle; what he'd done to me, forcing me to do something that had been my worst fear.

Kali was still looking at me, and I felt the anger fade away. This was her circle, but it was also mine. I'd helped cast it, and she was giving me the opportunity to deal with that other ten percent.

How the hell does a seventeen year old get to be so wise? How could she have known? Maybe it was because she had lost so much herself. Maybe this was the up side to losing your family.

It hardly seemed worth it, though.

"A year and a half ago, I shot and killed Ronald Brandau," I heard myself say. "He was a murderer and drug addict, but nothing that he did to me was personal. From both his and my points of view, I was in the wrong place at the wrong time. From Danielle's point of view I was in exactly the right place at exactly the right time. If I hadn't stopped him Ronald would have killed more people. Maybe that's my gift to him, that he doesn't have to answer for anything more than what he did before we met. Maybe... maybe, killing him was enough." I stopped, and looked at the ground. Kali waited patiently, then reached out and took my hand. I cleared my throat again, and said the most difficult words I'd ever spoken.

"Ronald, I forgive you. I wish you peace."

Kali brought out a pack of juice boxes, and a Tupperware container. She placed them in the middle of our circle, then grasped George's hand as well as mine. I took Jordan's hand and, after a moment, he held hands with George.

"Great Mother and merciful Father, we ask you to bless this food and drink. So mote it be."

"So mote it be," I echoed, followed by the two boys.

The container held four *alfajores*, Colombian caramel-coconut cookies. *Doctora* Rojas used to make them for us all the time, and they were Kali's favourites. She handed around the juice boxes, and we each took a cookie. I savoured the flavour, and although Kali had made them, I imagined her mother's love flowing into me. My eyes started tearing up again.

We sat, eating and drinking for maybe ten minutes. When the last crumbs were gone, Kali asked us to rise, and we again held hands while she thanked the Gods and Guardians for attending, again in Spanish.

We packed up, and started back to the car, each of us carrying one of the glow sticks. It was important that we not leave any litter behind. For a group of teenagers on grad night, we were very quiet.

"How do you feel?" Jordan asked me as we walked back.

I thought about it. "A lot better." It really was a graduation night.

Maybe there was something to Wicca after all.

CHAPTER 24

Moving On

For as long as I can remember as a child, a nice lady named Sandra would come to see Mum and Dad twice a year. The three of them would go into Dad's home office and talk for an hour or two, then she'd leave. If I peeked, they'd be talking about things that made no sense, and doing a lot of stuff with papers. It was pretty boring to a little girl.

When I was eleven, we were having supper, and Dad reminded Mum that they had a meeting with Sandra in a few hours.

"Why does Sandra come over?"

"She's our financial adviser. She helps us to have more money."

That was something that made sense to me now that I was out of the closet.

I've always been a bit obsessive. One of the other presents I got for Christmas when I was nine was a huge piggy bank. Mum explained that I should start saving because I'd need a lot of money to become a detective. They probably thought I'd save the occasional penny. I'm showing my age; that was back when Canada had pennies.

At first, most of my allowance went into the pig. Later, I started collecting bottles and cans from neighbours and the parks. My parents helped me to recycle them. By the time I was eleven, the pig was full. A lot of it was bills.

After supper, Sandra arrived with her briefcase. I always thought she was cool because she wore a fedora and trench coat like Sam Spade. Almost before the front door was closed I was on her.

"I have a question," I said to her.

"What is it, Veronica?"

"How do you get Mummy and Daddy more money?"

"I take some of your parents' money, and loan it to businesses, like your father's restaurant but bigger. The businesses use it to become bigger, so they can make more money. Then they pay back the loan and some extra. For every dollar that your mum and dad loan out, they get an extra five cents each year."

"I need more money. Can you do that for me?"

"How much do you have?"

I got my piggy bank, and Daddy helped me to get the plug out of its tummy. When we'd finished counting, the total was $478.75.

"That's amazing," Sandra said to Dad. "I know adults who have trouble putting away over $25 per month. You should start a youth bank account for her so she can learn how to handle her money. We'll also set up an investment account for her as well so she can start earning interest. That, in addition to what you're already doing, should give her a nice amount by the time she's eighteen."

Talking about my investment portfolio at the age of eleven did not help me to pass as normal at school.

When you are a kid, everything happens too slowly. My investments weren't growing fast enough for me, so I kept bugging Dad to give me a job at his restaurant. The problem was the labour laws; he couldn't hire me until I was twelve. On my twelfth birthday, I started busing tables and washing dishes.

By graduation, I had done most of the jobs in the restaurant, from bus girl and cashier to purchasing and line chef. Dad was paying me fifteen dollars an hour, and most of that went into my investment account.

When I started my business I knew that there could be several months before my first case. I was determined to have enough to live on until then. There was no way I was going to run short, and come crawling back home.

By law, while I was in school I could only work two hours on weekdays, and eight hours on weekends. After graduation I worked full-time, and Dad promoted me to assistant sous-chef. I was stunned.

"You're kidding."

"Not at all. You've been in a kitchen since you were five years old, and working here since you were twelve. Nobody here doubts your qualifications. What little you don't know, Cliff will teach you. That's why I'm making you his assistant. By the way, you get a raise too."

I still had trouble believing it. A seventeen year old assistant sous-chef was unheard of. In this case it helped that my father owned the restaurant, and had taught me everything I knew. That would help to establish my authority, but it wouldn't buy me respect. I'd have to earn that myself. Preferably, without punching anybody.

It was an actual shock when I gave Shannon, our saute chef, a pointer and she responded with "thank you, chef."

Instead of sitting around the house, Kali asked Dad for a job as a hostess. Like her parents, she refused to fall into the life of the idle rich. Patrons of the restaurant loved her accent, and she charmed almost everyone who came in. She had to wear normal dresses at work, and it was funny seeing her in something other than her Romantigoth clothing. She kept the red-tipped hair, putting it back in a pony tail. It was actually an elegant look for her.

About three weeks later, Dad hired a new vegetable chef. Ivan had an impressive resume for a young man, having worked in several high-end restaurants in Europe and the US. It didn't take me long to figure out why he moved around. He was an arrogant prick. He was at least ten years older than me, and seemed to think that following my directions was beneath him. He'd listen to Cliff, mostly, but constantly ignored me. It was humiliating, and I had difficulty giving orders to someone who treated me with so much disrespect.

My first impulse was to knock his lights out, preferably with a forty centimetre fry pan. After two days of that crap, I went to see the sous-chef about it. It wouldn't be right to bother Dad without going through the proper chain of command.

"Chef, can I talk to you about a problem?"

"Let me guess: Ivan?"

"He's been giving me attitude, and I was hoping you could give me some advice on how I could talk to him about it."

"Don't you want me to talk to him?"

"Not unless I can't solve the problem."

"Good for you. I'd suggest you find somewhere you can talk to him alone. Express your concerns, and give him a chance to explain. I know it can be difficult, but keep calm and be professional. If you can't reach an understanding with him, come and see me."

The next day I set things up for our talk, then cornered him in the pantry as he was getting potatoes.

"Ivan, I need a word with you."

"I'm busy."

He tried to leave, and I closed the door, standing in front of it.

"This will only take a few minutes. You seem to have a problem working for me. I'd like to know why."

"The only problem I have is a little girl who thinks she knows more than a professional chef."

It took me a moment to believe what I'd heard. It took another moment for me to get my temper back under control. I replied very calmly and professionally.

"Is it my height, my gender or my qualifications that you resent?"

He snorted.

"I have work to do." He grabbed my arm, and tried to yank me aside like a child.

There's a time and place for professionalism. There's another for self defence.

I ground one knuckle hard into the back of the offending hand. He yelled at the sudden pain, and tried to pull his hand back, but I was pressing too hard. It stayed put on my arm. I let him flap around for about two seconds before releasing him. Frankly, I was proud of myself for not breaking his arm. He looked at me in shock for a moment, which gave me time to take a breath.

"Assaulting a co-worker was a mistake. You're fired. Pack up your knives and leave."

He held his bruised hand to his chest.

"You can't fire me."

"Yes, I can."

"We'll see about that."

I let him out of the pantry, then retrieved my phone from the shelf where I'd placed it earlier. I followed him from a distance.

If he had a problem with me, Ivan should have gone to Cliff. Instead, he went straight to the executive chef. He also didn't bother to close the office door before he started yelling.

"Your sous-chef just attacked me!"

Dad was sitting at his desk. He said "I'll have to call you back," and took a Bluetooth headset from his ear.

"Why would Cliff do that?"

"Not him, that *girl*."

He said *girl* like it was a dirty word. I saw Dad's eyes narrow slightly.

"All right," he said calmly, "why would Veronica attack you?"

"I don't know. She cornered me in the pantry, and damned near broke my hand."

He held the offended limb out to my father. There was a really impressive bruise forming. Dad spotted me hovering outside the door.

"Veronica, could you come in, please."

I closed the door behind me. There was enough rubbernecking going on in the kitchen as it was. Ivan looked smug. *I hope he tries to touch me again*, I thought.

"Veronica, Ivan has made a serious accusation. What's going on?"

"Chef, I think I'll let my witness speak for me."

"Bullshit," Ivan yelled. "She's lying. There was nobody else in the pantry with us."

I handed my phone to my father. He put his headset back in, then played the video I'd cued. Ivan looked worried.

"What's that?"

Dad took out the earpiece, and looked at Ivan.

"She's right. You're fired. You have ten minutes to pack your knives and leave."

"What?"

"The alternative is that in eleven minutes I'm calling the police, and having you arrested for assault. They may not have covered this in your training, so let me give you some advice. When the executive chef appoints a sous-chef, it is wise to assume that he knows what he's doing. Despite her age, Veronica has six more years experience than you do. You're fired."

Ivan glared at us, then left, slamming the office door behind him.

"Damn," Dad said, handing back my phone. "Now we need a new vegetable chef. You're on that station until we can hire someone else."

"Yes, chef," I said.

Crap. No good deed...

Toward the end of July, George told Kali that he had received a scholarship from the University of Toronto, and would be leaving at the beginning of September. They were sure that they could sustain a long-distance romance until he graduated and moved back to Calgary.

That night, while his parents were visiting relatives, Kali finally made up her mind, and dragged him off to have her evil way with him. From her description, it was tender, loving, wonderful, and in an actual bed. Unlike Adam, George had been paying attention. He made sure their first time was not only memorable, but also that there was enough time for cuddling afterwards.

When I saw her the next day, Kali seemed a bit put out that I couldn't immediately tell what had happened. She was bouncy, verging on giggly, so I knew something was up. Apparently, it had been George. I knew she'd been out late, but considering how chaste they'd been until then, I assumed that they'd fallen asleep watching a movie or something.

Once she started, Kali was nearly as insatiable as me. She kept him in her room most evenings. They usually started right after dinner so that George could get home at a reasonable time. Now it was my turn to be happy for her while she spent most of her time getting laid.

My happiness was incomplete. Not because she was too busy to spend much time with me, but because I could see trouble on the horizon. In six weeks he'd be going away, and their new sex life would end for four years, with the possible exception of semester breaks, and maybe summers. I got cranky after a week or so without sex; I couldn't imagine what several dry months would be like.

Then there were both the stresses and temptations of being apart.

His parents were another issue. They didn't approve of Kali at the best of times. Her two-tone hair, her dress, her faith, her choice of career, and even her skin colour were problems for them. I had no idea how George had turned out to be so nice. Their religion didn't believe in premarital sex, and if they found out what was happening they'd make his life a living hell. I tried to imagine what I would do if Mum and Dad actively hated someone I loved. It wasn't a pleasant thought.

I kept my mouth shut. Except for my unusual friendship with Jordan, my own relationship track record was not a good resume for counselling someone else. Maybe it would all work out. It worried me, though.

Mum and Dad also remained silent on the subject. As with me, after making sure that she'd had The Talk, they let Kali run her sex life to suit herself. She'd known where she was heading, and had gone to the doctor for birth control well before it was necessary.

At least there was one smart daughter in our family.

George left on September first. We all went to the airport to say good-bye. He and Kali did a lot of crying, kissing, and fairly tasteful groping. I thought it was sweet. So did Mum. Dad looked a little uncomfortable. Little princess number two wasn't a virgin, and he probably thought that he was letting Diego and Laura down. George's parents stood to one side looking like a pair of Weeping Angels. I thought they were going to bring out the flaming crosses while their son defiled himself by kissing a girl who wasn't as white as they were. If only they knew how "defiled" he really was, the lucky boy.

Mum and Dad, wonderful people that they are, were letting us live at home rent-free, as long as we were working toward our career goals. I was working as many hours a day as possible, and banking around $2000 per month. I was taking the investigator's course online, and I felt like a traitor to my bank balance when I withdrew a thousand for tuition.

There was also the course so I could be certified to carry my baton. Mum knew someone who knew the man who taught it. She convinced him to let me challenge the test for a relatively minimal fee. I had no trouble passing it.

A week or so later the courts finally stopped fooling around with the wills, and Mr. Flynn began executing the estate. For such a large estate, things were fairly simple.

Kali got everything except for Ramón and María's pension. The Colombian cousin tried everything he could think of, short of hiring cartel hit men, to be named as Kali's guardian, to overturn the will, and to have himself be named as a trustee. The bastard even tried getting Kali's old family doctor to declare her incompetent due to the shock of her sister's death. He got nowhere against Mr. Flynn, who told Kali that he thought Ricardo would have a stroke if he got much more worked up about his flood of petitions. Kali suggested that it wouldn't break her heart if he did.

She wouldn't become a trustee until her eighteenth birthday, on October 26. In the meantime, she had several meetings with Mr. Flynn to discuss the estate. She wanted to get the ball rolling on some specific things she wanted to accomplish immediately.

The first was selling the house. Not only was it far too big for her, it held too many memories. We'd gone to visit the Morenos several times, and Kali was always sad afterwards. They seemed depressed to be living there too.

That would leave the Morenos without a place to live, so Kali was going to buy them a house. All they had to do was to find something they liked. It wasn't like price was any object.

Her third project was to find a location for her occult shop. She settled on a property in Marda Loop that had a good-sized suite for rent. Instead of renting it she had her lawyer make an offer on the whole building. That way she would have income from the other tenants instead of just paying rent to someone else.

The last thing she wanted was to build a new house for herself. The location she picked was just south of Marda Loop so that she could walk to work.

Having a lot of money may not make you happy, but it makes a lot of things easier.

Clearing out the old house was both physically and emotionally difficult.

Kali started four piles. One was stuff that she would immediately need for her new place, such as bedroom, kitchen, and living room furniture. The second was things that belonged to the Morenos. Kali insisted that they take one of the vehicles as well.

The third pile included things like the antiques that would go into storage, at least for now. Some of the pieces had been in her family for over a hundred years. She'd decide what to do with them later.

The last pile was the hardest: her parents' belongings. The bedding and much of the clothing went to the women's shelter or Salvation

Army. She kept her mother's jewellery. A few of the items held special memories from her childhood and she would sit, and hold them in her hand for a long time before moving on.

On the last day, we went though the whole place again, making sure that nothing remained but an empty shell. That was even more depressing.

I stood on the porch while Kali took one last look at the empty living room, then pulled the door closed. She handed the keys to the realtor, who thanked her. We were both silent as we got into Dad's car, and he drove us home.

She didn't look back.

On October nineteenth, I mutated again. I was now officially an adult. The four of us celebrated by going to Maison Chandler for dinner. That might seem like an odd choice, but we were determined to let someone else cook for a change. And where, outside of our home, would we get better food?

We started with a spinach salad with mangoes, pine nuts and Dad's special vinaigrette, accompanied by freshly-baked focaccia dipped in olive oil and balsamic vinegar. Next was French onion soup with asiago cheese. The prime rib was accompanied by the tallest Yorkshire pudding I'd ever seen, and a 2008 California Cabernet Sauvignon. For dessert we had an Italian Moscato d'Asti that went beautifully with the hazelnut and chestnut cheese cake. Everybody conveniently forgot that Kali was a whole week underage.

I paid no attention to Colombian customs, and finished every bite. I thought I would explode. The entire kitchen staff came out to receive our compliments.

When we got home, Mum and Dad gave me my birthday present. They'd been putting money away since I was born in case I wanted to go to university. Half of it was in a tax shelter that had to be used for education, the rest was free to use as I wished. Mum suggested that a criminal justice degree would look good on my business cards.

My birthday present was $25,000. I could afford to quit my job at the restaurant and become a PI.

Kali was told that her new house would be ready around November, and suggested that we move in together until I was ready to get my own place.

Apparently, slipping deadlines are a tradition in the construction industry. For various reasons, house construction was about three weeks late, so she took possession a bit before Christmas.

That turned out to be a good thing. We had just started packing when George came home for Christmas break. He didn't bother to tell his parents that he was in town. Instead, he was staying with a friend. Kali spent a lot of time at the friend's house instead of packing.

Moving has to be the least convenient activity ever invented by humans. Kali made it easier on us by hiring some nice men who had also moved everything from her old house to storage. They were about as wide as they were tall, and made lifting massive furniture look easy.

The new house was amazing: five bedrooms (one for her, one for me, one spare and two for office space, if needed), three bathrooms, a living room with a vaulted ceiling, a three car garage, and heated driveway and walkway.

Around this time Binky entered my life. I'd gotten my driver's license when I was seventeen, and I'd even been known to drive myself, occasionally, over to Casa Hernández instead of requiring a chauffeur. Mum and Dad's mechanic, Doug, went over the white 2000 Cavalier from bumper to bumper, making sure it was in perfect mechanical condition. Kali wanted to know why I named it Binky, so I loaned her my Terry Pratchett books.

Kali was clever about her shop. Instead of just opening it and assuming that she would have a clientele, she talked to everybody she could reach in the Calgary occult scene, regardless of their affiliations. After she'd found out what they *really* wanted, she then did the same with the various New Age communities and, for good measure, the Hindu and Jewish communities. She then spent weeks pouring over catalogues. She even hired a marketing consultant.

One evening in February, Jordan and I were lying in my bed, resting after a vigorous, and thoroughly satisfying, round of benefits.

"I have some good news, and some bad news," he said as I ran my fingers through his chest hair.

"Not in the mood for bad news." I gently bit the nipple that I could reach.

"The oil company likes my work, and I'm being promoted."

"That's wonderful," I said. I gave up on his chest hair, and went exploring further afield.

"The bad news is that the job is in Vancouver."

I'd been about to dive under the covers, and my mind was on other things. It took me a moment to make the connection.

"You're leaving?"

"In about two weeks. I just found out today."

I tried to be philosophical about it. We'd always known that we were just friends, and it would be a disaster for us to get married.

"I'm happy for you."

"Liar," he said tenderly. "You think this sucks as much as I do. We knew that life would get in the way some day."

"I know. I just hadn't thought it would be so soon."

We were quiet for a few minutes, lost in our own thoughts. My fingers started playing with him again. I got up on one elbow, and gave him my best seductive smile.

"You know what else sucks?"

On April thirtieth, BhadraKali opened its doors. It was named after the Hindu goddess of martial arts. She was the daughter of Shiva the Destroyer, and Durga the Demon Slayer. I didn't really get the connection with *mi hermanita*. On the other hand, it had Kali's name in it, so maybe that was good enough.

For an occult shop opening in Calgary, the crowd was huge. There were at least fifty people there, enjoying the wine and cheese as well as live music from a pair of local artists, Vanessa Cardui and Sora. Kali sold so much stuff that, even with the cost of the event, she made a profit. I know the musicians were happy with the number of CDs they sold.

Back when I'd first heard Kali's life story I promised myself I'd never whine about anything trivial. Now I had a problem, and it was difficult to talk with anybody about it. Not only was it embarrassing, it was ridiculous.

I was horny.

While Jordan was available it was tolerable. By now, Jordan had been gone for two months, and he'd taken my sex life with him. I was constantly nervous, hyperactive, lonely, and cranky. It was like having constant PMS without the cramps. It got so bad that I began to worry that I had some kind of mental illness. I looked up nymphomania on a psychology website but the description didn't fit. Satisfaction wasn't elusive; I could get it, I just didn't have anyone to help me with it.

I went to see Trinity when I couldn't take it any more. I'm not sure what I expected. Perhaps some kind of sage advice or coping skills. Maybe she'd recommend cold showers. Instead, she listened for half an hour, and then gave me a requisition for blood work in her MD persona. Two days later she called me to set up another appointment.

In a normal doctor's office, the people sort of acknowledge each other, and sometimes even say hello. In a psychologist's waiting room, people watch you furtively in case you're crazier than they are. A guy in his thirties kept looking at me when he thought I wouldn't notice. Maybe he sensed that he was in real danger of being molested.

Another woman came out of the office, glanced at the two of us, and then scurried out, head down, without making further eye contact.

"Veronica, please come in," Trinity said. Once the office door was closed she wasted no time.

"The good news is that you aren't crazy. You have a condition known as hyperthecosis. It's not particularly dangerous, although it probably explains your irregular periods, and certainly explains your libido. Basically, your hormone levels are too high. Fortunately, you haven't developed hirsuitism, at least for now. If excess hair is a problem later on you can always get it removed if it bothers you."

"So there's nothing really wrong with me?"

"It depends on your point of view. You have an extremely high sex drive. At your age, there shouldn't be any physical complications, but later on you may be at increased risk of breast cancer, heart disease, or stroke. There are several treatment options available to you."

"Thank God. I'm so horny that I seriously thought of seducing the guy in the waiting room. I feel like I'm out of control."

"One of the options is getting laid more, but I understand you aren't in a relationship at the moment."

"Yeah, having random sex isn't my thing. Or at least I hope it isn't."

"Since you are already taking birth control pills, the least invasive will be to get you a pill with more oestrogen. If that doesn't work, I could give you a prescription for an anti-androgenic drug to decrease your libido. That would be a last resort, however, as there can be adverse side effects."

"In other words, the same stuff they give to sex offenders."

"Yes, but in a lower dosage. As I said, that would be a last resort."

I walked out with a new birth control prescription, and went back to drooling over guys on the street. As for getting laid more (or, at all) I was desperate enough to seriously consider one-night stands. That really worried me. I liked to think that I was more discriminating than that, and it could be dangerous. I started to feel like a sex offender.

It didn't help that I wasn't getting any work. I put announcements in the papers, tacked up notices on bulletin boards, and even did a radio interview about being a woman in a traditionally male field with a professor of Women's Studies on the university radio station. To keep myself sane, I asked Dad for my old job back. It wasn't available, but he did hire me part-time to fill in as required. At least that kept me somewhat occupied.

My social life, apart from hanging out with Kali, was close to zero. I'd never been into the bar or club scene, and now I wasn't sure that I dared go out. Whenever Kali and I went anywhere, I found myself checking out guys the way some drunk men check out girls. If a guy had come on to me, I don't know if I could have stopped myself from saying yes.

I felt like a combination of a drug addict and slut.

After a while, I checked out online dating sites. For some reason, "female PI with a raging hormone problem, deadly martial arts skills and permanent PMS" didn't get me many matches.

Our home life was also a source of stress, at least to me. Kali would have been fine with me staying with her forever without paying a nickel. I wasn't wired that way. I insisted on paying half the utilities and food, which was all she'd accept. I needed to get out before it put a strain on our friendship.

My search for an apartment and office space was going slowly. There weren't that many rentals available during the spring. Offices were in even shorter supply, and expensive when they existed.

Yes, there was an office/bedroom in the house. I just couldn't see myself bringing clients to another person's house. Especially when George was there.

George came to live with us for the summer. He told his parents that he'd found a job in Toronto, then moved in with Kali while he searched for one here. I liked George. He treated Kali like she deserved.

She and I had gotten used to wearing whatever we wanted around the house, and now I had to get dressed to leave my bedroom. Kali still wandered around in lingerie and combat boots.

One morning, Kali got up, and found me sitting at the kitchen table, looking at rental notices in the paper.

"*Hola, chiqui,*" she said cheerfully.

"Piss off," I said without thinking. It was a reflex, like a dog with a wounded paw snapping at a veterinarian. I was so angry that I didn't even feel badly when she looked hurt.

"What's wrong?"

"Nothing. Nothing's wrong. Everything is great. There's no office space in this damned city that I can afford. Once university gets out I'll probably be able to find an apartment, but I still won't have an office. How the hell can I run a business without an office?" I threw the paper across the kitchen, and watched the pages separate and flutter to the floor. Served them right.

"That isn't it. You've been looking for a place for a month. What's really wrong?"

My eyes watered.

"What do you think? I'm lonely. I miss Jordan."

"I thought you were just friends."

"We are. Were. But he kept me from going crazy."

"Aren't your new pills working?"

"Trinity is still figuring out the dosage. In the meantime I'm ready to molest Binky's shifter," I blurted.

She looked surprised. I blushed, but my hormones were still talking.

"You have no idea what it's like. I'm like teenage boys are supposed to be. I'm obsessed with sex, 24 hours a day. And you know what the worst thing is? You and George! You think you're being quiet, but I can hear you every night, even with our doors closed. God, how many times a night do you guys do it? Five? Six?"

"Once," she said. "Usually." I ignored her.

"I'm so frustrated I could scream! It might help a bit if George wasn't so cute, and if I didn't know how nice he is. I keep thinking that he could handle two women as easily as one."

My brain finally got the brakes to work. I couldn't read the expression on Kali's face. Was she angry? Horrified? Disgusted? All of the above? Those were definitely the feelings going through me at that moment, along with shame.

"I'm sorry," she said quietly. "I had no idea it was that bad." I could see the light bulb go on in her head. "What if you used your home as an office?"

"I'm not bringing clients into your house."

"I meant, what if you used part of *your* home as an office? Most apartments I've been in, everything opens off the living room. Maybe you could use the living room as your office."

I wanted to say something rude, simply because that's how I felt. I forced myself to rationally think about what she'd said, despite the fog of hormones.

"That could work," I said after a minute. I looked up at her, standing there in a night shirt that was very thin and very short. It reminded me of the noises in the night, which pissed me off unreasonably. She looked at me like a dog who expects to be beaten. Now I felt badly.

I jumped up, and hugged her. "*Hermanita*, you are a genius. Now all I need is an apartment, and some furniture. Brilliant. Absolutely brilliant."

My emotions were flopping back and forth like a beached haddock. When I realized that, I started laughing hysterically. I pictured Trinity solemnly writing me a prescription for men: Take two with meals as needed.

All I needed to do was find a pharmacy where I could fill it.

CHAPTER 25

Korean Fried Chicken

There was nothing more that I could do about Beleth until Mum called back, so I switched back to the problem with Parker.

Chances were that I was in the same boat. If I couldn't get any information on Beleth, I probably wasn't going to find any on Horse Boy either. There was one big difference that I might be able to exploit: I had a personal connection with Parker through Kali.

Approaching Parker was risky. If he wasn't as committed to his relationship with Keith as I'd been led to believe, or if he was more into Horse Boy than I suspected, then approaching him could backfire badly.

If he told Horse Boy about my interest, Beleth would probably find out too. That would compromise both investigations. I might find myself with a restraining order against me. Much more likely, they could decide to cut their losses, and disappear along with the answers I needed.

On the other hand, this was an opportunity for what my friends on the force called "generating leads:" poking trees more or less randomly to see what dropped out and hit them on the head. Spooked suspects sometimes did stupid things that left them vulnerable to investigation.

Just before lunch time I drove to Kimu Visuals. The place was a candy store for photographers. I'd heard of Hasselblad cameras, but I'd never seen one before in real life. Considering that just a camera body cost enough for a down payment on a house, this would probably be the last time too.

I saw Parker immediately, standing behind the counter typing something into a computer. Nobody asked me if I needed assistance as I made my way over to him. I guess I didn't look rich enough. That was fine by me.

After a few seconds he realized that someone was standing in front of him and looked up.

"May I help you?"

"Hello, Parker," I said grimly. "We need to talk."

"I'm sorry, do I know you?"

"Not yet. I understand you're about to go for lunch. It'll give us an opportunity to get acquainted."

"Look, I don't know what you think you're doing but..."

I pulled out my ID wallet and flashed my badge and license. I did it quickly, held low as if I wanted to spare him the embarrassment of having his co-workers aware that he was being questioned. By law, a private investigator can't represent herself as a "detective" or anything else that might be confused with a police officer. It's not my fault if he saw a glimpse of a badge, and assumed that it said "police" when it clearly says "private investigator." People see what they expect to see.

"Co-operation would be in your best interest."

I thought that was quite clever, sounding like a threat of some kind without actually saying anything. He actually turned white, something else I'd never seen before in real life. This case seemed to be full of those moments. For a second I thought he'd faint. He swayed, but caught himself on the counter, and took a deep breath.

"All right." He raised his voice and spoke to the only other woman in the store. "Tessa, I'm going for lunch now." Tessa waved in his direction without taking her eyes off her customer who was playing with one of the Hasselblads equipped with a Hubble-sized lens.

We took my car. I drove to a small, family-owned restaurant called Olive Chicken that served KFC – Korean Fried Chicken. He was silent during the drive. I told Parker that I'd buy, and he let me order as well. He seemed resigned to whatever was about to happen. I took out my notebook, deciding to start with the familiar, and get to the bizarre later.

"I understand you know Keith Bonsell." He nodded.

"How would you characterize your relationship with him?"

"I – we're getting married."

"Congratulations. So you love him?" He nodded again. I made a show of dipping one of my french fries into the Korean hot sauce and munching it. Delicious.

"And how would you characterize your relationship with the man at 147 Millward Place North East?"

He became even quieter, and again I thought he was going to faint. He didn't turn white, though. He turned bright red, and looked down at his untouched lunch.

"Well?"

"I don't know."

"What do you mean, you don't know? It seems like a simple question."

"It – it's complicated."

"I'm sure Keith would agree." Parker became quietly frantic.

"Please, don't tell Keith. I don't want to lose him." Silent tears streamed down his face.

I handed him one of my paper napkins, then let him stew for a minute to get him in the right frame of mind. I reminded myself that he'd cheated on the man he loved and, regardless of his tears, he hadn't felt enough remorse to stop.

"I can't promise anything, but maybe we can work something out if you tell me what happened. Start at the beginning."

He looked down at his lunch, and seemed to see it for the first time. He picked up a fry and ate it, stalling for time.

"It was near the end of September. Keith was visiting his sister in Edmonton, and I was just going to go home after work and watch TV. This really short man came up to me in the parking lot, and offered me a coin. I took it sort of by reflex, you know? I figured I could give it back if it was something illegal or something."

"What kind of coin? A quarter? A loonie?" ,

"No, it was more like, I don't know, a medallion. It felt funny."

"What do you mean?"

"It's hard to explain. There was a tingling in my fingers for a moment. I couldn't take my eyes off it until the man spoke, then I couldn't take my eyes off him. My head felt mushy, like I was floating around inside myself or something. Have you ever been so short on sleep that it's like you leave your body, and watch it walking around? It was sort of like that."

It sounded a bit like my experience with Beleth. I began to see how Frank and Parker might have been sucked into this mess, and I realized that I might have narrowly escaped the same fate. The only reasonable explanation was that there must be drugs involved.

"Do you still have the coin?"

He fished in his pockets, and held the coin in his open hand. I didn't try to touch it in case it was coated with something. This case was making me paranoid. Given the stakes, that sounded like an excellent idea.

The medallion was about the size of a one dollar coin, but silver and engraved with a weird scrawl: some wandering lines, a Valentine heart, a figure eight on its side, and several Maltese crosses attached to other things. It took me a moment to realize that there were also equidistant capital letters engraved around the edge, all pointing outward. Once I figured out where the word started I could read it.

The word was BELETH.

I looked at Parker. From his expression, I got the feeling that he'd wanted to tell someone about this for a while. He put the coin on the table.

"Can you describe the man?"

"He was really short, with chestnut hair to his shoulders, brown eyes, young looking but built like a professional athlete. Definitely not a kid. He was wearing a muscle shirt, and pants that really showed off his package."

"How short?"

"A bit higher than my belt." That would make him about the same height as the Beleth I'd encountered.

"And you're sure he was male? Could it have been a woman impersonating a man?"

Parker looked startled by my question.

"I don't think so. No, not a chance."

"All right. What happened after he gave you the coin?"

"Like I said, I couldn't take my eyes off him. He started talking to me."

"What about?"

"I don't know!" He raised his voice, frustrated and scared. Some other patrons glanced toward our table.

"Take a deep breath and calm down. Your lunch is getting cold."

He looked at his plate again, and ate another fry.

"I honestly don't remember. It's like the whole thing was a dream, or something."

"Or a drug experience?"

"I don't know. I've never done drugs. I suppose it's possible."

"What next?"

"We got into my car, and drove to his place. I don't remember agreeing to any of it. We just went. I don't know why."

"And when you got there?"

Parker looked like he was going to be sick. I put one hand on my plate so I could save it if I had to. Seriously, their fried chicken is that good. Besides, I'd paid for it.

"We – did things."

"Things involving pony play and dressage," I said quietly. There was no need for him to go into details when I'd already seen it. He looked panicky.

"How did you know?"

"Never mind. Had you ever done anything like that before?"

"No! I'd never even... Keith and I met in high school. We were each others first. I've never done anything with anyone else before. I'd never even kissed anyone before I met Keith."

I made notes while thinking about what I'd heard. Parker sounded completely sincere, which either meant that he was a world-class actor, or yet more strange things were going on. I was starting to lose track of how many weird things were associated with these cases.

"Do you enjoy it?"

"No! I hate it! Keith and I, we're, um, kind of vanilla in bed, you know? This isn't something I've ever done, or even thought about before. That's what freaks me out. I have no idea why I went, or why I keep going back. It's like a compulsion, and I can't fight it."

"Maybe he scratches an itch you didn't know you have." I suggested.

"You don't understand. I *hate* what he does to me. I *hate* that I can't stop. I *hate* not knowing why I can't stay away. I *hate* that I can't make myself leave once I'm there." He took a breath, and calmed down a bit. "And I *really* hate what it will do to Keith when he finds out."

"Does this guy have a name?"

"Beleth. That's all he's ever said. I don't even know if that's a first name or a last name."

"How does he contact you?"

"That's another crazy thing – he doesn't. It's like I just know when to go see him. I'll get this urge to go that I can't fight, and he's there. He's always ready for me, too, just as if I'd called ahead."

"But you never do."

"No. I just show up whenever I get the impulse, and there he is. I know how it sounds, but please, you have to believe me."

"Is there ever anybody else there? Has Beleth ever mentioned anyone else to you?"

"No, we're always alone. And he doesn't really talk much. Just to tell me what to do."

I ate another piece of chicken with sauce while I thought about all that Parker had told me. My mandate from Kali was to find out what Parker was doing after work. Technically, I'd done that, but the happiness of two of her friends was also on the line. It was time to address the spirit of the assignment.

"Would you like to stop seeing this guy?"

"Oh God, yes. I'd do anything to get away from him. Please, can you help me?"

"All right." I passed him one of my business cards. "I know a doctor who may be able to help you. I'll call her, and see what she says."

He looked at the card for the first time.

"You aren't with the police."

"No, I'm Kali's friend. She asked me to help you. If you're serious about getting away from this guy, you need to promise me three things."

It was the first time since I'd spoken to him that he looked hopeful. I think he had been very close to believing that there was no way out of this situation alive. I hoped that I was doing him a favour.

"Firstly, you have to give me the coin."

His hand started to slide it toward me, then slowed. I saw a determined look on his face, and his hand twitched, like he was trying to drag it back and push it forward at the same time. It knocked the coin across the table. As it slid toward me he almost grabbed for it, stopping himself at the last moment. He reminded me of Bilbo trying to leave the One Ring behind.

I quickly pushed my chair back before the coin ran into me, stopping it just before the edge with my sleeve. I wrapped it carefully in a napkin, then put the bundle in my pocket. Given the way that this case was going, I wasn't going to take any chances with something that might lead to me wearing a saddle. He stared at the pocket containing the coin as if he expected it to burn its way out. Taking my cue from Gandalf, I purposely shifted in my seat to hide the pocket from his sight. He blinked and relaxed. I was beginning to feel like I was in some cheap horror movie. I really hoped that the coin couldn't affect me just by being in my pocket.

"Good. Secondly, I want you to promise me that you won't do anything stupid or crazy until we get this sorted out. That means no suicide, confronting Beleth, or confessing to Keith."

He hesitated, then nodded.

"Say it."

"I promise not to do anything stupid or crazy until this is sorted out."

"Good. I can't give you the details, but you aren't alone in this. When we get to the bottom of it, I want Beleth to be the only casualty. Got it?"

"Yes. What's the third thing?"

"Eat. Wasting that chicken would be a real sin."

CHAPTER 26

The Godmother

A few days after my lunch with Parker the weather was getting nicer. A Chinook wind had blown in during the night, raising the temperature to plus five Celsius. If we were lucky, it might last a few days. From my balcony window, I watched the snow melting, and tried to think of where my investigations could go next.

When the phone rang, Yoko Geri teleported out of my comfy chair where he'd been sleeping. He was half way across the living room before he landed, his back arched like a Halloween cat. He stalked off into the bedroom as I tried not to laugh at him.

"Chandler Investigations."

"Veronica, Trinity here. Would you be available for lunch? There's some business I'd like to discuss."

"I'd love to, but I really don't have time for another client right now. Perhaps in a week or so?"

There was a pause, as if she was choosing her words very carefully.

"The matter I wish to discuss actually bears on at least one of your current cases."

"Oh?"

There was a pause.

"All right, where do you want to meet?" I said.

"There's a charming little restaurant at Fortieth and Northmount Drive called Puspa. Do you know it?"

It sounded vaguely familiar. Maybe I'd driven past it some time.

"Just a second."

I opened my laptop and typed the name into the search bar. It took me about twenty seconds to find it.

"It's Bengali, right?"

"That's the one. Can you make it at noon?"

"I'll be there."

Puspa is one of those tiny, family-owned places that usually have the best food.

As soon as I saw it, I recognized it as the same restaurant that Adam had taken me to the night we'd parked. I told myself I was stupid to blame the restaurant for things that he, and I, did that night. Maybe it was fitting that I go there with my shrink.

Once inside, spotting Trinity wasn't difficult. There were only about ten tables.

"Veronica, I'm so glad you could make it."

"You know damned well that I couldn't stay away after a teaser like that. Are there more..."

She held up her hand to stop me.

"Let's order first, if you'll trust me."

"You helped me to bring the wiring in my head up to code. It's a little late for me to start doubting you now."

The host, a distinguished-looking Indian man I vaguely remembered from last time I'd been here, appeared by our table as soon as she looked up.

"Rupak, I think we'll have the butter chicken combination with *chai* and *lacchi*."

"Very good, Doctor." He disappeared into the kitchen as quietly as he'd arrived. His accent was just enough to complement the exotic decor.

"You must come here a lot."

"As often as I can."

Lacchi turned out to be a smooth yoghurt milk shake with rose water and mangoes. I was glad this wasn't a Colombian restaurant. We didn't have to leave anything behind on the plates.

The combo included mulligatawny, salad, rice, naan, and butter chicken. The butter chicken was a religious experience all by itself. The menu said it all: "mild, but essentially most flavourful." We ate in silence for a while, not wanting to spoil the gastronomic spirituality of the moment. After a while, though, my curiosity got the better of me.

"This is wonderful, but you said that you have information relating to my cases."

"Actually, I can *get* you information about your cases. I understand that you might be in possession of some evidence that the police wouldn't be interested in processing at this time."

"How did you – oh, Parker."

"It would be unethical of me to say, of course. But I know some people with forensic expertise and facilities who could look at the evidence for you."

"That's kind of you, but it sounds expensive. How much would it cost to get results from a private lab?"

"Nothing."

I put down the naan with which I'd been about to scoop up some butter chicken sauce. It took some serious impulse control for me not to lick the plate.

"Dr. MacMillan, my parents taught me to beware of Greeks, or even Irish-Indians, bearing gifts."

"Did they also mention gift horses and mouths? I have some colleagues who do each other favours on occasion. This would be just another favour."

"In return for...?"

"Someday, I'd like to be able to call upon you to do a service for me, if I get a case that warrants your talents."

"How Godfather-esque, or should I say Godmother-esque. This smells to me like something bigger than a few favours."

Trinity expertly tore a piece of naan using only her right hand, then twirled the bread fragment on the plate to pick up a piece of butter chicken and sauce. As it passed her lips she closed her eyes reverently, and chewed slowly. I politely let her finish. One should never be interrupted during a sacred ritual.

"I know you've spent a lot of time around police officers," she continued. "Surely you must have heard the complaints about the difficulty of getting results and resources in a timely manner."

I snorted. "You aren't kidding. It takes hours to collect evidence, and days to process it. By that time, the bad guy could be in another country. Don't even mention DNA analysis. On television, it takes moments to get a match. In real life it's more like six to eight months."

"Exactly. How would it change their world if they could match a DNA sample in two days?"

That was a stunning thought. Calgary was lucky, the police had their own forensic lab, at least for most common things. They still had to send DNA to the RCMP forensic labs, three of which had recently closed due to budget cuts. Having access to independent labs would be a God-send for investigators.

"There has to be a catch somewhere. If outside labs could do the work, why don't they already?"

"An accredited forensic lab needs certified technicians, meticulous accounting procedures, and iron-clad physical security. If there's the

slightest possibility that a sample was contaminated, processed incor-
rectly, handled by the wrong person, or even substituted, it's literally a
'get out of jail free' card for the offender. Of course, all of that assumes
that you require a pristine chain of custody to satisfy a court. If your
requirements are less stringent, you may be able to use a less prestigious
facility."

"So what you are saying, is that I can get my evidence analyzed, but
the analysis won't stand up in court?"

"Correct. Of course, if your entire case rests on one piece of evidence
then you probably have issues anyway. It can, however, tell you whether
a certain suspect is involved, saving many otherwise fruitless hours of
investigation. You can also get fast results so you know that the investigation is moving in the right direction while waiting for the certified results for court."

"Under those conditions I can see where it's a big help, but I don't
have a lab. Why would you need my services?"

"As you are aware, despite what television shows suggest, most criminal investigation has nothing to do with fancy science. Frequently, what
is needed are boots on the ground; competent people who search for
clues or keep watch on suspects. It may be that someone in law enforce-
ment will find themselves in a situation of limited manpower, or other
non-technical resources. Your skills may be invaluable to them at that
time."

I thought while eating. This was huge. I wondered why nobody had
thought of it before. Then I thought about the strings SSgt. Mott had
pulled to get me an internship. Maybe I'd been groomed for this from the
beginning.

"Not many people know about this, do they?"

"No, they don't. The police service would come under considerable
fire for using outside, civilian consultants in sensitive investigations,
regardless of how well it works in practice. There are people in the press,
and in the government, who wouldn't care if a serial killer was caught
and lives saved, if there was the slightest hint of irregularity in how he
was caught. Only certain officers know about our network. They can call
on us at any time for help, for themselves or their colleagues, but it must
remain secret so that we can continue to assist others."

"That would explain some of the 'intuitions' about investigations. I'm
guessing that your help doesn't always work out."

"Sadly, no. Detectives are allowed to have hunches, but if they can't
convince others to follow it by persuasion, they can't reveal the information's source. It's one thing to say, 'I have a gut feeling we should look at
so-and-so.' It's quite another to say, 'I asked some unlicensed civilians to

put so-and-so under illegal surveillance for two weeks before gathering samples that were tested in a non-accredited laboratory to prove that he's our killer.'"

By now, Rupak had taken away our plates, brought cups of *chai*, and rice pudding with cardamom for dessert. After the first taste I resisted the urge to gobble the pudding, and took tiny spoonfuls so it would last longer. Trinity was doing likewise but I caught her watching me.

"You're taking a chance on telling me this," I said after I thought I'd made her wait long enough to pay her back for her silence when we arrived. "What's to prevent me from getting my fifteen minutes of fame by blowing the whistle on you?"

"I don't believe for a moment that you're serious, but there are several things. I haven't named any names, so you actually have nothing but a fanciful story that I'll deny having told you. Your supposition about certain detectives is nothing but speculation. If you did manage to bring down part of our network, I doubt that any of your police friends would ever speak to you again."

I looked at the empty dish before me, and ran my spoon around it one last time just in case I'd missed anything.

"Fair enough. You're right, there's too much of a need for me to jeopardize what you're doing. Out of curiosity, how big is this network of yours?"

"If you mean in terms of people, I'd have to consult my records. I do know that we have assets in 127 countries so far."

She caught me just as I was sipping my *chai*, and escaped the blast only because I was looking toward the batik hanging on the wall at the time. Fortunately, I contained the spray behind one hand, so only I got wet.

"One hundred twenty-seven countries?"

"Yes. It's amazing how quickly a grass-roots movement grows when it fulfils a deeply felt need."

I'd thought her offer was bigger than it seemed but this was ridiculous. My psychologist was – at first words failed me, and then I thought of the exact term.

"You're an anti-Moriarty."

She laughed, but my timing was off. She managed to get the cup away from her lips before she sprayed me with *chai*.

"That's rather good. I'd never thought of it that way before, but yes, I'm the mastermind at the centre of a web of agents who thwart criminals. The Napoleon of crime fighters." She arched her eyebrows, and lowered her voice. "My spies are everywhere. Or, at least, by number of countries, about 65 percent of everywhere." She drained her cup. "The appellation is particularly amusing considering the name of our group."

"Which is?"

"BSI." I raised one eyebrow. "I'm confident that you'll figure it out."

I reached into my pocket, and brought out the coin I'd taken from Parker, now doubly-encased in two small plastic sample bags. I looked at her for a moment, then handed it over. She examined it curiously through the bags.

"Parker's obsession seems to have started when he handled this. I thought it might have some kind of drug or toxin on it."

"You haven't touched it?"

"No, that seemed like a bad idea."

"I'll see what we can find," she said. She looked at her watch. "I'm afraid we'll have to cut this short. I have an appointment with a client in less than an hour."

She left cash on the table, including a hefty tip. This visit had thoroughly washed away the bad taste of my previous visit. I'd be back.

The sun was warm on our faces as we left the restaurant.

"I'll let you know as soon as the lab has anything," Trinity said. "I think this is the beginning of a beautiful friendship."

"Please tell me you did not just quote from Casablanca. That would make me the corrupt policeman."

"But it would make me the freedom fighter and bar owner. Aren't bartenders supposed to be therapists in disguise?"

I wondered if all private investigators had such crazy lives, or whether the universe just had it in for me. What was next, being offered a position by MI-6?

Of course, from what I'd read, MI-6 had around 3200 personnel, so the BSI might be bigger than them.

Madre de dios.

CHAPTER 27

You Aren't Going to Like It

The next day, Mum was sitting on my living room couch with a glass in her hand. "You aren't going to like it."

"Now there's a surprise," I said. "So far I haven't liked anything about this case. I'm beginning to appreciate why fictional PIs drink so much."

From the depths of my comfy chair, I lifted my glass of homemade beer in illustration. I paused for a moment, and let the aftertaste develop. It wasn't quite as smooth as I wanted, so I made a mental note to try reducing the hops by five percent next time I brewed.

Left to myself, I tend not to be a morning person, and her phone call at eight had woken me. I wondered if drinking in the morning was a bad sign, even if it was just one beer. Especially since this was my first case.

Mum was on duty so she was having water. She'd insisted on coming over to give me her report, refusing to say anything over the phone. That could be good or bad. I thought back to what I'd learned about Trinity, and wondered if Mum knew. I felt guilty not telling her, but it wasn't my information to share. I'd have to ask Trinity before it drove me nuts. This case was full of secrets, few of which made any sense at all.

I took another sip from my glass. Yoko wandered in, and sat on Mum. I could hear him purring from across the table.

"I assume that you found out something that will cause me to lose even more sleep."

"Are you absolutely certain that you gave me the right address?"

"Yes."

"And have you had breakfast yet?"

"No. Why does that matter?"

"Because you're going to need to believe at least six impossible things."

It's never a good sign when a homicide detective starts quoting Lewis Carroll before giving a briefing. Mum opened a file folder on the coffee table.

"First, it wasn't easy to get the information. You owe me big time."

"I know, FOIPP. I hope you didn't put yourself at risk."

"None at all. I called in a favour from someone in District Four who called in a favour from a friend. It seems that Crime Stoppers got an anonymous tip that people were squatting in a house on Millward Place."

"Really? That's convenient. That let you open a case file."

"Honestly, haven't you being paying attention? Until there's a body I'm not involved. A general investigations detective at Four, on the other hand..."

"Duh, my bad."

"A Mr. Ming Chang bought the property last year. He applied for a development permit, but so far hasn't done anything with the house."

"He hasn't rented it to anybody? So my source was right, the Beleth Twins are squatting."

"That's what the tipster said. Wait, twins?"

"I forgot to tell you. It looks like Beleth has a male accomplice who also goes by the name of Beleth. They look like fraternal twins."

"Wonderful. It gets better, though. You said that you were there at night?"

"Yes, around six or seven. When I spoke to her it was around eight thirty."

"And the lights were on?"

"Yes, of course. It was well after dark."

"Mr. Ming had all the utilities shut off last summer."

I sat up, and put my glass on the table.

"That's impossible. The lights were on. People were the next thing to naked in the living room without any goose bumps. I can show you the video I took, and nobody's breath is showing. Hell, I was sitting in the living room in my winter coat and almost melted." That brought back an awkward memory that I suppressed. "There has to be at least heat and light on."

"Not unless they ran their own power lines and gas supply."

"I suppose that's possible. Marijuana growers do it all the time."

"The problem with that is that there's no missing power, and no increase in the gas consumption in surrounding houses. The investigator called the utilities company to confirm that the power is off, and everything is perfectly normal. They even sent someone to look it over. No power. No gas."

"Then what the hell was going on? A generator in the basement? Big propane bottles?"

"Maybe. Did you hear anything like a motor running?"

"Not a whisper."

I downed the rest of my drink, and decided it would be best if I didn't get another one. Instead, I got up to pour myself a bowl of cereal. Mum followed me to the kitchen, and leaned on the peninsula counter.

"Somehow, I need to get inside that house again. There has to be some clue as to what's going on." Mum smiled her "I know something you don't" smile.

"By a strange coincidence, the detective at District Four who asked to handle this investigation owes you a favour. I'm led to believe that she's contacted Mr. Ming, and is going to meet him there this afternoon to see if anything is amiss. He doesn't want any trouble, and is extremely interested in letting her poke around. I don't suppose you'd like to tag along, purely as an interested observer?"

"No wonder I never got away with anything when I was growing up. That's brilliant. Who's the detective?"

Danielle Shuemaker met me at the District Four office so we could ride over together.

She'd let her hair grow since the last time I had seen her, and now wore it in a pony tail. She caught me staring as we were about to get into the car.

"There's a bit of a scar where I got hit, so I changed my hair style to cover it."

"It looks good. Congratulations on becoming a detective. Are you sure you won't get fat sitting behind a desk all day?"

She laughed as we both opened our doors and paused. The laughter died as we remembered the last time we were in a car together.

"I don't think we'll go to Peter's today," she said, a bit too conversationally to be real.

"No churches either." I hoped that I sounded calm.

We got in the car, each pretending that we were completely relaxed about the whole thing.

Ming Chang was, I suspected, somewhere in his seventies. He looked like one of those elderly Chinese gentlemen you see doing T'ai Chi in a park who could probably bench press our vehicle. He got out of his car as we pulled up. Danielle rolled down her window to talk to him.

"Have you gone inside?"

He gave us a startled expression, like an owl.

"You think I'm crazy? Who knows what's in there. Come get me when it's safe. Very dangerous, you go first."

Every afternoon of poking around a haunted house should start with an old guy with hair like Einstein spouting Indiana Jones quotes.

He handed the key to Danielle, then retreated to his car.

We started by walking around the outside. As before, the sidewalk and walkway to the front door were clear of snow, courtesy of Mr. Ming complying with city by-laws. Apart from some squirrel and rabbit footprints, and the larger mail carrier ones, the snow was undisturbed. For the sake of paranoia, I checked the gas meter. I pointed out to Danielle the smudges on the pipes where I'd stood on it. This was the right house. All the blinds were down, and the drapes drawn, so we couldn't see inside.

Danielle examined the door before opening it. There were no signs of forced entry. Danielle put the key in the lock. It opened easily. I pulled slightly on my baton to loosen it in its holster. She rested her hand on her Glock.

I followed her in so she'd have a clear field of fire. Once we cleared the front hall I'd watch her back.

The first thing I noticed when the door opened was the lack of warmth on my face. The heat was off, and must have been for at least a day. The front hall was empty.

I put my hand on Danielle's arm to stop her while I looked past her. The walls were completely bare. I got out my camera, and started recording what I was seeing. I'd stood on this floor just a few days ago, dripping muddy snow from my boots. There was no sign I'd ever been here before. If the floor had been clean I'd have dismissed it as someone trying to erase evidence. Instead, the floor was slightly gritty with dust. I could see Danielle's footprints in front of me where she'd stood, but no others. If we were in a movie, now would be the time for the ominous music to start.

The only thing in the living room was the wall-to-wall carpet. There was no sign of where I'd walked across it, and sat on the couch. No sign of the couch, either. A low haze of dust was raised as we walked through. I could see bulbs in the ceiling light so I flipped the wall switch a few times. The bulbs remained dark.

Danielle relaxed slightly, taking her hand off her gun, but the emptiness just made me more nervous. I didn't know how long it took for a carpet to recover from having furniture on it, but I suspected that it was months. There were no flat spots on the living room carpet to indicate where any of the furniture had been.

"Police!" she yelled. "Is anybody home?"

We waited for a count of ten. There were no sounds. Nothing. She motioned me toward the kitchen while she checked the bedrooms in back.

Apart from the occasional mouse droppings, and an old can of peaches, the kitchen cupboards and drawers were empty. There were gaps where the refrigerator and dishwasher had been removed. I tried the faucet, and found that it was already open, probably from when the plumber had drained the system. The handle and spout were uniformly dusty except where I had touched them.

Danielle startled me by appearing around the corner.

"Nothing here."

"Let's check the basement," I said, thinking of every horror movie in which the monsters lurk in the dark. I don't know what I expected to find there if the ground floor was abandoned.

More nothing, that's what. There was a furnace and hot water heater, both stone cold. The main gas valve was closed. I watched the electric meter for a few moments, but the disc didn't budge. There were a few bits and pieces of junk that hadn't been disturbed for months: a broken kitchen chair, some rags, a child's doll staring blankly at the ceiling. Creepy.

"The owner said he hasn't been in here since last summer," Danielle said. "I'm willing to bet that's the last time anybody has been in here."

I nodded my agreement, still trying to understand what was going on.

We went outside and locked the door behind us. Ming Chang was standing outside, fidgeting.

"Well?"

"It looks like a false alarm. Nobody's been inside for months," Danielle said. "I'll send you a copy of the investigation report. Sorry to have troubled you."

"Well?" Danielle said as we drove back to the station.

"I'm sorry I wasted everybody's time like that," I said. "I must look like an idiot."

"We all make mistakes."

"The problem is that I didn't. You saw the scuffs on the gas meter. That's the house I surveilled. I have videos of the inside, warm, lit up and full of furniture on two occasions within the last two weeks. I was sitting on a couch in that living room a few nights ago. I wish I had some idea what the hell is going on."

"There's nobody there now."

"Thank you, Detective Obvious. This case is driving me completely bug-house nuts."

As we went back to the station to pick up my car, I noticed that, compared with the first time we'd been in a car together, Danielle paid extra attention when driving through intersections. On the other hand, so did I.

At the end of the week I got a phone call.

"Hello, Ms. Chandler?"

"Parker, what can I do for you?"

"You've done enough, thanks. I wanted to let you know that Dr. Mac-Millan referred me to a friend of hers. Dr. Sterling is cool, and I think I'm really making progress. I haven't felt like visiting that house for over a week now."

"That's excellent. I'm still trying to get to the bottom of what happened to you and others. I promise you I'll let you know as soon as I discover anything."

"That would be good. I still don't know how I'm going to explain this to Keith."

"Don't worry about it. If you want, once we figure out what's going on, I'll be there to answer any questions he might have. At the very least, I can assure him that whatever happened to you was completely non-consensual. In the meantime, let the doctor help you to get yourself together."

"I will. Thanks again."

After I hung up I was both glad and depressed. At least one person involved in this was making progress.

What was the Beleth Twins' game? There are three main reasons why people do bad things: money, sex, and power.

I had a sudden inspiration and called Sofia.

"Hello?"

"Mrs. Reinkemeyer, this is Veronica. Can you talk?"

"Yes, Frank is at work. What have you discovered?"

"My investigation is ongoing. Do you know if Frank has a silver coin with an odd symbol on it, and the name Beleth engraved around the out-side?"

"That's a strange question."

"The possibility came up during my enquiries. He may be keeping it in his suit, or a coat pocket. Could you check when he gets home?"

"I suppose. What's this about?"

"Believe me, I wish I knew. I'll let you know as soon as I have something. By the way, wear gloves while going through his pockets."

"Whatever for?"

"There's a possibility that the medallion is contaminated in some way. Better safe than sorry."

"Very well, if you insist. Is that all?"

"For now." She hung up.

Until I heard back, I'd assume that Frank had a coin as well. As far as I knew, no actual money had changed hands. Neither of the victims seemed ripe for blackmail. I supposed they could be grooming Parker to steal cameras for them, but it seemed like a ridiculously complex way of going about it when all they had to do was drive a truck through the front door some night and start loading.

Frank was a better candidate for blackmail. At least he had an interesting amount of money. Sofia had gone through their personal finances at my request, and she couldn't see any missing funds. Blackmail seemed unlikely unless he was syphoning funds directly from his company. To do that he'd probably have to have the CFO covering for him, which also seemed unlikely. In real life, criminal conspiracies are difficult to pull off without somebody leaking information. Unless, of course, Frank was blackmailing his CFO in turn. I could hear Occam spinning in his grave, wondering why his razor was so dull.

The sex angle seemed most obvious, but that didn't track either. According to Parker, Beleth hadn't touched him apart from the occasional correction with the riding crop or spurs. Parker certainly wasn't having a good time. I watched the video of Frank again to be sure, and saw the same thing. There was no actual contact with Beleth apart from the equipment and riding crop. I would have expected a horse rider to pat the mount's shoulder or rump when he did something right, but even that didn't happen.

Power seemed like the winner, but even there I had my doubts. There's no point in having power over someone else if you don't use it somehow. Nobody keeps slaves just so they can clutter the house. They exist to follow your orders, and show others that you are rich and powerful.

True, she trained Parker and Frank as dressage horses, but why? They couldn't be entered in a real horse show. Maybe there was a human equivalent, some kind of BDSM pet show. It was worth looking into. You don't spend the hours necessary to train a dressage horse, and then just let them sit in the figurative barn.

When I re-watched the videos I couldn't shake the feeling that the Beleth Twins were doing this with an almost clinical detachment. It wasn't personal, as it would be in a BDSM setting. It was a task. Maybe they were doing it for someone else, an as yet unknown employer. I tried to figure out how to get to the boss, if he or she existed. The problem was how to follow one or the other of the Twins, especially now that Parker was out of their grasp. I'd never seen either of them outside the house, and only once when a victim wasn't present.

The idea of a mastermind being behind the twins didn't really make sense to me, but I decided to keep the idea around just in case.

For the sake of something to do, I transferred the photos I'd taken of the inside of the house to my laptop. Something bothered me about the empty living room, and I had to go through the pictures several times before it jumped out at me.

There was no telephone jack anywhere in the room. There was one in the kitchen, but there was no way to hide a line running from it to the living room. I even went back to the videos. There was no extension cord.

That was just wonderful. I'd been chasing a prop telephone that wasn't even plugged in. If the Twins had phones at all they were probably burners. I'd need a number to get a handle on their communications. To do that I'd have to break in while one of them was there, and find a real phone. Maybe I could sneak in a bedroom window while they were doing their thing with Frank.

It took only a moment to reject that idea. Apart from the illegality, the blinds in the back windows were down, so I'd have to go in without knowing if the other twin was in that bedroom. I'd have to leave tracks in the back yard, bring some kind of ladder, and jimmying a window creates noise. Being caught half way through a bedroom window by the Twins seemed like a bad idea. I might even have to fight off Frank. I'd be shocked if he had any fighting skills, but if he sat on me I'd be in real trouble.

All right, forget that. Maybe I could get them to unmask themselves by starving their communications. If they couldn't sit inside and communicate with the boss, they'd have to come out. I'd heard of cell phone jammers, and information wasn't hard to find online.

There were several problems. The biggest one was that they were illegal in Canada, so if I wanted one I'd have to order one from the U.S. That meant somehow getting it through customs without being caught. They were also expensive. Sure, I could get one for $65 but a really useful one was over $2200. Apart from being illegal and expensive, I didn't have the time.

Forget that. I'd have to go old school. That was illegal too, but I'd have to be caught first, and squatters wouldn't have much legal recourse against me. I considered making the whole thing completely above board by going through Ming Chang, but if the theoretical boss existed it might well be him, or somebody he knew. That could explain the use of his house. He could have cleaned the place, then blown dust around to make it look like nobody had been there in months. The mystery of the appearing – disappearing -- appearing furniture still bothered me. At this point, I wasn't going to put anything past these people. They seemed to have ridiculously large resources.

Maybe it was time to invest in a tin-foil hat. Or ask Trinity to give my brain a tune up and oil change. I wondered if free therapy was covered under our new business arrangement.

I thought about anti-Moriarty, which my mind transformed into Auntie Moriarty. She'd said that the nickname was appropriate given the name of the network, and that I'd figure it out. Maybe it was time to give myself a small win.

I had too much wandering around in my brain as it was, so I cheated and used Google to look for "Moriarty BSI." The answer popped up immediately: Baker Street Irregulars, the name of Sherlock Holmes' informant network. I was unreasonably pleased that I'd figured it out. At this point it was probably the only thing that made sense in my life.

My life had been taken over by mysterious midgets, haunted houses and murky motives, and now was also a Conan Doyle conundrum. I resolved to stay away from any waterfalls. What was next, space aliens?

A brief thought ran through my brain, sticking its tongue out at me as it passed by: Maybe Beleth really was a demon.

Yeah, sure. I could believe that the one I'd met *thought* she was a demon, but the whole furniture thing had to be a gimmick. If I started trying to run down paranormal leads I'd be led away by nice men in white coats to be fitted for a designer jacket with long sleeves.

I wondered if they still used straitjackets in mental hospitals, or indeed if they still had mental hospitals. Maybe they'd gone out of fashion, or were called something else now.

Marvellous. On top of everything else, I was apparently coming down with ADD.

CHAPTER 28

Oh, Bugger

I braced myself for what I was about to do. This was going to hurt a lot.

I looked at the total on the online order form for a moment longer, buyer's regret already setting in, then clicked on the "Pay" button. I'd chosen expedited shipping, so in only 48 hours I would be the proud owner of a $600 smoke detector.

Once I'd decided to get eyes inside the mystery house, I had to figure out how. The bugs you see in movies, the little black boxes hidden under tables or in light fixtures with wires dangling down are *so* old school. Modern ones are tiny, and made to blend in with the other furnishings. A clock can contain a video camera, the lens hidden as the dot over the i in the brand name. Watch it, nanny: Those plastic eyes in the child's stuffed animal are watching you. The lens of a camera at the end of a fibre optic cable peering through the ceiling is almost big enough to see if you stand on a chair – and are looking right at it. People are suspicious these days; video and audio bugs like these were relatively cheap, and locally available.

Problem one: this house had no electricity. Anything I planted had to be battery-powered. That meant a limited lifespan before I'd have to change the batteries. Somehow, they forget to mention that in movies.

Problem two: a lot of battery-powered bugs these days don't transmit, they store the information because transmitters use a lot of power to get a decent range. By "decent" I mean outside the house. You need a radio license to operate the high power ones. Bugs that store the information use memory cards like the ones for cameras. It's a relatively cheap and easy system, but the memory is a limited resource.

Problem three: Almost all civilian bugs hide in plain sight in common items, but this house was empty. A teddy bear on the kitchen counter would be obvious. The only thing that hadn't been cleaned out was the smoke detector on the kitchen ceiling. Fortunately, bugs that looked like smoke detectors were available. They'd even let you know if there was a fire.

Problem four: Bugs like that were special order items. I needed something that would last for several days or, preferably, weeks and store a hell of a lot of data. I couldn't be sneaking into the house every day or two so that I could change memory cards, and replace the batteries.

Problem five: I needed a model with a motion detector so it would only record when somebody was there. That was part of the solution to the limited memory/battery problem.

Problem six: The model had to look at least approximately like the one in the house.

I found a video bug that would do what I needed from a supplier in Toronto, but it was expensive, especially when I specified air shipping. I couldn't wait "twelve to fifteen working days" for delivery.

I had no doubt that I'd be able to use it in future cases, but in the meantime the outlay still stung.

Yes, I could have asked Kali to buy it for me. She'd have done it without blinking an eye.

That wasn't going to happen, ever. Kali was rolling in money, and she'd happily give me any amount I wanted. This wasn't just a matter of pride. I knew that once we started down that road it would only lead to dependency and resentment. I thought too highly of her, myself, and our friendship to ever do that.

That doesn't mean that I wasn't tempted on occasion.

Two days later, on Friday, a Canada Post truck pulled up outside my building, and I buzzed in a nice young man who had me sign for a package. Considering the involvement of Mr. Murphy in this case so far, I was slightly surprised when I tested the product. It worked perfectly, and was exactly what I needed.

Maybe there *was* a Santa Claus.

Timing was everything. Sofia confirmed that, so far, Frank had never gone to the house on weekends, so that was my window of opportunity. I called Parker. He still had his key to the house, and was happy to give it to me. As far as the owner was concerned, the key wasn't legally in Parker's possession, so technically I was still trespassing. Of course, if anyone asked about it, I would have no idea that the key wasn't legitimate. Parker in turn could pass the blame on to Beleth, where it belonged.

Being a private investigator requires being a world-class athlete: we're frequently skating on thin ice.

I asked Nick if he knew anyone with work coveralls I could borrow. Wisely, he asked no questions. He knew a woman about my size who worked for an electrical contractor, and convinced her to loan her uniform for the weekend for "an undercover operation." Later he told me that her big concern was bullet holes in the fabric: she thought it would be cool to have some. Along with a black wig from Don's Hobby, sunglasses, a wad of cloth, and makeup so that I looked older and darker, I now had a disguise.

George had a friend named Tony with a white cargo van, and convinced him to loan it to me for the weekend. All it would cost me was gas and beer. Tony had asked for a case of Bud Light but I couldn't force myself to be that cruel. He'd get a case of my best homemade instead.

A quick trip to Home Depot got me a tool belt. A helpful associate in the electrical department recommended a few tools that I probably needed anyway. It was a good thing that I was charging Sophia for expenses.

After borrowing a stepladder from Dad I was ready to go.

My apartment didn't have a smoke detector, but Mum and Dad had a couple. They also asked no questions as I practised pulling a detector down, then replacing it with my surveillance camera a few times until there were no problems. I wanted this to go quickly and smoothly.

Saturday morning, at the hideous hour of 7 A.M., I picked up the van from Tony, then drove over to my parents' place to get the ladder. I was getting thoroughly sick of Millward Place.

It was unlikely that the Beleth Twins were home. If they were, I had a 50/50 chance of the woman answering the door. She was the only one who might recognize me. Even if she did answer, I had been in a much different disguise that time. The wad of cloth was stuffed in my cheek, a one-sided version of what Marlon Brando had done for his role in the Godfather. If asked, my story was that I'd just had oral surgery. The cloth not only gave me a chipmunk cheek, but also gave me an excuse to mumble, disguising my voice without a chance that I'd slip up and forget. A clipboard with an authentic-looking work order completed my kit. If anybody was home, I'd just pretend I was at the wrong address, and leave to try again some other time.

I was hoping that all this preparation was overkill. From what I'd observed, I didn't think they stuck around the house if they weren't expecting a "client." It bothered me that I still didn't know how they were getting in and out without being seen. Maybe there really were secret tunnels in the basement.

I knocked, in case anybody was home, or a neighbour was watching. Nothing happened. I waited a bit, then knocked again. There was still no answer, so I used the key.

The house was still empty. Or maybe empty again. It was hard to keep track. The footprints in the dust were still visible from our police visit.

I carried the ladder to the kitchen, and set it up under the smoke detector. The unit was supposed to twist off but somebody had gotten paint on it. I had to use my new utility knife to cut away the excess from the casing before it would move. I was very careful so it wasn't too obvious that someone had been digging at the ceiling.

Once the unit was loose, I tried to detach the detector from the ceiling, and ran into a snag. The damned thing wasn't the battery-powered kind I'd been expecting. It was permanently wired in.

Crap. All the detectors I'd seen were battery operated. It hadn't occurred to me that there was another kind. Not only that, but the wires were stuck into the back of the detector instead of being attached with those little plastic cone things. I wasn't an electrician, and I had no idea how in hell the thing came off. I tried pulling the wires but they didn't budge, and there were no screws that I could see.

As usual for me, that's when there was a knock on the front door. Oh, bugger.

Now what? The Twins wouldn't knock, they'd have their own keys. Ditto for Mr. Ming or Frank. Maybe it was somebody wanting to know if I'd found Jesus.

Danielle and I had looked everywhere in the house. There was no Jesus here. Dust bunnies, yes. I didn't think that there was a Church of Dust Bunnies. Damn, my brain was wandering off without me again.

The knock was repeated, louder this time. The door knob rattled as someone tried it; odd behaviour for missionaries unless they were frighteningly zealous. I was glad I'd locked the door behind me.

There was another knock, still louder. Whoever they were, they weren't taking the hint. Somebody knew I was here. I got off the ladder, retraced my steps, and carefully looked through the peep hole.

It was Mr. Galvan from next door. At least nobody had summoned the tactical team. That would have been fun for me to explain at District Four. I opened the door, and gave him a lop-sided smile due to the stuffing in my mouth.

"Yeth?" I mumbled.

"Who are you?" He demanded, suspicion all over his face.

"Who're you?" I mumbled back.

"I'm the neighbour. What are you doing here?"

"I' here to fikth the shmoke detector."

Mr. Galvan looked at me shrewdly. "I thought that Chinese guy was going to tear the house down. Why would he need a new smoke detector?"

"Don' as' me, I just do wha' I' told." I waved the clip board at him. "Shee?"

Mr. Galvan hadn't brought his reading glasses, and he moved the fake work order back and forth trying to focus on it. I don't know how much he could make out, but after a minute he seemed satisfied.

"Humph. It's a crying shame, young man, the way people get thrown out of their own homes these days, and other people profit from it."

It was my surveyor persona who had heard the story, not Ms. Fix-it, so I tried to look confused by his oblique reference to the previous owners. I had a sudden, silly urge to ask him if the Lambs had stopped screaming yet.

"Sorry, 'ut I haf to – ulp – get 'ack to 'urk now." The cloth, saturated with spit, shifted in my mouth, and I almost swallowed it. I wasn't sure that I understood what I had said. Mr. Galvan gave me an odd look.

"Tooth problems?"

"No' any 'ore. They 'ulled it out yeshterday."

"Gargle with warm salt water. That'll make it feel better in no time."

"Thank you." I edged backward and started to close the door.

"How much would you charge to change a light bulb?"

"Wha'?"

"The light burned out at the top of my stairs. I have a ladder, but I can't reach it by myself."

"I'll be o'er af'er I finsh here."

"Thank you. My house is the one next door."

He pointed, then wandered away as I closed the door.

The interruption had actually been useful. It had allowed my subconscious to work on the problem, and I realized that I was being an idiot. Like most people with no electrical skills, I had an instinctive fear of shocks, or doing something wrong, and causing whatever it is that burns down houses. Now I remembered that the power was off, and would probably never be restored. I just cut the wires, covering the ends with some black tape just in case, and tucked them up in the electrical box. After that, the camera went into place without a hitch.

I still didn't relax until the ladder was in the van. I shut the back doors, then headed over to Mr. Galvan's house.

Fortunately for me, his problem wasn't the height of the ladder, it was his inability to climb due to a bad knee. He already had his ladder set up, and he insisted on holding it for me. It took me only a few seconds to change the bulb for him.

He handed me a twenty, but I refused to accept it. It didn't seem right taking money for five seconds work while pretending to be a handyman. He called me "young man" again as he thanked me for being so courteous.

I was wearing unisex coveralls, but really. Maybe I should put breast implants on my Christmas wish list.

Exactly one week later, I went back to swap in a new memory card. Frank had been to the house twice during that time, so there should be lots of exciting things to see.

My second break-in was almost identical to the first, except that the van wasn't available. I managed to stuff enough of the ladder into the trunk of my Cavalier, a cheerful red rag tied on the end of the legs that stuck out, and a bungee cord mostly holding the lid closed. Every time I went over a slight bump, it jumped up, and then clattered down. I expected something to break every time it happened, but I made it there without incident.

Again, nobody answered the door, and this time everything went perfectly. I was back in my car within five minutes at most. I don't think that even Mr. Galvan saw me.

The dull pain behind my eyes was a fitting companion to the knots in my shoulders that were spreading up the back of my skull.

It wasn't that the camera had failed, or run out of memory or anything simple like that. The hardware had worked flawlessly.

The trouble was that what it had recorded was impossible. Ridiculously impossible. It had to be fake. Maybe this was one of those reality shows, trying to convince me that spooky things were happening. If the host jumped out and yelled "boo" he was going to get a face full of fist.

The camera was set to come on at the first hint of movement in the room. I'd cranked up the motion detector sensitivity to maximum since there shouldn't be anything in the house that could create a false alarm: no open windows, blowing drapes, pets, or people. A mouse couldn't have run across the floor without being recorded. The camera also would stay on for about fifteen seconds after motion stopped, so it wouldn't drop out if people were still for a few seconds.

The first part of the video showed me finishing the installation, packing up, and leaving. The next time stamp was Tuesday night, a few seconds before Frank arrived.

There was just enough light filtering through from the street lamps to show that the living room was as empty as it had been the previous weekend. I wondered what had triggered the recording. Maybe a stray air current, although there shouldn't be any with the windows closed and the furnace turned off.

Within a second, a short figure was standing in the middle of the room. A moment later the lights came on, and the furniture appeared. There was no sense of it being a process. When I went through the video in detail later, everything appeared in the time between two frames.

The figure was Sister Beleth dressed, as she always did for Frank, in her equestrian outfit. She went around the room, making sure that everything was just right, including the neatly arrayed BDSM items on a side table. Then she sat in the same chair she'd used when I'd come as the survey taker. At no time did she look toward the kitchen.

She draped her leg over the arm in the same porn-star pose, looked up toward the kitchen ceiling, and wiggled her fingers directly at the camera as she smiled. Her timing was perfect. Frank sadly waddled in about two seconds later, and she turned her attention to him for the rest of the evening.

I rubbed my aching eyes, and wondered which question to tackle first. I decided to leave the whole David Copperfield thing with the furniture for later.

How the hell did she know that the camera was there? It would take a very close examination to detect the camera lens. Once the camera was on, it would record any attempt to get close to it. At maximum sensitivity, a fly couldn't walk within half a metre of the unit without triggering it.

From the moment I'd left the house, there was no recording until Tuesday night. Even if she'd been looking for it, she couldn't have seen the lens from outside any of the windows because the blinds were closed.

I'd more-or-less joked about it before but now I really did feel like I was going crazy. All right, Sherlock, back to first principles.

I had a recording, therefore the camera had recorded. The unit had no mechanical apparatus that could jam. Either the electronics worked or they didn't. Therefore, the record must be complete to the best of the camera's ability. How could the camera have been compromised?

The only way to turn the camera off was the switch on the top side that was hidden in the ceiling. It was barely conceivable that someone could have broken through the ceiling from the attic, and approached the camera from its blind side. However, there was no evidence of that when I took it down to change the memory card. Breaking through the ceiling would have left pieces of debris on top. There was no chance that I had simply missed them. Any debris would have fallen straight into my eyes when I tilted the unit.

The other problem with that theory was that the detector was mounted to one of those octagonal steel boxes. It would take a brain surgeon to break through from above and then wiggle a probe through a screw hole to operate the switch. I seriously doubted that it was possible. They'd have to find two screw holes in just the right places to turn the unit off and then on again.

The only sane possibility was that someone had entered the house, taken the memory card out, edited the images, and then replaced the card. It was not impossible that someone could have done that on Friday after Frank left the second time, the day before I came to swap cards. If they did the whole thing in complete darkness, the motion detector wouldn't have turned on the camera as it was being reassembled. Coming up with a viable theory made me feel better.

I felt much better for about twenty seconds, then something tickled the back of my mind. I got out the user's manual for my toy. There it was, under the specifications section. The motion detector was infrared, not visual. Trying to get to the camera in darkness wouldn't work. Even in pitch blackness, body heat would have activated the camera. The blank video would show that someone had been there.

Was it possible for somebody to hide behind a shield or something to fool the motion detector? The company I'd bought it from had a 24/7 service number, so I called it.

Could someone fool the motion detector? Short answer: no, not unless they were very lucky and extremely good. Unless whoever did it took fantastic precautions, the detector would pick up a temperature difference between the shield and the background. They sold this model to government agencies for covert surveillance; it had to be nearly foolproof.

I was out of ideas. As much as it pained me, it was time to call for help. Again.

The phone rang as I toyed with the business card, bending it back and forth between the fingers of one hand.

"Dr. MacMillan."

"Hi Trinity, it's Veronica. Are you busy?"

"Not at all, I was just about to call you. I have the results from the analysis of that medallion."

"Ah. I'd forgotten about that."

"Really? I take it that there's something else, then?"

"I was wondering if you know anybody who could look at a video, and tell me how it could be faked."

"Certainly. Is it short enough to e-mail it to me?"

I held the phone with my shoulder while typing on my laptop.

"Done. It's edited to preserve client confidentiality but the good parts are all there. I've also sent you a description of the circumstances, and camera set up."

"Why do you think it was faked?"

"It'll be obvious, given that the recording is real-life, real-time video. What did you find on the medallion?"

"I've just e-mailed you the report. The medallion is nothing but pure silver with one set of finger prints on it belonging to Parker. There is one peculiarity, though."

"Oh goody, a peculiarity. Why am I not surprised? Weren't there any drugs or chemicals on it?"

"None. Just the trace contaminants that you'd expect from it being handled."

I was beyond swearing. Blowing out a long breath had to do.

"What's the peculiarity?"

"All silver is composed of two stable isotopes with mass numbers 107 and 109, each in almost equal amounts. Does that make sense to you?"

"I know what isotopes are. Same element, different weights."

"Good. The medallion is 38% Silver-107 and 62% Silver-109. That's far outside the limits of any possible laboratory error."

That was *very* weird.

"Could the silver have come from a meteor or something?"

"Good thought. I asked about that, but no. As far as we know, all the silver in the universe has about the same isotope ratio. The only theory the lab can come up with is that someone purposely obtained pure samples of the individual isotopes and alloyed them."

"That doesn't make sense either," I said. "I know just about nothing about nuclear chemistry, but I do remember reading that the Manhattan Project spent about two billion dollars to separate uranium isotopes. No matter how much more advanced the technology has become these days, it would be crazy expensive, and pointless to make a silver alloy like that. Why would anyone bother?"

"The chemists have no idea. One of them suggested that the silver is from another universe. "

"You know, I really, really hate this case."

"You sound bitter."

"Good for you, you must be a psychologist," I said bitterly. "Nothing about the case makes any sense. Does the mysterious isotope ratio bother you?"

"I must admit that it is perplexing."

"Imagine having your career depend on finding out why it's that way.

Now imagine having an entire case file full of crap like that. Every time I follow a lead it either goes nowhere, or ends up down the rabbit hole."

"I can see where that would be difficult."

"Wait until you see the video."

"I'm sure there's a rational explanation for all of this. If your brain overheats too much, come see me."

I thanked her, and considered her offer.

Screw that, I had a better idea.

"Hola, chica. ¿Cómo estás?"

"Muy bien, hermanita," Kali replied. *"¿Et tú?"*

"Mierda. I'd really appreciate it if we could have a girls' night."

"Sure. Give me an hour to lay in extra supplies."

I gave her two hours. At three o'clock, I parked in Kali's driveway. She had everything we'd need set up in her basement rec room.

The first course was lime-cumin chicken and tempura vegetables. We cooked the individual pieces in her deep fryer, the morsels skewered on forks like a fondu.

I told her, in blistering detail, how her case was going. I also told her, without mentioning any names or identifying details, about the Reinke-meyer case. I was fed up with the whole thing, and my language was even less lady-like than usual.

"May I see the video?" I passed her a USB drive with the same edited video I'd sent to Trinity. All Beleth, no Frank.

She plugged the drive into her television, and we watched it in silence.

"Amazing," Kali said when it was done. "If it was anybody but you was showing me this, I'd say it had to be a hoax."

"I wish it was. No wonder I can't find out who she is. She's a god-damned wizard from another universe." I pulled my fork from the fryer, blew on it so I wouldn't burn myself, and popped the chicken in my mouth. I have no idea how it tasted.

"You sound bitter."

"You aren't the first person to tell me that."

"Is this how all your cases are going to affect you? Because if they are, I think you should consider another line of work."

"I can't imagine another case like this one. Trust me, if I do get another one of these, I'll quit so fast your head will spin."

"Don't you have any idea who the woman is?"

"All I have is the name she and her brother go by: Beleth."

"I've heard that name before, somewhere."

"Yeah. It's supposed to be the name of a demon king. Or queen. Depending on how he or she feels that day, I guess. Maybe the Beleth

Twins are the same person.”

“Give me a minute. You get dessert.”

Kali got her laptop and started browsing, sometimes reading a site for several minutes at a time. I looked in the refrigerator, and found sliced bananas and more tempura batter. Excellent! There was coconut ice cream in the freezer. Kali truly is a goddess.

After about ten minutes she sat back, looking like she was trying to decide how to tell me something awkward.

“I don't think it's a trick.”

“I did not want to hear that. How can it not be a trick?”

“Everything you've told me about Beleth, both of them, corresponds to information about Beleth the demon.”

“I know. So they can read. Criminals have posed as things they aren't before. That's the whole basis of running cons.”

“Maybe the reason your surveillance video looks like magic is that it is.”

I mounded ice cream into bowls for each of us, thinking about how to respond. Finally, I carefully put the scoop down on a plate.

“Kali, that's crazy.”

“Is it? It explains how Parker, and your other client's husband, were ensnared, the lack of motive, how Beleth got in and out of the house without anybody noticing, the disappearing furniture, and waving at the camera. Occam's razor.”

“I think that Occam is slitting his wrists with his own razor at this moment. Remember Sherlock Holmes' saying: 'When you have eliminated the impossible, whatever remains, however improbable, must be the truth.' I'm pretty sure that introducing something more impossible to explain the impossible doesn't count.”

“You're probably right. It's just that what they are doing fits the description exactly.”

“That just means they're using the mythology as a smoke screen. Anybody trying to find out who they are gets tangled in the legends. And that means that they are intelligent and organized. They believe that they've thought of every loop hole. All I have to do is to find the one they've missed. I have experts looking at the video, and I'm betting that they figure out how it was done. Once I know that, it'll tell me something about Beleth that they don't want me to know.”

Kali had swapped our forks for bamboo skewers. She had four of them in the fryer, the bubbles seething as if the slices of tempura banana were being devoured by piranhas. How symbolic.

“I hope you're right.” She didn't sound convinced.

“Apart from stage magicians, have you ever seen, or heard reliable reports of, magic like this? Even in books?"

"No."

She pulled the fried bananas from the oil, and used a fork to push them off into our bowls.

"Eat your ice cream. It's melting."

We settled in to watch the movies I'd selected. I'm a bad-assed, hard-boiled detective with mad martial art skills and a big baton so I picked an action movie.

Twilight: Breaking Dawn. Both parts.

Bella really should have gone with Jacob.

CHAPTER 29

Clubbing

There was one lead to Beleth that I hadn't followed yet. The research promised to be unusual, at least for me.

I admit that my rampaging hormones have caused me to fantasize about having several men at once, but never about other women, whips, chains, or ponies. I know, I'm boring. Too bad.

As usual, my first step was the internet. There was plenty of information about pony play, including human show ponies. That was good. Now I knew that human pony shows existed. I just had to find out if there were any local ones.

That was easier said than done. There weren't any specific pony show listings for Calgary, at least not human ones, so I broadened my search to all kink.

Three hours, a lot of cat-petting and two beers later, I had the contact information for some kink organizations. That was all. With luck, somebody would be willing to talk to me.

I called the first number.

"Hello, this is the Chinook Kink Association. Please leave a message and we'll get back to you." *Beep.*

"Hi, I'm looking for information on pony shows in Calgary and..."

The line picked up.

"Hello, this is Lady Shibori. Are you an owner?"

"I'm a private investigator. I'm looking for..."

The line went dead. At least I knew by implication that there were pony shows in Calgary. I just had to find someone who was less sensitive about talking to me.

My next three calls ended in much the same way, so I called someone whom I hoped wouldn't hang up on me.

"Hello?"

"Hi Mum, it's Veronica. Your daughter. Just in case you were wondering."

"How much is this going to cost me?"

"How sharper than a serpent's tooth. All I want is the name of a contact."

"Would you like some irony instead? The full quote is, 'How sharper than a serpent's tooth it is to have a *thankless child.*'"

"*Thank you* for correcting me. Seriously, I need the name of somebody in vice I can talk to."

"What is it that you're looking for?"

"My two bad guys are either victimizing people for no reason, or are training human ponies for a dressage competition."

Silence.

"Excuse me?"

"Didn't I tell you? Sorry about that."

Silence.

"Some people's children. Call Peggy Jorden. Her home number is 403-555-0187. If anybody knows anything, she will."

"Thanks. You're my favourite mother."

"I'd better be. Give me a few minutes to call her first."

Peggy didn't sound like a cop on the phone. She had an elegant voice that sounded like someone who made her living narrating audio books.

"Detective Jorden? This is Veronica Chandler."

"Hello! Janet said you'd be calling. And call me Peggy, It's Sunday and I'm off duty. What can I do for you?"

"I'm a private investigator, and I've encountered a pair of dwarf twins who do non-consensual training of people to be dressage horses." I paused to let her process.

"Holy crap, you do get the interesting ones, don't you?"

"Have you ever heard of anybody like that in Calgary? Or elsewhere, for that matter."

"I can't say that I have. You did say dwarf twins, didn't you?"

"Yes, and they both go by the name Beleth."

"It reminds me of a story I once read about triplets all named Donna. I'd remember something that unusual if I'd encountered it. Can you come by my office tomorrow? I have some people on file you might get information from."

"That would be great. Around ten?"

"Perfect."

I'd never worked with vice during my internship. Being underage, I certainly couldn't go out in the field. Besides, the subject matter was deemed too sensitive for my sixteen year old eyes. From what I'd seen as an investigator since then, perhaps that was for the best.

Now that I was just another civilian, Peggy had to come down to the front desk to escort me upstairs. She was a bit taller than me, pushing fifty with shoulder length blonde hair. She looked like somebody's doting aunt. Her face was too sweet to imagine her undercover on a hooker stroll.

Peggy wasn't kidding about the office. She was one of the few people in vice who wasn't in the bull pen. The reason became apparent soon after we arrived. She needed the quiet.

There was a power bar on her desk. Plugged into it was a line of cell phones, all low end burners. Held in place beneath them was a big paper calendar. One of the burners rang as she closed the door.

"I have to get this," she said. She sat down, and picked up one of the phones. I noticed a piece of tape across it that said "Cherri" in black marker.

"Hi there, this is Cherri," she said. Her voice had taken on a silky, sexy tone. If I closed my eyes I could easily believe that she was in her twenties. "What would you like me to do to you?" I couldn't hear the other end of the conversation. "Oo, you naughty, naughty boy. Tonight at seven? I can't wait." She sounded like Ashley Borenstein trying to seduce a new boy, if Ashley had been older, and more experienced at real seduction.

Peggy hung up, and made a note of her "appointment" on the calendar.

"Sorry," she said in her normal voice. "We're running a sting operation." Another phone rang as she was typing notes into her computer.

"Shit, don't these guys take a break?" She picked up another phone.

"How dare you call me, you worthless piece of cow dung? Of course this is Mistress Kimberlee. What's the matter, did you accidentally dial a real woman with your pathetic pee-pee? That's nice, but I don't know if I want to make an appointment with you. I have a few minutes around eight, if you think you can remember that."

"Interesting job," I said. "How do you keep your personalities straight?"

"At first I needed a cheat sheet. Now I just do it." She pulled a piece of paper out from under her computer keyboard.

"Try this woman for information. She owes me after a problem her club had last year. Tell her I sent you, and she'll talk to you."

"Thanks."

"Let me know how it goes." Another phone rang. "I have to get back to work. Lust never sleeps."

"Tell me about it."

I got up, and left as quietly as I could. Behind me I could hear someone very young.

"Hello, Daddy? I've been a bad girl..."

I wondered who would win if Peggy had a creep-off against Beleth.

The club wasn't easy to find. I suppose that was the whole point. Peggy's note said not to go before about 2 P.M.

No matter what time it is, Seventeenth Avenue South West bustles. There's always too much traffic, and too much going on. Heaven help you if you don't know exactly where you are going, and don't have someone riding shotgun to navigate for you.

The instructions I'd gotten from Peggy read like a cross between an Easter egg hunt, and a bad spy novel. My first break was finding a parking spot. By a miracle best known to St. Christopher, it was only two blocks from my destination.

Crossing the street, I found a narrow alley between two buildings. At the back of one of them, a small sign was attached to the wall. The sign was drawn in medieval style, showing a fat pony with a small dog prancing around its feet inside a circus ring. The message was obvious to those in the know: The Dog and Pony Show. Beside it was a barred glass door with a "CLOSED" sign hanging inside.

Despite the sign, the door was unlocked, and I went in. Rather than leading to the store at the front of the building, there was a flight of stairs leading down. At the bottom was an unmarked, heavy steel door of the kind usually found on boiler rooms. Beside it was an equally unmarked button. I pushed it.

A few seconds later, there was a click from a hidden speaker.

"Yes?"

"I'm here to see Lady Godiva." There was no obvious microphone, so I spoke to the button.

"What's the password?"

I had an impulse to say "chocolate" but instead went with the approved response.

"Spank me."

There was another click, then a man rolled the door back just far enough so I could enter. He was dressed for a leather club, complete with chaps and a leather police hat. I started forward, and he put his hand out to stop me. He was trying to look menacing.

232   G. W. RENSHAW

"You aren't a regular."

"Peggy Jorden sent me."

That changed everything.

"Come with me."

At that hour the club wasn't open. He was the only other person I saw. He led me past a coat room, dance floor, lounge, dungeons – all the things a good night club needs. We stopped at a door that said "Manager," and he knocked.

A few seconds later I heard "come in."

Lady Godiva wasn't what I expected. Instead of a tall, blonde Valkyrie with a leather bustier and whip, she was a middle-aged woman of medium height, with grey-streaked brown hair and glasses. Her clothing was what you'd expect on a housewife her age doing the grocery shopping.

"Thank you, Bruno. You may go." The doorman tipped his hat, and closed the door behind him.

"Please, have a seat. How is Peggy these days?"

The office was small, with a lot of filing cabinets, and too much paperwork on the desk. There was a sturdy looking chair in front of the desk, so I sat. Of course, the upholstery was leather.

"She's well. Keeping busy." I wasn't going to give out any details without Peggy's permission.

Lady Godiva put a file folder in one of the drawers and closed it, then sat behind the desk.

"Good. Did she tell you what she did for us?"

I shook my head.

"Last year a gang decided we'd make a good home for their drug trade and prostitution ring. Peggy was in charge of a joint operation with Guns and Gangs that got rid of them for us. We owe her. What can I do for you?"

"I'm looking for two people who appear to be forcing men to become dressage ponies."

"What exactly do you mean by 'forcing?' The common meaning, or the technical meaning within the show pony culture?"

"I mean non-consensual. The victims haven't asked to be trained, don't want to be trained, and their lives are being ruined. What's the technical meaning?"

Lady Godiva's face hardened.

"All training is consensual, in the sense that the ponies have asked for it at some point. Forced training is still consensual, but I suppose that, in a way, it's similar to a rape fantasy. If these people are actually doing what you say, I'll do anything within my power to help you stop them. It soils the reputation of the entire community."

I brought out some pictures I'd printed from the videos.

"Both of them go by the name Beleth. They are about three foot eight in height and, as you can see, very similar in appearance."

She studied the pictures, then shook her head.

"I don't know them, and I've never heard of them. I'll ask around; e-mail some of my friends in other places. They certainly are distinctive enough."

"That's what I'm hoping. Is there a dressage competition in the near future?"

"There's a pony show next weekend."

"I have to assume that there's a reason for the training. The only thing that I can think is that the victims will be entered in a show."

"That makes sense. If the trainers have told the victims lies about the culture, they might be too afraid to ask for help during the show."

"It's not likely they would anyway. They seem to be incapable of stopping what's going on or saying no. I suspect some kind of drugs or something."

Her expression became a lot harder.

"That's even worse, and definitely not what we do here. If you can remove perverts like this from our community, we'll be in your debt."

We exchanged business cards.

"Thank you. I'll look forward to your call."

Damn, more waiting.

On Wednesday morning I was lying on my couch reading a book, Yoko Geri snuggled against me, when the phone rang.

"Veronica, is there anything you'd like to tell me about that video?"

"Hi Trinity. Like what? It should all be in my notes."

"Are you certain that your notes on the circumstances of the recording are complete and accurate?"

"Of course. Why?"

"And you didn't have it produced as a joke?"

Oh hell, no. It couldn't be.

"Oh shit, are you telling me that the video is genuine?" I didn't need this.

"It's impossible, but yes. There's no sign of any tampering. The frames are all intact and there are no artifacts in the video. Your initial asser-tion was correct. What it shows is impossible."

"*Mierda.*"

"Can you tell me what's going on?"

"Believe me, I wish I knew. As soon as I find out, I'll let you know. I don't know whether this makes me feel better or worse."

"In what way?"

"I thought I was going crazy. Now my therapist tells me that I'm not delusional. Instead, reality has gone out for lunch."

"I see your point. I'm looking forward to an explanation."

"You and me both."

CHAPTER 30

Show Time

Saturday was a busy day. I'd called Lady Godiva, and told her what I wanted to do. Set up for the pony show was supposed to start at ten o'clock in the morning, with the show itself starting at noon.

At eleven I arrived at the house on Millward Place, assuming that the Beleth Twins would have left by then. Swapping the memory cards went off without a hitch. There wasn't time to view the past week's video before heading to the club.

The gods of parking were not smiling on me a second time. I had to walk eight blocks to the Dog and Pony Show. This time Bruno let me in without question, and led me to Lady Godiva's office. There was a leather fetish costume laid out over her guest chair.

"The outfit will prevent you from standing out," she said. This time she was in a sleeveless, corset-laced leather leotard with a top hat, riding crop, and thigh-high leather boots. She actually made it look good. "You can change here. Since you said that you don't have experience, I selected something that should be comfortable for you."

She left, closing the door, and I examined my disguise.

There was a sort of spiky butterfly-like mask in red and gold, a spiked black leather choker, a black leather leotard much like hers, black riding boots, and a matching red and gold micro skirt that I assumed went on over the leotard. Mercifully, the boots didn't have six inch spike heels.

The outfit was surprisingly comfortable, at least physically. It made me nervous to think that I'd be going out in semi-public in it in a few moments.

The irony was that, even though I was undercover, my duty belt, baton, and handcuffs fit in nicely with the outfit. I wouldn't have to conceal them.

I brushed my hair out, and put it back in a pony tail. It was show time.

The club had been an underground warehouse back in the day, so except for washrooms, storage, and the manager's office, it was mostly one large, open space. The dungeon equipment had been moved back against the walls, and the ring was set up in the centre.

My discomfort with the outfit lasted about twenty seconds. That's how long it took me to realize that, compared with most of the people who crowded the club, I was dressed like a Sunday school teacher.

My outfit had been chosen well. Nobody bothered me as I wandered around, looking for the Beleth Twins. I guess speaking to a dominatrix without permission was against the rules.

At noon the show began. Owners brought their ponies into the ring, paraded them before the judges, longed them, and demonstrated their obedience. Most of the ponies were two-legged because it afforded them more ability to perform. There were some, however, who remained on all fours. The two classes were judged separately.

Around one thirty the ring was cleared, and obstacles were set up for the show jumping. There were no four-legged ponies in that event. The jumps were pathetically short by equestrian standards. However, each pony was wearing a padded harness that allowed their riders to sit behind them in piggy-back position. Most of the jumpers were male, and the riders tended to be on the small side. None, however, were small enough to be either Beleth.

The last event was dressage. The Radetzky March was a favourite for the routines, and I have to say that I was impressed by the athletic prowess of the ponies.

None of them were Frank, and none of the riders were dwarfs.

I didn't bother to stay for the awarding of prizes. The club employees were also on the lookout for the Beleth Twins, and nobody had signalled me that there was a sighting. I went back to the manager's office, and changed back into my regular clothes.

Lady Godiva came in soon after.

"It looks like they didn't come," she said.

"No. Any luck with your other contacts?"

"None. Nobody has heard of these people, or anybody like them. There was one non-consensual trainer in Montreal a few years ago, but he was kidnapping women, and holding them in his basement. Apparently one of his slaves managed to strangle him with her lead line so he's definitely not one of your twins."

"I'll keep working the case from other angles. These two are beginning to piss me off."

Lady Godiva laughed. "You sound like Peggy."

"I'll take that as a compliment. Thanks for your help."

I hadn't had any lunch, so I made myself a sandwich before reviewing the surveillance video. Yoko sniffed at it but wasn't interested. My cat, the culinary snob.

I didn't expect to learn anything new, so I fast-forwarded through. Monday, 6 P.M., Frank. Wednesday, 6:15, Frank. Thursday, 10 A.M., Sofia.

What the hell?

I went back to the beginning of that segment. As usual, the house was empty, then everything appeared, including the female Beleth. A minute later she went to the front door, then returned, Sofia trailing behind her. Beleth was leading her with a piece of string looped loosely around Sofia's neck.

She had my client stand in the middle of the living room and disrobe. When she was naked, Beleth walked around her. On one occasion, she swatted my client across the buttocks to get her to stand up straighter. After that she opened Sofia's mouth and looked inside.

She was checking her conformation, just as if she was buying livestock. I was furious, and had to remind myself that this had happened over two days before. There was nothing I could do to affect the outcome now.

Sofia looked stoned, passively letting Beleth do whatever she wanted. By this time, it was a look I knew well. My suspicion was confirmed when Beleth pried open Sofia's right hand, and took something from her.

She'd found Frank's coin.

I didn't know whether to feel angry, or sorry for her. I'd told her to wear gloves when searching for the coin. Maybe she had, and touched it later, by accident. I was a little freaked at the implication that if I'd made one tiny mistake with Parker's coin that would be me on the video.

I skimmed through the rest of the video. I didn't need to see the details of Sofia getting into her horse outfit, or being saddled. Nor did I need to see the dressage training session. Eventually I'd have to speak with my client, and I imagined that she'd be grateful that I'd skipped those parts.

There was one thing I noticed in passing. Any sensible trainer would go easy on a new student, since she couldn't possibly know what was expected of her. Beleth didn't, and there were multiple streaks of blood on Sofia's sides by the time the session was done.

Afterwards, Beleth removed the foreleg gloves, and then sat in the chair watching while Sofia removed the rest of her tack and got dressed.

She left in tears, without even looking at her trainer.

Beleth looked at the camera and waved, smiling. Then she and the furniture disappeared. The house was once again cold and empty.

I checked the ends of Frank's two sessions. Neither time did Beleth wave at the camera.

By now, I was willing to believe that, somehow, Beleth knew that Sofia's session was the only one I'd watch. It was getting harder not to give in to Kali's theory about demons.

I poured myself a beer, and wondered what I would do next. There were several possibilities, and there was no room for error. I had to pick the right one the first time.

I could confront Sofia, as I had Parker. It had worked once. That might or might not have been a fluke.

Another possibility was just to present her with the information about her husband. Maybe seeing that they were trapped the same way would save their marriage. Maybe she'd break free. Maybe he would, if she told him what she knew. Or maybe they'd both be pony slaves forever.

There was another anomaly in Sofia's video, given that this was her first time. At no time had Beleth handed her a house key. I wondered why the two men got one but she didn't.

I briefly toyed with the idea of calling the police. The problem was the same as it was before. Unless one of the victims complained, or at least was willing to admit that they had been coerced, no crime could be proven. It would be my illegally-obtained word against the Twins, assuming that the police could find them.

Maybe I should confront Frank. The shock of finding out that his wife had hired somebody to find out about his situation might shake him out of it. Parker was getting help; I could offer the same to Frank.

One thing I was not going to do was to waste any more of Trinity's time on this. It was a good bet that Frank's coin, even if I could get it, would turn out to be just clean, pure silver with a weird isotope ratio.

Something that Slut Beleth had said came back to me. I'd told her that I wasn't into mathematics, and she's said that was why I had trouble getting things to add up. Was the solution mathematical? In what way? How could I find out? Contacting a professor at the university would be easy, but how would I phrase the question? "Hi, here's a bunch of perverted videos for you to watch. The woman told me my lack of math skills was preventing me from solving the mystery. Have at it." Yeah, right.

Maybe she was just playing with me. That would be entirely in character.

I was most certainly under a time constraint. I'd heard from Parker

that his coercive sessions had left him with post-traumatic stress dis-
order. Frank was probably in the same boat, but Sofia was a fresh victim.
If I acted immediately, Trinity could probably help prevent further psychological damage instead of having to repair it.

That made the decision easier. I had to see Sofia right away.

"Reinkemeyer residence," said a masculine voice.

Damn.

"Hi, this is Veronica from Dorinda Designs. Is Mrs. Reinkemeyer at
home?"

"One moment."

"Hello?" Sofia's voice was guarded. As far as either of us knew, there
was no Dorinda Designs.

"I have some news on your case. Can you meet me at my office?"

"I don't know. It's inconvenient right now."

"Tell your husband that you ordered a dress, and you have to come in
for a fitting. Please, it's important."

She hesitated, then gave in. I was reminded of Parker's reaction to my
visit to his workplace.

"Very well. I'll be there in half an hour."

That went well. Now I had another call to make. It felt like a spy calling my handler.

"Trinity, this is Veronica. I may have another couple of clients to refer
to you."

"Really? Any connection with the previous one?"

"I think you'll find the two cases *extremely* similar except that this is a
married couple."

"Interesting. Have they agreed to treatment yet?"

"No, I'm about to talk to her. I wanted to know what their options
were first."

"I'd be glad to see them."

"Good. I'll let you know."

"I appreciate your discretion. We'll have to provide you with a more
circumspect means of communication. I'll be in touch."

I wondered if I'd be told to put future messages behind a certain brick
under a bridge somewhere. In addition to the rest of the literary crowd,
my life was now turning into an Ian Fleming novel.

The living room was tidy, and this time I made sure that there was
nothing hidden under the sofa. I also made sure that Yoko Geri was actually in my bedroom before closing the door. The buzzer sounded, exactly
on time. This time she knocked before entering.

Her outfit was less upscale this time. Her body language was a lot less arrogant or confident. My guess was that her experience with Beleth had shaken her badly. After giving me her coat to hang, she sat on the sofa. I didn't ask before placing a bottle of water in front of her.

The last time, she would have demanded to know what I'd discovered. Now she just sat and waited.

"Sofia, I've discovered what your husband is doing when he is late from work."

"He's having an affair, isn't he?" Tears formed in her eyes and rolled slowly down her cheeks.

"No, he isn't."

The look on her face told me that I'd just thrown her a life preserver.

"You husband is in a very difficult situation at the moment. He's going to need your help to recover from it. Are you willing to do that?"

"Yes! Anything!" She sniffed and grabbed a tissue from the box. "People always assume that I married him for his money. I'll admit that was part of it, but I really do love him. Are you sure there isn't another woman?"

"Not in the sense you mean. Do you remember the coin I had you look for?"

She stiffened at the mention of the coin.

"Yes."

"I know that you found it, and what it did to you."

I've never seen such a look on a person's face, even when Nick told Kali about her parents. She went straight from wide-eyed terror to wailing like an infant, her face buried in her hands.

"Sofia," I said. She continued sobbing. I moved to the couch and pulled her wrists down. "Sofia."

"I'm so ashamed."

"Why didn't you use gloves as I asked you?"

"I did. I wore gloves the whole time."

That didn't make sense. Not that anything in this case did. Unless...

Oh shit. I'd had Parker's coin in my jacket pocket for several hours. It hadn't affected me, but there was one thing I hadn't done.

"Did you stare at the coin for a long time?"

My question seemed to calm her slightly, probably because it made no sense to her. She blew her nose.

"Yes, I mean, it was so unusual. I looked at it for several minutes, and I felt my head swimming like I'd had too much to drink."

"And your gloves were on the whole time?" She nodded.

"Excuse me." I grabbed my phone, and called Trinity's number. I started speaking as soon as it picked up.

"This is Veronica. Is there any chance that a lab technician stared at that coin for more than a few seconds?"

"That's a rather odd..."

"I know. Is there?"

"Do you mean the whole coin or part of it? During analysis someone would have had it under a microscope but they would have been looking at a small portion at a time."

"I'm guessing that it would have to be the whole thing, but to be safe you should call your lab, and find out if anyone is or has been acting oddly in the past few days. I think the problem we discussed can be created just by looking at the coin for a while."

"That doesn't make sense." She paused. "I'll do it, of course. Nothing that I've been privy to in this case seems to make sense. Are you saying that the coin has some kind of psychic aura?"

"I have no idea. Maybe the design affects the brain. All I'm sure of is that someone was affected while looking at it and wearing gloves."

"Thank you for letting me know. I have calls to make."

After hanging up I looked at Sofia. She was staring at me like I'd gone crazy.

"There's another coin?" She asked.

"At least one other. The one you found was given to Frank by that woman you went to see on Thursday. It had the same effect on him that it did on you – with identical results. You couldn't stop yourself, could you?"

"No."

"You might remember that when you are talking to him. I'm certain that he's as much of a victim in this as you are."

She started crying again, less violently this time.

"Listen, I know a therapist who has dealt with *exactly* this kind of thing before. I can give you her number, for both you and Frank. She can help."

She nodded, and I put one of Trinity's cards into her hands.

"I want to assure you than none of my records will ever see the light of day. I stopped watching the video soon after you entered that house. The details weren't something I needed to know."

"Thank you." She had a drink of water. "She said that her name was Beleth."

"I know."

"Do you know who she is?"

"I haven't been able to find anything, and believe me I've tried."

"Can she be arrested for anything?"

"Probably not. If you lodge a complaint with the police they'll investigate, but they'll need my surveillance videos as evidence. Without them they won't be able to do anything. Even with them, it will be difficult proving that you were coerced." I didn't mention that there was a police report stating that the house had been empty for months.

"Oh, God, no. I couldn't live with it if any of what happened got out."

"Then I'm sorry. She's going to get away with it."

"So we'll never know why she did this to us?"

I sighed. Life was not fair.

"No. Unless a miracle happens, this case is closed."

CHAPTER 31

Mirabile Visu

I quietly closed the door behind Sofia Reinkemeyer as she went home to her husband. I didn't envy either of them the conversation that they would be having. She had promised me that she'd call Trinity the next morning, so at least they had a chance to come out of this reasonably intact.

From a mercenary point of view, the good news was that she'd been so grateful that she'd not only paid her bill, but tacked on an extra thousand dollars. Despite my assurances of confidentiality, I think her secondary purpose was to ensure my silence about the videos. That would have been insulting. I chose to take it as just a tip for a job well done.

I called Trinity again. She said that none of her technicians were acting oddly, and she cleared some time on her calendar for the Reinkemeyers. It looked like things were really wrapping up.

Two hours later, I was pondering what to make for supper while lying on the sofa with Yoko Geri on my chest. I had a truly epic disinterest in doing anything at that moment, including cooking.

The phone rang. I managed to grab it without disturbing Yoko's esteemed repose.

"*Hola, hermanita.*"

"*Hola, chiquita.* You have good timing. I could use some cheering up."

"Then it's a good thing I'm calling to invite you to dinner."

"*¡Mi hermana maravillosa!* I take it back, your timing is perfect. I'll be right there."

She waited until dessert to ask the questions I didn't want to think about.

"How's your other case coming along?"

I sighed.

"Mostly closed, I guess. I got paid, and life goes on."

"What do you mean by 'mostly?'"

"There are some details that are obscure, but my client is satisfied, or at least can live with what she has."

"What about Keith and Parker?"

I sighed.

"You had to ask, didn't you?"

"I'm paying. I get to ask."

"Parker was under the mental control of someone who used him for unknown, non-consensual purposes. He's getting help for the psychological damage, and wants to tell Keith about it. I promised I'd be there to help him explain if he wishes."

Kali pursed her lips. It wasn't an attractive way for her to express thoughtfulness.

"What do you mean by 'mental control'?"

"I really wish I knew. Beleth gave all the victims silver medallions. I had them analyzed, and there's nothing remarkable about them other than a weird composition. Yet, somehow, the victims all acted like the medallions were able to infect them with a compulsion – to go to that house every so often, and passively allow Beleth to do whatever he or she wanted. It has to be some kind of drug, but I haven't figured out how it's delivered. And don't tell me it's demons again."

"You still haven't identified the people doing this?"

"Apart from their assumed name, no."

"Or why they were doing it?"

"No."

"That's not very satisfactory."

"No."

"Did you ever figure out the trick with the surveillance video?"

"No. I sent it to a lab, and they decided the whole thing was impossible."

"Occam's razor."

"Bite me, *miquita*."

I got home around ten, but I was still too wound up to consider bed. I filled Yoko Geri's water and food bowls, then wondered if I should sprawl on the couch and read a book, or sprawl in the bathtub and read a book. The promise of warmth won out. I was in the bathroom filling the tub when there was a knock on the door.

"What the hell?" Unless a resident blindly let in a stranger, nobody could get into the building without buzzing the intercom. I didn't really know any of the neighbours yet. I looked through the peephole, and barely saw the top of somebody's head. Maybe a child was locked out of their apartment. I opened the door.

Even though Beleth was wearing headphones, I could hear the music clearly. It sounded like a brass band.

"Mind if I come in?" she said, turning off the music, and draping the headphones around her neck.

"Yes, I do. How did you get in? And how the hell did you find me?" I saw no reason to pretend that I didn't know who she was. At least she'd gotten dressed before stalking me, if you could call an outfit that would make Daisy Duke blush being dressed. She wasn't even wearing a coat. Her hair hung loose down her back, and was perfectly combed. Once again, her clothing made concealed weapons highly improbable.

She laughed. "I have resources. I'm leaving town, and it would amuse me to answer some of your questions."

"What are you talking about?"

"Now that you've spoiled my fun, I'm going home. You're the first person in a long time who hasn't been either terrified of me, or wanted to control me. I find that refreshing. Not to mention intriguing."

I kept my eyes firmly fixed on her, not letting them glance toward the storage unit beside the door. On one shelf there was a small wicker basket where I always threw my keys, handcuffs, and baton when I got home.

I looked down at her. Why was I feeling intimidated by someone who was almost half a metre shorter than me, and couldn't weigh more than two thirds of what I did? There was something about her, an aura of perfect confidence, like she believed that nothing she did could ever fail. Apparently, my interference in her activities had put an end to that, and for some reason that intrigued her.

"Fine," I said, letting her in. While her back was turned, I palmed my baton and keys from the basket. Fighting fair is a concept that Mum and Nick had literally beaten out of me when were sparring at the gym. Fairness sounds really noble until it gets you killed. If Beleth so much as smiled the wrong way, I was ready to take her head off.

"Nice place. May I sit?"

"Be my guest." If she got violent, being seated would put her at an initial disadvantage.

She wriggled over to my comfy chair with a lot of hip action, hopped up onto the seat, and crossed her legs. She was so short that her feet didn't reach the floor. I let her have her way, hoping for some answers. I would stand as long as she was here.

I wasn't happy about this, but it might be my only chance to get some answers. It was certainly the only time I knew of when she'd appeared outside the house.

"Who are you?"

"I told you, my name is Beleth."

"Beleth is the name of a demon."

She shrugged.

"Sticks and stones may break my bones..." I swear, she giggled. "No, actually, they don't."

"Why did you have a telephone in your living room?" That honestly seemed to confuse her.

"Why shouldn't I?"

"It wasn't hooked up. Why have it at all?"

It took her a few seconds, then she laughed.

"How foolish of me! I forgot, you all use mobile phones now, don't you? Thank you for pointing that out."

"How did you meet Frank Reinkemeyer?"

"I noticed him having coffee one day, and thought he'd make a good experiment. It was a whim, really." She twirled her hair around one finger. "I get bored so easily."

"Have you ever trained anyone like that before?"

"Of course not. That's what made it a whim."

"What was in it for him?"

I seemed to have a knack for confusing her.

"Why would you think that there should be something in it for him?"

"That's usual in a BDSM relationship. Otherwise, why did he agree to participate?"

Another puzzled look, then she raised her arms like I'd told her to "stick 'em up." The gesture tickled something in my memory. I couldn't quite remember where I'd seen that before. In a movie somewhere?

"That's why you're confused. You think that this is about sex. I told you, it was an experiment."

"To prove what?"

Again with the confusion.

"Why would I need to prove anything?"

"Isn't that usual in the scientific method? You have a hypothesis, and you perform an experiment to test it."

"No, no hypothesis. I just wanted to see what would happen."

I was getting pissed off.

"Like a child pulling the wings off a fly. You ruined four lives just for the hell of it."

"Four?"

"Frank, his wife, Parker and his fiance." She shrugged again.

"Oh. That wasn't my intention. Honestly, I never thought about it."

"What's the deal with the medallions?"

"It's my – logo – I suppose you'd say. They're just a concentration focus for my subjects."

She seemed to delight in giving me just enough of an answer to make me ask the next question.

"Focus? Is that how you controlled them? By hypnotism?"

She opened her mouth to speak, then closed it again. She looked thoughtful, like I'd asked her something complex.

"No. Not hypnotism."

"How, then?"

"It would be difficult to explain."

"And the isotope ratio?"

She gave me that confused look again.

"The isotope ratio in the silver is abnormal."

"Interesting, I'll have to look into that. The silver is quite normal where I come from."

"And where's that?" She smiled.

"That would take a lot of explaining. These days the official name is Downland."

I decided to change subjects.

"Why were the two men given house keys but not Sofia?"

"I told you, I'm going home. There was no point."

"Who's your partner?"

That also seemed to confuse her.

"I don't have a partner."

"Then who is the guy who was doing similar training with Parker?"

She laughed as though I'd said something hilarious.

"You thought there were two of us? No wonder you are confused. No, there's just me. One plus one equals one."

"Bullshit. The two of you look similar, but there's no way you could pass for a man unless you were dressed for the Antarctic."

There was a shimmer, like she'd turned to smoke for a moment, and the male Beleth was sitting in my chair. One moment I was talking to the sister, and then her brother was there, in the same pose. The outfit that had looked slutty on her looked ridiculous on him. It also didn't fit very well. The shorts in particular must have been very uncomfortable for him.

"I told you, there's just one of me." Even the voice was male.

He changed back into the female form. I still wasn't buying it. Her big, spooky mind control secret must be an aerosol drug. She could have given me a spritz of hallucinogen when she came in. Maybe she had fil-

ters of some kind up her nostrils where I couldn't see them, or maybe
she just didn't care that she was tripping.

"How did you do that?"

"That would be awkward to explain, but it isn't difficult. How's your
knowledge of advanced quantum mechanics?"

I was not going to follow her down that rabbit hole. Time for another
subject change.

"Did you know about the camera?"

"Of course. That's why I waved at you. I thought it might cheer you
up."

"How?"

She wiggled her fingers at me. "Like this."

I could feel myself losing what little patience I had left.

"I mean, how did you know that the camera was there?"

"I felt it." She lowered the pitch of her voice. "There was a disturbance
in the Force."

This was going nowhere. I decided to go for the big question.

"Why me? It can't be a coincidence that my first two cases as an
investigator just happen to involve you."

Again, she made that "stick 'em up" gesture with her arms. It suddenly
came to me where I'd seen it before: in then 1956 movie *The Ten Com-
mandments*. It was the ancient Egyptian expression of astonishment. She
dropped the levity.

"That's marvellous! I'm impressed. No, it wasn't a coincidence. You're
going to be crucial to a lot of people in the next while. I wanted to see
how you'd react."

"React to what?"

"Weirdness, in the old sense."

I'd had it with her non-explanations.

"This is bullshit. Leave now."

"That's rude."

I flicked the baton, and it sprang open with a satisfyingly solid thunk.

"Leave. Now. And don't come back."

She laughed.

"Wrong quote. It's, 'go away and never – come – back.'"

The last was said in an excellent imitation of Gollum from the movies.
That was the last straw.

"Are you seriously trying to tell me that demons watch *Lord of the
Rings*? What's *Criminal Minds* to you, a sitcom? Get out."

She hopped off the chair, smiling.

"Make me."

As quickly as possible, I threw the keys at her face, underhand, to distract her, then snapped the baton at her knee. She spun aside so quickly that she was literally a blur. I'd never seen anything move that fast in real life. Regardless of her speed, when her hand pushed me it was gentle.

At least it felt gentle. I flew over the coffee table, spinning in midair, and landed face first on the couch. I used the bounce of the cushions to flip over, so I could meet the attack that would follow.

She was gone. The apartment door was still closed, and the deadbolt was set, as it had been after I'd let her in.

Cautiously, I scouted the apartment. Yoko Geri instinctively seemed to recognize that I was hunting something, and bounced around my feet, helping me kitten style.

Beleth wasn't in the kitchen, bedroom, closets, or bathroom. I even checked the cupboards. For completeness, I checked the balcony, and the hallway outside.

Dammit, another mystery. I really loathed that woman. Or man. Both. Whatever.

I sat on the couch for the next half hour with my baton, expecting Beleth to pop out, phone me, or something. I paid close attention to my surroundings, expecting more hallucinations. Nothing happened. There was nothing strange that I could see.

I let the cold water out of the bath tub, and then refilled it. As soon as the water started running into the tub, my phone rang. I marched out into the living room, and snatched it from the coffee table.

"What?" I snapped, expecting Beleth.

"I hope I didn't wake you," Kali said. I relaxed a bit.

"No, I was just about to have a long soak."

"Good, I forgot to mention it earlier, but I wondered if you were free for lunch tomorrow. There's a new shawarma place just down the street. I thought we could check it out."

"Sure, that sounds wonderful," I said, my gaze darting around the apartment in case Beleth was somehow still here.

"You don't sound enthused."

"Sorry, I had a visit from Beleth earlier. I'm still cranky."

"¡Mierda! How did she know where to find you? Forget that, how did she know about you in the first place?"

"I did meet her once, not that I gave her my real name. I have no idea how she found me."

"That's creepy and scary. What did she want?"

"She said she's leaving town, and it would 'amuse' her to answer some of my questions."

"So who is she?"

"Beleth, that's all she said. I did ask her if she's a demon."

"And?"

"Her reply was, and I quote: 'sticks and stones may break my bones... no, actually, they don't.' I tried to throw her out."

"What do you mean, 'tried?'"

"She's fast, much faster than me. She dodged my baton, threw me on the couch, and then she was gone when I looked for her."

"Veronica, I've seen you fight. I can accept that somebody might be faster than you, but much faster? As in supernaturally fast?"

"Forget it, I'm not buying the whole magic and demons thing."

"Why not?"

"It doesn't make sense."

"But it's the simplest explan–"

"No! No demons! Not now, not ever!" Both Kali and I stopped in shock. I never yelled into the phone. Even when my hormones were raging I'd sworn at her, but I'd never truly yelled. Now I'd done both.

"I'm sorry," I said quietly. "I just can't accept that there is magic in the world; that there are creatures who wander around making bullshit of the laws of nature."

"Why not?" She repeated, equally quietly. I took a deep breath and let it out.

"When I was eight my grandmother died of cancer. I prayed, because that's what they tell you to do. I asked God not to take my grandma from me. She got sicker. Then I found a book in the library that was supposed to contain magical spells for all kinds of things: wealth, love, power, health. I did every spell that was even remotely related to making grandma better, and every time I went to see her she was thinner, more pale, and in more pain. If magic works, it should have worked then."

"I'm sorry. You never told me."

"I'm sorry too. Now you know why I couldn't get into Wicca either."

"Why didn't you say anything before?"

"It wasn't important. Just because I can't follow your path doesn't mean it isn't right for you."

"Mum told me something a year ago." Kali always referred to my parents as Mum and Dad. Her own parents were always Mama and Papa. "She said that, in her career, she has run into eight cases that had no solution. These were cases where things didn't make sense, where she finally had to give up because what she found had no explanation that she could take to a Crown Prosecutor."

"She never mentioned that to me."

"You know Mum, she lets us figure things out for ourselves."

"So how did she handle her inexplicable cases?"

"She said she learned to live with the fact that sometimes there is no explanation. She also said that she hoped that you could learn the same thing before it drove you crazy."

"I'd suspect that you are making this up to make me feel better, but it sounds too much like her. Fine, so there's no explanation. Life goes on. Today, psychotic magical dwarfs. Tomorrow, shawarma."

"That's my girl."

I let the cold water out of the tub, again, and then refilled it, again. It was a good thing I wasn't paying for utilities. While that was happening, I put the book I'd selected back on the shelf, and picked a new one. I wasn't in the mood for another mystery at the moment; Sherlock Holmes would have to wait for another day. A romance by Mercedes Lackey seemed like a better choice.

I put the baton and phone beside me, just in case, and oozed into the hot water. I opened the book to the first page. I might be having trouble being a hard-boiled PI, but tonight I could at least be a poached one.

Sometimes, it was nice to be a normal teenage girl.

GLOSSARY

There are quite a few non-English phrases in this book. For those of you who don't speak a multitude of languages, here are the nearest English translations.

Ahora – (Spanish) Now!

Arroz amarillo – (Spanish) Rice coloured and flavoured with achiote seeds.

Bananos con Salsa de Naranja – (Spanish) Bananas with orange sauce.

Bienvenida a nuestra casa – (Spanish) Welcome to our home.

Buen provecho – (Spanish) Bon apetit.

Chica – (Spanish) girl.

Chiquita – (Spanish) little girl.

Cómo estás? – (Spanish) How are you?

De nada – (Spanish) you're welcome.

Doctora – (Spanish) female doctor.

Encantada – (Spanish) Enchanted ("pleased to meet you").

Esto es para ti – (Spanish) This is for you.

Estoy encantada de asistir – (Spanish) I would be happy to attend.

Et tú? – (Spanish) And you?

Fuerzas Armadas Revolucionarios de Colombia – (Spanish) Revolutionary Armed Forces of Colombia.

Führer – (German) leader or guide. To avoid associations of Hitler, modern Germans tend to use *Leiter* instead to mean leader. In this case Veronica means both senses.

Gracias – (Spanish) Thank you.

Granhijueputa – (Spanish) Fucking son of a bitch.

Hijueputa – (Spanish) Son of a bitch.

Hola – (Spanish) hello, hi.

La cena esta servida – (Spanish) Dinner is served.

Madre de dios – (Spanish) Mother of God.

Malparida vida! – (Spanish) Bastard life!

Mi hermana maravillosa! – (Spanish) My wonderful sister!

Mi hija no nos dijo que usted habla español – (Spanish) My daughter didn't tell me that you speak Spanish.

Mierda – (Spanish) Shit.

Mijita – (Spanish) "Little daughter," a term of endearment.

Miquita – (Spanish) Small female monkey; "monkey girl"

Mis papas son unos cerrados de mierda! – (Spanish) Shit, my parents are closed-minded.

Muchas gracias – (Spanish) thank you very much.

Muy bien – (Spanish) Very well.

Perdóname, no habla Español – (Spanish) Sorry, I don't speak Spanish.

Perro – (Spanish) Lit. Dog; an adulterous man.

Pichar – (Spanish) In Colombia only: Fuck!

Por favor – (Spanish) Please.

Shibori – (Japanese) Twisted, as in wet cloth you are trying to wring. Also idiomatic for 'kinky.'

Tenemos una invitada que tiene mejores modales que ustedes – (Spanish) We have a guest with better manners than you two.

Traidor – (Spanish) traitor.

Vengan acá! – (Spanish) Get out here!

Yoko Geri – (Japanese) side kick, in the martial arts sense.

ABOUT THE AUTHOR

G. W. Renshaw is a writer, martial artist, Linux druid, and actor who lives in Calgary, Alberta, with his lovely wife, and the twin cats Romulus and Remus. He has a wide range of interests, from flint knapping to quantum cosmology. He will happily watch just about any film with monsters in it.

You can connect with G.W. at:

Twitter:
www.twitter.com/GWRenshaw

Facebook:
www.facebook.com/pages/GW-Renshaw/287045931461429

Website:
www.gwrenshaw.ca/

Made in the USA
Charleston, SC
30 May 2016